Mrs May

A PsychoSexual Odyssey

DAVID PICK

YELLOWBAY BOOKS

Published by YellowBay Books Ltd 2013
www.yellowbay.co.uk

YellowBay Books Ltd
9781908530547

YellowBay Books is dedicated to edgy,
daring and radical new writing.
Let us know what you think at info@yellowbay.co.uk,
Or visit Amazon and give the book a review

For Jo
and for
Dulcie and Poppy

"Men are so quick to blame the gods: they say
that we devise their misery. But they
themselves – in their depravity – design
grief greater than the griefs that fate assigns."
— **Homer,** *The Odyssey* **(circa 800 BC)**

"There's Nature and there's Nurture. Is there also some X,
some further contributor to what we are? There's Chance. Luck.
This extra ingredient is important but doesn't have to come from
the quantum bowels of our atoms or from some distant star. It is
all around us in the causeless coin-flipping of our noisy world,
automatically filling in the gaps of specification left unfixed by
our genes, and unfixed by salient causes in our environment."
— **Daniel C. Dennett,** *Freedom Evolves* **(2003)**

Chapter One

Hickety Pickety Pop
How many times before I stop?
One ... two ... three ... four ...

She is flying in a blur of skipping rope beneath a fierce sun.

Slap, slap, slap
On the hot tarmac

Her feet kiss the Earth, and the Earth kisses back.

Ticky-tacky, tarmac
Black, black, black.

She is dancing on glue.

Sticky-sticky, tarmac
Stick, stick—Stuck.

The truck passes with its customary roar, wheel after giant wheel, wheeling by, the belch of burnt diesel hot on her leg. She cannot breathe. She cannot move.

And the truck labours on, dragging itself to the summit of the hill ahead. She prays that it will vanish beyond the crest but the monstrous tyres refuse to turn and, with remorseless predictability, break free, begin to roll, back down the hill towards her, six abreast, rank after rank, a tide of tyres with treads like teeth, jagged, gigantic, tearing up tarmac to devour her.

With a start, she is awake. Her face is wet. But the sun is making the curtains glow. It is morning....

She hadn't told him. She wanted to see if he would remember— and he hadn't. From the moment he got in the car, he was in full spate: who was for him, who was out to get him, who was on the fence? By that tally, his chances didn't sound good. She wanted him to get his wretched Chair, of course she did. The last time he'd been passed over, he had crumpled and gone to bits, a full nervous collapse that no one would expect of the charismatic Dr May. God knows how he'd be if he bombed again. And for her own sake, it would be nice to get even with the snoots in the Department, especially the wives. 'Professor May' had a ring to it. And he did deserve it. Today though, especially today, he should have left a tiny corner of his selfish mind for her—for them. Not a lot to ask.

"Hey, I've forgotten the paper." He signalled a turnabout with a twisting finger. "Can you do a twirl?"

"Yes, sir!" She touched her forelock. "Right away, sir."

They were driving down Erasmus, one of the leafy academic avenues which radiated like the spokes of a wheel from The Hub, a large roundabout with a vast modernist bronze at its centre, the heart of the campus. Ginny dropped the old Saab into second gear and slipped into the traffic behind a couple of bicycles. Simon shifted in his seat and looked over his shoulder.

"Why don't you overtake, for God's sake?" he said.

"What's the rush?"

"There is no rush—but you're doing three miles an hour! We must look like a couple of old ladies."

Ginny slowed to a crawl.

"Sorry, I forgot—the dashing Dr May is without his penis extension today! Golly-gosh, I hope nobody notices!"

She resented his sports car. It was an indulgence so wildly out of character that her suspicions had flared when he appeared in it, and they still smouldered a year later.

"Face it, Virginia, the glorious complexity of the male psyche is way beyond your puny understanding," he said, not for the first time.

Back on Erasmus, she accelerated with unnecessary enthusiasm before braking hard to bring them into the lay-by outside the terrace of campus shops.

"Pop off and buy your paper then," she said. "And why don't you raid the top-shelf while you're at it."

She gave him a sideways glance and raised her eyebrows. His reaction was almost, but not quite, instantaneous. Slapping both hands over his face, he said, "Christ, I forgot. You've been to the clinic." He pulled his hands down from his eyes to cover his mouth. "How did you get on?"

She heard the note of dread in the question. What exactly did he want to hear?

"I'm officially pregnant—again," she said.

"And everything's OK?"

"As far as they can tell, it's all systems go!"

"Wow!"

Was there more bewilderment than elation in his voice?

"Is that all you can say?" she said, glaring at him. "Aren't you pleased?"

He took hold of her hand and squeezed it. "Of course I'm pleased, but I'm also terrified," he said. "We've been here too many times."

For a moment she sat with her head bowed. "It's grim, isn't it," she said quietly, "to be too scared to be happy? They tell you to relax and let Nature work its miracle, but you can't, not really."

"At least the fallible follicles did the business this time," he said cheerfully.

"True," she replied, responding to his initiative. "And your little feller's scored a bull's eye too. It's a team game."

"It's the solo performance I'm not partial to," he said, "at least, not with a bunch of medics sniggering outside the door."

Simon's struggles with the dirty magazines and the sample bottle were the only feature of the IVF routine which they could ever laugh about, so they exploited every variation on the old joke with gratitude.

She nudged him with her elbow. "Go on...get a copy of 'Electric Blue'...just in case."

"No way... I'm going to give the tennis-elbow a chance to mend."

She put her hand on his forearm. "Perhaps our luck really has changed," she said, "perhaps you're going to be a Prof and a dad all in the same year."

He leaned across and kissed her. "I do hope so, Mrs May. We've been waiting too long."

A man in a Panama hat was fumbling to release a Jack Russell terrier that was tied to the railing outside the mini-mart. There was something familiar about him when he looked up to acknowledge Simon's greeting, but it took Ginny a moment to place him. It was David Gurjieff. Back in her student days this place had been his fiefdom. 'One of the few intellectual beacons in the provincial fog,' Simon used to say. He'd been a big factor in luring Simon from Cambridge, or so Simon maintained in his more pompous moments. Hardly recognisable now—just another old man with a dog, toddling up the hill to buy his cut-price *Guardian* with all the other retired dons. Amazing how far the old boys would hike to save 40p. Or drive, for that matter. The carbon-cost of cheap newspapers must be astronomical.

She rarely came up the hill during daylight hours—not once since they came back from California. When they did go to the Jesmond for a film or a play, it was always in the evening. Yet it was all so familiar—the stark university buildings, rescued from their prize-winning brutalism by the new foliage of an early spring; the variegated clumps of swots and lovers dotted around the lawns among the trees; the strip of silver sea where the avenue dropped to the city. Nothing had changed.

A leggy creature, arms folded defensively below her breasts, was tripping along the pavement beside an animated young man. Her head was bowed, and an uncertain smile played on her lips. It was like watching herself: '*Will you, won't you, will you, won't you, will you join the dance?*' Different faces, same old tune.

God, it had been exciting though, all that forbidden fruit! She used to tease him about his 'hands-on' teaching methods and call him a cradle-snatcher. Was it really as risky as he made out? Probably not. One hell of an aphrodisiac though.

Back then, he'd been the Department dish. When he made his first move, she had assumed he was joking, and laughed. He could have had his pick of any number of the bright young things, strutting their assets with '*available*' tattooed on their foreheads. Not that she'd been entirely plain herself. The legs weren't bad, and the bumps and curves were in the right places, but everything moved as though the joints needed oiling. It had been hard to look happy then, which was a shame because the dimples were pretty and brought the sun out when they did show up. Sixteen years on, with the joints better oiled, the dimples appeared to order, and it was easier to hide the discomforts inside.

And there was Simon, closing fast on fifty now: desperate to have his due, desperately clinging on to youth. Above the neck, all patrician gravitas; iron-grey hair falling long on the upturned collar of his denim shirt; eyebrows, still a luxuriant black, writhing above those restlessly intelligent eyes. Below the neck, the physique of a has-been rodeo star, slightly stooped, but virile and still dangerous...waving goodbye to the grand old man that he intends to become...turning towards his supportive young wife... still the academic groupie; still teaching other people's children; still waiting for a child of her own.

Ginny closed her eyes and put her hands on her belly. Was there really a child growing inside her? She could feel nothing but a vague unease. *Hickety Pickety Pop. How many times before I stop?*

The passenger door opened.

"Why don't you let me drive?" Simon said.

"Don't be an idiot. I'm not an invalid."

"Why take chances?"

"Hop in, you prat! You bequeathed me this old banger and I don't want it wrecked by boy-racers. OK?"

"Dr May is prescribing cotton-wool," he said, fastening his seat-belt, "wads of it. You've got to cocoon yourself in the stuff."

"It didn't help last time, Doc," she said, and started the engine.

"Never mind the last time. Gloomy thoughts are strictly forbidden."

"Okay, let's be positive!" Ginny said, pulling away from the kerb. "Let's focus on the things that really matter. Let's go collect the love of your life."

Simon sighed ostentatiously and folded his arms.

"Let's face it, Simon," she continued, "you lavish a damned sight more money on that car than you do on me."

He sighed again and looked out of the window, losing himself in the drab expanses of the science and engineering blocks. They drove in silence until they reached the coast road and became caught up in the heavy traffic.

"Bit of luck running into old David," Simon said. "He was very complimentary about that piece I did for the Quarterly. Well argued and long overdue, he said."

"Do you think he'll put a word in for you?"

"He's not one of the referees unfortunately, but, if he's consulted, I'm sure he will."

"Surely they'll ask his advice. Isn't that what Professors Emeritus are for?"

"They'd be nuts not to, but you know Klugman. He's a clown and the VC's barking. It's a lottery."

The garage was on the far side of town, tucked away down the back streets. By far the quickest option, if not the most direct, was to scoot down the Esplanade and cut back into one of the Regency squares a mile or so down the coast. On a whim though, as she approached the Clock Tower roundabout, a place where three roads meet, Ginny veered to the right and joined the streams of vehicles funnelling into the High Street. Looking back at this day, as she would obsessively throughout her life, it was at this precise instant that everything changed. It was as if, presented with two futures, she had chosen at random a life that did not belong to her.

The town swallowed them up in the bustle of a busy Friday. Traffic was stop-starting its way along the High Street in both directions and shoppers dodged between the bumpers to exchange one teeming pavement for the other. Then a siren began yelping, urgent but unseen and impossible to place. Ginny checked her mirror. To her astonishment, she saw a uniformed police officer sprinting up the white line in the narrow gap between the two lanes of traffic about fifty metres away.

"Watch it, Gin!" Simon yelled.

Her eyes flicked back to the road and she stamped on the brake just in time to avoid a collision with the motorcycle in front. Her heart leapt.

"Jesus, that was close," said Simon. "What the hell were you…?"

"Look behind. I got distracted by the plod."

Simon swivelled in his seat.

"I wonder what all the excitement's about," he said.

Blue light was dancing up ahead, reflected and re-reflected in distant windows along the Upper High. The traffic began to part as vehicles hugged the pavements and a squad car emerged in the centre of the road, blues spinning, headlights flashing, speeding towards the junction with Union Street. Indifferent to the drama of the moment, the traffic lights ran through their mindless routine. At red, the siren's high-pitched yap became an insistent scream and the police-car began to weave a path through the confusion of uncertain drivers struggling to clear its path.

"Get your wheels on the pavement, Gin. I don't trust these cowboys."

Ginny obeyed, leaving as much road as she could.

"Look!" Simon shouted, pointing across her face to the opposite side of the road.

A slender figure was charging down the alleyway between the bookshop and the bank. A much larger man was in pursuit, but he was losing ground.

A siren-shriek burst in Ginny's head, and the world turned frantic blue. The squad car was almost on them when its passenger pointed towards the alleyway. With a squeal of rubber on tarmac, the driver swerved.

Ginny's hands went to her mouth. Sliding flank-first down the High Street, the gaudy chequerboard of blue and yellow became gigantic.

"Oh Christ, he's lost it!"

She didn't hear the impact for the screech of siren and skidding tyres, but the Saab rocked violently.

"He's clipped us!" Simon yelled.

Despite being thrown around in her seat, Ginny's eyes never left the police-car. It was a miracle that the driver kept control, but somehow he managed to haul the car to a halt just short of the pavement by the alley, panicking the crowds of shoppers.

"You macho bastard!" she shouted, thumping the window with her fist.

With a lingering groan, the siren died and the doors opened.

"There he is," Simon said, pointing across the road, "the master criminal!"

A youth had run out of the alley. When he saw police car, he seemed to lose heart and came to a stop. Bending at the waist, he put his hands on his knees and rocked back and forth, sucking in air. He looked beaten.

"All this mayhem for a kid!" Ginny said.

The boy raised his hands in a gesture of surrender but, as the policemen approached, he took off again, running between them, straight for their car—one foot on the bonnet and onwards, upwards to the roof. Stamping and kicking out at the frenzy of light at his feet, he began a war-dance, shaking the tangle of straw-coloured hair and punching the sky with his fists.

"May as well enjoy himself while he can," said Simon. "It won't last long."

Something passed Ginny's window, obscuring her view. It was the policeman they had seen sprinting through the traffic. He was breathing heavily now, advancing on the police car, a menacing figure, swollen in his body armour, with all the tools of the trade hanging on his hips. He was beckoning the boy down with both hands, inviting him to jump.

"He'd love to get his paws on the kid," Ginny said. "You can feel it!"

A second police car bullied its way noisily down the High Street, and slewed itself diagonally across the road to block all movement. From the alleyway, the boy's pursuer made an appearance, shouldering his way through the crowd of shoppers, a warrant card brandished above the silver helmet of closely cropped hair that crowned his head.

"The entire police station's turned out," Simon said, opening his door. "You wait here and take it easy. I'm going to have a word."

Some of the youngsters in the crowd were shouting encouragement to the boy as he applied his Doc Martins to the light-box on the car-roof, and the detective was trying to use the mood of the crowd to his advantage, clapping his hands above his head.

"OK, Billy-Whizz! Well done!" he called out. "You've made us all look like prats. You've had your bit of fun. Now it's time to get down, before somebody gets hurt."

The boy leaned forward. "Make me!" he said.

Impatient car-horns were sounding all along the High Street. The detective checked his wrist-watch.

"I'll give you precisely one minute to see sense," he said. "Come on, Whizz, you're not daft."

There were now five uniformed officers surrounding the car, waiting for the signal. The boy was taunting them, but it was all for show. His wariness betrayed him.

"Who's in charge here?" Simon asked, arriving on the scene.

"I am," replied the detective, "but this is not the time, sir."

"It damned well is the time!" It was Ginny, her voice quivering with rage.

Simon turned to her. "Ginny, please—leave it to me!"

Ignoring him, Ginny advanced on the police car. "One of these clowns should be charged with dangerous driving," she said. "Just look at that!" She pointed to the damage on the rear wing of the police car. "That smashed into me at God knows what speed. And I was parked over there, wheels on the pavement."

The detective was struggling to hide his exasperation. "If that's true, madam, we'll deal with it as soon as..."

"What do you mean, 'If it's true!'?" Ginny shrugged off Simon's efforts to calm her down. "Of course it's true. This could have been a blood-bath. We could have been killed...any one of these people could have been killed..."

"You tell him, lady," the boy on the roof interjected. "The pigs are out of control in this town."

Without pause, Ginny turned her fire on the boy. "I think we've all heard more than enough from you, young man," she said, surprising herself with her classroom voice. "Get yourself down here, at once!"

For a moment the boy stared intently at Ginny, then spread his arms out as though to fly away and jumped gracefully from the top of the car to land in front of them.

"Hello, Mrs May," he said, as he straightened up. "Do I get a 'Smiley Face'?"

Chapter Two

The boy was dragged kicking and cursing to one of the squad cars, and when the crowd had stopped its sarcastic applause, the High Street returned to business. Immediately the mood of the police changed and the detective in charge began to compete with the anxious police driver to show consideration and kindness. Their lucky old Saab was destined to be better than new and in double-quick time; and of course they would want to make a formal complaint, that was only reasonable in the circumstances. Ginny and Simon swapped wry looks.

Whisked off to Police HQ, they were soon in the presence of a solemn Chief Superintendent who listened intently. A statement was taken, a full enquiry was promised; stern disciplinary action loomed for the driver if fault was found. All the boxes were efficiently ticked. But whenever Ginny enquired about the boy and the crime that had provoked the massive police response, she received the same guarded response: The boy was wanted for questioning in relation to a very serious offence.

It was only on the way to the garage to collect Simon's Mazda that they encountered a police driver who was less tight-lipped.

"You know that young thug they pulled in this afternoon?" Ginny began. "Believe it or not, I used to teach him when he was a sweet little thing at infant school.

"Not exactly your star pupil then?" the driver replied, glancing in his driving mirror to see how his witticism was received.

"You can say that again!" she said, offering a grin. "Looks as though he's deep in doo-doo this time…"

"The kid's a menace. Needs locking up before he kills someone. The joy-riding's bad enough, but they torched the car in the underground car-park and the Heywood Shopping Centre nearly went up in smoke. The sooner he's banged up in Fulford the better."

Simon attempted a mildly liberal critique of the Youth Justice system which produced a stony silence. When the police car finally pulled onto the garage forecourt, Ginny suspected that the driver was just as pleased to wave them goodbye as they were to be out in the fresh air.

"Not the most sensitive of souls," Simon observed.

The mechanic behind the reception desk explained a few of the 'little extras' on the bill and handed the print-out to Simon, who gave it a cursory glance and was about to push it into the back pocket of his jeans when Ginny filched it from his fingers.

"I can see why you're desperate for this promotion," she said dryly. "You have an expensive mistress."

But the money appeared to have been well spent. A spin along the Esplanade was achieved at sixty without the wheel-wobble that had previously caused him distress and the engine was adjudged to be 'running sweet'. By the time they had turned into Highfield Avenue the whole transaction at the garage had become a bargain.

For a moment it was like night as they passed under the canopy of the big copper beech and scrunched onto the rough gravel drive. Simon backed expertly into the ramshackle shed that served them as a double garage and there it was—the house, dappled by the late-afternoon sun through the lime trees; a hodgepodge of architectural oddities, clapboard with hanging tiles, red brick, steel and glass; a century or more of haphazard evolution.

Ginny raised her arms and stretched luxuriantly. "I have never, ever been so glad to be home," she said through a yawn. "What a day!"

Simon pressed a button on the dash and with a low hum the roof reared up over their heads. "You haven't forgotten the Bryants, have you?" he asked, wincing in anticipation.

"Oh, no way!" Ginny said, shaking her head. "Absolutely no way am I going to the sodding Bryants'! Not today! Not after the day we've had!"

Taking the keys out of the ignition, Simon got out of the car, grabbed his leather satchel from behind the driving seat and left her seething while he let himself into the house. He was in the kitchen filling the kettle when she finally appeared.

"A nice cup of tea, a good, long soak in the tub and . . ."

"I don't get this, Simon," Ginny interrupted, sitting down at the pine table. "All afternoon you've been treating me like I'm made of glass and balsa wood, and now, when I'm strung out like a violin, you want me to spend a grisly evening with the rotten Bryants!"

"Oh, come on, Gin! You get on fine with Jane, and we don't have to stay until..."

"Ring up and cancel, Simon. I'm not kidding!"

"I can't, Gin, not with the state of play up the hill. It's not going to look very collegiate if I'm not there to welcome a new colleague, is it?" He observed the pained look on her face, and pressed his case further. "That's what this bun-fight is all about—a new woman in the department. She's a poet from Nottingham or somewhere..."

"OK, that's it!" Ginny said, and slapped the table. "I really couldn't take another of your poets, not today!"

"Now that is ridiculous."

Ginny screwed up her face in distaste. "Do you remember the last one you brought home—that woman with the shaven head and the born-again gleam in her eye...Sappho in dungarees?"

Simon said nothing. She watched him go through his meticulous ritual with the kettle, warming the pot, spooning in the loose leaves. God knows why tea-bags are liturgically heretical.

"Seriously," she said, "why don't you go on your own?"

Pot to kettle, water poured at boiling point, precisely; oven timer set for four minutes.

"I don't like to leave you on your own," he said.

Liar, she thought. You can kiss arse with gay abandon if I'm not there to snigger, that's the truth of it.

"I really should get my feet up," she said.

"That's true," he agreed.

"And there's no need to tell porkies this time!" she said. "You can lay it on thick about how traumatised I am after the accident."

"And you really don't mind if I go on my own?"

"Of course I don't."

It was the perfect negotiation. Everybody gets what they wanted in the first place, with no loss of face.

She opened the French doors into the Edwardian conservatory that had been built on to the back wall of the house. Simon called it her 'studio'. She called it her 'playroom', and, now that she was job-sharing, she spent more time in here playing with clay than she did at school. It was her domain: papier-mâché masks flew like a flock of surreal birds, slung from the old vine that smothered the wall and infiltrated the stained-glass roof-space; families of rag-dolls lived on top of cupboards; vivid canvases leaned against the window-ledges, bent under the weight of pots and primitive figurines.

It amused her to think of Simon's eyrie, perched at the top of the house, three storeys above her head, the antipodes to her playroom—a stark and scrupulously organised space in which the only decorative features were a parchment scroll of Chinese calligraphy and a large poster of the footballer, Zinedine Zidane, brooding in black and white above the desk. As her shrewd old Gran had observed on a snoop not long before she died, the house was like their marriage: 'chalk, cheese, and a muddle in the middle.'

The beeper beeped in the kitchen and Simon announced tea.

"Won't be a tick!" she called, her head buried in the cupboard where she stored the miscellany of her life.

The chaos in the cupboard disguised a filing system which rarely let her down. On the bottom shelf she found what she was looking for. Taking the lid off one of the shoeboxes, there he was, at the top of the pile—in the whirl of the Maypole, in a blur of girls and ribbons, an exuberant little boy. The only boy, his mouth gulping sunshine, joy in his eyes, and his blood drumming with the dance.

"There he is," she said, handing the print across the kitchen table. "I knew I'd got it somewhere."

"Wow!" said Simon. "That's some photograph. Did you take it?"

"Don't be daft! It was a student we had—he spent more time taking snaps than he did with the kids."

"Doesn't look much like our reprobate..."

"Oh, that's him ok. Little Will Buckley aged five."

She tipped the photographs on to the table and began to shuffle them.

"Here we are, the whole gang—Class 1 with their brand new teacher." Ginny looked closely at one of the pictures and shook her head. "God, I look a sight!"

Simon pinched the photograph from her hand. "You look like a schoolgirl yourself. Very fetching."

"Gran was right," said Ginny. "You really are a dirty old man,"

He turned the photo towards her and pointed at one of the children. "Is that him?"

Ginny followed the finger. "That's him. It's hard to believe that little angel is the yob we saw today!"

"It's sad," said Simon, "I'm not surprised you're upset."

Ginny sighed. "I'd really love to know what went wrong."

She began flipping through the frozen moments of that distant Sports Day as though they might provide an answer. Eventually, in the crowd of parents at the sack race, beyond the row of out-of-focus bundles bounding for the tape, she saw them—the Buckleys. She was a pretty woman, blonde hair mussed up by the wind, eyes bright with life. He was behind her, a tall, athletic-looking man, leaning forward with his fist clenched. Both intensely focused on their son, both willing him to win.

"Look at the poor parents," she said, passing the photo across, "on the other side of the tape, cheering for Will."

Simon gazed thoughtfully at the picture. "Thank God we never know what the Fates are cooking up for us," he said, then frowned and looked more closely. "Hey, isn't that Jude, at the back of the group?"

"Yeah, she'd be there!" Ginny exclaimed. "Give me a look..."

"Was their Caroline in the same class?" Simon asked.

"No, she's older than Will. She was in the same class as his sister, a couple of years ahead."

Ginny sat back in her chair, cradling the big teacup in both hands. She took a sip and, with a shiver of relish, said, "Oh, goodie, goodie!"

Simon looked suspicious. "What are you plotting now?" he asked.

"A good goss with Jude, that's what!" she replied. "It's just what I need."

Jude Holroyd had been Simon's friend long before Ginny appeared on the scene. Their parents had been near neighbours in one of the upmarket London suburbs and, when the prep schools emptied out for the hols, Simon and Jude had ended up in the same posh gang. Years later, by sheer fluke, they had become neighbours again.

Jude lived at the top end of Highfield Avenue, in the heart of what she called 'The Ghetto', the sprawl of Edwardian and Victorian villas half-hidden in the leafy lattice of avenues and lanes which had been colonised by academics and administrators as the university spread its tentacles down the hill. It was a source of great frustration to Jude that her husband, who ran the University Medical Centre, took his Hippocratic Oath seriously, thus denying her many a juicy titbit that would have added to her already encyclopaedic knowledge of campus gossip.

'You and I are extras in the academic soap-opera,' she had once said to Ginny, 'non-speaking parts, but very close to the hanky-panky.' That was only partly true. Jude had lots to say, and the acid on her tongue ensured that her contributions were enjoyed and feared in equal measure. On the endless circuit of university dinner-parties it was always a relief to hear her boisterous laughter as you came into the room.

A large woman, who dressed to flaunt her stature, tonight Jude was wearing what looked like a bell-tent of cream silk, covered in large red flowers to match her glossy lipstick. In her hand she brandished a bottle of Rioja.

"Lead me to a corkscrew!" she ordered, and marched down the hallway.

Ginny tagged on behind. "No wine for me, I'm afraid," she called, "I'm on the wagon."

Jude brought herself to an impressive standstill. "You're preggers again, aren't you?" she asked.

Ginny nodded. "Two months," she said.

Jude crossed her fingers. "Third time lucky," she said. "I feel it in my water."

Ginny collected a half-empty bottle of *Badoit* from the fridge, and Jude got to work with the corkscrew.

"According to my little bird," she said, tapping her nose conspiratorially, "you're going to be cracking open the bubbly before too long."

"Since when did the VC start confiding in you, Jude?"

"You'd be surprised what a discreet soul like me picks up on her travels."

Ginny slumped down on one of the kitchen chairs. "Oh God," she groaned, "I do hope he gets it this time."

The last rejection had almost scuppered them. For most people a two-year exchange with the University of California would have been a spectacular consolation prize. Not for Simon. He'd gone into a spiral of despair. And if it hadn't been for a chance encounter with the potter's wheel she might have joined him.

The cork popped and the wine glugged.

"You must not be doomy!" Jude instructed. "Trust me. Lady Luck has definitely turned a somersault." She raised her glass. "Here's to the three of you—you, Simon, and the baby."

Ginny raised her own glass and took a sip of fizzy water. "Take a look at these, Jude," she said, pushing the shoebox across the table. "They'll take you back a bit…"

Jude put on the half-moon spectacles that had been dangling round her neck, removed a handful of photographs and spread them on the table. "Great God!" she exclaimed. "That's me, three stones ago!"

"Let's see!" Ginny scrambled to her feet and leaned over Jude's shoulder.

The woman in the refreshment tent had been snapped mid-lick as her ice-cream cone threatened to go into melt-down.

"I look positively anorexic, don't I?" Jude said.

Ginny gave a snort. "I wouldn't go that far."

"Bitch!" Jude muttered, and began sifting through the pile of photographs. "Here they are!" she said, pointing to the Buckleys at the sack-race.

"I only met them a couple of times at parents' evenings," Ginny said. "They seemed a nice family."

"They were. When you and Simon were in the States, we saw quite a lot of them. Our Caroline and their Chloe were like that…" Jude crossed her fingers to illustrate. "We were invited round for supper, and the Buckleys came to us. We all got on very well. For a used-car-salesman, he's remarkably civilised, and she was lovely."

"So how come the past tense?" Ginny asked. "What went wrong?"

Jude gave a grimace. "I feel terrible about the Buckleys," she confessed, "…especially her. I dropped her like a stone, I'm afraid." She took another swallow of Rioja, and reached for the bottle.

"Sounds a good story…" Ginny said, folding her arms on the table-top, "tell me more."

Jude poured another glass and leaned back in her chair. "They were worried about the lad. He'd just started at the local comp and it wasn't going well. They asked me to put in a word for him at St Ninian's. Boy, I wish I hadn't!"

"Bad news, even then?"

"A nightmare, from the word 'go'. Fighting, thieving, you name it. According to the Bursar, he was working his ticket…"

"And what does that mean?" Ginny asked.

"Trying to get expelled," Jude explained.

"But why?"

Jude shrugged. "God knows, but he got his wish. They kicked him out—well, to be strictly accurate, the Buckleys were persuaded to take him away. Mustn't have any nasty publicity for St Ninnies, must we? Stops the big cheques rolling in!"

"And you dropped the Buckleys?"

"I did, I'm afraid," Jude acknowledged. "As school secretary, I knew all the gory details, and I simply couldn't face them. The Head couldn't prove anything, but your 'sweet little Will' almost certainly put a match to the new science block."

Ginny was exhausted, but the events of the day jangled around in her head and sleep would not come. Eventually she heard the crunch of gravel on the drive and the security light flared, throwing the roses on the bedroom curtains into silhouette. The front door opened and closed, and the crack around the bedroom door lit up. Floorboards creaked on the landing and the light went out again. Simon tip-toed into the darkened room and she watched him undress through half-closed eyes.

"Are you awake?" he whispered.

She said nothing. He would have lots to tell, he always did. But not tonight. Not tonight.

Lying in the darkness, her fingers explored the flatness of her stomach, and she tried without success to drain her mind of the clatter of the day.

Chapter Three

She was spared the nightmare, but after a night of fitful sleep woke to find herself a prisoner in her own body. Only her eyes were alive, darting about in their sockets, frantic. In a short while her mind would regain control of her limbs—she knew that because the psychiatrist had told her so. But, for those few helpless moments, reason was small consolation.

After the bad start, Saturday continued to be grim. She looked in the mirror and saw a face that did not belong to her, a face that was sallow and drawn. Why 'drawn'? Stretched out like a wire, perhaps? Or drawn like a turkey—goodbye giblets, unreliable innards. She gave herself a sour smile and felt sick.

Simon fretted over her. She responded with peevishness and drove him away to his desk. He cooked for her and she took refuge from the reek of garlic, distracting herself in the playroom, clawing at the clay, searching for something that would not come out. He read a book and she resented his absorption. He closed the book and asked her if she would like a walk. She was irritated by his forbearance and refused. Sniping and harrying, she grizzled the day away, unable to relent—poking away at his patience like she poked at the clay, producing nothing. And later, as they lay together in the big double bed, the weight of guilt pressed down on her and the hand that should have stretched out to give and to receive reassurance refused to move.

On Sunday morning she insisted on hoovering the house and Simon escaped to play five-a-side football with the other middle-aged boys up the hill. The whine of the vacuum cleaner almost swallowed the chime of the doorbell but her ear picked it out and she opened the door to find Doc Holroyd on the doorstep carrying the Sunday papers. Jude had told him about the baby and, as he was passing...Doc was not an accomplished liar. Simon had obviously been on the phone making a fuss.

Curiously enough though, after half an hour chatting to Doc about not very much, she felt calmer, and when Simon returned from football she surprised him with a peck on the cheek and apologised for being a shrew. She cooked an omelette for lunch and they argued companionably about the nonsense in the paper. Then Simon went upstairs to the sitting-room and tinkled jazz abstractions on the baby-grand while she went back to the clay. By the end of the afternoon, she had created a nest of highly satisfactory vipers—six writhing serpents which raised their heads, mouths gaping for the slender candles they would eventually hold.

Monday morning came and she felt lousy again. When Simon suggested that she should call in sick, it was tempting to crawl back under the duvet. If he had not persisted, she may have relented, but he kept on and on and her resolve stiffened. Terrified that she might vomit, she asked him to open the roof of the car and, despite the chill wind and scudding cloud, he obliged. But he couldn't resist making one last attempt to persuade her to stay at home.

"Jesus, Simon!" she exploded. "It's called 'morning sickness'—not cancer! Just drive the bloody car. I want some wind in my face."

They drove in silence until they were approaching the T-junction at the bottom of the avenue. "Go the long way, over the Wold," she snapped.

He checked his watch. "Have we got time?" he asked.

"Drive fast!" she said. "That's what this damned thing is for, isn't it?"

"Oh, for Christ's sake!" he cursed and threw the wheel over, slamming through the gears to accelerate up the steep winding road, pressing her back into her seat and shifting her from side to side at every bend. She swallowed to control the queasiness and felt sweat on her brow. But as they reached the summit and rounded the Devil's Elbow the sun broke through in a dazzle of gold and silver, and the wind off the sea slapped her awake. They plunged like a roller-coaster, plummeting down the escarpment towards the city and she shrieked with the sheer joy of it. By the time they pulled into the school car park, she felt renewed.

Using the heels of her hands to rub away the cold tears on her cheeks, she said, "Jesus, Simon! That was a real trip! I'm sorry I lost my rag."

"Me too," he replied, reaching across her lap to open the door for her. "Are you sure you're OK?"

"I feel loads better. Can you pick me up about quarter to four?"

"No problem. I'm teaching till lunch, then I'm back on the book and the day's my own."

Ginny reached behind his seat for her shoulder bag and kissed him on the cheek. "Have a good day," she said.

She waved as the car pulled out into Murray's Road and watched him waiting at the corner of Dorset Avenue while gaggles of children and pram-pushing mums crossed in front of the Lollipop Lady.

Banter or bickering; that was all they seemed to manage these days. The niggling was down to her, of course. She could see that. Small wonder that he retreated into his own private spaces. And when did that begin, that sense of being shut out? A year ago? Five? When she was his student, he used to rehearse his thinking out loud, and she would get glimpses of his mind at work. Not anymore.

She arrived at the classroom to find her assistant, Jan Lockwood, buried in the big corner cupboard. She had already retrieved numerous pairs of kitchen scales in brightly coloured plastic.

"Hi, Jan!" she called. "Good weekend?"

"Too blinking good," came the muffled reply.

Jan emerged from the cupboard.

"My God, you do look rough," exclaimed Ginny.

She had a frazzled expression on her face and a large cardboard box of toys in her hands.

"We took Dave's mother home on Saturday and we spent yesterday celebrating," Jan explained.

When she'd returned from California to find that a bright young thing had taken her job, the idea of sharing the work had seemed ludicrous at first. But it had worked brilliantly, for both of them, thanks in huge measure to the wonderful Jan Lockwood, who was the best teaching assistant on the planet.

"Go and get yourself a cup of coffee, for goodness sake," said Ginny. "I'd have brought 'the hair of the dog' if I'd known."

The bell rang. It was all about to begin again. She took a deep breath and, before she had time to exhale, the room began to seethe with little people. A hand tugged at her skirt and she looked down to a pair of eager eyes and a happy smile.

"My granddad died on Friday, Mrs May."

"Oh, that is sad, Jarvis. I am sorry."

Now that he had her attention, the smile broadened. "My mum has been crying all the time."

"Oh, poor mummy! You'll have to be very kind to her."

"I've got a headache, Mrs May." It was Chantelle Babcock, lower lip trembling, eyes huge with tears.

"Go and get a nice drink of cold water, Chantelle. That will make it better."

She began to shoo her charges towards their tables, promising stars and smiley faces. Clapping her hands, she said, "Come on now, I'm going to count to five and I want everybody at their tables, as quiet as little mice. One…two…"

She felt a warm presence against her thigh and looked down. He was there again—the albino head, the thick glasses, the thumb stuck in mouth. "Come on, Jason, off we go…" Taking hold of the skinny shoulders, she pushed him gently towards the table by the window. "Four….four and a half….four and three-quarters… sh!... sh!...sh!"

By now, Jason was in place, his finger sealing his lips just like hers, his enormous eyes gazing adoringly at her as she shaped her mouth to form the magic number.

"Ffffff-ive!" she shouted and cupped her hand behind her ear, turning around to listen intently to every table. A cough was smothered. "Brilliant!" she exclaimed. "Quieter than the quietest mouse!"

Standing in front of the white-board, she pronounced the ritual greeting, "Good morning, Class One." And, in the eternal sing-song of the infant school, the chant came back, "Good morning, Miss-sis May. Good mor-ning, Miss-sis Lock-wood."

While Mrs Lockwood distributed the worksheets for Literacy, Ginny began to check the register, listening to the piping voices around the room, the cheeky, the confident, the sullen, and the mousy-quiet like Jason—poor, clingy, little kid. What nightmare do you live in, little man?

The morning passed. Pens struggled with the curly 'c', and then the kicking 'k'. Teddy bears were weighed in the scales. A song was sung in the hall and the vicar told a joke that nobody understood. Playtime came and went with a cup of cold coffee in the squally rain. Then wild animals roared on the white board courtesy of the Internet and a herd of thirty-three eccentric elephants were daubed on posters. Hair was sucked, noses were picked and nails were bitten.

The lunchtime bell was a relief. She had started lining up the children, girl-boy-girl, ready to crocodile their way into the school hall when the school secretary, Mrs Appleby, popped her head around the door.

"Can you give your husband a ring, Mrs May?" she said. "He called about half an hour ago."

"Thanks, Mrs Appleby," Ginny replied and fished in her bag to retrieve her mobile. He had never called her at school before.

"Can you take the children through to lunch, Mrs Lockwood? I won't be a moment." The cheerful crocodile set off, every hand waving her goodbye as though they were leaving for ever.

Simon answered on the second ring.

"Hi, Gin. . ."

"Is there a problem?"

"I can't pick you up as arranged, I'm afraid. I'm up before the Dean. . ."

"Jeez," she said, with an intake of breath, "is this it?"

"Could be. . ."

"Hey, that's terrific. . ."

"Hang on a mo, Gin. It wasn't good news the last time out. . ."

"This time is different—I can feel it!"

"Come off it, witch, you'll have me jinxed. . ."

"Oh, don't be such a sad-socks," she teased, "remember 'Batty' Bettelheim in California!" She assumed a manly trans-Atlantic drawl and went on, "'Positive Mental Attitude, Dr May! PMA's the only way!'"

"Personally, I'd rather expect the worst . . ."

"Well, Jude thinks it's yours—and Jude is never wrong! Anyway, I have fingers and toes crossed for you. And don't worry about me; I'll catch a bus home."

"No, don't do that. I'm seeing Klugman at 3.30 so I should be with you by 5 at the latest. Can you hang around?"

"Oh, I'll keep myself out of mischief. . . And Simon, you deserve it. You really do. . ."

"Thanks, Ginny....Thank you for everything," he said, suddenly serious. "I really mean it."

She looked at the mobile to check that he had disconnected. It was an odd thing for him to have said. Quite unlike him.

The eager anticipation on the sea of faces as Ginny prepared to read them a story convinced her, as it always did, that this was the most precious part of their day together. Arms folded on their tables, heads resting on their arms – just as Mrs Osborne, her own infant-teacher had instructed all those years ago – Class One waited to be transported into the world of *Borka*, the little Russian gosling, born without feathers, whose mother had to knit a pullover to save it from the icy winter. And as she read, the silence around her reading voice grew heavy with the children's dreams.

When the story ended, the classroom erupted with noisy questions that refused to die away, even when the end-of-school bell rang out. Mrs Lockwood took charge of the scrimmage by the coat-rack while Ginny coped with the more persistent children. Jason Nolan was back at her side, rubbing a pleat of her skirt between his finger and thumb, savouring the sensation as he sucked on the other thumb, and when she crossed the room to her locker, he shuffled along beside her.

She looked at her mobile and switched on. The digital clock appeared. Simon would be on his way to see the Dean this very minute. Please, please, bring good news.

Prising Jason's hand from her skirt, she slipped the phone back into her shoulder-bag and led him through the long corridors to Reception, out along the path towards the school gate, searching for his mother in the throng of parents and their skittish offspring. A furniture van passed by with a gust of exhaust and there on the opposite side of Murray's Road was Jason's mum with pram and toddler, waiting with other late-comers at the traffic lights. But what caught her eye, and made her take an involuntary step forward, was a face glimpsed for an instant at the back of the crowd. Was it the Buckley boy? Surely not? A convoy of school buses wiped the crowd from view and, by the time the road was clear, the figure had vanished.

As the pram approached, she said, "Hello, Mrs Nolan, I've brought a young man to meet you."

The woman extended her hand towards Jason and the little boy scuttled to her side. "Has he been good?" she asked in a low, flat voice.

"He's been very good, haven't you, Jason?" Ginny returned her gaze to the mother. "You would let us know if there was a problem, wouldn't you, Mrs Nolan? We're here to help, you know."

The tired eyes were defensive. "We're fine….aren't we Jason?"

Ginny watched the Nolans make their way to the traffic lights, with Jason sneaking glances over his shoulder to check that she was still there, his mother moving with slow solemnity, as though she were too tired to push the pram.

Preoccupied, Ginny turned away, her gaze travelling absently across the parade of shops on the opposite side of the road, then back, drawn instinctively to the newsagent's shop, sensing watching eyes in the shadows behind the window display. Her suspicion seemed to trigger a movement, and she knew for certain that he was there. On the next green light she crossed the road.

He was standing at a carousel of picture postcards, spinning it with his forefinger, rhythmically, aimlessly, his face turned away from her. The shopkeeper was serving two little girls, keeping a wary eye on the children who grazed the shelves of sweets. Ginny took an Evening Gazette from the stack and fumbled in the shoulder bag to find her purse.

"Good afternoon, Mrs May," said the newsagent.

The postcards stopped spinning.

"Hello, Mr Aziz," she said, handing over a twenty pound note. "Sorry to take all your change."

"That's no problem at all, Mrs May."

Ginny thanked the beaming newsagent and turned as though to leave.

"Good gracious!" she said. "Is that Will Buckley?"

The shoulders stiffened under the T-shirt.

"What a coincidence!" she exclaimed.

"Hello, Mrs May," he said, doing his best to sound surprised.

His eyes were pale blue and flecked with violet. The wildness that she had seen in them had vanished. This wasn't the thug who kicked the world in the teeth. This was the boy who had danced the Maypole. She could see him clearly.

"How did you get the scar?" she asked, speaking without thinking.

His hand went up to his right eye where a small pink scar tugged the eyelid downwards towards the cheekbone. It gave a piratical cast to an otherwise unexceptional young face.

"I had a spot of bother," he said.

"You and 'bother' seem to go together," she replied. "I'm quite surprised to see you out and about, to be honest!"

He stuck his hands in the pockets of his jeans and eyed her warily, head cocked to one side. Seeing his features harden as he reconstructed his defences, Ginny's instincts took control.

"Would you like to come across to the school and take a look at your old classroom?" she asked.

"What for?" he said, as though she were crazy.

"Oh, I don't know—for old time's sake."

He looked at her with undisguised pity.

"It's not changed that much," she went on, "a bit more hi-tech perhaps...do you like computers?"

The boy followed her out of the newsagent's putting on a show of sulky indifference, but by the time they were crossing Murray's Road it was as though the expedition had been his own idea, and Ginny could hardly keep pace with his loping stride as he swaggered up the school path, thumbs hooked into his studded belt, shoulders rolling like an East Side hoodlum.

"I've got a visitor, Mrs Appleby," Ginny called through the open window at reception. "He's an old boy, aren't you Will? Can we sign him in please?"

The school secretary placed the visitor's book on the ledge.

"They want your autograph, Will," said Ginny, as the boy hung back. "Come on, don't be shy!"

The boy scrawled an indecipherable signature with a nonchalant flourish and threw the pen back on top of the book.

"Believe it or not, that says 'William Buckley'," Ginny said, pulling a face. "And to think—I taught him how to write!"

"He'd make a good doctor," Mrs Appleby said, reaching for the switch below the window.

With a metallic click, the inner glass door trembled on its hinge, and Ginny pushed it open for her guest. "Lead the way," she invited, "if you can still remember."

As though he had been in the school only yesterday, Will made his way unerringly through the labyrinth of corridors to Ginny's classroom.

"Ten out of ten, and a Smiley Face!" Ginny said. "You've got a good memory, Will."

"I'm Whizz now," he said. "I don't like 'Will'."

"I'll try and remember that, but it won't be easy," she replied. "How come you're out, Whizz? They told me they were going to lock you away for a long time."

"I didn't do it, did I?" he snapped, defying contradiction. "I told them I didn't do it and they made prats of themselves, cos I could prove I didn't do it." The yob was back.

Ginny threw open the classroom door, and issued a challenge. "I bet you can't find your old place."

With a sneer, he slouched towards the window beside the playing field and pointed to the chair that nowadays belonged to the pushy Miss Levinson.

"That's it!" he said.

Ginny pulled back the tiny chair, expecting him to baulk at the invitation, but he sat down, unable to squeeze his knees under the table. Like Gulliver in Lilliput.

Ginny perched herself on a table in front of him. "How long is it since you were at Murray's Road?" she asked.

There was no reply. He was gazing about him at the paintings on the walls, a gentle smile on his lips.

"How old are you now, Will?"

"Whizz," he said, emerging from daydreams. He gave her a pointed look. "My name is Whizz."

"Sorry, I forgot. How old are you, Whizz?"

"Eighteen," he said, swallowing the 't'.

Ginny wrinkled her nose. "Pull the other one! You're not eighteen—I can do the sums."

"You do 'em then," he grunted.

"You always were a terrible fibber, Whizz, even when you were little. You were the worst fibber I ever had."

The strange violet-blue eyes shone. He liked this idea, and he wanted more.

"You told the most outrageous porkies ever, and, silly old me, I used to swallow every word. Do you remember the day you told the whole class that your dad had had his leg chopped off in a car accident, and we all fell for it, even the Head?"

The boy wriggled with pleasure as he re-lived the moment.

"And when your mum came to collect you," she continued, "there we all were, so sympathetic. 'Oh, Mrs Buckley,' I said, 'how dreadful for you! How is your poor husband?' . . . And your poor mum didn't have a clue what we were on about!"

At the mention of his mother, he had stopped smiling.

"Do you remember that? You monkey!"

With a twitch of his head Will became Whizz again, but in the microsecond between then and now, as the barricades went up, she glimpsed the panic in him.

"What is it you want with me, Whizz?" she asked.

The boy's brow furrowed, and his eyes narrowed.

"What's that?" he asked, looking over Ginny's shoulder.

She turned to follow his line of vision.

"The white board, do you mean?" she said, puzzled and disappointed. "That's new since your day. It's got all the latest bells and whistles." She went over to the computer to give him a demonstration. "To be honest, I preferred our old blackboard. I'm so kack-handed on this thing. The kids are all much better at it than I am..."

A muffled version of her mobile's tinny tune began to play inside her shoulder-bag.

"I'm sorry, Will," she said, retrieving the phone and checking the display. "It's my husband, and it's important, I'm afraid."

She turned her back on the boy and, saying a silent prayer, wandered to the back of the class. She clamped the mobile to her ear.

"Hi, Simon," she said, conscious of the tension in her voice.

"Guess what?" he said, and went silent.

"Stop teasing…"

"You are talking to the new incumbent of the Herbert Quayle Chair of English and American Literature."

"Oh, Simon, that is fantastic! I am so, so happy for you." Forgetting the boy, she whooped in triumph like a cheerleader at an American football game and wagged her fist in the air.

"It does feel pretty good, I must say," he agreed.

"'Professor May'," she rehearsed. "That'll take some getting used to."

"You can call me Prof for short, if you like. . ."

He was playing it down, but as he went over the meeting with the Dean and the Vice Chancellor she could hear the relief in his voice, and she felt so pleased and proud that her eyes began to fill with tears. Everyone said that he should have been given his Chair years ago, and it was miserably unjust that he'd been overlooked. Wiping away the tears with the back of her hand, she suddenly remembered that the boy had been a silent witness to her un-teacherly behaviour, and turned round to give him a friendly wave...only to find that she was staring at an empty room.

"Oh, Christ, he's gone!" she exclaimed, interrupting Simon in full flow. "Look, something's cropped up and I've got to go."

"What on earth's the matter?" he asked anxiously.

"I'll tell you when you get here," she said, and snapped the mobile shut.

Scurrying along the corridors, checking the empty classrooms to left and right, she stopped to peer through one of the round porthole windows of the school hall and, in the dim light, saw a figure disappearing through the double doors opposite. She hurried in pursuit and eventually burst into the foyer where she narrowly avoided a collision with the Head. He was standing outside his office, jaw set and arms folded. Through the glass doors she could see the Buckley boy stalking angrily up the path towards Murray's Road. One of the fathers, who was shepherding a group of older children out of the building, seemed anxious to be elsewhere. There had been a confrontation. That much was obvious.

The Headmaster gave her a sour look. "Last time that young man paid us a visit it was three o'clock in the morning and the police had to pull him off the school roof."

"I'm sorry, Mr Croft," Ginny said, "I got distracted and he slipped away."

"He shouldn't have been here, Mrs May. He's bad news."

Ginny returned to the classroom to collect her things. To her puzzlement, the shoulder bag was not on the coat-hook where it ought to be. It was lying on the table where she had been sitting with the boy. She opened the leather flap to drop the mobile inside. Suspicious, she began to check the contents of the bag: keys to the house; headscarf; appointment card from the clinic; Building Society book. And the purse: a single twenty; the fiver folded inside the tenner from the newsagent; credit card; switch card. Nothing missing.

Feeling relieved, she put on her coat and, before turning off the lights, cast her eye over the room, still pestered by an intuition that something was not as it should be. And then she saw what it was. The storybook had gone from her table. Intrigued, she checked her bookcase to see if she had put it away out of habit, but there was no mistake. The boy had taken *Borka*.

Puzzled, yet strangely gratified, she turned off the lights and made her way through the deserted building to the car park where Simon's Mazda was waiting.

"Sorry," she said, as she opened the door, "I got held up."

The ignition fired and the engine revved with a fruity roar.

"Hey, not so fast!" she shouted, and knelt on the bucket seat so that she could put her arms around him. "Let me give my clever husband a big sloppy kiss."

Simon laughed and kissed her back. "Shameless hussy!" he exclaimed. "We're not out of the school car park yet."

"You must be chuffed!" she said, holding him at a distance to see him better.

"You can say that again," he replied with conviction. "I thought I was going to have to go chair-chasing all over the damned place."

"I did wonder if you'd permanently blotted your copy-book," said Ginny, performing contortions to get her legs under the dash.

The Mazda nosed its way into the stream of traffic, and Ginny immediately started to thumb her way through her contacts on her mobile phone.

"Who are you calling?" Simon asked.

"Only the 'charmed circle'..."

"Oh, do we have to?" he moaned. "Can't we just have a quiet night in?"

"Don't be such a misery, Simon, they've been rooting for you for years—and anyway, I want to do some boasting."

The car edged forwards in the heavy traffic.

"Hey, Jude," she said, when the phone answered, "guess what? You were right."

Simon nudged her with his elbow. "Look, Gin . . ." he shouted, "look back there... across the road, in front of Boots ..."

"Hang on, Jude," Ginny said, craning her neck, "the Prof is being a pain."

For a moment the chemist's shop was obscured by a passing bus but then she saw a police car parked with two wheels on the pavement, and Will Buckley, leaning back against the shop-window, legs spread and arms raised high above his head, mouthing off to another crowd of on-lookers while a uniformed policeman conducted a body-search.

"I didn't think we'd be seeing him again," said Simon, accelerating to keep pace with the traffic. "I thought they were going to throw away the key."

Chapter Four

It started in the lounge bar of The Halfway House, just the six of them, sharing a bottle of fizz while they studied the menu. Charlie Mullen, whose elevation to the Chair in Psychology had been meteoric and apparently effortless, could barely contain his joy at his old friend's success, and Ginny was relieved to see that his wife, Bee, had managed to shake off the blues. Even good old Doc sparkled in his own quiet way. Only Jude seemed oddly out of sorts.

Charlie, who had charge of the bottle, topped up the glasses and embarked on a caustic little speech, marvelling that, in offering a professorial chair to their good friend, the Vice Chancellor and his lackeys had displayed judgement and intelligence which the entire university had hitherto believed they lacked. In his best oratorical blarney, he went on to torment Simon with a lavish eulogy and was raising his glass to propose a toast when the door opened and half the English Department spilled in from the car-park.

"Ok, who put the word out?" asked Simon, with a sigh.

Everyone looked at Jude, who affected a smile of purest innocence. And before anyone could protest, their table was surrounded by well-wishers, all anxious to shake Simon's hand.

"Come on, Prof, it's your round!" someone shouted at the back of the crowd, an idea that was taken up enthusiastically and eventually propelled Simon towards the bar where he pleaded poverty, pulling out the linings of his trouser pockets to prove it.

"Yer man's a pauper, can't you see," Charlie Mullen intervened, "reduced to penury by skinflint governments, just like the rest of us. So, we'll have a whip round to help the poor divil out. A fiver each from every impoverished teacher, and not a penny piece from those poor beggars who bear the iniquitous burden of the Student Loan ..." There was a loud cheer, and then Charlie held his hand out to Simon. "And twenty quid from you, Professor May, if you please."

With a display of reluctance, Simon produced his wallet from the back pocket of his cords and, to the acclaim of the crowd, parted with two ten pound notes, adding an extra tenner with a flourish to milk the applause.

"I sometimes think Charlie loves your husband more than he loves me," Bee said, taking a swallow of champagne.

"You know, I'd forgotten about all this..." Ginny mused.

"....about our husbands' wild affair?" exclaimed Bee with a snort.

"Don't be daft... I'd forgotten how much he loves all this...camaraderie."

"It's his natural habitat," Jude observed. "He loves them, and they love him, simple as that."

A young woman with spectacular spiked hair, jet black and tipped with scarlet dye, was leaning forward to catch something that Simon was saying. Suddenly she put her head back and laughed. Simon buried his smile in a pint of bitter before wiping the foam from his upper lip and acknowledged a raised glass at the back of the scrum. Ginny watched as he moved among the crowd, seeing him across almost two decades of time. For a moment she was unaware that he was looking directly at her, puzzled by her lack of response. Feeling foolish, she raised a hand in greeting and surprised herself by blowing him a kiss.

Simon threaded his way out of the knot of drinkers and sat beside her. "You seemed miles away," he said, putting an arm around her shoulders.

"I was," she replied, "I was an age away, when life was always like this . . ."

"Ah yes, those halcyon days . . ." he said, mocking her gently, "those 'days of wine and roses.'"

"Don't be so cynical. I was remembering why I used to fancy you."

"Used to?"

"You bet—past tense! Don't run away with the idea that you are anything but a stuffy old professor." She squinted at him and added, "Who's the spiky little minx?"

Simon nodded towards the bar. "Do you mean, Mel?"

"The one they're all drooling over, the pretty little punk."

Simon started to laugh. "That's Melody Vance...your 'Sappho in dungarees'. She's the poet I wanted you to meet."

"You're kidding."

The girl had her audience spell-bound. Her face was geisha-white, with a jet-black spiral drawn just below her right eye, her lips a vivid scarlet like the spikes. She was outrageously different and twinkled mischief like a sprite.

"Not what you'd expect, I must admit," Simon said. "She's a performance poet, and a very good one at that."

Doc Holroyd advanced on them, a near-empty champagne bottle in his hand. "This is all Jude's fault, I'm afraid," he said. "She's robbed us of a nice, quiet dinner. I hope you two don't mind."

"Hooray for Jude!" cried Ginny. "We haven't had a spontaneous party for yonks."

"And what about you, Simon . . . ?"

"Oh, don't worry about old sad-socks," Ginny blustered, "he's loving every minute of it."

"Well, what say I order some sandwiches?" suggested Doc.

Ginny put a restraining hand on his arm. "No, hang on a mo," she said, struck by a brainwave. "Better still! Why don't we do a Pizza Party like in the olden days?"

Simon looked skywards for inspiration. "I wish you could make this woman see sense, Doc," he said. "She's supposed to be leading the quiet life."

Ginny gave him a challenging look, and began to tick off a list on her fingers.

"Take-away pizzas—no cooking! Plastic cups—no washing up! Bring a bottle—no booze to buy! There's absolutely nothing to do, Simon. Except live a little!"

Jude insisted on settling up with the taxi driver while Bee helped Ginny to carry the bulging Tesco bags to the front door. The twilight of evening gave way to the glare of a security light and a dog barked loudly in the house. Bee took a step backwards.

"My God! When did you get the dog?" she asked.

"We didn't," replied Ginny. "It's Simon's virtual guard-dog."

When she unlocked the door there were more intimidating snarls and a conventional burglar alarm started to whine. She began to enter the code in the touch-pad, then lifted her finger into the air, saying, "Down, Rover!" before pressing the final button. The barking stopped. "Good, isn't it?" she said in a voice rather too loud for the sudden silence.

"It scared the pants off me," said Bee.

In the gloomy hallway, the red light on the telephone was blinking brightly. "Blimey!" said Ginny, looking at the display. "Eleven messages. We've never been so popular."

Flicking the lights on, Ginny led the way into the sprawling kitchen, issuing instructions as she went.

"Can you dig out some dishes for the nibbles, Bee? You'll find them in the cupboard under the dresser... And Jude, you're in charge of candles..."

"Oh, very Freudian," quipped Jude. "And where do you keep your candles then?"

"Top shelf in the pantry—you'll find two big boxes full of stuff. We haven't lit the place up for years, but there should be plenty, especially with the night-lights we got from Tesco's."

Hunting through the profusion of postcards, invitations, and business cards that were pinned on the soft-board beside the fridge, it took Ginny a while to locate the take-away menu from The Pizza Place.

"How many pizzas do you reckon we'll need?" she called out.

"I counted twenty-six people back at the pub," Bee replied.

"And I think we should rustle up a few more..." Ginny said.

"Don't go mad, Ginny," Jude cautioned, "twenty-six is plenty."

"There are some of Simon's buddies in other departments that really should be here... I'd like to surprise him, if I can." Ginny picked up her purse and headed for the telephone in the hall, calling out over her shoulder, "I'll get a few for eight-thirty and a second delivery for later."

Her hand was reaching for the receiver when the doorbell rang. She opened the door expecting to greet another well-wisher and was surprised to find the silver-haired detective on the threshold.

"Hello, Mrs May, I'm glad I caught you," he said, pushing his warrant card forward. "D.S. Carmichael."

"I know who you are, sergeant—will I ever forget?"

He looked more like one of the yobs he chased than a policeman—scruffy jeans, blue trainers and a hoodie. But he was far younger than the hair would suggest, and handsome in his way, with the cool, suspicious gaze that comes with the warrant-card.

"I don't suppose you've seen Whizz Buckley hanging about round here this evening?" he asked, folding the wallet and returning it to the back pocket of his jeans

"Not round here, no...But I did see him this afternoon at school."

"I know you did..." Carmichael said. "We found this on him." From the patch-pocket in the hoodie he produced the missing copy of *Borka*.

"I gave it to him," Ginny said, the lie slipping easily to her tongue. "I used to read it to him when he was little."

"I'm not interested in how he got it," the policeman said, opening the book and turning the inside cover towards her. "But I would like to know why he's written your address in here."

Ginny leaned forward and read the child-like scrawl on the book's frontispiece.

"This is not your handwriting, I take it?" Carmichael asked.

Ginny took the book and looked more closely, frowning.

"No, it's not mine," she said.

Carmichael reached for his back pocket again. "I'd like you to call me if he shows up," he said, and handed her a business card.

"You seem to spend your life chasing this boy," she said.

The policeman looked at the floor for a moment as if debating how to respond. "He's not one of your five year-olds anymore, Mrs May," he said. "He's very screwed up is our Billy Whizz, and he keeps bad company."

"Why do you keep calling him that?" asked Ginny.

"Billy Whizz is the old street-name for speed, and that's his drug of choice..."

"And he prefers 'Whizz'?"

"Good name for an outlaw. That's how young Mr Buckley sees himself. He's at war with the world."

Carmichael put his hand out to take the storybook back. Instinctively, Ginny held it back.

"Do you mind if I keep it?" she asked.

Carmichael gave a noncommittal shrug, and studied her face for a moment.

"Look," he said, "I can understand why you're concerned for the lad, but he wrote down your address for a reason, so I'd be careful. Give me a call if you're worried. Despite what you may think, I don't spend my time chasing Whizz Buckley for the fun of it. To be honest, I've got a soft spot for the lad, but for some crazy reason he's gone haywire. The lad's a danger to himself and to everyone else. That could include you, Mrs May."

Ginny was intrigued and would have liked to learn more, but there was no time. Thanking the detective for his concern, she watched his shabby saloon car drive out of the gate, and wandered back to the kitchen, tapping the book against her lower lip. It was hard to believe that the boy was dangerous. Erratic, yes; needy, for sure; but she hadn't felt threatened, not in the least. She was uneasy now, though. There was no denying that. God knows why he wanted her address?

"Shall I open some wine," said Bee, breaking into her thoughts.

"Oh, yes...good idea," Ginny replied distractedly. "While you're at it, open a few. I know it's bring-a-bottle, but we don't want to run out."

Jude popped her head into the kitchen from the conservatory. "Do you want me to put candles in here as well?"

"No, I wouldn't bother," Ginny replied, squeezing past her. "I never take the Christmas lights down. It's too much of a fag, and they're impossibly tangled with the foliage by now." She knelt down beside the kiln, putting the copy of *Borka* on the floor, and unplugged one cable to replace it with another.

The effect was magical. A swarm of fireflies had appeared in the tresses of the vine producing myriad reflections in the angles of the glass and forming new constellations in the darkening sky.

"Just look at this Jude," Ginny said, picking up the book as she got to her feet. "This is spooky."

She showed Jude the page with the address scrawled across it and explained about the detective's visit.

"My God, Gin," Jude exclaimed, "that's scary—you've got a stalker!"

"I've found some absolutely delicious Sancerre," chirruped Bee as she teetered in from the kitchen. She held out two plastic beakers of white wine.

"Not for me, thanks," replied Ginny.

"Nor me," said Jude, "I'm on red."

Bee took a generous swig. "Well, I'm getting in the mood," she said, and boogied her way back to the kitchen, wagging her backside.

"Jee-sus!" Ginny exclaimed, slapping her forehead with the palm of her hand. "I forgot to order the pizzas. How stupid can you get?" She snatched a look at her watch. "My God, we'll never be ready in time!"

Jude blocked her way as Ginny made a dive for the kitchen and took hold of her by the shoulders. "For goodness' sake, calm down, woman," she said. "It's just a few mates round for drinks, that's all it is. Think about the baby, Ginny."

"I know, I know," Ginny groaned, shaking her head, "I've been totally manic for the last few days. Simon's been going spare, and I can't say I blame him."

"It's this wretched accident, isn't it? And the Buckley kid?"

"It hasn't helped, that's for sure," Ginny replied. "Believe it or not though, I feel tons better today. We've had so many 'downs' in the last few years, I'd forgotten that, you can actually get some 'ups'. It's like a great weight's been lifted, and I feel...well, I feel liberated." As though to demonstrate her feelings, Ginny lifted Jude's hands from her shoulders and grasped them in her own. "It's going to be all right this time, Jude, it really is. As soon as tonight's little celebration is over, I shall settle down like a broody old hen and quietly lay my egg. That's a promise."

Jude gave her a cock-eyed smile. "A reformed character, eh?" she said sceptically. "Well here's a test for you...Let me order those pizzas while you go and put some glad rags on."

The big sitting-room looked terrific. The Chinese yellow walls that she had fought for so doggedly worked well in the subdued lighting and set off the splashes of colour she had used in the collages. Standing in the doorway with her tray of pizzas, listening to the babble of conversation and the squalls of laughter, Ginny experienced a surge of relief. Her impetuous schemes did not always blossom, but tonight had been a success. The ludicrously expensive Max Mara frock that she'd bought for the wedding last year was worth every penny, and she was glad she hadn't been stuffy about the make-up. She didn't do glam as a rule, but tonight was different.

By the bay window, old Prof Gurgieff was holding court, his arm linked with Simon's in a gesture that spoke more of possession than comradeship—the elderly scholar proudly presenting his prodigy to a younger generation of students and dons. And Simon, evidently moved by what was being said, was smiling shyly, his eyes so unnaturally bright that she wondered if he was close to tears.

A gust of laughter drew her eye to the far side of the room where Jude was dispensing wine from two bottles as she entertained the crowd by the piano. It was clear from the pinched look on the face of Cordelia Bryant that Jude was baiting her again and, as Ginny approached with the tray of pizza-segments, she was in time to hear the twist of the knife.

"Well, I know you have me down as a fat philistine, Cordelia, but I don't care," Jude was saying. "Those uncrackable codes that you people call poetry leave me totally cold. Maybe these new-fangled 'poetry slams' that you're so sniffy about would turn me on." She turned to the spiky-haired poet. "What do you reckon, Mel? Could you make poetry come alive for a dim old trout like me?"

"I'll send you a ticket for my next gig," Mel replied.

"Oh, why wait so long?" Charlie Mullen interjected. "Now is the hour. . ."

"Hey, hey, hold on there." Mel had her palms out to ward off the challenge. "I'm a fully-fledged, professional poetry-tart and I only spout for money...."

"Well, that's no problem then," responded Charlie, taking out his wallet, "we'll have another whip round."

Mel raised her hands high, surrendering to the enthusiastic clamour. "Ok then," she conceded, "I'll spout a bit for you, but I'm not going to be the only show-off...Who else has got a party-piece?"

"Wild horses wouldn't stop Charlie giving us a dose of Yeats," said Jude.

"Oh, what a happy thought," agreed Charlie, rubbing his hand together. "Indeed I just might allow myself to be persuaded. . ."

"And Simon could play some jazz. . ."

The suggestion came from Cordelia Bryant. The silly woman had once called round when Simon was doodling on the piano and caught him unawares. If only she knew how much he loathed performing in public. Unfortunately her unwelcome suggestion had been greeted with enthusiasm and poor Simon was already being bullied to the piano, desperate for rescue, but beyond help.

He began with a tentative rendition of *Bye, Bye, Blackbird* and received a rapturous reception that was not entirely deserved, but it seemed to boost his confidence because he moved straight into a sequence of apparently aimless minor chords and looked around the room until he caught Ginny's eye. He gave her a secret little smile, and the chords began to shape themselves into a haunting version of *September Song*. She closed her eyes and the familiar words played in her head, "*Oh, it's a long, long while from*

May to December..., but the days grow short when you reach September..."
Then, all too soon, he segued into *The Birth of the Blues* and the
sentimental spell was broken. His fingers were teasing out ever
more complex variations on the old tune—'gymnastics for the
mind' he called them, and they absorbed him totally. His
students were impressed. She could see the glow of admiration in
their eyes and was reminded of that night long ago, when she'd
arrived early for one of their clandestine 'tutorials' and found him
at the keyboard lost in the same trance. Until that moment it had
been his intellect that dazzled her, but the intense focus that he
gave to his music betrayed a depth of feeling that she had not
previously fathomed. Was it then, perhaps, that she had
committed herself to him?

Wriggling her way through the press of people, the tray of
empty plates held high above her head, she made her way to the
stairs. It was a relief when she reached the kitchen to have the
place to herself. There was debris everywhere but the mess was
superficial, and by the time she had filled one of the big black
bin-liners with pizza-boxes, paper plates and plastic cups, order
was quickly restored. Tearing off another bin-bag from the roll,
she went into the conservatory and began working her way
towards the kiln. It was some time before she spotted a high-
heeled shoe lying on its side beside an empty wine bottle and
realised that she was not alone. The shoe was Bee Mullen's. She
was asleep, slumped in the battered upholstery of an old
armchair, a plastic cup of wine held precariously in her lap and a
frown on her brow. Ginny reached over and carefully removed
the cup, then tiptoed out of the conservatory, leaving the
sleeping woman to whatever dreams were troubling her.

Picking up the other bag of rubbish on the way, she went
through to the pantry. The night was black as ink and she could
see herself reflected in the grubby glass of the back door, but the
instant she threw it open the patio was lit up like a film set
waiting for actors. Walking out into the glare of the security
lights, she made her way round the side of the house. As she
turned the corner towards the lean-to where they kept the
wheelie-bins, the light clicked off and she was engulfed in
darkness. She paused for a moment to allow her eyes to become
accustomed to the dim light of the crescent moon. From the
sitting room above she could hear a woman's voice – Mel's
party-piece, she assumed – a rap of some kind, interrupted by
occasional laughter...and the piano picking up the syncopated

rhythms, weaving patterns round the voice. So focused was she on the thin sounds from the room upstairs that the voice that spoke out of the shadows was as loud and unexpected as a gunshot.

"Issis Nay… Issis Nay," it said in a husky whisper.

Paralysed by fear, she dropped the plastic sacks.

The voice spoke again, an incoherent mumble, as though through a mouthful of food. She turned to run, but a hand grabbed her wrist, and the voice spoke again, louder this time, and more urgent. Finally she understood.

"It'th Whith… It'th Whith…"

The hand relaxed its grip, and Ginny broke free, spinning away towards the patio, triggering the blinding whiteness of the security light. At the pantry door she turned, squinting at the boy who stood on the edge of the darkness.

"Don't be thcared," he said, slurring his words like a drunk, lurching unsteadily towards her.

Ginny slipped inside the pantry and closed the door, turning to rest her forehead against the glass, finding comfort in its coldness. With an effort of will, she relaxed the tension in her shoulders and steadied her breathing, saying a silent prayer that he would be gone when she looked up. When she was calmer, she raised her eyes. But he was there still, standing in the middle of the patio, stooped as though exhausted at the end of a race. Her fear began to dissolve, first into resentment and then to anger. How dare he terrorise her like this, in her own house?

She opened the door a fraction, ready to slam it shut and turn the key if he chose to make a rush.

"For God's sake, go away, Will," she shouted. "Just leave me alone or I'll call the police."

He shouted something and stumbled towards her. Quickly she closed the door. The garish light had sucked all colour from the scene, bleaching his hair an ashy white and turning his face into a mask she did not recognise. She turned the key and watched him, mesmerised by the sway of his shoulders as he shuffled closer. Finally, when he was no more than a couple of metres from the door, she saw what fear had forbidden her to see. Huge swellings had swallowed his eyes and the features of his face had all but vanished. A black gash had replaced one eyebrow. Congealed blood had welded his nose to his swollen mouth, and his lips were pouting like some ghastly fish.

Ginny unlocked the door and opened it. She could hear him now, whimpering like a child who has cried himself to exhaustion, his entire body trembling with the effort of breathing.

Hand outstretched, she went to him and took him gently by the arm. She began to whisper to him, slowly and tenderly, coaxing him towards the open door.

Chapter Five

A tipsy choir of undergraduates was giving a raucous account of *The Party's Over* as it lurched its way down the stairs. Ginny pinned a grin on her face and tried to look like the happy hostess as she battled against the tide of bodies. Spotting Charlie Mullen on the landing, she called out, "Is the Doc still up there?"

Charlie put his hands to the side of his mouth. "As far as I know, he's with Jude," he called back. "Have you seen Bee?"

Ginny wriggled herself past a noisy trio. "She's in the conservatory," she mouthed, pointing downstairs.

"She's not pissed again, is she?" Charlie asked, as they met on the staircase.

Ginny did not like the look on his face. "She's lonely, Charlie," she said, brushing by, "hadn't you noticed?"

It appeared that the entire senior common room was on the landing waiting for their inebriated students to disperse, fluttering like over-excited moths about the bright flame of their exotic new poet. Ginny was keen to winkle her husband out from the throng and tell him about their uninvited guest, but old Prof Gurgieff had had too much and was leaning heavily on Simon's arm.

In the sitting-room, the hard-core was making sure that no wine was wasted, and Jude was busily dumping empties in a cardboard box.

"Do you know where Doc is?" Ginny asked.

"Search me, sweetie," Jude replied. "He went missing hours ago."

Ginny explained what had happened in the garden, and Jude listened, open-mouthed.

"Ch-rist!" she exclaimed. "He really is stalking you!"

"You wouldn't say that if you saw the state of him," Ginny replied. "Ask Doc to pop down if he shows, will you? I've got him hidden away in the little pantry off the kitchen."

She hurried out of the room, but as soon as she reached the top of the stairs it became clear that something was wrong. The babble of voices down below had died away leaving an uneasy silence. Taking the stairs as quickly as she dared and side-stepping the two drunks who were slumped near the bottom, she came into the kitchen to hear an anguished voice screaming, "No polithe... No polithe..."

The departing guests were in a frozen tableau, all eyes turned towards Whizz, cornered like some hunted creature, wounded and dangerous.

Simon's voice said, "Well, let me get you an ambulance then..."

He was standing in a group with David Gurgieff and the Bryants, an expression of horror and distaste on his face as he confronted the boy.

"No amb-uh-lanthe," said Whizz. He was twitching slightly, as though a muscle in his neck had gone into spasm.

"Then I'll have to get the police," Simon said.

Whizz grabbed a wine bottle from the table. "I said...no pol-ithe!" His arm swept across the table sending several bottles crashing to the tiled floor. "No pol-isse," he screamed again, and brought the bottle down on the table-top with a ferocity that seemed beyond his strength. As the bottle shattered, arms went up to protect faces and the whole room seemed to gasp.

Ginny pushed her way through the crowd. "Put the bottle down, Whizz," she said, extending both her hands, palms out, as she approached him.

Whizz raised the broken bottle to his face, peering at it through the swellings that hid his eyes. The tic in his neck and the twitches of his head gave the impression that he was astonished, as though the jagged glass in his hand had appeared by magic.

"Ginny, be careful," Simon warned.

"Put it down, Whizz, there's a good boy," Ginny said, using her calm, classroom voice.

"You prom-ithed... no pol-ithe..." he said, rocking from side to side, his shoulders swaying. "No pol-ithe... no pol-ithe... no pol-ithe... " The mantra became more insistent, its rhythm broken by the spasms that shook his body. And the broken bottle twitched erratically with every convulsion, barely a metre from Ginny's face.

"It's all right, Whizz," she said, extending her hand to take hold of his wrist. "Let's put it down."

Abruptly, the chanting stopped. Gently she pushed his arm towards the table-top and took her hand away. After a pause, the boy released his grip on the broken bottle, and withdrew his hand—quickly, as though pulling it out of a fire. One of the students at the front of the crowd darted forwards and swept his forearm across the table top, sending the broken bottle spinning to the floor, causing Simon and the Bryants to dance out of its way.

The boy was wary now and raised his hands to ward off any attempt that might be made to restrain him. He was surveying the remnants of the party through the slits in his battered face, his head held back, the twitches more frequent now, as though charges of electricity were pulsing through his nervous system.

"Has anybody here seen Doc?" asked Ginny in a loud voice.

Bee appeared at the conservatory door. "Doc's in here with me…we've been getting some air in the gar…" Her hand went to her mouth. "Oh, my God, what's happened?"

Doc Holroyd put his hands on Bee's shoulders and eased her to one side.

"Could you take a look at the boy, Doc?" Ginny said. "He's taken a bit of a beating."

Doc sucked in his breath. "You should be in Casualty, young man," he said.

"I'll go and call for an ambulance," Simon said.

The boy's agitation intensified and the chanting resumed, louder than before and more desperate. "No pol-ithe…no pol-ithe…"

"I made him a promise when I found him in the garden…" Ginny explained.

"Ginny…" pleaded Simon, "you heard what Doc said."

Whizz began to pound the table-top with his fists, first one, then the other, thumping out the rhythm of the chant.

"I made a promise," Ginny repeated slowly.

"Just look at him," hissed Simon, trying to contain his growing frustration. "God knows what he's on, but he's out of his skull on something…"

"He's not the only one out of his skull, is he?" Ginny said, sweeping her finger across the assembled party guests. "Look at this lot."

Simon shook his head. "That is ridiculous…" he whispered, enunciating each word distinctly.

"Simon," Ginny said in an ominous tone, "I made a promise to the boy, and I intend to keep it." She fixed him with a glare.

Simon clamped his hands around his head. "That is quite the most stupid thing…"

"Do not call me stupid," Ginny said menacingly.

She saw contempt in his eyes. Somewhere inside her, a dam burst, releasing a torrent of vitriol, uncontrolled and uncontrollable.

She was vaguely conscious of the doctor playing peacemaker, the white skin of his palms close to her face, and his voice, calm and insistent; and Jude going on and on about the baby; and Charlie repeating her name, over and over; and Simon's face, pale with anxiety. And then they were on the stairs, Jude's podgy arm around her shoulders, following Doc Holroyd as he helped the boy climb painfully up the stairs to the spare bedroom. She had won.

Ginny inhaled deeply to steady herself and raised her eyes to the mirror. The makeup had been a mistake, she had to admit. She blamed Little Miss Poetry-Punk for that. The coal-black spiral on the clown-white cheek; the sexy slash of that oh-so-scarlet mouth—they were ridiculous, but they'd made her feel old and drab, and she'd gone ferreting at the back of the knicker-drawer like some demented teenager.

She turned her head and squinted at her profile. To be fair, she hadn't overdone it. A dab here or there had helped—shame about the eye-shadow though. On its own the blue-green base would have been fine, but the glitter was naff and didn't deliver the sparkle that was promised on the tin. Perhaps it had lost its lustre when the night turned sour.

In a series of vicious tugs she pulled lumps from the cylinder of cotton wool and gave the bottle of pink fluid a shake before soaking one of the pads. She sniffed the synthetic peachiness and wrinkled her nose. But it was like cool balm when she pressed it against her eyelid, and she took a moment to relish the sensation. Behind her, the door to the bedroom swung open.

"Don't let it spoil a lovely evening," Simon said. "It's not worth it."

She began to wipe away the makeup from her eye. The 'lovely evening' had ceased being lovely the instant she saw that look in his eye. It was an un-lovely look by any calculation. There had been no pity in that look.

She tossed the swab into the waste-bin and picked up a fresh one.

"You could see the state he was in," she said, raising her smeared eyes to accuse him in the mirror. "It didn't stop you though, did it?"

"Stop me what?"

"Stop you threatening him with the police..."

"Oh, come on..." he said.

Working the swab into the other socket, she said, "Any fool could see that the kid was petrified, but you just kept on and on..."

In the mirror she saw him raise his hands and start ticking off his fingers.

"He's sixteen years old; he was high as a kite; and he's been beaten to pulp." He leaned closer to the mirror to emphasis his argument. "He should be in a hospital or at home with his parents. It's a simple as that."

Ginny turned to face him. "The truth is, Simon, you don't give a damn about the kid. You just wanted him tidied away so he wouldn't spoil your precious party."

Simon perched himself on the edge of the bath and crossed his arms. "There's no reasoning with you, Ginny," he said wearily. "Just believe whatever you want."

Ginny went to work on the rest of her face.

Time was when she had to stop him wading in to help the waifs and strays. Time was when his principles were everything. Time was....

"That was some tantrum you threw down there," he said. "The Bryants were impressed."

"Bugger the Bryants," Ginny snapped, and tossed another swab into the bin.

In the airing cupboard, the boiler gave a groan and died for the night. A surly silence was beginning to fester when, suddenly, Simon laughed.

"I suppose you're right," he said. "Bugger the Bryant. Bugger the lot of them."

She looked over her shoulder and eyed him sceptically. He could be prissy about her colourful vocabulary, and rarely swore himself.

"Bollocks," she said, tearing off a fresh lump of cotton wool. "You don't mean that for a moment." Leaning forwards close to the mirror, she began wiping away the last smears of lipstick from the corner of her mouth. "And by the way," she went on, "I do not throw tantrums."

Not true. She'd behaved badly.

She turned her head first one way, then another. Her skin was shiny and fresh, and she looked years younger without the mask.

Simon appeared behind her in the mirror. "Can we call a truce?" he said. "If I've behaved like a pompous prig, I'm sorry—but you rattled me."

"Good," she said.

"You did call me 'a right-wing prick' in front of half the Department."

Ginny stifled a snigger. "Did I really say that?"

"You did...with a few choice expletives thrown in."

"Oh God, I'm sorry."

"No, you're not. You meant every word, but let's call it a day, eh?" He took hold of her shoulders and squeezed her gently. "We're supposed to be celebrating, Gin."

He was right, of course. He'd been right about everything really.

She tidied up the bathroom and they went through the regular rigmarole of bedtime trying to pretend that nothing untoward had happened. Simon prattled on about his great day, as though his words could rekindle the warm glow of the evening. Ginny lay jack-knifed on her side facing the bedroom wall, glad to be silent. The words that conjured up some comfort for him worked no magic for her, and ill-feeling lingered about her like a foul smell.

Staring at the wallpaper, she thought of the injured boy lying beyond it, in the room they no longer dared to call 'the nursery'. He had looked so vulnerable in the glare of the security light. Like a lost child.

The mattress sagged as Simon slipped under the duvet and, with a click, the bedside light went out. For him, the heady optimism of the evening had returned and he talked on and on, as though he couldn't bear to stop.

"You should have seen Bryant's face when David made his little speech. 'The university had frittered away my intellectual gifts,' he said. 'I should have had my chair years ago, but I'd been undermined by lesser men.' Pure hokum, of course and I should have been pink with embarrassment, but, you know what? I almost wept with relief."

Simon turned on to his side and shaped himself around her. Without thinking, she raised her elbow to allow his arm to encircle her, twisting so that her left breast lay cradled in the palm of his right hand.

"I know it's all ridiculous hyperbole," he went on, "but I felt like one of those poor devils on the steps of the Old Bailey when the judge has quashed their conviction. They had finally let me out and I was free again . . ."

An image of Bee drifted into Ginny's mind—flaked out in the conservatory, saliva dribbling from her lower lip, her forehead crumpled in a frown. Anyone could see she was falling apart... except her husband, the great psychologist...

Simon kissed the nape of her neck and hugged her close. "And what about the jazz?" he said.

Oh yes, the jazz... the gymnastics of the mind...

"I've always thought of jazz as a kind of meditation," he said, "gymnastics for the mind...and strictly solitary. Not tonight though. I really surprised myself tonight."

She'd been straining to hear the piano when the boy spoke to her out of the night. The very thought of it made her heart thump almost as wildly as it had then.

"...considering I'd only heard that poem once before, it went really well... Mel wants us to put a set together for 'The Follies'. What do you think?"

Ginny raised her head from the pillow and spoke over her shoulder. "I think you're rather too taken with that little minx, if you really must know."

"Don't be so silly," he said.

His hand moved and she felt her nipple harden between his thumb and forefinger. The automatic response of her flesh irritated her.

"No!" she said, taking his hand away. "Not tonight!"

For a moment he froze. "I'm sorry," he said, "you've had a rotten time of it. Best get some sleep."

He kissed her shoulder and pulled away, easing his weight back on to his own side of the bed, taking care that the movement sent no signals of petulance. She felt the space grow cool between them. She could feel him staring up into the darkness, waiting for her to say something. It was a silence he didn't deserve, but she had nothing to say.

To her surprise, she began to weep. It was as though her tear-ducts had taken on an independent life, pumping cataracts of ludicrous tears with no instructions from her emotions, soaking her pillow in complete silence. The disconnection was mysterious, and the tears continued to flow even as her conscious mind observed the oddness of the phenomenon.

Then Time slipped. She was a child again, summoning up the same hot, silent tears in her bed at home, grieving for some imaginary loss, an exquisitely contrived fiction that brought delicious misery and was strangely comforting.

And soon, the rhythmic click of the skipping rope lulled her to sleep.

> *Hickety Pickety Pop*
> *Hickety Pickety Pop*
> *How many times before I stop?*

Chapter Six

Ginny tapped lightly on the spare bedroom door and listened for a response. After a while she tapped again then turned the handle and cautiously pushed the door open an inch.

"Hello, Whizz," she called, keeping her voice low in case he was still sleeping. "It's Mrs May."

There was no response. She eased the door open a little further and looked inside. He was standing in front of the window, oblivious to her presence as far as she could tell. One hand was resting on the window-catch above his head and the graceful arc of his arm was highlighted by the early morning sun, caught lemon-yellow in the halo of his unkempt hair. He could have been one of those classical statues of androgynous Youth— the slender back, the sinuous curve of the spine, the shadowy cleft in the buttocks. Like a torso in a museum, the figure was truncated below the waist, but not by the sculptor's chisel. Her Greek god had a studded belt slung low below his hips and baggy blue-jeans that barely defied gravity.

"Whizz!" she called, her voice much louder. "How are you this morning?"

The reply was unintelligible.

Ginny went closer. "Say again..." she said.

"Nice motor," he said.

His speech was slurred. If she had not followed his gaze to the old shed that housed Simon's Mazda, she might not have understood him.

"I don't get it..." he went on, turning towards her.

"Ouch!" Ginny exclaimed, wincing in sympathy at the state of his face. "That looks painful."

Overnight, the puffiness around his eyes had been suffused with bilious shades of yellow, green and blue, and his right eyebrow was encrusted in a scab.

"Who on earth did this to you?" she asked.

The boy picked up his thought as though there had been no interruption. "That MX5 Roadster is better than the new one," he said, trying to speak without moving his bruised lips and sounding like a bad ventriloquist. "So why frow out a good motor for a pile of crap?"

Ginny persisted. "Was it the police?"

In the slits where his eyes were hiding, she detected a glimmer of interest, but he said nothing.

"I ought to give your mum and dad a ring, but they're not in the book. Could you tell me their number? "

Whizz made a strange, stuttering noise in his throat, and it took her a while to realise that he was laughing. When the noise stopped, the stillness was chilling.

"Why did you come here?" she asked quietly, looking for an answer in his ravaged face.

The boy said nothing, but began to rock back and forth on his heels, twisting his head slowly from side to side, as if flaunting his wounds in a display of insolence and defiance. But then, the rocking stopped. For a moment he was fascinated by the ceiling above her head, then his head lolled onto his chest and he pitched forwards. Ginny let him fall against her, bracing herself to take his weight, but the pain of contact must have shocked him back to consciousness, because he groaned and tottered backwards, colliding with the old tallboy and upsetting the family of rag-dolls that were arranged on top.

Ginny took hold of him by the shoulders. "Come on, Whizz," she said. "You should be back in bed."

"I'm all right," he complained, wriggling free of her hands.

"Don't be silly!" she said, and put a hand gently on his arm above the elbow. "You got up too soon."

"I'm all right," he repeated tetchily, but he allowed her to lead him to the bed and sat down cautiously on the mattress. "I'm just hungry, that's all." He let himself flop back on the bed, legs bent at the knee, bare feet dangling to the floor.

Sprawled out against the terracotta of the duvet, he seemed more vulnerable than ever. Bruises mottled his fair skin and a criss-cross of angry welts was overlaid on the fragile arches of his ribcage. It was a violation.

"I can't believe someone could do this to you. How did it happen?"

"I ain't had nuffin' to eat for ages."

"Who was it?"

"The last time was down the cop-shop," he said to the ceiling. "A crap sandwich, wiv a cuppa tea, weak as piss."

Ginny abandoned the cross-examination. "How would you like some porridge?" she asked.

"That'd be cushty," he replied, "wiv cream…And d'you know what I'd like for afters?"

Ginny's hand was on the doorknob. When she turned round, he had propped himself up on one elbow and was waiting until he had her full attention.

"A nice st-liff, that's what I'd like."

Ginny made a face, not quite believing what she might have heard. "What did you say?"

"A sp-liff," Whizz said, making a painful effort to be understood. "A nice fat joint. That'd be good."

"Don't be cheeky," she said. "You'll stick to porridge, and like it!"

Ginny closed the door behind her, marvelling at the boy's resilience. Despite the kicking, all his swagger was still intact.

Fragments of discordant music were drifting up from the kitchen, which meant that Simon's breakfast rite was underway: *The Guardian* propped up against the Tupperware box of unsweetened muesli; the extra oats for roughage; the tubs of cod-liver-oil and the garlic capsules arranged next to the low-dosage aspirins, strictly in descending order of size; the pot of camomile tea devoid of caffeine; and *Radio Three*. Most mornings she would retreat to the playroom with a piece of toast and play *Kiss FM* loudly on the old transistor, or she would stay and disturb his ritual, teasing him about his hypochondria. Not today.

Bracing herself for the battle to come, Ginny went downstairs.

"Good morning, Professor May," she said.

"Ah," he exclaimed, smiling up at her. "How's the boy?"

To her surprise, instead of *The Guardian*, his head was buried in Yellow Pages.

"What are you after?" she asked.

"The boy's father…" Simon replied, "I've tried the number Doc and Jude had for them, but they must have changed it. I'm trying the garages now. The problem is: which one? He's got branches everywhere. He must be rich as Croesus."

"There's no rush," said Ginny. "I'll track him down later."

Simon took off his reading-specs and let them dangle on their lanyard, then pinched the bridge of his nose between finger and thumb. "I think I'll call in and get somebody to cover my nine o'clock lecture," he said.

"Don't be daft," said Ginny, leaning across the table to pick up the box of Quaker Oats, "the new Prof can't go AWOL on Day 1."

As she turned to move away, Simon took hold of her forearm and held her back. "Please, Ginny..." he began, begging for reason, "I know you're concerned about the boy..." The fingers tightened their pressure on her arm. "But I'm concerned about you...and I'm concerned about our baby."

"Will's not going to hurt me," countered Ginny, and removed the hand from her arm. "The poor lad's not in a fit state to hurt anybody." She shook the box of oats in front of his face. "I'm sorry to rob your bowel of its precious roughage, but I'm going to make him some porridge."

The doorbell rang, bringing their sparring match to an end before a punch had been thrown.

"That will be Doc," said Simon, getting to his feet. "I'll be interested to hear what he has to say about this."

Aware of the mumbled voices conspiring at the end of the hall, Ginny busied herself in the galley. Turning the box of oats to check the instructions, she caught sight of the old Quaker in his blue hat and white collar, beaming his well-fed smile. Instantly, as though a tap had been turned full on, her mouth flooded with saliva. Beyond all sane desire, she craved porridge...Thick, creamy porridge, with the crunch of brown sugar...and lots of it...

"Good morning, Ginny," Doc said, giving her a cursory salute. "I gather your uninvited guest has survived the night."

Ginny swallowed hard, and snuffed out the string quartet on the radio. "He looks a bit of a mess, but he's quite chirpy."

Doc dumped his ancient medical bag on the work surface in front of her and pointed an accusing finger.

"Thanks to you, young woman, I did not sleep easy in my bed last night," he said. "That lad should have gone straight to Casualty, no arguments."

"But he didn't want to go, did he, Doc?" she said, giving him a sweet smile.

"Scared of a blood-test," he said, and gave her a knowing look. "I'm going to be perfectly blunt with you, Ginny. If you want to carry this baby to term, you're going to have to control that temper of yours..."

"I do have control of my temper but..."

"Good!" he interrupted. "Let's keep it that way. And while we're at it, your husband is one hundred percent right. You should not be in the house on your own with that young tearaway, and that's an end of it."

Leaving her with a piercing stare, the doctor picked up his bag and headed for the stairs.

Ginny called after him, "Do I have your permission to make the boy some breakfast?"

One foot on the first step, Doc paused. He was considering a riposte, but confined himself to a contemptuous flap of the hand, and went up to see his patient.

Ginny poured milk into the saucepan and began to measure out two cupfuls of the dried oat-flakes, which floated on the surface like a thousand small scabs. The craving had vanished.

Simon was on the phone, being shunted from garage to garage, and getting nowhere. Ginny wielded the wooden spoon, stirring morosely until she began to meet sticky resistance in the pan. The porridge was acquiring the consistency of warm wallpaper paste and still looked revolting. But, when she lowered her nose to sniff, she was instantly transported back to childhood, and her mouth watered again.

"This is a wild goose chase," said Simon, tossing his mobile onto the table. "Nobody knows what Buckley's movements are. His PA's not in yet, and they won't give me his mobile or his home number." Tipping his chair back precariously, he reached behind him to the Welsh dresser. "I know you're not going to like this," he said warily, "but it looks as though we may have to use this."

Ginny stopped pouring porridge into the bowls. Pinched between two of his fingers was the card that Carmichael had left when he returned the copy of *Borka*. She resumed pouring porridge.

"I told the boy we wouldn't call the police," she said, calmly, and began to scrape porridge from the sides of the pan, coaxing it into one of the bowls with the spoon.

"Would you prefer to talk to DS Carmichael yourself?" Simon asked. "You said yourself he's not a bad chap…"

"No way will I be talking to the police," said Ginny, picking up the tray. "The boy trusts me, and I want to keep it that way."

Simon sighed, and looked up at her as she passed. "I will keep trying," he said, and I promise I will do my level best to get hold of his father. But we've got to do something."

"Oh, I know you'll do what's best," said Ginny, sweetly. "You and Doc have a direct line to the Almighty, I know that."

Chapter Seven

Whizz was sitting on the bed, propped up by pillows against the wall, his chest swathed in bandages. He was holding his bowl close to his chin so that it caught the dribbles of porridge that escaped as he spooned it into his damaged mouth. It was a clumsy process but, despite the scuffed knuckles and swollen fingers, he wielded the spoon with gusto.

"He'll need a sweatshirt or something, Ginny?" said Doc, as he packed his stethoscope into its box. "You'll have to junk his T-shirt, I'm afraid."

Whizz reached across to the bedside table for the sugar bowl and, before Ginny could stop him, proceeded to empty most of the Demerara into his porridge.

"Hey," she protested, "leave some of that for me."

She had pulled an old bentwood chair to the side of the bed in preparation for their heart-to-heart, and she was relieved to hear the click of the doctor's bag.

"I know you fancy yourself as a bit of a tough guy, young man," Doc said, shrugging his way into his coat, "but, if I were you, I'd get myself down to Casualty and have those ribs X-rayed. And remember what I said about the other stuff—leave it alone! Have you got that?"

Whizz gave no signs that he had been listening. He stuck out his hand to grab the mug from the bedside table, and began lapping noisily at his tea. Ginny debated whether to play schoolteacher.

"Aren't you going to thank the doctor, Whizz?" she said.

After a calculated pause, the boy took the mug from his mouth and gingerly wiped away some dribble on the back of his hand. "Thanks mate," he said, loading both words with insolence.

"Well, there you are, Doc!" said Ginny. "Another satisfied customer!"

Doc Holroyd laughed and opened the door. "You take it easy, Ginny. No excitements, remember—doctor's orders!"

As soon as the door closed, Ginny began to devour her porridge. It was already lukewarm and tacky, but her tongue searched out the rough granules of sugar and she crunched them between her teeth, adding sweet decadence to the wholesome oatmeal.

"W...o...w," she said, exhaling through the word and stretching it out as she opened her eyes wide. "I haven't had porridge for a hundred years—not since Merry made a wish and turned kitty-cat into a king."

"What's all that 'kitty-cat' crap?" sneered Whizz.

"My Grandma was always coming out with daft things like that," she replied. "Her favourite was, 'You'll never be merry if you moan,' and she meant it. She never moaned, my Gran. Not once, and she had a really tough life. When I was a little girl and my mum went into hospital, I went to live with Gran, and it was like going to live in a story-book...The dolls she made became her imaginary friends, whole families of them, and she talked to them all day long...she used to make them out of scraps she picked up at jumble sales... "

As Ginny spoke, the back parlour of the old terraced house came alive: the whirr of the sewing machine; Grandma with a mouthful of pins; Granddad slumped in front of the fire, stinking of beer and snoring; the black cat, slinky by the fire; the box of buttons that were her jewels and treasure; and the dolls—rag-dolls everywhere, sitting on the mantel-shelf, propped up on the window-ledge, on the sideboard, on top of every cupboard. As the memories crowded in, she became entangled in the web of her own story, and it was some time before she remembered that she had an audience.

His head was tipped back against the pillows at an odd angle, the battered moon of his face strangely serene. He could well have been asleep, but some part of him was alert, she could sense it. Once again she discarded all plans to quiz him about his injuries and returned quickly to the land of the dolls, to the hundreds of rag-dolls that Grandma made to sell in the market, the Mildreds and the Megans, the Mirandas and the Millicents, the whole, vast tribe of Merry Maids, each with her own jolly frock, each with a magic secret that it was Ginny's job to discover.

But even as she told the tale, evoking her childhood in language as vivid as she could muster, the strangeness of her situation did not escape her. They could have been back in the classroom where he had been that happy child, with his tiny arms folded on his desk and his head resting on his arms...but there he was, sprawled out on the bed, a teenage thug, utterly lost in the make-believe world of Grandma's dolls...

A tap on the door broke the spell.

"Can I have a word, Ginny?" called Simon, from the landing.

"That's my husband," she said.

"He's a tosser, your old man," said Whizz.

Ginny opened the door a fraction. From the guarded expression on Simon's face she could tell that he had not brought news she wanted to hear. She asked anyway.

"You didn't get hold of him, did you?"

"No," he said, speaking in a half-whisper. "He couldn't, or wouldn't, speak to me." He beckoned her to come out of the bedroom.

"You've phoned the police, haven't you?" she said, when the door closed.

Simon nodded. "Carmichael's on his way...And I didn't make any trouble for the lad, if that's what you're thinking. Quite to the contrary, as it happens. I said he'd been no trouble at all."

"Well, that's all right then, isn't it?" Ginny said, folding her arms.

"It's still possible that Buckley or his wife will call. I left our numbers with his PA, and she promised to pass them on."

Ginny shook her head. "I think the Buckleys have washed their hands of him. In fact the whole world seems to have ditched him." She opened the bedroom door, and gave him a defiant look. "Not me though, Simon!"

The breeze from the window helped the door to close more firmly than she had intended. After the slam, there was a pause before Simon's muffled voice called, "I'll wait until he gets here, then I'll have to dash. I won't be late tonight."

"Who's he hanging about for then?" Whizz asked.

Ginny weighed her options, and decided to be direct.

"He's been on the phone to Detective Sergeant Carmichael," she said, watching his reaction carefully.

Whizz accepted her news impassively. Eventually he said, "What a twat!"

"You don't have to go with the policeman if you don't want to," she said, sitting down beside him. "If you want to stay here and have a chat, I'm all yours. I'm not working today."

"What's your old man's problem?" Whizz said, sounding surly. "I ain't done nuffin' to him."

"He's worried about me…"

"Why?"

"He doesn't think I should be left alone with you."

"Why not? Do he fink I'm going to rape you or somefin'?"

"I'm going to have a baby," Ginny said. "He doesn't want me upset."

"So what's he fink I'm gonna do to your baby?"

Ginny gave a little shrug. "Husbands are funny creatures…"

"Yours is a twat...but he's done me a favour."

Ginny looked puzzled. "What do you mean?"

"Saved me a walk..."

The strange disconnects in the boy's thought processes were not helping communication, and his sore mouth was still mangling his meanings.

"Can you say that again?" Ginny said.

"The pigs…" he said, "They can give me a lift into town."

Far from fazing him, the policeman's impending arrival, seemed to animate him.

"Can you get my trainers?" he said, wincing with the effort as he struggled into a sitting position at the edge of the mattress.

Apart from a single brown bloodstain, the Nikes were a startling white. Ginny picked them up and took them to the bed. She knelt down and began tugging at the laces to ease one of the shoes open.

"Don't mess with those!" he barked angrily. "Just put them down for me…"

Ginny flinched. "There's no need to shout," she said.

His feet were filthy and she held one of the trainers at arms' length while he slipped a foot inside. Whizz lifted the other foot in readiness, then froze, distracted by the sound of a car on the gravel outside.

"That'll be my taxi," he said.

She was supposed to be impressed by his cool. In a sad sort of way, she was. It was time to go back to the streets, whether he liked it or not. He was getting togged up, inside as well as out— psyching himself up.

Putting his hand on Ginny's shoulder for balance, Whizz got himself vertical

"I'll get you a shirt," she said. "Would one of mine be alright? It would be more of your size."

"Whatever," he said, and shuffled over to the window trying to catch a glimpse of the visitor.

Ginny picked up the stained T-shirt from the chest of drawers, went into her own bedroom and dropped it in the laundry basket. Sliding open the mirror-door to her wardrobe, she cast a cursory eye over the array of blouses, and then riffled through the pile of sweatshirts, pulling out a couple in plain colours. On a mischievous whim, she slid aside the door to Simon's side of the wardrobe and pulled out an old-fashioned granddaddy of a shirt, a stripy creation, with no collar and long tails.

As the wardrobe door slid smoothly back on its track, Ginny's heart gave a lurch. A monstrous face was leering at her in the mirror, its bulbous features a livid scarlet, its huge protruding eyes bursting with rage.

"What's this?" asked a muffled voice.

Furious, Ginny turned on the boy. "Put that back!" she snapped.

The red devil-mask was one of the set of Noh masks they had brought back from the stop-over in Nagasaki.

"What is it?" asked Whizz, looking down at the hideous face that he held in his hands.

"It's the demon *Shikami*, if you must know. Give it to me, please."

"How come he's bright red?"

"I'll tell you another day," Ginny replied, taking the mask away from him. "We haven't got time for Japanese theatre, not right now."

As she put the demon with the other Noh masks in the chest by the window, there was the sound of laughter from outside the house. Simon was standing with DS Carmichael beside his beloved Mazda, swinging his leather satchel by its strap to drop it into the passenger seat. Pulling back the sleeve of his jacket, he checked his wristwatch and gazed anxiously up at the spare room, then turned away, only to catch sight of them at the wrong bedroom window. He looked puzzled for a moment, but gave a wave of his hand and forced a smile.

Whizz curled his fingers and gave a lewd wag of his hand, chanting, "Wanker! Wanker!" in a playground sing-song.

"Stop that!" cried Ginny, the schoolmistress back in her voice.

"Well, he is! He's a total tosser!"

"That's quite enough," she said, pulling the boy's arm to turn him away from the window.

"Which shirt do you fancy?" asked Ginny, holding out the shirts. She raised the two sweatshirts. "These will be a better fit..." She see-sawed his choices. "...but you may prefer one of Simon's."

Whizz pointed. "I'll have that one."

"I thought you might," Ginny said, with a grin. "It's Simon's favourite."

The sleeves were too long and she had to roll them up. Whizz held out his injured hands warily. They were badly scuffed and swollen.

"I need a piss," he said.

There was a moment's hesitation as Ginny pondered the implications of this announcement. She finished an adjustment to the boy's sleeve, and stepped back.

"The toilet's in there," she said, pointing to the *en suite*. "I think you'll manage."

Outside, the Mazda's engine roared into life and its wheels crunched gravel on the drive. The university's new Professor of English and American Literature had obviously despaired of waiting.

Ginny opened the front door to find Carmichael sitting on the dry-stone wall that bordered the front garden, his right hand cupped below a cascade of purple fuchsias that spilled from the stone urn beside him.

"Good morning," she said.

He looked up. "Good morning."

"You're on a fool's errand, sergeant. Public Enemy Number One has behaved impeccably."

"I'm glad to hear it," he said, strolling towards her.

He looked different - no jeans, no hoodie, no trainers. He was wearing the smart-casual clobber that would not look out of place in a fancy golf club.

"My husband is a neurotic," she said. "He shouldn't have called you."

She extended a hand towards the front door, and followed the policeman as he made his way down the hall.

"He was lucky to catch me," he said. "I was hoping to get a round of golf in..."

Ginny congratulated herself on her perspicacity. "Are you on a day off ?" she asked.

"I'm on nights."

She looked at him with undisguised curiosity. "So how come you're volunteering to baby-sit?"

"Well, first off, your husband's quite right. Young Mr Buckley is not good company for a woman in your condition..."

"My 'condition', as you put it," she protested, "is none of your business."

Carmichael pressed on. "The main reason is the boy," he said. "Something's up. I don't know what, but I've got bad vibes. He's on the edge of something nasty."

"And you'd like to help him?" Ginny asked, watching him carefully.

Carmichael noted her scepticism. "Yes, I would, funnily enough."

"So would I," Ginny said.

"Can you do my buttons?"

Whizz was at the foot of the stairs, his shirt open to reveal the strapping around his ribcage, the shirt-tails hanging down almost to his knees.

"Stone me!" said Carmichael. "It's Wee Willie Winkie."

Whizz shuffled into the kitchen. "I can't do me buttons," he complained.

"Good morning, William," Carmichael said, peering at the boy's face. He sucked in his breath through pursed lips. "That's not nice, Whizz. Did Moon do that to you?"

Whizz ignored the detective and held his injured hands away from his sides as Ginny began to fasten the shirt buttons.

"Who is Moon?" she asked.

"Moon is a scum-bag," Carmichael said, "but Whizz thinks he's Robin Hood—don't you, Whizz? God knows why anybody would choose Moon Rivers for a role-model, but Whizz managed it...didn't you, Whizz?"

The boy had adopted a pose of bored indifference. It was obviously a scene that they had both played before.

"This is what a 'punishment beating' looks like," said Carmichael, presenting the boy like an exhibit in a freak show. "This is what Moon does to a grass, isn't it Whizz?"

"I'm not a grass."

"Oh, no, Whizz Buckley doesn't grass!" Carmichael mocked. "The problem is: Moon *thinks* he's a grass. And that's enough. Poor old Whizz gets a kicking."

Ginny frowned at the policeman. "So who set him up?" she asked. "Is this down to you?"

"Not me," Carmichael said, with a dismissive shake of the head. "Not my style."

Ginny studied his face, wondering if she'd got him wrong.

"You don't have to go with him, Whizz," she said, "not if you don't want to. You can stay here with me if you like."

"Nah, it's alright," Whizz said, "I got things to do..."

"And so have I," said Carmichael. "Come on, young man. Let's get you back where you belong."

Ginny was ushering them down the hallway towards the front door when a thought occurred to her.

"Hang on a second, would you?" she said.

Bending over the hall table, she picked up the felt-tipped pen and began to write on the notepad beside the phone.

"I'm writing down both my numbers," she said, "my mobile . . . and my home number." She ripped the page off the pad and offered it to Whizz, looking hard into his swollen eyes. "If you need help, you're to call me. Do you understand?"

The boy nodded. "Thank you, Mrs May," he said, and carefully pocketed the slip of paper before he turned away.

The expression on DS Carmichael's face could have been one of admiration, or it could have been one of sympathy. Ginny couldn't decide.

"Are you going to be around all morning?" he asked.

"I expect so," she replied.

"Then I'll try to get back. I think we ought to have a chat, Mrs May."

Then he turned and followed the boy to the Mini, waving a finger above his shoulder in farewell.

Chapter Eight

Ginny gave the mound of clay a satisfying slap, and experienced a release of tension. With the other hand, she slapped it again. Simon was right; the doctor was right; the policeman was right; they were all one hundred percent bloody right. She was drunk on hormones; living out some crackpot maternal fantasy; and the policeman would soon be back to tell her so.

Her mobile rang, vibrating on the board beside her, buzzing like a bee. It was not a number she recognised. Curious, she thumbed the green key and listened.

"Hello," she said.

There was no response, only an empty space around the whine of a drill and snatches of music from a distant radio.

"Hello," she said again.

Someone whistled tunelessly in her ear, close and shrill. She shouted to attract the whistler's attention, but he moved away and his whistle was swallowed in the echoes.

"This had better not be you, Whizz," she said. "I am not amused."

Papers rustled close to the mouthpiece, and somewhere in the distance metal clanged on metal.

Ginny was becoming distinctly uneasy when something scraped against the other phone, and a breathless voice said, "Sorry… Got called away. Are you there?"

"I'm here alright," Ginny said. "I've been here forever. Who is it?"

"It's Andy at Seaborough Saab. Your 900's ready anytime you want to pick it up."

Surprised and pleased, Ginny offered her thanks and terminated the call. She looked at the mobile in her hand. Why so neurotic? If the boy rang, he rang. She put the phone down on the prep table, and returned to the clay.

In California, it had been her salvation. Closing her eyes, she savoured the coolness of the clay, searching out its textures with the tips of her fingers, just as Takashi had taught her, kneading it gently, communing with its inner nature, smelling the earth, primal and raw. Every day, before they began work in the studio, Takashi would wrap a blindfold round her head and tell her to 'find the clay'. She could hear his deep voice now, mesmeric and compelling.

It was the only time she had been tempted to be unfaithful. Having dragged her half-way around the world and dumped her in the leafy luxury of Santa Barbara, Simon had withdrawn inside himself and shrivelled up. Night after long night she lay beside him, aware of his wakefulness, frightened and rejected by his refusal to speak...or weep, or do anything remotely human. It was a nervous breakdown she supposed, but she could not persuade him to see a doctor, and it was never properly diagnosed. She would have gone mad herself if it had not been for the clay – and Takashi.

The pleasure she derived from watching him at the wheel was shameful. Those fingers furrowing the silky surfaces, that masterful hand on the swell of the pot: they were erotic clichés as crude as the phallic thrust of missile launches and the insinuations of chocolate-flake commercials, worth a snigger perhaps, but nothing more. And yet, during those dark nights of rejection, she could think of little else, and in the morning, when she gazed into those almond eyes, instead of seeing the inward stillness of the Zen, she would see the flicker of his desire. Or was it a reflection of her own lust? She never discovered which, and she remained a good and faithful wife. But she often wondered what might have been.

The clay was warming to her touch. It had come to life in her hands and she could feel its suppleness and strength. Scooping up the mound, she centred it on the wheel, and began to shape a crude bowl with rough pinching movements of her fingers and thumbs. Then she settled herself on the bench, wetted her hands in the bowl of slip, and engaged the treadle with her foot, rocking back and forth, listening to the creak and click of the ancient wooden contraption as the wheel gathered speed. Gently, she cradled the outer wall of the spinning vessel with one hand, and began to caress its inner surface with the other. Slowly she drew her hands together, lifting them upwards and outwards, then back again in a fluid, sinuous arc, bestowing a generous swell to the belly of the new vase and a flourish to its slender neck.

She was pleased. The clay did not always respond so obediently, but today she felt inspired.

The doorbell rang.

"Bugger!" she said out loud.

Wiping her hands on her smock, she swung her legs over the bench, already bracing herself for a lecture from the policeman, but curious too. There was much she wanted to know about Will Buckley.

But it was not Carmichael on the doorstep. To her irritation, it was Bee, full of *joie de vivre* and looking better than she deserved to be, her make-up immaculate and not a hair out of place. She was so busy twittering on about a lost earring that she failed to notice that her welcome was not as warm as it might have been, and scuttled down the hallway, flapping her hands like a flightless bird. Ginny sighed and shook her head. The missing earring was no more believable than the false gaiety. These visitations were not unusual. They usually ended in smudged mascara and a box of Kleenex. And what infuriated Ginny more than anything was Bee's assumption that they were sisters in misery, both doomed to a lesser life in the shade of their brilliant husbands.

In the playroom, Ginny pointed out the vase, still wet on the wheel, and explained the necessity of adding decoration before the clay hardened, hoping that her visitor might draw the appropriate conclusion. But Bee cooed her admiration for the pot and insisted that Ginny 'carry on creating' while she searched for the earring. Thrusting her hand down the side of the baggy armchair where she had passed out the night before, Bee scrabbled about in its dubious depths and – hey presto – on the very first trawl, fished out a dangly confection of pink coral which she brandished in triumph.

"Mission accomplished!" said Ginny dryly. "Now please bugger off, Bee. I'm desperate for some peace and quiet with my pots."

The light went out of Bee's eyes. Cracks appeared in the make-up where the smile had been. And Ginny felt awful.

"Did I do anything stupid last night?" Bee whispered.

"If you did, I'm sure my own exhibition eclipsed it," Ginny said.

"He never says anything," Bee went on, "but I can always tell when Charlie's cross." A tear squeezed its way below a false eyelash and slowly ran down her cheek.

A morning of mopping-up with the paper-hankies seemed unavoidable, when – Alleluia – the doorbell rang.

"That will be my policeman," said Ginny.

Bee looked bewildered.

"My policeman," Ginny repeated, leading the way into the kitchen, "the one who called at the house when we came back from the pub with Jude."

No policeman seemed to feature in Bee's hazy recollection of the previous evening.

"It's about our accident…" Ginny said, pausing in the hallway, "…when the police-car rammed us…?"

Comprehension dawned at last, and Bee seemed relieved to be re-connected to reality. As she blinked back her tears and began to re-build her defences, Ginny took pity.

"You had a bit too much, Bee, that's all." She took hold of her hands and squeezed them. "If you get any grief from Charlie, just remind him of the time he disgraced himself at the wedding in Bishops Stortford. That'll shut the bugger up."

At the precise instant that Ginny turned the catch, the doorbell gave another chime. When she opened the door, Carmichael's finger was still poised over the bell-push.

"I was beginning to wonder if you'd gone out," he said.

Ginny attempted an introduction, but Bee had already become her giddy self, shaking the earring and babbling on about lost treasure. When she finally teetered off down the path, Carmichael gave Ginny a look that mixed amusement with sympathy.

"Would you like some coffee while you tick me off?" she said, leaving Carmichael to follow as she went back into the house.

"What makes you think I'm here to tick you off?" he said.

"Well, it's pretty clear that you've got me down as a silly woman who's playing with fire." She held up the jar of *Nescafé*. "Will instant do?"

"That's fine…" he replied, "…and as a matter of fact, I think you're anything but silly. 'Formidable' is the word our Chief Super used."

Ginny inclined her head to acknowledge the compliment. "I'm flattered," she said. "Perhaps he got them to extract their digits down at the garage—my old Saab's been fixed in record time. They called a few minutes ago."

"I could run you down if you like," Carmichael suggested. "We could have our chat on the way."

"That would be great," she exclaimed. "Thank you."

She hadn't realised how oppressive the house had become until an opportunity to escape presented itself. It was as though someone had thrown open all the windows and let fresh air come in.

"It's the least I can do," said Carmichael.

Ginny poured boiling water on the coffee granules.

"Just out of interest," she said, "where did you take the boy this morning? When you left here?"

"I took him straight to the YOT, the Youth Offending Team. They're the people who know what's best for him...."

"Not his parents?"

"The parents are not in the equation. They kicked the boy out."

There was a moment of silence. Although she was not surprised, Ginny was shocked.

Carmichael read her mind. "You shouldn't be too hard on the Buckleys," he said. "Whizz is not your average mixed-up kid."

"But you don't abandon your kids when things get difficult, do you?" she said. "Not in my book you don't."

"Depends what you mean by 'difficult," he said. "How about hoovering out all the goodies from your parents' house and flogging them at Boot Fairs? How about nailing up the doors, and holding your mother hostage with a hammer at her head? How about launching a war on your father's business?"

Carmichael watched her carefully, weighing up the effect of what he had said.

"So what went wrong?" Ginny asked. "Has anyone bothered to find out?"

"Lots of people have been trying, but nobody can get through to the kid. He spits on anybody that tries."

"He didn't spit on me," she said, handing him a coffee mug.

"No, he didn't," replied Carmichael. "He seems to trust you...which is why I wanted to talk to you."

Ginny looked at him in surprise. She was being treated like a grown-up, and by a policeman no less. The colour rose in her cheeks, and she turned away.

"I'd better clean up then," she said.

The smock came over her head and she tossed it on the side of the bath. Sluicing her hands under the tap, she splashed her face and towelled herself dry as she went into the bedroom. She took out the pins in her hair and shook it free. From the wardrobe she selected a slate-grey shirt which, according to Simon, brought out the blue in her eyes, and looped a necklace of chunky wood around her neck. As a final touch she wrapped a broad belt of plaited leather around her waist, turning the shirt into a tunic-top that emphasised her slim figure. She ran the brush through her hair, and liked what she saw in the mirror. For the first time in weeks, she felt buoyant and confident.

Chapter Nine

DS Carmichael drove a Mini Cooper, black and silver with chrome trim—striking, and just short of flash. He was in no hurry to talk about Whizz and, as he negotiated the leafy avenues of the 'ghetto', he subjected the university to some gentle scorn.

"Never felt like the real world when I was at uni," he said.

Ginny was surprised. "Did you come here?" she asked.

"No, Southampton. Did law—but I dropped out after a year."

"That's a shame."

"No it's not," he said. "I like my life a bit more edgy."

At the traffic lights he did the unexpected and headed away from the city, turning into the maze of ugly prefabricated buildings and gaudy advertising that was the Hillbrook industrial estate. Ginny was intrigued but chose not to ask him for an explanation, leaning back in her seat and watching him as he drove.

He pulled up on the opposite side of the road to a steel-and-glass edifice with sculptural pretensions and an indiscreet graphic which trumpeted William Buckley Motors along its entire length. New models glistened in the showrooms and the forecourt was crammed with second-hand vehicles, six of them on angled plinths designed to catch the eye.

Carmichael pointed into the sky. Clusters of cameras perched on pillars encircled the site.

"That's state of the art closed-circuit gear; cost his old man a fortune…plus a couple of round-the-clock security guys thrown in. It started about two years ago with a bit of tyre-slashing then he upped the ante with a can of paint-remover. We nicked him for that and he got two months in a Secure Training Centre—that's nick for babies; one month inside, one out on licence."

"And the father wanted him prosecuted?" she said

"They thought a short, sharp shock might sort him out." He laughed. "How wrong can you be? It got worse while he was inside—somebody chucked petrol bombs at the forecourt. He's got nasty friends, has Whizz."

Carmichael checked for traffic before releasing the hand-brake, and did a U-turn. Parked cars and an endless stream of juggernauts made driving awkward, but he wove a confident path back towards the coast road, talking full throttle at the same time.

"When they tightened the security at the showrooms, Whizz turned on the old man's customers and we started finding cars all over the city. Anything with a Buckley sticker in the back window was fair game for a bit of joy-riding and a match in the tank. That's how we know Whizz was involved with the fire at the hypermarket."

"So why didn't you lock him up for it?" Ginny asked, voicing the question that had been troubling her.

"Because the little bugger was elsewhere when the car was torched—doing good works with the Vicar of St Stephen's, would you believe, with the half the WI to back up the alibi. Didn't even bother to keep the grin off his face when he told me that one."

They travelled for some while in silence before Ginny said, "If you've been trying to frighten me, I think you've succeeded."

"Good," he said, giving her a nod, "not that I think he means you any harm personally. You seem to be the only person on the planet he's got any time for…"

"I get the feeling Whizz has not been a happy bunny since he was a very little kid," Ginny reflected. "That's probably why Murray's Road has been such a magnet for him."

Carmichael took his eyes off the road to look at her. "And how about you?" he asked. "How come you've stuck your neck out for the kid?"

Ginny gave a little chuckle. "A psychiatrist would have a field day, wouldn't he, sergeant?" she said. "Well, I'm sorry to disappoint you, but there's not a sniff of anything Freudian going on. He was a sweetie when he was little, but I didn't want to hug him to my bosom, and I certainly don't want to now."

Carmichael looked left before leaving the T-junction and briefly caught her eye.

Ginny smiled. "I find it hard to say 'no' to a kid who needs my help. It's an affliction of mine."

They were in heavy traffic on the sea-front and approaching the Clock Tower roundabout. Carmichael kept to the left-hand lane while Ginny watched the cars filtering right towards the

High Street, reflecting on how much had happened in the four short days since the Fates began to play tricks with her.

"I'm not trying to stop you helping the boy," Carmichael said, changing down the gears to crawl behind a garbage truck. "I don't like the idea of you going solo, that's all. It would be far better if we joined forces."

Ginny pulled a sceptical face. "Are you trying to recruit me?"

"You've got an allergy to policemen, I know that," he said, giving her a grin, "but think about it. The kid won't talk to probation officers, or social workers, or shrinks, and he sure as hell won't talk to us, so what chance have we got to straighten him out?"

"But he'll never open up to me if he thinks I'm in cahoots with the police," she protested.

"Why should he know?"

The mobile phone on the dashboard started to play Beethoven's fifth.

"Sorry," Carmichael said, and leaned forward to flick the speaker on.

A north-country voice launched into a long list of arrangements for his sister's wedding and reminded him that he had a speech to write. She was very Lancashire and unstoppable. Carmichael looked embarrassed. Ginny was amused. Her Old Gran would cross a road to avoid a copper, but this one seemed surprisingly human.

She pressed the toggle-switch on the door-handle and the window beside her slid down. The spring breeze had a nippy edge, but she relished the ozone: acrid bladder-wrack on the tide-line; chip fat and doughnuts; diesel and candy-floss—the eternal smell of the English seaside. And you could see why the bucket-and-spade brigade used to invade the place in their thousands: the sandy crescent of beach with its dinky row of swing-boats; the harbour jetty crowned by its black and white lighthouse; the yacht bobbing in exactly the right spot; everything posed for the perfect picture postcard.

Time was when the seafront was proud to be vulgar, like a brassy tart shaking her goods at the maiden aunts. Now it was just sad and tacky. One or two guest houses clung on to respectability, but most were boarded up or hid their squalor behind filthy net curtains. A Victorian playground turned Elizabethan slum, home to the homeless and the dispossessed, the over-spilled and the underfed.

They had been brought to a standstill outside *Xanadu*, a collection of tat-and-trinket shops, bingo-bars and fast-food joints, all sheltering below a sky-blue dome that was liberally flecked with seagull-shit. The lights at the road-works turned green at the same moment that the unstoppable Mrs Carmichael finally ran out of instructions.

"Sorry about that," Carmichael said, switching off the phone as he released the clutch. "I've got to give my sister away next...."

"Pull over!" Ginny shouted.

"What?" exclaimed Carmichael.

"Pull over," she said again. "I've just seen one of my kids from school..."

Ginny kept her eye on the little figure, her hand ready on the door-handle waiting for Carmichael to clear the road-works and bump the car up the kerb on to the promenade. Then she was outside and running risks with the traffic. Jason Nolan was not far ahead and she was gaining on him when, quite suddenly, he vanished into one of the arcades. It could have been *The Nugget* or *Las Vegas*, it was hard to tell. She peered into the gloomy interiors, but saw no sign of the boy. There were children in *The Nugget*, a small group watching one of the dads fish for tat with a toy crane. She decided to explore and she was quickly swallowed up in the din of a zillion machines, all blinking and winking and buzzing as they competed for attention.

The place was bigger than it looked. At first the only punters she met were disappointingly old, sitting in a solemn row feeding their pensions to a line of hungry fruit-machines. She was beginning to despair when ultra-violet lights started to flash, picking out two teenage girls bopping about like robots as they placed their feet on numbered mats at the dictate of a lurid screen called *Dance Crazy*. Drawn deeper into the electronic chaos, she began to encounter more youngsters: two vacant-looking lads racing virtual motorbikes at *Indianapolis*; an outsized girl-jockey on a metal horse jumping her way round *Aintree*; and a round-shouldered youth with unfashionably long hair who was warding off *The Invasion of the Undead* with a pump-action machinegun, spraying the big video-screen with virtual bullets and causing horrid mutilation in the ranks of the zombies.

And then she saw Jason, perched on top of a pin-table with a bag of crisps. He was watching the slayer-of-zombies, his round spectacles filled with reflected mayhem. As though sensing her presence, the little boy turned towards Ginny, and she ran towards him, narrowly avoiding a collision with the gunman.

"What on earth are you doing here, Jason?" she shouted, pitching her voice against the pandemonium.

The boy gaped at her, but before he could find words to reply, a hand grasped her arm above the elbow and a shrill voice screamed in her ear, "What the fuck do you want, darling?"

It was the slayer-of-zombies. He was shorter than Ginny by a few inches, but there was violence in him, and the pale face that he thrust close to hers had a wayward look.

"I'm Jason's teacher," she explained, still battling with the noise, "and I want to know why he's not at school?"

"I bet they'd like to know where the fuck you are too!" he shouted.

This witticism pleased him so much that he wanted to share it with his mates, who had materialised out of the gloom and were crowding round them.

"Get a load of this!" he yelled, jabbing his finger at her. "This is Jason's teacher doing a bit of bunking off."

The gang found this hysterically funny and began making strange animal noises. The zombie-slayer dropped his gaze to Ginny's feet and slowly let his eyes travel up her body before leaning forwards to put his mouth close to her ear.

"I bet you could teach me a thing or two, darling," he said in a breathy whisper, then leaned back and bellowed, "What do you think guys? Not a bad bit of cunt for a teacher?"

Amid the whoops and catcalls, a voice shouted, "Filth!" Instantly the crowd scattered. Glancing towards the seafront, Ginny could see why. DS Carmichael was standing beside the two trance-dancers, silhouetted against the distant daylight, scanning the arcade, making no attempt to stop the runaways as they escaped into the sunshine.

Feeling bolder, Ginny turned to confront the youth who had menaced her, but he had moved up close to Jason and was whispering in his ear.

"Come on, Jason," she said, pushing her tormentor to one side, "let's get you home."

As she lifted the little boy down from the pin-table, he threw his skinny arms around her neck and clung to her, clamping his legs around her waist.

DS Carmichael was suddenly at her side. "Is the boy OK?" he asked.

"He's fine, aren't you, Jason?" she replied, hugging the boy close to reassure him.

"You take him outside and I'll be with you as soon as I can," Carmichael said.

As Ginny carried the boy towards the daylight, a fresh battalion of ghouls was already marching out of Hell. Their nemesis paused in his slaughter to flutter his fingers in a little wave to Jason, then re-engaged the enemy, nonchalantly dispatching more of the undead while Carmichael shouted in his ear.

When they reached the fresh air, Ginny lowered Jason to the pavement and disentangled herself from his clutches, reassuring him that she wasn't in the least bit cross and that everything was going to be all right. By the time Carmichael emerged from *The Nugget*, the boy was much calmer. Ginny pulled another tissue from the sleeve of her shirt and encouraged him to blow his nose.

The detective squatted down beside them. "Did Moon give you anything, Jason?" he asked.

Ginny looked at Carmichael in amazement. "Did I hear you right?" she asked.

"Not now!" Carmichael said brusquely.

"Was that really Moon Rivers?" she repeated.

He turned and glared at her. "I said, not now."

Ginny bridled.

Carmichael flipped open his wallet. "You know what this badge is, don't you Jason? It means I'm a policeman, and it means you've got to tell me the truth." The little boy gazed up at the detective, his wide eyes magnified by the lenses. "I need to know if Moon gave you anything."

The eyes filled with tears and Jason began to nod his head.

"Let me see, then," Carmichael said.

The boy fumbled in the pocket of his baggy tracksuit bottoms and produced a fifty-pence piece.

Carmichael gave a snort.

"Is that your wages, Jason?" he asked.

The boy nodded.

"What you did you have to do for all that money then?"

The child's chin dropped to his chest and his shoulders began to heave.

"Have you been running errands for Moon?"

Jason was snivelling now and rubbing his eyes.

"Come on," coaxed Carmichael, "I'm not going to bite you. Just tell me what you were doing for Moon."

The policeman had been speaking quietly, but there was something steely in his persistence that grated on Ginny.

"For goodness sake," she snapped, "he's five years old!"

Impulsively she grabbed Jason by the hand and stalked off towards *Xanadu*, the boy in tow, half-running to keep pace.

"You're going the wrong way," Carmichael shouted. "The car's this way."

Anger had brought a rush of adrenalin, but now, just as suddenly, it gushed away leaving her dry-mouthed and faint. She stopped walking and hung her head, feeling queasy.

"Are you all right?" Carmichael asked when he caught her up.

"I have felt better," she replied, giving him a stony look.

He looked concerned and took hold of her elbow. "Would a cup of coffee be a good idea?" he said.

"No thank you," she said, shrugging off his hand.

"I do have a job to do, you know," said Carmichael, giving her a pained look.

"Well, go and get on with it," Ginny snapped. "I'm going to get this child back home to his mother."

Carmichael looked out to sea and chewed his lower lip. "OK then," he said, "please yourself! There's a lift if you want one."

Ginny watched him stride away and turned to the boy. "Do you live far from here, Jason?"

The child gazed up at her blankly.

"Never mind," she said, giving his hand a reassuring squeeze. "Can you remember your address?"

The pallid face brightened. "24, Falcon Street, East Farley, Seaborough," he parroted confidently.

"Brilliant!" she said. "You've just got yourself a Smiley Face."

She hadn't a clue where Falcon Street was. It could be miles away. She looked along the seafront. Carmichael had stopped outside *The Nugget* and was looking back to see if they were following. He beckoned to her and mouthed his invitation again.

Ginny raised her hand in acknowledgement. "OK Jason," she said brightly, "shall we go and ask that nice policeman the way home."

There was a moment of giddiness as she straightened her back but she was determined not to make an even bigger fool of herself and swallowed a deep breath of sea air to clear her head before setting off down the pavement. Jason meanwhile had come alive and skipped along beside her with all the bounce of a beach-ball.

It was a tight-lipped journey. DS Carmichael drove straight to Falcon Street. He knew the place well. He knew number twenty four, and he knew Jason's mum. Above all, he knew Jason's dad, Kenny.

"Hello, Mary," he said, holding his ID to the crack of the door, "just look who we've brought home."

The door swung open to reveal a befuddled Mrs Nolan in a grubby pink nightdress, her hair lank and limp, eyes puffy and red-rimmed. On her hip she carried a baby with a big yellow dummy stuck in its face. Behind her, another child, wearing little more than an ominous nappy, was coming backwards down the steep staircase on all fours.

"Where's your dad then?" she said to Jason. "You're supposed to be with your dad."

Jason was clinging on to Ginny's shirt, rubbing the material between finger and thumb, and sucking furiously on the other thumb. She prised his fingers away and took him by his skinny shoulders. "Off you go to your mum then," she said, pushing him gently away.

The little boy scurried to his mother and pressed his head against her thighs, his hand eager to explore the textures of the cheap satin nightie. The baby wriggled and made a lunge for Jason, trying his best to swat him about the head. Mrs Nolan struggled to control the child who lashed out with his little foot making her gasp in pain.

Carmichael waited until the baby had been subdued. "We found Jason in one of the arcades on the seafront," he said, "with Rivers, of all people. That's not good, Mary."

But the woman's eyes were fixed on Ginny, the pupils dilated and black as tar, hostile and resentful. "I weren't well this morning," she said dully. "That's why he weren't at school."

With a shriek of defiance the baby spat out his dummy and arched his back in another break for freedom. Mrs Nolan groaned and doubled up.

Alarmed, Ginny held out her hands towards the baby. "Can I help?" she offered.

Mrs Nolan snatched the child away and hugged him to her breast. "No!" she shouted. "We'll manage…"

Ginny glanced at Carmichael. If he shared her sense of intrusion, it did not show.

"We'd better have a chat about all this, Mary," he said. "Can we come in?"

Mrs Nolan showed no willingness to move, but continued to rock the baby, watching Ginny out of the corner of her eye.

"Not me," Ginny said. "I'll wait in the car." She held her hand out for the car-key, adding, "We've got a guide dog coming to see us tomorrow, Jason. You wouldn't want to miss him, would you?"

The boy gazed back at her, his glasses blank with sky.

"I'll get him there tomorrow, Mrs May," his mother said, and she wedged the baby on her hip, leaning down to grab the toddler by an arm so that she could drag the protesting child up the stairs. Jason followed, turning at the bottom of the stairs, just in time to give Ginny a timid wave before Carmichael closed the door.

In the patch of wilderness that had once been a garden, the buddleia was in a death-struggle with the bindweed. Ginny walked towards the broken gate and pointed the car-key at the Mini Cooper. The side-lights winked as the doors unlocked. It was the only sign of life in the dead road. House after dreary house, quiet as tombs.

Tilting the passenger seat back, she stretched out her legs and tipped her head back. She wanted to shut it all out. Back there on the pavement outside *Xanadu* she had feared for her baby. That giddiness, that gnawing emptiness in the stomach...she knew that feeling well. Yet again, at the first available moment, she would be head down in her underwear, searching for 'spotting'.

Too soon the driver's door opened. "Sorry to wake you," Carmichael said.

"I wasn't asleep," she replied, sitting up to fiddle with the lever that raised the seat-back. "I was trying to meditate, would you believe?"

Carmichael took the car-key from the top of the dash where she had left it.

"I'd better get you to that garage," he said, "or I'm going to be late for work."

He drove down Falcon Street until he found a stretch without parked cars, then executed a neat three-point turn and returned the way they had come. Ginny stared across the road towards number twenty-four.

"They've tried to take her kids away, haven't they?" she said.

"It's Kenny that's the problem," he replied. "When he's away, Mary's OK. She copes just fine. The sooner we put Kenny away for a good long stretch the better. And that goes for Rivers too—you know what that 50p was for, don't you?

There was an edge to his voice. He had not forgotten their difference of opinion outside the Pleasure Dome—but then neither had she.

"Tell me about Moon Rivers," Ginny said. "He wasn't what I expected at all."

The policeman gave a grunt. "What did you expect? Al Capone?"

"Well, I didn't expect that little pip-squeak."

Carmichael raised his eyebrows and snatched a quizzical look at her. "And here's me thinking he'd put the frighteners on you!"

"He surprised me," she countered.

Carmichael was quiet for a moment. "The first time they banged Moon up, car crime in the west of the city fell by two-thirds. He was a legend down the nick before I came…."

"And you've gone on 'banging him up' ever since?" she interrupted.

"If we can catch the sod we certainly do."

"So prison works then, does it?"

"Well, let's put it this way," he said, "a lot of people sleep easier if Moon is off the streets."

"Doesn't solve the problem though, does it?" she said.

Carmichael sighed and gave her a weary look. "Mary Nolan's social worker is probably a fully paid-up member of your Hearts and Flowers Party," he said, "but I bet she does a little dance every time we put Kenny away."

They were on Strand Street, the only road that cut through the maze of narrow lanes in *The Shacks*, inching along behind a pedaled rickshaw, with local bo-hos milling around the car as though traffic had no right to be there. In the doorway of a tattoo-parlour a young black guy was blowing jazz on a flugelhorn, his cheeks inflated like two balloons on the point of bursting. On the pavement beside him, a coven of Goths had forgotten to be depressed and were dancing enthusiastically to his music.

Carmichael leaned forward and pointed to the pavement on the opposite side of the road. "Here comes Shirley," he said.

There was no mistaking Shirley, an Amazon of a woman even without the mountain of back-combed hair. Wearing a leopard-skin coat over a red satin ra-ra skirt and fishnet tights, she sashayed along on sky-scraper heels, oblivious to the attention she was attracting from passers-by.

"My neighbour," explained Carmichael, and lowered his window to shout a greeting.

Shirley brought herself to a standstill with a theatrical flourish. For a moment it looked as though she might bob a curtsey, but then she bent her head towards the hairy bundle in the crook of her arm and poked it with a finger. A mouthful of small teeth were bared, and the bundle barked.

"Morning, Captain Baxter," shouted Carmichael, easing out the clutch as the traffic moved.

Shirley wagged the dog's paw at Carmichael, and in a deep, manly voice called out, "Bye, Sherlock. See you later!"

Carmichael shifted up the gears. "Shirley was in the Grenadier Guards," he explained. "Calls the big hair-do his 'bearskin'."

Ginny was impressed. "Do you live in *The Shacks*?" she asked.

"Why so surprised?" he replied.

"Well, it's a bit of a thieves' kitchen for a copper, isn't it."

He shot her a glance that was full of mischief. "Give me rogues and vagabonds any day," he said, "much better company than all those clever sods up the hill."

From the depths of her shoulder-bag, Ginny heard the muffled tones of her mobile phone. Excusing herself, she flicked it open and checked the number on the display. It meant nothing to her.

"Hello," she said, "Ginny May."

"You fucking slag!" a voice said. "Why did you dump the filth on Moon?"

"Is that Whizz?" she exclaimed.

"Why don't you mind your own fucking business, twat?"

Ginny switched on the mobile's speaker and held out the phone so that Carmichael could hear. Whizz ranted on. Mangled by his damaged mouth, the abuse barely made sense. When the stream of insults gave signs of drying up, Ginny put the phone back to her ear and waited for a lull.

"I was looking for the little boy," she said eventually, "that's the only..."

"Don't give me that, you slag," he interrupted.

"And don't you dare call me a slag," she countered angrily. "I've heard more than enough filthy language from you. That's enough!"

There was a pause, then: "Listen, you slag. I know where you fucking live, and don't you fucking forget it."

The connection died with a click.

Ginny snapped the mobile shut and dropped it in the bag. "That's that then," she said. "I don't expect I'll be hearing from him again. Probably just as well."

"That wasn't for your benefit," Carmichael said. "He'd got an audience."

Ginny repeated the boy's parting shot, mimicking the tough-guy tone. "I know where you fucking live and don't you fucking forget it."

"He was talking to Moon," Carmichael said, checking his watch, "trying to prove he's still a bad-boy."

At the junction with Station Road they escaped the narrow confines of *The Shacks* and Carmichael took the first opportunity to duck out of the traffic, weaving an intricate route through a labyrinth of unpromising streets, and driving with the urgency of someone who was late for work.

"If you're right, and Moon and his cronies beat the daylights out of Whizz," Ginny, "why on earth would he go back for more?"

"Same reason," replied the policeman. "To prove himself to Moon."

Ginny shook her head. "That doesn't make any sense to me."

Carmichael turned right and found his way blocked by a removals van disgorging office furniture into the road. Undeterred, he slammed the mini into reverse and retraced his path at speed.

"They don't work to our rules, these kids," he said, raising his voice above the whine of the engine. "Logic doesn't come into it. Whizz has put himself outside all that. Don't ask me why, but he's kissed goodbye to a cosy middle-class billet and he's turned himself into an outlaw." To Ginny's relief the backward charge had come to an end, but Carmichael had not. "He lives by Moon's rules now, because Moon is the only family he's got."

Carmichael chose another unpromising service alley that ran behind Ramages Department Store and MacDonalds.

"And here's another thing," he said, shifting rapidly through second to third gear. "Moon Rivers just loves having a kid like

Whizz to play with. It's his revenge—watching the rich kid go down the toilet, giving him a gentle push now and then. It's more fun than a train-set."

By some miracle of navigation, they had arrived at a junction with the main road only a few blocks away from *Seaborough Saab*. As he waited for the traffic, Carmichael checked his watch again.

"Are you going to make it?" Ginny asked.

"With a bit of luck," he replied.

Ginny watched his fingers tapping the top of the steering wheel like a pianist practising scales. He was eager to be moving but there was no tension in him, no impatience. He seemed able to look the world coolly in the eye and deal with what he found, no illusions.

"I would have helped, if I could," she said.

"But it's not a lost cause yet," he said, and eased the Mini into the main road.

"He won't call again," said Ginny, "not now."

"Don't put money on it…"

They drove past the opulent showroom with its shiny display of new models and turned into the compound where rank on rank of second-hand Saabs boasted their ludicrous price-tags. Alongside the other motors on the apron, the old Saab looked out of place. Despite the best efforts of the wash-and-wax, it was distinctly shabby. She was delighted to see it.

"Thanks for the lift," she said. "It's been an interesting day."

"Seriously," Carmichael said, "if anyone can get through to that kid, I reckon it's you. If he does call, you will give me a bell, won't you?"

He extended his hand so formally that Ginny was taken by surprise and failed to respond at once.

"No going solo though," he warned. "No heroics, OK?"

The pressure he had applied to her hand to emphasise his meaning was disconcerting. Ginny responded by shaking his hand a little over enthusiastically, as if she had just sold him a car.

"OK," she said, showing the dimples, "that's a deal."

Chapter Ten

For the next couple of weeks life in the May household was tranquil. To Simon's professed irritation but un-disguisable glee, a Harvard celebrity had inconveniently over-dosed and left the Vice Chancellor with a yawning hole in the University's fiftieth anniversary celebrations. Instead of delivering his Inaugural Lecture to the customary audience of friends and dutiful colleagues in a gloomy lecture hall, Simon would be pushed into the spotlight in full academic pomp to sound off in the *Hexagon*. With less than a month to prepare, he was rarely away from his desk. And when he wasn't working, he was making music on the piano—not the usual 'gymnastics for the mind', but jaunty variations on hackneyed seaside tunes for this year's *Follies*. It was a pleasant change. And it was all down to Mel, who had gone off like a firework in the English Department.

To the strains of *A Life on the Ocean Wave* drifting down from the sitting-room above, Ginny splashed glazes on a dinner service of wonky plates and bowls that she had created with deliberate disregard for symmetry. Simon was happy. She was happy. The bad dreams had fled and she felt rested. What's more, the new serenity had brought a sense of perspective so sharp that her priorities were, for once, breathtakingly simple— baby first and second, Simon third. Whizz Buckley and his dysfunctional universe had almost faded away, and might well have vanished entirely if it were not for Jason Nolan and the change in his end-of-school routine.

Ever since the visit to Falcon Street with Carmichael, it was not Mary who came to collect the boy, it was his dad...and Kenny Nolan was a disconcerting presence in the crowd of mothers that waited at the gate. His good looks had long since been squandered on whatever poisons he was partial to, and they were probably numerous. When she asked after his wife, his eyes would skitter about as if they were loose in their sockets, and he would mumble something incoherent about Mary's state of health. Were it not for the image of Mary clinging desperately to her children, Ginny would have phoned Social Services, and she never ceased to feel guilty as she watched little Jason trail reluctantly after his shambolic father as they made their way to the crowd of no-goods who hung around outside the bookie's shop. It was then that she found herself looking out for Whizz. She couldn't help it...

Ginny dipped her brush deep into a jar of oxide and flicked an arc of cobalt across the table, spattering a cohort of up-turned soup bowls.

"We need a referee."

Mel was standing at the door to the playroom. Her scarlet spikes had long since gone, replaced by tuft upon tuft of jet black hair tied in a forest of multi-coloured ribbons. Today she was wearing a black leotard under an electric blue mini-skirt no wider than a belt, and a flash of blue lightening was painted on her cheek. Anyone else would have looked ridiculous.

"Your husband thinks I'm taking vulgarity to new depths," she said, "but I think he's being a stuffed-shirt."

"My money's on you," Ginny replied, flicking another random shower of glaze across the table.

"Could you spare a mo to have a look?"

By the time Ginny had peeled off her rubber gloves, and discarded the wrap-around pinny that looked like a Jackson Pollock, the piano was giving a sentimental account of the old Jaques Trenet song, *La Mer*. When she finally made it to the top of the stairs and peeped into the sitting-room, Mel was standing behind Simon, swaying to the gentle rhythm, her hands resting lightly on his shoulders.

"Doesn't look raunchy to me," said Ginny, folding her arms like a battleaxe of old.

"Oh, no," said Mel, spinning round, "this is the sloppy bit. The dirty bit is right at the beginning." Reaching behind the sheet music propped up on its stand above the keyboard she produced a wooden rolling-pin. "You've got to imagine that this is a giant stick of Seaborough rock."

"Wait till you see what she's got planned for it," interjected Simon, with a pained look on his face.

"Don't be such a fuddy-duddy, Prof. The kids are gonna lap it up."

"It's not the students I'm worried about..."

"Come on, stop bickering you two!" Ginny said, flopping down in one of the Chesterfields. "I am eager to be shocked."

Simon interlocked the fingers of both hands and began to flex his wrists. "Do we really have to?"

"Yes, we bloody do," insisted Mel.

Simon began to play *Oh, I do like to be Beside the Seaside,* producing a string of lunatic changes of key. Mel, meanwhile, was standing behind the baby grand with her back to Ginny. Slowly she turned, offering her profile. Then she raised the rolling-pin, and extended her tongue.

Ginny sniggered. Fellatio at *The Follies*! Small wonder Simon's nerve was being tested.

As the piano jangled out the last few bars of the intro, Mel slowly trained the rolling-pin on Ginny like a gun, and began to intone, hissing out the sibilants and rolling out the 'r's like a side-drum:

Scarlet letters running through the rock, (circles finger on end of rolling-pin)

from the first suck until the very last, (sucks, then inverts the rolling-pin)

a tart of a town where they learned to love, (caresses Simon's shoulders)

and helter-skeltered down their gaudy days, (pirouetting throughout)

drunk on laughter, ravenous for life, (collapses languorously on pianist, sucks again)

chasing the sun across the seaside sky. (leans back and opens herself to the heavens.)

Simon, who had been decorating this performance with flourishes on the piano, banged out a discordant chord, shouting, "We can't possibly get away with it. No way!"

He was laughing, but he meant it.

"What do you think, Ginny?" asked Mel, rolling onto her stomach, as playful as one of the kids at school.

"It'll bring the house down," Ginny said.

Simon had folded his arms over the top of his head. "It will bring my career down, that's for sure," he said.

"Rubbish!" retorted Mel. "It's pure McGill, straight off a saucy postcard and it's just what *The Follies* needs—a good kick up the arse. I'm right, aren't I, Ginny?"

On the window-ledge at the far end of the big sitting-room, the ring of the telephone provided Ginny with a timely excuse.

"You're both right," she said, hauling herself out of the sofa. "It'll go down a storm...and Simon had better look for a new job."

She picked up the phone. Although there was silence on the line, for some inexplicable reason, she knew who was calling. She turned her back on the piano.

"Mrs May?"

The piano had resumed *La Mer*. Ginny cupped her hands around the mouthpiece.

"What's the matter?" she said. "Are you all right?"

"They done me this time…"

"Who's done you? Have they beaten you up again?"

"The cops… They done me for thieving."

"Where are you?"

There was another moment of silence.

"If they send me to prison will you come and see me, please?"

His voice had changed: the pitch; the clarity of diction; the grammar—everything was transformed. He was a different person.

"Of course I will," she replied, "if that's what you want."

"Thank you, Mrs May."

"Where are you? I'll come now, if you like…"

But the phone was dead. Ginny stared out over the garden wondering if she should try 'ring-back'.

"Is there a problem?" It was Simon calling from the piano.

"Not really," she said, putting the phone back in its charger. "I was supposed to be seeing that woman who runs the craft fairs at Castle Rock but she's cried off."

As soon as she could escape, Ginny left Simon and Mel chuckling over another risqué stanza, and went back to the playroom to put in a call to DS Carmichael. A recorded voice apologised and invited her to leave a message. Ginny issued a silent curse, but obediently left her message.

It was impossible to concentrate on the pots while she waited. The upside-down soup bowls looked like rows of bare backsides with chronic acne. They were crying out for extra attention but she needed a spark of energy that simply wasn't there, so she distracted herself by cleaning brushes and mopping up the worst of the mess she had made.

When Carmichael returned her call, he said, "The kid's done it this time! They caught him in the act, no arguments."

"Can I come and see him?" she asked.

"No chance," he replied. "The Custody Suite is a madhouse on a Friday night. You might get to see him in court tomorrow morning."

"Surely they won't get him to court so soon?" she said.

"Not for the full hearing, that'll be next week probably. But they'll have a quickie with the magistrates to decide whether to bail him or stick him on remand. From what I've heard, we're opposing bail so they'll probably bang him up for a few days until the next Youth Court sits."

"It's that serious, is it?"

"He was caught knocking off a Community Centre, and he's 'ticked' a lot more."

"What's that mean?"

"It means he's asking for other offences to be 'taken into consideration'. It clears the decks, so they can't come back to haunt him."

"He sounded scared when I talked to him."

"Well he's not been acting scared down the nick. According to my oppo, he's been a pain in the bum."

Chapter Eleven

"Don't you think we should pack some blankets around them?" asked Simon, putting the stack of fruit bowls into the boot of the Saab next to the box of miscellaneous pots.

"They'll be fine," she said, checking her watch as she closed the hatchback. "I'm not the racing driver in this family."

She was late. According to Carmichael, the magistrates would start their list at nine o'clock, and it was already a quarter to.

"These boxes are heavy," warned Simon. "You'll get some help, won't you, Gin?"

He'd been sweet: abandoned the conference speech he was writing; insisted on bubble-wrapping everything; and then packed the car.

Ginny gave him a peck on the cheek. "Don't worry," she said, "I'll be careful."

She felt guilty about the subterfuge, but she couldn't face another dose of his disapproval. And anyway, she intended to appease her conscience by visiting several craft galleries when the court case was over.

The Magistrates' Courts looked deserted. Below the Royal Coat of Arms there was not a glimmer of light in the gloomy foyer, and Ginny was surprised when the heavy glass door opened. The silence of the building swallowed her up. Three security gates with metal-detector frames barred her way to the staircase ahead, and the security cubicles at either side were unmanned.

She was beginning to suspect that Carmichael had been wrong about the Saturday sitting, when a man appeared up some steps from the basement.

"I sorry, madam," he said, heading for one of the gates with a bunch of keys. "We got short crew on Sat-days."

He was immaculate in a dark green blazer, with razor-creased slacks and highly polished shoes—ex-Gurkha soldier, by the look of him.

Ginny put her shoulder-bag into the plastic basket beside the scanner, and walked through the frame. The security man searched the bag and handed it back to her.

"Switch off mobile, please madam, if you go to court," he said.

"The Magistrates are sitting today, then?" she asked.

"One court only on Sat-day. Court Number 2."

Ginny climbed the stairs and found herself in a huge waiting room, with groups of chairs and side-tables, and a phalanx of brand new vending machines. Everything was clean and neat, and waiting for Monday when the place will be full of bustle and seething with anxiety. A notice-board which promised 'Today's Court List' had been left blank, and when she knocked at the door marked 'Duty Solicitor's Room' there was no reply.

The empty building was intimidating. As she went through the imposing archway that led to the courtrooms she felt like a trespasser. The glazed panel in the door of Court One showed a narrow rectangle of darkness within. Further down the corridor, the identical panel in the door to Court Two was illuminated. She peeped through. There was another Coat of Arms above a raised dais with three leather thrones awaiting the arrival of the magistrates. At the table below, in the well of the court, two men in suits were riffling through a pile of documents. A third man sat hunched over his papers some distance away.

Easing the door open, Ginny slipped into the back row of what she assumed was the Public Gallery. The two men looked up from their task. They seemed surprised that a member of the public had shown up, but voiced no objection. Ginny waited, feeling conspicuous.

After a while, the first defendant was brought into the dock, handcuffed to a custody-officer. After he was un-shackled, he sat down, looking docile and bemused as he stared out through the bullet-proof glass. Everyone stood as the magistrates trouped in, and it soon became apparent why Saturday morning justice was not a popular spectator sport. It was deadly dull.

The presiding magistrate made his pronouncements in a sepulchral voice but, for all his *gravitas,* it was clear that he was not running the show. The Clerk of the Court was the man in charge, a sharp-suited individual with bulbous eyes and a bald head that sat on his shoulders without the benefit of a neck. The villains, who had been dragged from all over the county and beyond, turned out to be a sad miscellany of drink-drivers, petty thieves and violent drunks who had had the temerity to do their sinning at the fag-end of the working week. Each of them was made to stand in the dock while the Bench decided whether to grant bail or remand them in custody until Monday when the vast weekday army of legal functionaries would return from the golf-courses and leafy suburbs to dispense more considered justice. Although the formal niceties were studiously observed, with much 'Your Worshipping' and bowing, it was clear that every person present – Clerk of the Court, Magistrates and attendant solicitors – would all have preferred to be elsewhere this Saturday morning.

Ginny looked at her watch. An hour had crawled by. Despite the efforts of the Clerk to hasten proceedings, only four miscreants had been dealt with. Smothering a yawn, she wondered bleakly if DS Carmichael had sent her on a fool's errand.

Then things looked up. The lawyer who had provided a token defence in all the cases so far stacked up his papers, and made way for an altogether more dashing replacement—a tall, rangy individual with a walrus moustache and a greying pony-tail that hung half-way down his back. When the new arrival took off his sheepskin overcoat and folded it over the back of his seat, he revealed a black jacket, cut ostentatiously long and left unbuttoned to show a splendid waistcoat in maroon brocade. It was as though Wyatt Earp had strolled into court, minus Colt 45 and Stetson.

The Clerk of the Court greeted the newcomer with exaggerated courtesy and exchanged knowing glances with the prosecuting solicitor. Wyatt Earp sat back in his chair, folded his arms and eyed the Clerk with scepticism that bordered on hostility.

"The court will rise!" announced the Clerk, and the magistrates filed back in.

The defendant was a small-time thief and heroin-addict who had admitted stealing perfumes from a local department store. He sat placidly on the wrong side of the glass watching the antics of the legal worthies on the right side of the glass with mute acceptance. The prosecuting solicitor explained that the police were opposing bail because the defendant had a record of absconding on previous occasions, and was already in receipt of a suspended prison sentence for a previous offence.

It occurred to Ginny that the magistrates would not waste too much of their Saturday on this case, but the defence had other ideas and embarked on a long and eloquent speech in mitigation.

'Prison is just an expensive way of making bad people worse', was Wyatt's text. As he developed his theme, the Clerk began a detailed inspection of the plasterwork on the ceiling of the court. The magistrates made notes, or doodled. The prosecutor flicked through his diary. Even the defendant looked bored. To her shame, Ginny felt some sympathy with the court. It had been a long morning. But then Wyatt moved on to give a harrowing account of his client's epic battles with many demons, and asked the court what possible advantage there could be in sending such an addicted individual to a prison which was probably better stocked with drugs than the average chemist's shop. It was a point well made, and brought Ginny back on side. When Wyatt finally sat down, she felt like applauding. However, after a very short adjournment, the magistrates did what they had always intended to do, and remanded his client in custody. Wyatt leaned back in his chair, hooked his thumbs in his trouser pockets and shook his head sorrowfully as if the world had gone mad.

The Clerk opened another folder. "The next case is one for the Youth Court," he announced. "We must clear the public benches." He was looking directly at Ginny.

Blood rose to her cheeks. "But I've been waiting all morning," she exclaimed.

"I'm sorry, madam," the Clerk said, "but unless you are the young man's mother or a very close relative, you must leave the court."

Ginny clenched her fists, and seethed with rage. The Clerk's protruding eyes were unblinking.

"Perhaps the court would allow me a moment?"

It was an intervention from Wyatt Earp.

"I would appreciate your help, Mr Bradley," the Clerk said, picking up the telephone on his desk.

The tall lawyer shambled across the courtroom, and shepherded Ginny into the corridor outside.

"I'm Joe Bradley, the boy's solicitor," he said, and offered his hand. "I'm sorry about The Toad, but technically he's right. Only mums and dads allowed I'm afraid."

"I'm Ginny May," she said, "I used to be Will's teacher in primary school. I thought he could do with a friendly face in court."

Bradley gave her a thoughtful look. "I'll tell him you came."

"I'll wait and see him afterwards," Ginny said. "Another hour won't hurt."

The lawyer crinkled his face and shook his head. "They're not going to bail him, I'm afraid." He paused, closing one eye while he wrestled with an idea. "I'll tell you what though..." he went on, "it's against the rules, but I'll try to wangle you a few minutes before they cart him off to Fulford..."

Through the narrow window, Ginny watched the maverick lawyer go back to the defence bench, and then moved her position until she had an oblique view of the dock where Whizz was gesturing wildly as he harangued the court. She could hear nothing through the door, but she didn't need to. The boy's performance would no doubt relieve the tedium of the morning, but then Their Worships would take considerable pleasure in teaching him a lesson.

The cappuccino from the machine was surprisingly good and the big waiting-room was airy and civilised. The architect had done a good job. It wasn't a bad place to wait, but she had waited far too long today. For the umpteenth time she checked her watch. It was almost time to feed more money into the parking meter but she didn't dare leave the building.

"Oh God, I could kill for one of those," cried Joe Bradley as he strode across the room, his hand deep in his trouser pocket fumbling for small change.

"How did it go?" Ginny asked.

"Remanded in Custody pending a Youth Court next week. They would have hanged him if they could."

"Can I get to see him?" she asked.

"We got lucky," Bradley said, pressing buttons on the vending machine. "I'll just wet my whistle, and I'll sneak you down."

"Whizz didn't help himself, did he?" she asked.

"The kid's a kamikaze," said Bradley, taking a sip of his coffee. "It's nigh on impossible to help him." He turned his eyes on Ginny. "So why are you bothering?"

"Because he's a lost soul, I suppose..." she said, "...and because his parents seem to have air-brushed him out of existence."

"Ah, yes," Bradley interjected, "the wicked parents! The Bench had a pop at them this morning."

"I should think so!" Ginny said. "Where are they, for God's sake?"

Bradley sniffed and rubbed the end of his nose with a forefinger while he gave the matter some thought.

"I went to their house once," he said. "It's like a big ice-cream cake plonked down on the headland at Coombe Bay, all very luxurious. They showed me the kid's bedroom. Every stick of furniture in splinters, every book ripped to shreds, every window broken, the carpet slashed, wallpaper ripped off walls... He'd trashed the lot...systematically. It was his way of saying goodbye to home and family."

Bradley tipped back the plastic coffee cup and took a swallow, leaving a trace of froth on his moustache.

"The kid's mother hasn't been out of the house for more than a year. She's a wreck. According to her husband, she spends most of her days at a telescope looking out to sea."

The lawyer raised an eyebrow to give her a cock-eyed look, then he wiped his moustache on the back of his hand and tossed the cup in the waste-bin next to the vending machine.

"Come on," he said, "let's go and see the little charmer."

The cell block reeked of disinfectant. A bunch of keys clinked on the custody officer's hip as he led them down the long corridor with cells on either side. Apart from a low-level hum from the nearby power-plant, it was the only sound. They were in the bowels of the building.

The jailer stopped at a cell door, looked through the observation window and rattled a key in the lock. "Mr Bradley has brought you a visitor," he said, swinging the metal door open.

There was a cot with a thin green mattress and a seat in the same material that was hinged to the wall. Whizz was lying on his stomach on the floor. He did not look up. He was tearing chunks of polystyrene from what looked like a coffee-cup.

"Mrs May has come to see you, Whizz," said Bradley.

Whizz ignored them, and continued to break the pieces of polystyrene into smaller fragments.

Bradley raised his eyebrows and shrugged a question at Ginny.

"Can I see him on my own, please?" Ginny asked the jailer.

"I could get shot for this," the man replied, but he gave her a brusque nod. "Joe and me'll be outside. Door open at all times, mind. And no malarkey, young man."

Ginny entered the cell and perched on the plastic mattress. On the wall opposite she could see the stain where Whizz had thrown the tea. It was still wet and glistening. She looked down at the boy. He seemed absorbed by his task.

"What are you doing, Whizz?" she asked quietly.

He muttered something incomprehensible.

"Sorry...What did you say?"

"I'm killing time," he said, making each syllable distinct.

He was working with the focus and intensity of a clockmaker, as though he were engaged in the most intricate and demanding task on earth.

"Moon taught me this," he said eventually. "You got to get as many bits as you can out of a cup. Moon got over a thousand one time. I only done seven hundred and sixty last time I was in."

Ginny watched him for a few moments. "You're going to have an awful lot of time to kill if you carry on like you did in court today."

Whizz stopped working, and leaned on one elbow to look up at her. "How do you fucking know?" he said. "You wasn't even there."

"They wouldn't let me in," she explained. "I was looking through a window."

The boy considered this for a moment, and then resumed his task, breaking up the fragments into ever smaller specks with his thumb-nail, pushing them into groups of ten with his index finger.

"When you phoned me at home last night," Ginny said gently, "you asked me if I would come and visit you in prison. And I will. I'll come as soon as I can."

"Moon done time in Fulford," Whizz said chattily. "Done it twice in fact."

"Would you like me to bring anything for you?" she asked. "Any books or anything?"

"What Moon says is...If they give you a plateful of shit when you're inside, you got to give 'em two platefuls back. That's what Moon says."

"I think Moon has far too much to say for himself," she said, and immediately regretted the note of schoolmarm in her voice.

Bradley put his head into the cell. "Time's up," he said.

"Just one more minute, if you can," Ginny appealed.

"Be quick," Bradley whispered. "The guy's done more than he should already."

Ginny squatted down close to the boy. "Look at me, Whizz," she said, touching his shoulder, "come on, please look at me."

The boy leaned over on one elbow and craned his neck, looking her full in the face. Apart from the little crescent scar that tugged at his right eye, he was unblemished. The marks of his beating had healed, and his eyes were clear and steady.

"The little boy I remember at Murray's Road was not cut out for a dreadful world like this," she said, parting her hands as though to encompass the whole cell. "I want to find out what went wrong for that little boy and I want to try to put it right. Are you going to help me, Whizz?"

She gave him a small nod to encourage a reply, but he was looking beyond her to somewhere far away.

Outside the cell, the jailer called, "Come on, let's be having you..."

"I'll come and see you next week. As soon as I can," Ginny said, straightening up and turning for the door. "That's a promise, Whizz."

"Thank you for coming, Mrs May."

Ginny turned round. The boy was on his stomach again, at work on the polystyrene, killing time.

The door slammed, the key turned and Ginny was soon in the lift with Joe Bradley, rising up, out of the stench of disinfectant towards the daylight and open spaces.

"He's scared stiff," she said.

"And with cause," Bradley replied. "He's a kid from the nice side of the tracks. He ain't going to find many soul-mates where he's going."

Chapter Twelve

There were no ominous signs or portents. Sunday had been glorious and they had walked for miles across the Wold, ending up in front of the log fire at The Pepperbox, an out-of-the-way pub with a bar wreathed in hop garlands. She had bought drinks all round and boasted of her triumphs in the craft shops the day before. Jude had been whacked and couldn't face the rest of the hike, so they sat in the ingle, savouring the wood-smoke and catching up with campus gossip while Simon and the others went back to collect a car. Pleasantly tired, she'd gone to bed early with a mug of hot chocolate and slept the night through, feeling buoyed up when she woke and ready for the week ahead. Simon was keyed up about the paper he was giving in Leeds, so she'd insisted he eat a proper breakfast and helped him pack. When she dropped him off at the station she was overcome by a surge of affection and embarrassed him with a sloppy kiss as they said goodbye.

Even the day at school had been quietly exhilarating. The spontaneity of the children was somehow newly fresh and miraculous, and at the end of the afternoon she rewarded them with one of her favourite stories, whisking them off to the sun-kissed countryside of long ago with the anarchic old scarecrow, *Worzel Gummidge*.

Only then, just as the end of school bell signalled the return to reality, did her body begin to reject the baby. A hand made a fist in her stomach and blood drained from her face. She could hear it gushing, drowning her, drowning out the tinkling voices of the children.

Somehow she made it to the staff toilets and bolted the cubicle door. She bent at the waist, arms crossed against the pain of the contractions which came in waves, growing fainter. She was cocooned in numbness. And the clock stopped.

"Are you there, Mrs May? Are you OK?"

It was her TA, Mrs Lockwood. Ginny checked her watch. It was almost three thirty.

101

"I've got the runs," she heard herself say. "Nothing to worry about, Jan."

"Are you sure?"

"Quite sure. You get yourself home. I'll be fine."

A cheery farewell followed by a hiss and a click as the pneumatic valve pushed the toilet door closed. Outside in the playground the sound of small feet scampering, a skipping rope slapping the tarmac, a ball bouncing, rivulets of children's laughter, squeals and raucous shouts, all moving away from her, into the distance, an extended diminuendo leaving behind only the sound of her own breath.

She kicked off her shoes and unbuttoned her skirt at the waist, letting it slip to the floor. With her foot she pushed the skirt out of harm's way beside the lavatory bowl and began to peel off her tights and knickers. She stared at the mess on the floor, oppressed by a weight of guilt and failure. The urge to hide everything away became imperative. Her cardigan, spread out on the linoleum, blotted it out. With wads of toilet paper she mopped blood from her legs and checked to see whether the flow had stopped. When she judged it to be safe, she retrieved the skirt.

Cautiously she opened the door to the corridor. At the other end of the building the choir was singing, stop-start, with bursts of piano and Mr Pearson's light tenor in between. She could see the door to the caretaker's storeroom, not far, but far too far. She steeled herself to walk, feeling soiled and naked, and soon found refuge in Mr Pettman's well-ordered empire, breathing deeply on the odours of cleanliness. Bucket, scrubbing brush and floor-cloths were on the draining board beside the sink, as though Mr Pettman had left them there just for her. She ripped off a black bin-liner from a roll on one of the shelves and was looking for disinfectant when she heard laughter in the corridor outside. It was Mary Braithwaite's unmistakeable cackle. She was with the new Year 4 teacher who had taken assembly that morning. Through the crack in the door Ginny saw them stop outside the staff toilets, and said a silent prayer. Mary brayed like a donkey again, and the two women walked on, turning the corner at the end of the corridor, their voices dwindling in the echoes of the empty building.

On her hands and knees, Ginny scrubbed the cubicle floor, and then started on the walls. She changed the water and scrubbed everything again, working until she was out of breath and sweating. When she had dried the floor with the cloths she rinsed them out, then smothered them with the thick green disinfectant and applied them to the toilet bowl, inside and out. The cloths went into the bin-bag with the cardigan and its shameful secret. She tied a knot in the plastic bag. Then tied another to be sure.

Back in the empty classroom, she opened her locker and took the faded tracksuit from its hook. Pulling the bottoms on under her skirt, she rolled the trousers up above her knees and smoothed the full skirt over them, checking that everything was hidden. The box of tissues on her table was half-full. She emptied it and, lifting the skirt again, fed the fat wad of Kleenex between her legs, hauling up the tracksuit bottoms to secure it and tightening the waistband of the skirt over the tracksuit for insurance. She put on her anorak and felt safe again.

They would have helped her, the friendly souls who sang out their goodbyes as she left the school. But she was inside a bubble of misery. She wanted to be home, and she wanted to be clean, and she wanted sleep.

The car took her home as though it knew the way. She was not in charge. One minute she was in Murray's Road, the next she was parked at the house, sitting next to a black bag that she could not bring herself to touch.

The phantom dog barked in the house as she set the alarms. Like an automaton, her body performed its routines and she was in the bathroom, tearing off her clothes and ramming them into the laundry-sack, hiding them away.

A fusillade of icy needles stung her face and took her breath away. The shower warmed. She looked down at her feet and watched the swirls of rusty water take her blood away. She soaped, and soaped again in an orgy of soap—shampoo, shower-gel, soap. She wanted every atom cleansed.

Hot water drummed on her head, drowning out thought, drowning out time. Eventually it ran cold, unbearably cold, and her mind came alive again.

The Clinic: she should have gone to the Clinic, of course she should…as she had done before…as she had done twice before. She would go when she was warm again, when she had spoken to Simon…

She pulled on a pair of knickers, then another, and wrapped herself in the big towelling dressing-gown. Sitting on the edge of the bed, she picked up the telephone feeling sick and dry-mouthed. What could she say? When the voice invited her to leave a message she returned the phone to its cradle. He would call her soon enough. He always did when he was away, soon after six. It was nearly that already.

Pulling the goose-down duvet over her, she lay on her side in the foetal position, eyes fixed on the phone, hands clasped together by her mouth: the synthetic scents of shower-gel and shampoo...a cloying jasmine mingled with sweet lavender... masking, but not obliterating, another note...faint, but insistent. She spread her hands across her face, sniffing it out, searching for the pungent traces below her fingernails. It was deep in her pores. The stink of disinfectant...disinfectant on the linoleum, disinfectant on the cubicle walls, on the lavatory bowl...the stink of disinfectant as the lift doors...a key grating in a metal door...cold tea dripping down a breeze-block wall...coffee-froth on a walrus moustache...an ice-cream house on a wild headland... a woman in grey gazing blankly out to sea at the grey waves... endlessly, eternally grey...wave after grey wave...

Miles out to sea, the phone rang. Then the bell was ringing in her skull. And her hand dropped on the telephone.

"Simon?" she said, her mouth tacky with sleep.

But it was Jude. And she blurted it out, the whole nightmare. She had intended to tell no one, not until Simon knew. But it would not stay in her head. The whole messy business spewed out. No hysterics, just the flat truth. She even managed a bitter laugh as she described 'poor Ginny-no-knickers' scrubbing her troubles away in the school lavvy.

"I'll be with you in five minutes," Jude said, and hung up.

Chapter Thirteen

Thank God for Jude. She'd taken charge. Thank God for Doc as well. He'd wangled a private room and even persuaded a consultant to forgo his pudding to check her over. They had prodded and probed and given her something to help her sleep. She would be right as rain after a good night's sleep and a few days rest. Right as rain.

Simon was still not answering. She had left messages but he did not ring back. Perhaps he'd lost his phone, or had it stolen.

Apart from the watery orange juice and a sliver of cardboard toast, she left the breakfast untouched on the table-top that they had swung over the bed. She made use of the outrageously expensive hospital telephone to ring the English department, and a helpful secretary managed to find the number of the hotel in Leeds where Simon was staying.

"Can I speak to Professor May, please?" she asked the receptionist.

A nice Yorkshire voice asked her to hold on, and she listened to the endless beep of the extension, not really expecting an answer. The morning sessions would probably have started already, or they'd all be having breakfast, nursing hangovers. When she was on the point of giving up, an irritable voice said, "Yes!"

"Had a bad night, did we?" she said.

There was a pause. "Oh, God!" he said. "I must have slept through the alarm."

"Thanks for the phone call," she said acidly.

"I'm sorry about that, Ginny. Last night's session just went on and on."

"I bet... I've been ringing your mobile..."

"I'm sorry. I must have forgotten to switch on again after the seminar. Are you OK?"

After all the detective work to track him down, now that she had found him, she didn't want to tell him, not over the telephone.

"Not exactly," she said.

"So what's the problem?"

"I lost the baby," she said.

The silence between them sang like a wire tightened on a ratchet.

"I don't believe it," he said.

She heard him swallow. "I'm sorry, Simon," she said.

He was weeping. She could hear his breath catching in his throat.

"I was feeling fine, absolutely fine..." she explained, "then right at the end of school, the cramps started..."

"Are you alright now?" he interrupted, as though unable to cope with more reality.

"I feel drained..." she said, "like I've had all the life wrung out of me."

He was trying to compose himself, breathing deeply. "I'm so sorry, Ginny, I really am," he whispered.

"You're not the one who can't hold on to babies."

"I'm sorry the wretched phone was off... I'm sorry you've had to go through this on your own...I'm sorry for the whole sad business..." He sounded more angry than sad. "I'll get the first train I can," he went on. "If I dash, I should make the ten-thirty."

He had pulled himself together, but she could tell that he was desperate to get off the phone. Surely there was more to say.

"With any luck I'll be back home by the time you get back," she said. "Jude's picking me up from the hospital later on."

He couldn't avoid asking about the hospital and they talked some more in a desultory fashion, still orbiting the void between them, never quite reaching out to make contact. When the conversation finally petered out they were both relieved.

It was strange that he should be the one to cry.

Bridget came up from the Clinic and stroked her hand. They could always try again. Lots of people did, time and again. More injections; more egg harvests; more pornography; more false dawns.

First time round, Simon had done everything that Bridget advised, and even conquered his squeamishness with the hypodermic to help with the injections. Second time, he had left her to inject herself. Third time, she was surprised when he agreed to provide samples. There would be no fourth time, she was convinced of that.

She channel-hopped around daytime TV but nothing claimed her attention and the newspaper demanded too much concentration. Lying back on the pillows she looked out of the grubby window at the small patch of sea framed by the functional grey of the hospital buildings and the grey sky. It brought to mind the house on the headland. She had spent the night in The Ice-Cream House. Every time the hospital had trespassed on her dreams, she had been there—when the old woman across the corridor began to wail, when the nurse crept in to check that she was sleeping, when the bin-men woke the wards with their clattering—each time she was stolen away from the seductive sadness of The Ice-Cream House, longing to stay...abducted by noisy reality, and yearning to go back.

Once, when she returned to the belvedere, the woman in grey had left her seat at the telescope to stand at the curved sweep of window, looking out to sea. Ginny had taken her place in the chair and put her eye to the telescope. The grey waves were at once enormous in her eye. At the same time, they were infinitely small in the vastness of the ocean, shape-shifting, going nowhere, moving, yet not moving.

"The shrinks would have fun with this, Gin," she said aloud, addressing the ghostly reflection in the glass, denying herself the indulgence of too much introspective waffle. "I am sick of this bloody place."

The dressing-gown that Jude had packed in her over-night bag was hanging behind the door and her mules were under the chair. She put them on and opened the door. In the room opposite, the old woman who had moaned like a fog-horn throughout the night was now sitting on the edge of her bed in a short nightie, all bones and bright eyes. She gave Ginny a toothless smile and waved. Ginny waved back and shuffled down the corridor to the nurses' station.

"Will it be OK if I get spruced up and ready to go home?" she asked the young woman behind the desk.

"I should think that'll be alright," the nurse replied. "I'll double check with Sister. Why don't you have a shower in the meanwhile?"

Before they allowed her to dress, she was subjected to a final examination, largely for the educational benefit of the adolescent houseman than for her own health and well-being. Then she sat primly on the little blue chair beside the bed, with her coat over her knees and her overnight-bag beside her feet, waiting for Jude. She remembered sitting like this as a little girl after she'd had her tonsils out, waiting for her Gran to come, wishing that her mum was coming too.

Eventually Jude breezed in, perhaps not as blustery as she could be at her expansive best, but breezy enough—it was a 'life-must-go-on' performance and Ginny was glad of it.

"I can't face going straight home," Ginny announced as she dumped her bag on to the back seat. "Have you got time for a diversion?"

"As long as it's not anything too exciting," Jude replied, with a sideways glance. "You heard what Florence Nightingale had to say when she discharged you..."

"I want to pop into town and see if Grey's Gallery has done the window-display they promised, that's all."

It was a fib, or at least a half-truth. God knows why she couldn't just come out with it. But she couldn't.

Jude was struggling to reverse the four-by-four out of its parking space, chewing on her lip as she misjudged the distances, abusing the power-steering as she spun the wheel this way and that. Ginny waited until they were pointing the right way.

"Do you think we could go by Coombe Bay?" she asked, trying to sound off-hand.

"That's a bit out of the way..." said Jude. "You're not flogging stuff there as well, are you?"

"No, it's nothing like that....I'd like to see where the Buckleys live, that's all…"

Jude raised her eyebrows. "Good God, you're not still obsessing about him, are you?" she exclaimed, risking a glance away from the hospital roadway.

"I dreamt I was in their house last night...couldn't get the place out of my head."

Jude pulled the Shogun up on the double yellow lines near the security office at the hospital gates.

"You're not planning to call in on them, are you?" she asked.

"No, no," Ginny said. She covered her face with her hands and pulled them down until her fingertips touched her lips. "I know it sounds silly," she went on, "but the house is haunting me, and I want it to stop."

Jude pulled a sceptical face. "And seeing the place will exorcise it?"

"I certainly hope so," Ginny said.

"That doesn't sound like the Ginny I know."

"I don't feel like the Ginny you know."

Jude thought about this for a moment, then engaged gear and edged away from the kerb. It wasn't long before she was prattling away, gobbling up the uneasy silence. For an extrovert, she was a surprisingly neurotic driver, knuckles white against the leather steering-wheel, each touch of accelerator followed by a stab of brake. Ginny felt car-sick.

Coombe Bay was not as she had dreamed it in the night. The wild headland had been tamed. There was no ruined lighthouse on the point. There was no Ice-Cream House perched in solitary splendour on the ridge. High hedges and stone walls offered only glimpses of the houses that hugged the hillside—on the left, red tiled roofs, swimming-pools like blue kidneys, neat lawns and flashes of sea; on the right, steep driveways curving up to houses hidden in the trees.

"This is them," Jude said, bringing the Shogun to a halt opposite a gate with the name *Halcyon* engraved on an oval of grey slate.

"What a lovely name for a house," Ginny mused.

"A bit of a misnomer, if you ask me," Jude remarked. "There's been nothing 'halcyon' about their days here."

"Can you get me a view?" Ginny asked. "I can't see a thing from here…"

She un-strapped herself to kneel on her seat and looked backwards through the rear window as Jude crawled the Shogun further up the road. "Hold it there, if you can," she called, "I think that's the best I'll get."

Through the trees she could see the upper storeys of the house rearing up towards the sky, a curvature of glass and cream plasterwork against the cumulus cloud-bank. It really did look like the upper deck of a cruise-ship.

"Do they have a telescope up there?" Ginny asked.

"How on earth should I know," Jude replied, "we only went for supper a couple of times. It wouldn't surprise me though. He had lots of toys."

"Looks a lovely house," Ginny said.

"It is. Very 1920s. The sort of place where *Hercule Poirot* could easily show up. Is it anything like your dream?"

"No, not really," Ginny lied.

"Has it done the trick?" asked Jude. "Sent your dream packing?"

Ginny offered a pale smile. "I'm glad we came," she said. "Thanks, Jude."

Chapter Fourteen

The old Saab was where she had left it, parked in front of the rickety lean-to, a black bin-bag on the passenger seat. She couldn't see it, but it was there.

Jude wanted to come in and make tea. Ginny wanted to be on her own and told her so. She had had enough lame conversation and was tired of politeness. As she turned the key, she felt guilty. She had been ungracious. After all that Jude had done, she deserved better. Turning from the door, Ginny watched the Shogun complete its three-point-turn, and motioned for it to stop. Jude crunched to a halt, and the window slid down.

"What is it, love?" she called.

"Do you really want a cup of tea?" Ginny asked.

Jude looked troubled. "There's nothing wrong with wanting to be on your lonesome, Ginny," she said. "If I were in your shoes, I think I'd feel the same."

"I didn't want you to think I'm not...."

"Don't be ridiculous," Jude said, and reached for the hand-brake. "Just remember you've got good friends if you need them."

Ginny turned the key in the front door. There was no barking from the dog; no hysterics from the burglar alarm. The house was quiet and smelt stale, as if nobody had lived there for a long time. In the gloom of the hallway a pin-prick of red light was winking on and off on the telephone table. There were seven messages. She put her overnight bag on the floor, sat down on the ladder-backed chair beside the little table and watched the light turning on, off, on, off, on, off... like it had something important to impart. She listened to the house instead. The gas-meter ticked in the cupboard by the door. The fridge shuddered and rattled in the kitchen, and went silent. The meter ticked away and the light blinked on. She put her finger close to the tiny bulb and watched her nail flush pink a few times then stabbed at a button to extinguish it... *Beep*, a tinny voice began to speak— Charlie Mullen being his charming Irish self, convening 'the

111

boys' for a needle match against the Engineers... *Beep:* A posh woman from the OUP wanting to commission an essay on the Dirty Realists... *Beep:* Bryant—pleased with himself about the eulogy he's written for the Inaugural and seeking plaudits, yuk! *Beep:* A get-together at The Jesmond to hammer out a running order for The Follies... *Beep:* "It's Joe Bradley...."

Expecting yet more of Simon's oh-so-busy life Ginny let the message pass in a blur, and it took a moment for Wyatt Earp to come into focus. She shuttled through the messages to listen again.

"If you want that lift to Fulford, I'm going on Wednesday. Give me a bell." Bradley rattled off a number that she didn't catch.

She sat back in the chair feeling leaden, as if her arms and legs were too heavy to move. She could have skipped through the calls again to retrieve the number, but instead she pressed 'Play' and sat motionless, listening again to the disembodied voices, lifeless as a lump of un-worked clay, but strangely comforted. This time, Bradley's telephone number was sharp and clear. She rehearsed it in her head and lodged it in her memory.

Car tyres ploughed the gravel on the drive outside. Simon was back.

The reflex would puzzle her later, but her first thought was to erase Bradley's message. Her fingers were light and nimble on the buttons.

A key turned in the lock and Simon came into the house. For a moment he stood in the doorway, silhouetted against the dying light of the afternoon, and she saw the taxi making for the gate.

"What are you sitting in the dark for?" he asked.

"I've been listening to the answer-phone," she said.

"Are you all right?"

"I'll survive."

It was impossible for him to embrace her while she sat in the high-backed chair. She chose not to get to her feet and suspected that he was glad. He looked uncomfortable, as though the last thing he wanted was to touch her.

"Before you do anything else," she said, "will you do something for me?"

"Of course I will," he replied.

"There's a bin-bag on the passenger seat of the Saab," she went on, "can you get rid of it, please?"

He cleared his throat. "Of course I can," he said, putting his suitcase on the floor. He seemed grateful for the chance of escape.

"Don't put it in the bin, Simon," she said. "I want you to take it to the dump and put it in the crusher. Wait until it's gone, will you?"

Chapter Fifteen

There was a haze of green across the wind-break of rowans and acacias that they had planted as saplings when they bought the house. The garden was coming into leaf and clumps of daffodils were dancing in the wind at the feet of the gnarled old apple trees. But last year's fruit had withered on the branch, unformed and discoloured. The trees were dying. They had consulted Bee's gardener, who scratched his beard and pronounced the death sentence. "Honey Fungus," he had said. "It's a swine—could choke the whole garden."

White tendrils knitting a mesh where the worms and beetles live, spawning pretty golden mushrooms and poisoning every plant they kiss. It wouldn't beat her though. She had plans for that patch. Root it out and scour the soil. Plant afresh—build an arbour perhaps, or a pergola.

Simon came out of the house patting his unruly hair into place, striding purposefully as though he was late. Desperate to be gone more likely. He vanished in the lean-to. She heard the car door slam and waited for the throaty growl of the engine. Nothing happened. Was he sitting at the wheel, numb with grief? Or was he on his mobile, getting his career on track? Laughing with a friend?

She couldn't read him any more...Last night they had drifted aimlessly around the house, and then sat stupefied in the armchairs beside the fire, lost to each other, unable to make a connection. True he had found some words of comfort, but they were hollow words. The things unsaid were the things that mattered, and he hugged those to himself, unable or unwilling to spit them out. He was clamming up, like he had in Santa Barbara, vanishing inside himself, shutting her out. She hated his reticence...

At last, the engine roared into life. The red Mazda nosed out of the lean-to and scrunched its way up the gravel drive. She was glad to see him go.

114

Ginny got up from the window-seat, and immediately sat down again. It was a moment of light-headedness, nothing more. She stood up again, taking her time...and felt fine.

She went to the roll-top desk next to the fireplace. Her passport was in the locked drawer with the birth certificates and the rest of life's bureaucratic paraphernalia. A passport seemed an odd thing to take to a prison, but Joe Bradley had been insistent.

"They're very fussy about who they let inside," he'd said. "They'll want to check you out."

Opening the flap on her shoulder-bag to slip the passport into the inside zip-pocket, she spotted her mobile telephone. For some unexplained reason, they had made her turn it off at the hospital and she had forgotten to switch on again. There were several missed calls listed—a queue of females, all eager to cluck their sympathy; plus one call from school, more of the same, no doubt; and one from DS Carmichael...

Her favourite policeman answered straight away. "Did you get to see Whizz at court?"

"I did," she replied, "and I'm just off to see him again, in prison—I'm going with his solicitor."

Carmichael laughed. "What do you make of Hippy Joe, then?"

"Is that what they call him?"

"Among other things," he said. "As defence lawyers go, he's not all bad."

"He's not very optimistic about keeping the boy out of prison."

"That's why I'm really glad you called me back," Carmichael said. "If Whizz is prepared to play ball, there's an outside chance the prosecution might not press for a custodial sentence..."

Ginny frowned. "What does he have to do?"

"Put the finger on Moon Rivers."

"He'll never do that..."

"He might if he knew it was Rivers who tipped us off about the Community Centre."

"And you want me to tell him this?"

"Well, he's not likely to believe a copper, is he?"

"I'm not a hundred per cent sure I believe it myself," Ginny said.

"Just ask him whose idea it was to knock over the Community Centre, and then ask him how come two squad cars were waiting for him when he came out of the toilet window." A siren had started wow-wow-wowing somewhere close to Carmichael. "I've got to go," he went on, raising his voice above the din. "Tell Whizz there are always deals to be done…Ask Bradley, he'll know the score."

Joe Bradley laughed like a horse and hammered his fists on the steering-wheel as the transit van flogged its way uphill in a noisy third gear.

"'Set a thief to catch thief!" he chortled. "Oh, the old ones are definitely the best! I'm surprised at Tom Carmichael." He gave Ginny a sceptical glance. "It'll never work, lady."

"But is it true?" she persisted. "If Whizz helped them put Rivers away, would they go easy on him?"

"They might," Bradley replied. "Probably would, in fact. But our lad won't grass. It's against his religion."

Ginny looked out of the window at the suburban sprawl rolling by, on and on, drab and unremarkable and never-ending. It was hypnotic.

"I'm not sure I trust coppers," she mused, surprised that she had spoken out loud.

"I certainly don't," said Joe Bradley. "When you're sitting in those interview rooms in the nick, you sometimes wonder who the biggest liar is—the little scrote you're defending, or the conniving bastard on the other side of the table."

"So what about DS Carmichael?" Ginny said, turning to look at the lawyer. "Do you believe him when he says that Whizz was set up?"

Bradley rubbed a forefinger vigorously under his nose as though he had an itch. "I do, as it happens," he said. "As coppers go, Carmichael's straighter than most."

Ginny leaned her face against the cool window. She was feeling weary and was tempted to close her eyes.

"How well do you know Moon Rivers?" she asked.

"Moon and I go back a long way," Bradley replied. "They pulled him in for mugging an old woman when I was Duty Solicitor. He was twelve years old, and I felt sorry for him. The poor little sod had a terrible life. The father was a thug, the mother was a waste of space, and Moon looked after his grandma single-handed…made quite a good job of it too."

They were on the slip-road to the motorway and Bradley accelerated to match his speed to the traffic flow. Skilfully he eased the transit into the gap between two juggernauts and settled for a steady sixty miles an hour in convoy.

"Whizz doesn't have Moon's excuse, does he?" Ginny said.

"Is that right?" There was an edge of sarcasm to his voice. "And how do you know what went on in the Ice-Cream House?"

"According to a friend of mine, they were a nice, well-balanced family..."

"Poverty is not the only breeding ground for criminality," said Bradley, interrupting. "It's the main one, I'll give you that, but the wealthy suburbs can fuck their children up just as well as the council estates."

Ginny sat up in her seat. She didn't like being smacked down, especially with an argument she would have made herself.

"So what's to be done, oh Source of all Wisdom?" she asked. "Are these kids beyond redemption? Or can we save them from themselves?"

"Once upon a time... I used to think we could..."

"And now you don't?" she interrupted.

"Now, I'm not so sure," he corrected. "I must've represented hundreds, maybe thousands, of lads like Moon. Precious few have come good. A handful, maybe, that's all."

"Doesn't that depress you?" Ginny asked.

The lawyer was quiet for a moment. "It depresses the crap out of me," he sighed. "The whole system stinks. We need more money, more education, more drug rehab, more mentoring, more everything—except jail. We need a lot less jail. But when all that is said, if I'm totally honest, I have to admit that most of these kids are so twisted that nothing in the world could straighten them out.

"That sounds like the 'counsel of despair' to me," Ginny ventured.

Bradley took his eyes off the back of the lorry in front, and raised his considerable eyebrows at her. "Listen, lady," he growled. "I used to play professional squeeze-box in a Zydeco outfit and I was happy as a hummingbird. I gave it all up to bury myself in a pile of dusty old law books, and every goddamned day since then I've choked myself in a collar and tie just to help these kids get a square deal in court. Do not accuse me of being cynical or I may just dump you on the motorway." He glowered at her out of the corner of his eye.

Ginny raised both hands and the lawyer accepted her surrender with a little nod, then he checked his mirror and flicked on the indicator to overtake. Back in the slow lane, the steady thrum-thrum of tyres on tarmac returned, and the motorway seemed to be spooling under the wheels like a never-ending ribbon of grey.

"Do you think I'm wasting my time with this kid?" she asked, watching Bradley for a reaction.

"Probably," he said, giving her a toothy smile. "But you're a screwball like me. If you weren't, I wouldn't have asked you along." He produced a cylinder of mints from his trouser pocket, eased one free with his thumb and offered it to her.

"No thanks," she said.

It was a curious accolade. Despite the weariness, being Hippy Joe's side-kick on his ramshackle crusade was better than being at home coddling herself and moping. She was glad she'd come.

"Is Carmichael using me?" she asked.

"Probably," he said again, showing more teeth before he popped a mint on his tongue. "But if you can keep Whizz out of this sewer-of-a-jail we're visiting, who knows….?"

"And what about Moon? I still find it hard to believe that he set Whizz up to get arrested. I thought 'grassing' was a cardinal sin?"

"You watch too much TV," Bradley said. "There is no honour among thieves."

"But why? What's the point?"

"For spite, for revenge, for the buzz, who knows? They don't need reasons." Bradley leaned forwards and drove with his forearms on the steering-wheel, leaving his hands free to gesticulate. "These kids don't see things like you and me. The nice comfy society we've constructed is there for them to plunder. That's how they see it. They're feral, like wild dogs, and they live by different rules. Our logic, our values don't apply…"

Ginny did her best to stay interested but, as 'The Joe Bradley Theory of Juvenile Delinquency' merged with the drone of the engine and the thrum of the tyres, she began to teeter on the brink of sleep. And then, with a start, she realised that the flood of words had dried up. Suddenly she heard herself say: "What's Zydeco?"

Bradley shot her a puzzled look.

"Sorry. It's not a word I know," she explained lamely.

Bradley pointed to a cassette which was poking end-out of the player below the dash. "That is Zydeco," he said, and leaned forwards to push the cassette home.

Abruptly the van was filled with fiddles and accordions, and Joe Bradley was jigging around in his seat, tapping out the washboard rhythms on the steering-wheel.

"You're going to love this next one..." he said, as the audience whooped and hollered at the end of the tune. "It's an old Cajun love song called *Joli Blon*."

Reaching forwards, he turned up the volume, and an electric fiddle began to slur and swoop its way through the opening bars of a folksy waltz. And when the vocalist joined in, Joe Bradley sang along in old Cajun French. His voice was a wheezy baritone and strangely beguiling.

Ginny let her eyelids droop and allowed the syrupy music to lull her to sleep. The earth beneath her dropped away and she was falling...free-falling...spinning slowly, round and round in a swirling, whirling vortex...ever downwards...

A hand gripped her arm... "Wake up, wake up..." Bradley was saying. "We've arrived."

Ginny wiped away the trickle of saliva on her chin.

"Welcome to Fulford," Bradley said, and switched off the engine.

Chapter Sixteen

The security fence was a mesh of steel, battleship grey and high as a house, topped off with coils of razor wire that glittered in the sunshine like twirls of silver ribbon on a gift-wrap. A prison van was waiting for the big gates to be opened. Through the black slits in its side, the latest delivery of young villains would be stealing glimpses of their new abode—not some grim survival of the Victorian penal system, but a sprawl of ugly, two and three-storey buildings, designed and built by bureaucrats, probably for the military in World War Two. It was grim enough.

Two large signs were riveted to the fence on either side of the gates for all new arrivals to read:

HM YOI Fulford
Secure College of Learning

Some wordsmith in the Department of Mission Statements would get Brownie points for the fancy euphemism, but how many of the new students would be able to read it? When she'd submitted the books that she brought to the man on the gate, she'd been told that no gifts were permitted, absolutely none: No books, no tapes, no CDs, nothing. The 'Secure College of Learning' had its own 'library resource'.

An irritable gust of wind sent a discarded paper cup skittering in the gravel and threw a swirl of dust into the air. Ginny blinked back a tear and wiped her eye with the heel of her hand. She was sick of waiting.

"Are you alright?"

Her escort had finally stepped out of the gatehouse, a dumpy, middle-aged woman in navy blue trousers and matching fleece. Only the keys that jangled on her hip announced her gaoler's status.

"I'm fine," Ginny said, "a bit of grit, that's all."

That wasn't true. She felt far from fine. The instant they had taken Joe Bradley to see his client, she had felt pathetically exposed and vulnerable.

"Are you sure you're ok?" Dumpy asked, scrutinising her face with the cool impudence of officialdom. "You don't look too good to me."

"If you must know..." said Ginny testily, "I'm sick of waiting for you."

The gaoler's eyes were unmoved. "This your first time?"

Ginny nodded.

The woman's upper lip twitched as though a grin might be forthcoming. "It'll be a disappointment," she said. "It's ages since we tortured anybody."

With the grin firmly in place, Dumpy turned her back, jangling the keys against her ample buttock as she waddled up the concrete path to a low-slung building that, in a different setting, could have been a cosy village hall. Below the homely gable of the roof, fixed to the white stucco of the walls, was a sign that read: 'Visitors Centre'. A notice threatening dire punishments for anyone caught smuggling was nailed to the wall beside the door. The list of forbidden articles was long.

Dumpy ushered Ginny into a small room that had been painted floor to ceiling in sludge-green.

"Take a seat," she said, pointing to a plastic chair. "I'll get one of my colleagues, and we'll give you a rub-down." The grin made a re-appearance. "I'll try not to keep you waiting, madam."

The door closed, and Ginny was alone in an airless box. Sticking a finger inside the collar of her polo-necked sweater, she ran it around her neck and eased the wool away from her skin. The place was as hot as a greenhouse. It was a relief when the door opened again.

"Stand, please," said Dumpy.

The second woman was younger and prettier. "Arms up, please," she instructed, miming the scarecrow position.

Dumpy leaned against the door-jamb and watched. The pretty one started the body-search, her fingers exploring Ginny's shoulders and her arms, then moving down to the flanks of her body.

"Won't take long...just routine...soon be done..."

The running commentary was non-stop, a gentle murmur of reassurance, strictly to the book, no doubt.

Ginny was not reassured. She could smell last night's garlic on the woman's breath, and she was too close.

"D'you ever find anything?" Ginny asked.

"You'd be surprised," Dumpy replied.

"Open your mouth, please." The pretty one stepped back and peered into Ginny's gaping mouth. "Tongue up."

The instruction was so bizarre that it took a moment before Ginny complied.

"Tongue down." The officer leaned her head to one side so that she could examine the roof of Ginny's mouth. "Feet apart now, please."

Dropping to one knee, the woman reached around as though to hug her. Hands lightly touched her buttocks, then began to feather their way up and down each leg.

Ginny was glad she'd worn trousers.

"Sit down, please... Nearly done...Just your feet now. Shoes and socks off, please..."

When the search was complete, the two prison officers led the way down a short corridor. Dumpy opened a door and motioned Ginny through.

It was uncanny. The visiting area was huge, totally out of scale with the building's homely exterior. Thanks to a diet of too many TV dramas, she'd been expecting a drab, functional space in shades of grey, but some enlightened soul had made an effort here. All the seating was upholstered and in cheerful colours. Each prisoner was provided with a blue seat. Visitors sat opposite on a curved three-seat settee, and there was a coffee table between them. This arrangement was replicated in three rows running the length of the room. And there was carpet, not the finest Axminster, but not the bare concrete or scuffed lino she'd imagined.

Dumpy took the white card that Ginny had been given in Reception and handed it to an officer at the raised observation desk. After consulting the card, he placed it in one of the numbered slots on the board in front of him, a layout that reproduced the distribution of seats in the room.

"Table 25," he announced.

Ginny followed her escort down the long room, casting her eye over the few tables that were in use, trying not to appear inquisitive. On one blue seat, an Asian boy in a turquoise tee-shirt was confronting two women in black *hijabs*, straight-backed and stern as judges. At another, a carrot-topped kid in a yellow tee-shirt was chewing the remains of his fingernails. His smartly-dressed visitor rattled a pencil between her teeth and stared up into the fluorescent lights in search of patience.

Dumpy hooked her thumb at a row of vending machines. "If you want a cuppa, it'll have to be the machines. On a proper visiting day, the canteen would be open and you could get a snack." She gave Ginny another grin. "No waitress service mind..."

Ginny ignored the jibe. "Do you keep the remand prisoners separate from the rest?" she asked.

Dumpy shook her head. "No way... If they got special treatment, there'd be trouble. The last thing you want in this place is to stick out from the crowd..." She stopped beside one of the settees and tapped her hand on the green backrest. "This one's for you. When the prisoner comes in, you can give him a hug or a handshake, but keep it brief, ok?"

Ginny was glad to sit down, and flapped her jacket to generate some air.

"You look like you could use a glass of water?" said Dumpy.

Before Ginny could respond, a squawk from Dumpy's walkie-talkie demanded her attention, and there was an incomprehensible exchange of radio-speak.

"It's not your day, lady," said Dumpy, taking her hand off the radio. "There's been a spot of bother with your lad...More hanging about, I'm afraid."

"What bother?" asked Ginny.

"Probably nowt to worry about—playing silly buggers, I expect."

With this reassurance, Dumpy raised her hand in a gesture of farewell and ambled away in the direction of the observation desk.

Ginny leaned back against the meagre padding of the settee, wishing that Dumpy had repeated her offer of a glass of water. She closed her eyes.

Somewhere a door clanged shut, then another; walkie-talkies crackled and yapped; keys clinked; raucous voices and coarse laughter; more door-slams; more quacking from the radios—the constant sound-track of prison, non-stop and inescapable.

She opened her eyes. At a table nearby, a large black woman wearing a purple turban and batik gown was haranguing her son, a handsome specimen with a face carved out of blackest ebony. His hands were clasped behind his head, and his biceps strained at the short sleeves of his red tee-shirt—a full-grown man, locked away in a prison for boys.

As though touched by her gaze, the object of Ginny's speculation turned his fine head, and glared at her, resenting her scrutiny. Fortunately, Whizz chose the exact same moment to make his entrance. Grasping the opportunity, Ginny smiled and raised her hand in greeting. Puzzled, the black prisoner glanced over his shoulder to see what she was looking at.

Whizz was approaching with wall-to-wall swagger—blonde hair in wild disarray, thumbs hooked in the pockets of his tracksuit bottoms, shoulders rolling inside the red tee-shirt. His escort wore an expression of weary resignation, and the woman in the turban stopped scolding her son to watch the performance. The black man showed a set of perfect teeth and made some comment as Whizz passed by. In response, Whizz stuck out his right hand and raised the middle finger.

"That's enough!" barked the officer.

Whizz shrugged and swaggered on. As he approached Ginny's table, he began to chant Class One's sing-song greeting.

"Good mor-ning, Miss-iss May."

Ginny raised her eyebrows, and glanced at the officer.

"Got a comedian, miss," he said.

Whizz arranged himself on the blue seat and swung his trainers on to the coffee table.

"Feet…off…" snapped the warder.

Whizz grinned.

"Get your feet off the table," Ginny hissed.

Whizz removed his feet from the table, and leaned forward to dust the table with exaggerated thoroughness.

The prison officer shook his head, and turned away.

"That was pretty stupid," Ginny said.

Whizz sniffed and puckered his nose. "Gotta have a laugh, ain't ya, Miss?"

"You need to keep a low profile in this place…" said Ginny in a fierce whisper, "make sure you don't stick out from the…"

"I'm not stupid," Whizz snapped. "I know what 'low profile' means."

His antagonism was breathtaking. She had been expecting some kind of welcome, perhaps even a small show of gratitude.

She forced a smile. "How're you getting on in here?"

Whizz shrugged. "Piece o' piss."

"No bother?"

The shoulders lifted again. "Nothing I can't handle…They give you shit, you give 'em double shit back…"

"The Gospel According to Moon Rivers...That will get you nowhere!'"

"Moon did alright in this shit-hole."

Ginny shook her head. "I think you should know that you're only in this place because of Moon."

Summoning up all the powers of persuasion that she could muster, Ginny explained what DS Carmichael had learned from fellow officers at the police station.

Whizz made it obvious that he wasn't listening. He examined her closely, wriggling forwards until he was at the edge of his seat, leaning towards her over the table, peering anxiously into her face.

"What's up?" he said, interrupting. "You look crap."

"Don't worry about me," said Ginny, struggling to maintain her patience. "Let's talk about Moon."

Whizz began to move his fingers back and forth across his cheek bones like a pair of windscreen wipers. "You've got great big bags under your eyes," he said. "Have you been sick?"

Ginny nodded. "Something like that...yes."

"Is that why you didn't answer your phone?"

Ginny nodded again. "That's right, but I'm better now...and I haven't come all this way to talk about me...I want to get you out of this place, Whizz..."

The boy looked about him furtively. "Are we going to swap clothes, or something?"

Ginny gave a little laugh. "It's a bit too public for that, don't you think?"

Whizz made as if to pull off his tee-shirt. "Come on, let's give it a go..."

"Stop it, you idiot..."

Suddenly, he was a different boy, playful and full of the right kind of mischief.

Ginny tried again. "Seriously, Whizz, there is a way you could kiss goodbye to this place..."

Whizz leaned back against the upholstery and cocked his head to one side.

"...but we do need to talk about Moon..."

The eyes hardened.

"Moon is not your friend."

"Bollocks," he said.

"Why do you think the police were waiting for you when you came out of that Community Centre?"

The eyes had turned hostile.

"Because Moon set you up, that's why."

"That's bollocks. Copper's bollocks."

"It's true, Whizz. You know it's true." He was watching her carefully. "It'll go well in court if you tell the truth about Moon Rivers. He deserves it. He's a menace."

Whizz screwed his face up, and seemed to come to an important conclusion.

"I reckon you fancy that copper," he said.

Ginny held his gaze, refusing to be provoked. "Mr Bradley thinks you could go down for six months, maybe a year."

"Wouldn't that'd piss off Professor Wanker Bollocks—if you went off and shagged the fuzz?"

Ginny clenched her fists, waiting for him to finish laughing.

"You won't be laughing if they lock you up for a year," she said.

Whizz scrutinised her face again. "I reckon you should see a doctor. You look like shit."

Ginny bit down on her lip. "If you must know, I lost my baby..."

His expression did not change. "That was very careless of you," he said.

And then he smiled.

Ginny let her head droop, and the entire visiting room keeled over onto its side. Fluorescent light flooded her eyes. Then, with a dull thud, the world went black.

Chapter Seventeen

She remembered a prison doctor flapping around like a white bat, and she remembered Joe taking her home in the old van. She remembered little else about that day, and not much about the days that followed. She cried until her eyes were raw. She cried until there was a pit of emptiness inside her. According to the general consensus, her collapse was a 'good thing'. Jude said that she'd 'bottled up her grief'. Bee thought it was 'best to let the poison out'. Doc prescribed sedatives.

Simon said nothing. He kept a wary distance, no doubt waiting until she was well enough to hear the truth. And the truth was he blamed her for losing the baby. Worse, he'd had enough of clinics, and injections, and masturbating to order. There would be no more babies. That's what he wanted to say.

Every day he brought her food, and then he took the unfinished food away, muttering words of encouragement, making his escapes as quickly as he could. And she was always glad to see him go, relieved that he had left his thoughts unspoken.

In the past, whenever Jude had tried to persuade her to go to the health farm on the annual 'gang pamper', she had always been quick with excuses. This year her resistance was low. It wasn't only Jude and Bee who nagged. Even Doc Holroyd sang Glebelands' praises. And Simon, usually so full of scorn for Jude's 'fat farm', was very keen for her to go...so keen that Ginny began to wonder why, and old suspicions bubbled up like marsh gas.

It was Bee who put her mind at rest. Simon, she had explained, was grieving too, in his own fashion. This was an insight that took Ginny by surprise and, recalling how upset he had been in Leeds the day she broke the news, she felt eaten up with guilt. Of course he would have his own sadness to deal with...and he must be sick of hers. What sane man wouldn't be?

Against her natural instinct, Ginny agreed to go...and, amazingly, Glebelands worked its promised miracle. After a mere two days of pampering, she was restored to something like her feisty self—not by carrot juice and colonic irrigation, but by a healthy hatred of everything Glebelands. The happy smiles; the minimalist meals of sculpted food; the pink carpets; the all-pervading smell of lotions and potions; and the never-ending ear-syrup that slurped from the sound system. The entire orgy of narcissism was nauseating.

Wrapping a towel round her nakedness, Ginny sat up on the treatment table.

"I'm sorry, Romaine," she said, "but I think I'm going to be sick."

"Oh dear," cried the masseuse, and flapped her muddy hands.

The shower washed away the nutrient-rich Glebelands mud and left Ginny feeling refreshed. She wrapped herself in the luxurious softness of a Glebelands bath-robe, wound a towel around her wet hair in the customary Glebelands turban, and, with Glebelands fluffy mules on her feet, shuffled into the adjoining lounge. A bevy of similarly attired inmates were sitting around the room in easy chairs, like plump Sultanas in a harem, great panda-eyes peering out of their grey face-packs.

Ginny approached the plumpest of the plump.

"I'm going to take a nap," she said.

An extra hole cracked open in the face-mask. "Are you ok?" said Jude, trying not to move her lips.

"Just a bit tired," she replied.

"You sure?" enquired the mask in the next chair.

The Glebelands' magic had certainly worked for Bee. Her eyes were clear, and the air of panic that usually fluttered about her had fluttered clean away.

"I'm fine, Bee, really." Impulsively, she reached forward to give Bee's hand a squeeze. "You mustn't worry about me."

She had learned to value Bee during their stay. Jude had meant well enough, jollying her along, steering clear of all things gynaecological. Bee had been prepared to sit and listen, and what she said made sense—particularly about Simon. She must give Simon time. No talk of babies for a while. Let the pain fade.

Sitting at the vanity table in the bow window of her room, Ginny made a call to reception and invented a domestic crisis to account for her sudden departure. She asked the girl to prepare her bill and call a cab, and on a sheet of Glebelands letter-head she scribbled a quick note to Jude. The letter to Bee took longer.

In the taxi she felt like a fugitive, and couldn't resist a peek through the rear window to check that no one was following. Thorn hedges on either side of the narrow lane hemmed them in, clawing at the car's paintwork. But then they emerged into the wide expanses of the chalk downs, and she felt free...free as the jet-plane she could see up above, scratching an arrogant white scar on the Wedgwood-blue bowl of the sky.

With a roar, the cab plunged into the dark tunnel under the motorway. A ghostly face appeared in the window beside her...her mother's face, uncomprehending as they drove her away in the black car. And she was little Ginny again, clutching her best rag doll, holding her granny by the hand...

Then the roaring noise faded and the day was bright again, and the ghost had gone.

The Saab was where she had left it, at the bottom of the fire-escape that zigzagged up to Bradley's office. It had been targeted by seagulls and looked shabbier than ever. Inside, the air was stale, but the old engine coughed into life at the first attempt. Coaxing a squirt of cleaning fluid onto the windscreen, she set the wipers to work, and then retrieved her mobile phone from the shoulder bag. After plugging the charger into the cigarette-lighter socket, she logged-on and scrolled down her contacts list to find the lawyer's number.

"It's Mrs May," she said to the secretary. "Could you let Mr Bradley know that I've picked up my car from the car park? I'm sorry if it's been in the way..."

Bird mess was now smeared in two over-lapping semi-circles and the windscreen was opaque. Ginny squirted more liquid and doubled the speed of the wiper-blades. As the glass began to clear, she saw Joe Bradley's transit bump its way up the kerb and drive towards her. With a sigh, Ginny returned his wave, and prepared for some unwanted sympathy.

Bradley pulled up next to the Saab. He lowered his window. Ginny did the same.

"Do you fancy a cuppa?" he asked.

"Sorry," she replied, "I've got to get home. What's the news on the boy?"

"Never mind him. You were in a real bad way. Are you on the mend?"

"I'm fine...just embarrassed about all the fuss. But tell me about the kid? Did you manage to persuade him to shop Rivers?"

"No way!" said Bradley. "Young Mr Buckley took his punishment like a man. Moon will be proud of him."

Ginny frowned. "You've not been to court already, have you?"

It was the lawyer's turn to look puzzled. "Two weeks ago...nearly three..."

Ginny grimaced, and rubbed her forehead.

"You've been sicker than you know, lady," said Bradley.

"What did he get?" asked Ginny.

"Six months—three inside, and three on licence. And he got off light, if you ask me."

"I don't suppose the parents showed up?"

Bradley shook his head. "They wouldn't have been welcome if they had. The kid's on self-destruct. Best leave him to it."

Ginny squinted up at him. "I'm going to pretend I didn't hear it." She reached forwards to engage first gear. "Tell him to send me one of those Visiting Orders. I'll go again."

Not waiting for an objection, Ginny bumped the Saab off the kerb and joined the traffic. Soon she was cruising down the High Street, past the alleyway which had delivered Whizz into her life, to the clock-tower roundabout where she had made her fateful right turn. No choices to be made today. Nowhere else to go but home. Left on to the Esplanade, past the Regency crescents and squares, and then left again into the suburban sprawl, street after street, into the leafy avenues, ever closer...

At least she would have time to make the house her own. Simon would be up the hill, teaching or working in his study. Or he'd be out of town, at the British Library, or at one of the innumerable conferences they treated themselves to...

In the gloom beneath the copper beech, the tyres seemed unnaturally loud on the gravel. Stupidly, as though to camouflage her arrival, Ginny found herself slowing the car to a crawl. As she emerged from the tunnel of rhododendrons, she braked to a standstill. Simon was home. The red Mazda was parked close to the house. And there was a bicycle leaning against the front porch. It was the punky poet's.

Slipping the car into reverse, Ginny backed up until she was hidden by the rhododendrons.

They would be rehearsing, sniggering over Mel's bawdy verse, her arm draped across his shoulders at the piano, her face pressed close to his face. Or they were not rehearsing...

Whichever scenario was in play, the role of the sad wife was not a role that Ginny wanted. Backing the Saab into a gap in the shrubbery, she turned around. At the gate, she was presented with a choice—left to the city, or right to the hills? The city was her habitat of choice, but not today. Today she would get lost in the crowds. Today she needed that big blue sky where the jet had made its mark, and she needed clean air from the sea.

It was a good decision. Parked in the picnic area at the Devil's Anvil, with her bottom perched on the bonnet of the car, she shaded her eyes from the sun and gazed across the undulating grey-green folds of the chalk downs to the Channel, glimmering in the distance like a sheet of beaten silver. She could see for miles down the coast, bay after hazy bay, until both sea and land melted into sky. And somehow, in the immensity of the landscape she found perspective.

She was not alone. Across the valley, a line of walkers trudged along an Iron Age track cut out of the chalk by countless generations of trudging feet, winding its way over the ridge like a thread of white cotton dropped by some careless giant. Above her head, a plastic kite flapped angrily in the breeze, hovering, then stooping on imaginary prey, then climbing again. Further down the hillside, a young man twitched the kite's invisible guides, hands moving like a conductor in the concert hall. The sheep were unimpressed, and continued to graze their land with total concentration.

In defiance of gravity a newborn lamb performed a vertical take-off, bounding high into the air as though its legs were spring-loaded. Repeating the trick to prove it had been no accident, the lamb settled for a humdrum existence back on earth and was soon bumping and barging for its mother's teats, competing fiercely with two greedy siblings.

Ginny watched the lambs suckle, and was transported back to the night when she first learned how cruel the countryside could be. It had been early summer, and the night air was warm and heavy with the scent of roses. She had stumbled out of the village pub with a girlfriend, squiffy on Pimms and giggling like schoolgirls. But the noise from the unseen fields demanded silence. It was the sound of inconsolable anguish.

"Them ewes'll be at it all night long," explained one of the locals. "They've took the lambs away…"

The shadow of a passing cloud was darkening the landscape, making the sea beyond dazzle with even greater brilliance. Ginny screwed up her eyes against the glare and looked again at the scalloped coastline, bay after gleaming bay. And all at once, with blinding clarity, she knew where she must go.

Chapter Eighteen

The wrought-iron gates and the blank eye of the security camera were forbidding. Ginny was tempted to turn back to the Saab, but stabbed her finger at the button on the squawk-box before her nerve could fail. To her relief, nothing happened. She decided to try again, just one more time, and then allow herself to quit. Raising her finger, she pressed firmly on the well-worn button.

After a crackle of static, a scratchy voice said, "Who is it?"

Ginny leaned towards the metal grille. "It's Mrs May," she said, "I used to teach Will at Murray's Road. Do you remember?"

There was a crackly pause, then: "What do you want?"

"I want to help him if I can."

Another burst of static, then: "Why?"

Ginny gave the box a puzzled frown. "Because he asked for help...I suppose."

She stepped back and looked directly into the camera lens. "Can we talk?"

"Come to the conservatory at the back of the house," instructed the voice.

There was a dull clunk, and the gates shuddered open. Ginny contemplated the tarmac drive and the darkness of the wood ahead. Welcome to *Halcyon*.

The drive snaked upwards through mixed woodland and ornamental rock gardens that eventually gave way to greensward, with the house crowning the hill. It was a pale cream confection, not unlike the ice-cream cake she had dreamed: three tiers piled up, each slightly smaller than the one below, all lozenge-shaped, with curved picture windows at either end, and port-hole windows along its length.

At the back of the house in a white-fenced paddock, she found a small stable block and some open garages that housed a huge power boat and an off-road buggy with outlandishly large tyres. She parked the Saab next to a mud-bespattered Range Rover and got out. The place was spookily quiet.

The conservatory was an ugly glass blister tacked on to the rear wall, an offence against the art deco spirit of the house. Ginny peered through the grubby glass. Someone had abandoned a passion for orchids, leaving only a few exotic survivors in a tangle of neglected vegetation. There was no sign of human life.

"Do come through, Mrs May." It was another squawk-box, mounted beside French windows.

Ginny went in.

"I'm in the house," said the tinny voice.

Puzzled and somewhat unnerved, Ginny made her way down the length of the conservatory towards a doorway framed by pilasters. She opened the door.

Mrs Buckley was standing on the far side of a small study-cum-library, arms folded across her chest. Everything about her was expensive: the neat knitted dress, the discreet jewellery, the impeccably coiffed blonde hair. She was smiling.

"I'm sorry about the cloak and dagger," she said, "but I'm a prisoner here. Please shut the door."

Ginny obeyed, and approached her hostess. No hand of welcome was offered.

"Silly, isn't it...being too frightened to leave your own house?" On closer inspection, the smile was icy. "When did you see my lovely boy?"

"About a month ago, I think," replied Ginny

"I trust he wasn't breaking into your house? Or stealing your car?"

She had the boy's eyes, and the same sculpted features. Without make-up she would have made a handsome man. As it was, her patience at the dressing-table had achieved a pleasing femininity, glamorous even, in its understated way.

"I saw him in prison," said Ginny, dispensing with tact. "Did you know he was in prison?"

Mrs Buckley barely blinked. "Best place for him," she said, and glanced down at her wristwatch. "If I'm going to help with your mission of mercy, we'd better get on. Would you like some coffee? "

"That would be nice," Ginny replied.

The thick carpet of the study gave way to ceramic tiles, and Mrs Buckley's kitten heels click-clacked across an impressive hall towards a staircase that swept upwards in a broken spiral, floor by floor to the top of the house. Ginny followed, admiring the cascade of Lalique chandeliers in the stairwell. On the walls, gazing out like ghosts from the pale pink plaster was a galaxy of film stars from Hollywood's golden age. She could see Bogart, Hepburn, Cagney and the rest, all ten times as large as life, but bleached-out, like memories fading into the fabric of the house. It was a celebration of kitsch that tiptoed on the very edge of naff, and yet the effect was triumphant. Someone in *Halcyon* had brave and expensive tastes.

"I've been going through the albums," Mrs Buckley said, pointing to an oval table between two scarlet sofas either side of the art deco fireplace. "Go and see...There are lots of you in there."

She had assembled a stack of albums. The top one was open. Ginny sat on the sofa and leaned forward. There she was, looking young and harassed, with a choir of dishevelled angels. It was Nativity at Murray's Road. One snap showed Will, aged five with a tea-towel on his head, offering a toy lamb to the manger. In another, the little shepherd was at prayer, the hands together and the eyes not quite as shut as they should have been.

Ginny looked across the room. The low sun was streaming through the big picture-window turning her hostess into an elegant silhouette. She was pouring coffee from a silver pot.

"These memories must make you sad," Ginny said.

"Oh, I'm way beyond sadness," her hostess said. "Milk...sugar?"

"No thanks," said Ginny.

"We've done sadness, and we've done self-recrimination, and we've done anger...We're trying to hate him now, and, you know, I think it's actually working...."

As she handed over a delicate cup and saucer she gave Ginny an acid smile, then sat down next to her on the sofa and pulled the album on to her lap. Her finger began to flick across the pages, pointing out the photographs that featured Ginny.

"'The Wonderful Mrs May', that's what we called you," she said. "Will used to talk about you morning, noon and night..."

She spoke fondly of Will and his sister, Chloe, smoothing each photograph with her fingertips. The pages were well thumbed. It was a journey through time that she had taken many times.

Ginny sipped her coffee, and watched the pages turn: family weddings, family holidays, birthday parties... She was watching the Buckley children grow younger and younger with every turn of the page.

"When did things go wrong?" she asked.

Mrs Buckley seemed not to hear, and turned another page:

Chloe pushing a doll's pram, wearing grown-up shoes; Will, his face painted like a cat, fingers clawing at the camera; Will again, blowing out three candles on a cake...

Mrs Buckley tapped the cat's nose with her forefinger. "Have you got children, Mrs May?" she asked.

"Afraid not," said Ginny. "We can't seem to manage it somehow."

More Happy Families: both children, naked in a plastic pool; Daddy, with Will on one shoulder, Chloe on the other; Will on the potty...

Another page turned. It was day one in Will's young life, in the Maternity Unit—proud father, weary mother, toasting each other with champagne; Chloe clutching baby brother in her tiny arms; the babe asleep in its cot...

Ginny looked at the picture of the newborn child, suckling at his mother's breast, and smiled at the irony of her situation. It could not have been engineered to be more exquisitely unkind.

Mrs Buckley, meanwhile, was tenderly stroking the blanket with her fingertip, as though frightened she might wake the sleeping baby.

"He says we brought the wrong baby home...said he didn't belong here. He meant it too..." She nodded her head towards the other albums. "Take a look in those..."

Ginny put the coffee cup on the table, and picked up another of the leather-bound volumes.

"Look at that," said Mrs Buckley, pointing at one of the photographs.

It was a family group in a restaurant. Everyone was saying 'cheese' at the camera. At first Ginny could see nothing untoward. Then Mrs Buckley's false fingernail picked out a child with no head.

"He really didn't want to be here, did he?" she exclaimed, and began to stab her finger at similar mutilations. "Look...look... look..."

In almost all the pictures there was a neat white vacancy where the boy's head should have been: dad on the riverbank, fishing with his headless son; a go-kart with a hole in the cockpit;

Chloe and her headless brother riding ponies; every cut executed with surgical precision.

"It must have taken him ages," Ginny said.

Mrs Buckley gave a snort. "Oh, he soon got bored with it..." She snatched up the remaining album and dumped it in Ginny's lap. "Take a look at this one…"

He had dispensed with the Stanley knife, and taken to scissors, snipping away countless triangles and squares before carefully re-mounting every print. The mutilations appeared more violent than the others, more desperate.

"I sometimes wake up to the sound of my teeth grinding together. Can you imagine that, Mrs May?"

She had moved to a cocktail cabinet near the window. Something rattled as she tipped it into the palm of her hand, then she slapped the hand against her mouth and drank greedily from a bottle of tonic water.

"We should never have moved here," she said, and turned to stare through the big window at the vast panorama of sea and sky. "We thought the children would be happy here. And we were right in the beginning. That first summer was perfection… it couldn't have been..."

Mrs Buckley stopped mid-sentence, and for a long time she was silent. When she spoke again, it was as though no time had elapsed.

"It couldn't have been more idyllic. But then the summer ended... Will got all dressed up in his brand new blazer and went off to big school carrying his new satchel, and suddenly everything changed. It was as if..."

Again, the words petered out.

Ginny waited, waiting for the mother in the same way that she had learned to wait for the son. And as she waited, she let her eyes wander across the spread of photographs, searching for clues.

The family likenesses were obvious: Chloe, dark and athletic like her father; Will, blonde, like his mother. Mother and daughter at ease with one another, playful and affectionate, always laughing. Father and son always doing something, water-skiing, canoeing, playing beach cricket, racing go-karts…happy snaps...but always striving...

"He became a monster very quickly..." said Mrs Buckley, emerging from her reverie. There was a harsh edge to her voice. "Petty things at first, then he excelled himself...."

She delivered a long list of Will's crimes and misdemeanours, with relish, as though she were boasting of his achievements at school. Ginny learned little new.

"Did you try to get help?" she asked, cutting her hostess short.

Mrs Buckley bridled. "Of course we tried to get help. We tried everything. But our lovely son would have none of it…"

With her forefinger, she pulled down the high neck of her dress and advanced on Ginny, angling her head so that her hair fell away to reveal a scar running down her neck from ear to collarbone.

"I was lucky," she said, tracing the scar with her fingertip. "I got a china plate. My husband took a table-lamp full in the face…and all because we arranged for a psychiatrist to come and talk to him…"

Her eyebrows were arched defiantly, as though they posed a question to which there was no rational response. She looked unhinged, on the brink of losing control.

In need of a distraction, Ginny reached for the first album she'd been shown, and opened it at random.

"This was my first teaching job, you know," she said, chattily. "I was green as grass. To be honest, I was terrified most of the time…" She was turning several pages at once, searching for the Nativity scenes. "But I couldn't have had a nicer class. They were such lovely kids…especially your Will…" She took a moment to study the pictures. "He could have been one of the Three Kings, you know, but he was determined to have that lamb. We couldn't prise it off him at the end of the play. He took it home with him…do you remember?"

Mrs Buckley's eyes shone with joy. She had folded her arms across her chest, and was hugging the memories to her heart, desperate for more. It was a craving that Ginny felt obliged to feed, and she dredged up every titbit of Will's childhood that her memory could supply, and then stole fragments of other children's lives when she ran short of truth. The truth did not matter to her hostess. She had found sanctuary in the stories, much as her son had taken refuge in tales of Merry Maids. It seemed unkind to stop.

Ginny ran the palm of her hand over one of the flimsy sheets that protected the photographs, and gently smoothed away the creases. The faint tick of the carriage-clock on the mantelpiece was the only sound in the room.

"For what it's worth," she said quietly, "I don't believe you've lost your son forever."

The woman was as still as a statue, but Ginny felt her interest quicken.

"I think your Will is in hiding. He's living inside the person he calls Whizz, and he'll stay there until someone persuades him that it's safe to come out..."

"And you are that person, are you?"

Her voice had been unnaturally loud, and her eyes flashed wildly.

"Maybe I am," said Ginny. "I think he still trusts me, like he did when he was little..."

Mrs Buckley had closed her eyes. She could have been praying, or she could have been closing her mind to a message of false-hope. It was impossible to tell.

In a corner of the room, a buzzer went off, an irritable noise that demanded attention. Mrs Buckley appeared not to hear it.

The buzzer buzzed again.

Mrs Buckley moved not a muscle.

Another burst of buzzing.

Ginny reached out and gently touched the woman's arm. "Don't you think you should answer that, Mrs Buckley?"

On the next buzz, as though the world had never ceased to turn, the figure of stone came back to life.

She smiled. "That will be Moira," she announced, and made for a lacquered cabinet near the door. "Moira does my hair every week. She's such a poppet. I don't know what I'd do without her..."

Mrs Buckley opened the cabinet door, peered briefly at a small black-and-white TV monitor, and then flicked a switch before re-closing the door.

"Thank you so much for coming, Mrs May," she said, offering her hand. "It's been lovely to see you again."

The handshake was limp and damp.

"Would you be kind enough to let Moira into the conservatory?"

Ginny was half-way down the stairs and feeling more relief with every step she took when Mrs Buckley called to her from the landing above.

"You will try, won't you, Mrs May?"

It was a scene from an un-made movie entitled *The Prisoner of Halcyon*: the lonely figure, slim and elegant, one hand clutching the balustrade, the other at her neck, framed by the giant ghosts of Garbo and Astaire on either side. If she had calculated the pose it would have been ludicrous, but it was not calculated.

Ginny nodded. "I'll do my best."

"You promise?"

"Please don't expect miracles," Ginny said, "but, yes…I promise. I will try."

The sun was setting behind *Halcyon*, bringing an early twilight to the paddock where the Saab was parked. Ginny filled her lungs. The air was cold, but never sweeter.

She looked about her at the rich man's toys, all rusting away in silence. No horses nodding at the stable doors-four black voids, and four horseshoes, nailed to the white weatherboards for luck.

Inside the Saab, her mobile began to ring, a muffled summons to her own life. But she was not ready. Not yet. She waited until the caller had given up and then unlocked the car door. Immediately the phone rang again. Whoever it was, they were persistent…probably Simon, alerted by Jude, anxious that she had gone missing.

The mobile lay on the passenger seat, still plugged into the charging socket. The jingle was obeying its programme and getting louder with neglect. Ginny picked it up, and checked the display. She was mistaken. It was a number she did not recognise.

"Yes," she said warily.

"Is that Mrs May?"

"Is that you, Whizz?"

"What I said about your baby…That was a crap thing to say…and I shouldn't have said it…I'm really, really sorry…"

He sounded close to tears, and the more he tried to explain himself the more incoherent he became.

"Shush, shush, shush…take it easy, Whizz. Everything's ok. We all say silly things sometimes…"

"Will you still come and see me then?"

"Of course I will…"

In the echoes of the prison, an angry voice imposed itself:

"Get off the phone, Buckley! Your time's up!"

Whizz was undeterred. "Have you got the 'VO' I sent?"

"I said get off the fucking phone…" The voice was close now, and menacing.

"Please come, Mrs May..."

There was a struggle and a commotion. And then the line went dead.

Chapter Nineteen

There was no sign of Simon's car in the lean-to, and the house was in darkness. As Ginny approached the front door, the security lights came on and the dusky night became electric day. The virtual guard-dog ran amok in the hallway.

Ginny unlocked the door, and quickly entered the code to kill the dog. A red light was blinking faintly on the hall table. She pressed 'Play' on the answer-machine.

"Sorry the pampering got up your nose." It was Jude, trying to sound bouncy. "Get on the blower if you need a chat. They can always drag me naked from the mud bath. A gruesome thought, I know, but we're here to help if you need us. Keep cheerful, love...Bye for now. See you on Friday for Simon's big night. We'll pick you up at seven..."

The message was timed at 4pm, about the time that she'd been driving down the coast to *Halcyon*. Simon must have left by then, so he wouldn't know that she'd escaped from *Glebelands*. He could be anywhere. With anyone.

Their bedroom looked innocent enough. Everything was in its rightful place. Turning back a corner of the duvet, she found Simon's neatly folded pyjamas exactly where they were supposed to be. And the pillows were respectably plump.

His eyrie was in a mess. Books and periodicals littered the desk. Yet more piles of books, some of them open, at the pillow-end of the futon below the eaves. It had been slept in; duvet and pillows crumpled and scrunched up. There were two coffee mugs on the floor.

Ginny pulled back the duvet and let her eyes interrogate the under-sheet. She picked up a pillow and buried her nose in it, detecting floral scents, perhaps a shampoo or an aftershave, maybe a light perfume. She sniffed the second pillow, still not sure. Then she turned to the coffee mugs, holding each one up to the hanging light bulb, searching the rims for smears of lipstick. Despite the lack evidence, on the way downstairs she subjected every room to the same suspicious scrutiny, aware that she was being paranoid, but indulging the sour pleasures of imagined victimhood with a degree of masochistic relish.

The envelopes in the kitchen brought her to her senses. There were two of them, propped up against the sherry bottles on the Welsh dresser, both addressed to her. Confident that she knew what it contained, she opened the drab one with the printed label. As expected, it was the Visiting Order from Fulford, a flimsy sheet covered on both sides with official-speak. Making a mental note of the visiting times, she folded the paper and put it in the zipped pocket of her shoulder-bag.

The second envelope, addressed in a florid hand, contained a single sheet of hand-made note paper, neatly folded three times to embrace a cheque...a cheque made out to her for the sum of three hundred and fifteen pounds. Astonished, she turned to the letter. It was from the craft shop on the quayside:

Dear Mrs May,

Congratulations! You have a wealthy patroness who adores your work and wants more. Come see what she has in mind – and bring more wonky pots. The shelves are bare.

Best wishes
Victor

Ginny re-examined the cheque, gloated a little, and then gave it a kiss.

With the exception of a couple of fruit bowls stored in a cupboard in the Welsh dresser, and an outsized ewer that hadn't been a great success, the only pots that would pass muster in the classy craft-gallery were the jugs that she used to display flowers around the house. Filling the kitchen sink with hot soapy water, she gave all the pots a thorough wash, drying each one with scrupulous care, taking her time, concentrating on every mundane task while her mind fretted about Simon and what best to do. By the time the pots were wrapped and packed away in a cardboard box, she had decided to do nothing. Simon would show when Simon chose, and anyway, she was still in dread about what Simon might have to say.

She settled for an early night, and took one of Doc's tablets. She lay on her back and closed her eyes, waiting for the drug to do its work. But her mind insisted on shuttling back and forth between *Halcyon* and Fulford prison, and sleep refused its invitation. To her surprise, she discovered that her arm was outstretched to the far side of the bed, her hand lying palm down on the cool sheet where Simon should be.

On impulse, she turned over and reached for the bedside table, fumbling for her mobile. It was just after ten o'clock. She keyed in Simon's number, and listened. After four beeps a recorded female made an announcement:

"The person you are phoning can't take your call. We will send them a text to let them know that you have called. Thank you."

Chapter Twenty

When Ginny set out for the craft-gallery she had no intention of going by way of Murray's Road, but the car was on automatic pilot and she found herself held up in a long queue of traffic directly opposite the school. Feeling like a truant, she shifted in her seat so that her back was to the window. When the traffic showed no signs of movement, she risked a furtive glance over her shoulder. No one was watching. And the buildings looked deserted.

Class One would be hard at work, little heads bent over work-sheets, faces contorting as their infant brains grappled with the immensity of the day's new challenge, all yearning for the bell that would release them into the playground...

A knuckle rapped on the passenger window.

Ginny turned. It was DS Carmichael, looking haggard, with several days' growth of beard on his chin.

"Can I get in?" he mimed, pointing at the door handle.

Ginny released the central locking.

"Didn't expect to see you," he said. "Are you feeling better?"

Ginny smiled. "When you tapped on the window, I was pining for the classroom, so I'm either totally nuts or I'm feeling better—you tell me!"

The truck in front puffed out a small black cloud of diesel fumes and began to move. Ginny released the clutch and joined the crawl.

"Can you park by the shops?" asked Carmichael, pointing ahead to the lay-by outside the newsagent and the bookies.

Ginny flicked on the indicator. "So what brings you to Murray's Road?" she asked.

"I've just been to see the Head..." replied Carmichael. "Jason's coming back to school tomorrow..."

Ginny frowned, and snatched a side-ways glance. "Why? What's been the matter with Jason?"

Carmichael looked surprised. "Have you not seen the news?"

"What news?"

"The news about Jason's dad..."

Ginny had drawn alongside a van that was already parked in the lay-by. Engaging reverse gear, she turned to look over her shoulder and began to back the Saab into the vacant space. Carmichael waited until she had completed the manoeuvre.

"They found Kenny's body in a rubbish-skip at the back of the fairground..."

Ginny's hand went to her mouth.

"We're still trying to work out whether he climbed inside for a bit of privacy while he shot-up, or whether some sweet-natured soul dumped him there. I know where my money is!"

"What about Mary and the kids?" asked Ginny.

"Social Services have been with the kids, and they're alright. Mary's gone to bits though..." He was about to say more when his mobile phone interrupted. "Sorry," he said, and took the call. There was a terse exchange of words, and then he turned back to Ginny. "Got to go, I'm afraid. They've just pulled in another low-life."

With a groan, the detective opened his door and made to get out.

"I think I should be at school when Jason comes back," said Ginny. "Is there anything else I should know?"

Carmichael checked his wristwatch. "What are you doing for lunch?"

"Nothing," replied Ginny, "I've got a bit of business with the craft-shop on the quay, then I'm free."

The policeman's weary face brightened. "If you're going to *The V&A*, that's perfect! Just ask Tweedledum or Tweedledee to show you the way to *The Cat*, and I'll meet you there. It's the best pub in the world, bar none."

According to the sign above the window, the gallery was called *Artefact*. To local artists and craftsmen, and to most of its customers, it had always been *The V&A*. Although Victor Burles and Albert Letouze pretended to disapprove of the nickname, in truth they understood its commercial value and did nothing to discourage its use. For nearly thirty years they had made a canny living selling seaside kitsch to the day-trippers who infested the Old Town during the summer, and top-end craft objects to the city's plutocrats and the rich sea-dogs who parked their fibreglass yachts in the marina.

"It's far and away the biggest commission we've ever had, dear," said Albert, a portly little man, prone to falsetto.

"Twelve of everything, from dinner plates to egg cups," added Victor in a chocolate baritone.

"And she's filthy rich..." confided Albert. From below the counter, he produced an embossed visiting card pinned to a swatch of curtain material. "Look...she lives in one of those grand houses in Cranbrook Square."

Ginny glanced at the card, and spread the material over the palm of her hand. "And what am I supposed to do with this?" she said.

Victor winced. "That's your palette, Mrs May. Ghastly, isn't it?"

Albert gave a snort of derision. "Just think of the money, darling," he said in a theatrical whisper.

Ginny re-examined the card. "I think I'll need to take a look at the dining room. Do you think Mrs Carfax would mind?"

"Of course she wouldn't mind," protested Albert. "She's a lovely old thing...pushing ninety, and bright as a button. Give the old girl a bell."

Ginny folded the sample of material and slipped it into her shoulder bag, then launched into an effusive thank-you to her two sponsors, who smiled indulgently and drank up her gratitude like nectar.

"Now...could you tell me how I get to a pub called *The Cat*? I've got a date."

Albert and Victor exchanged looks, obviously intrigued.

Ginny was amused. "I'm meeting a policeman, as it happens."

"Oh, that'll be Sherlock," said Victor, with evident approval.

"I hope you haven't done anything naughty, Mrs May?" added Albert, making it abundantly clear that he was hoping for the reverse.

With her *bona fides* apparently established, the gallery owners began to compete for the honour of being Ginny's guide, and a tight-lipped argument ensued about whose turn it was to have lunch in the pub.

"Why don't you both come?" she suggested. "Then I can buy you both a drink."

Chapter Twenty One

The Shacks sprawled over a couple of acres on three sides of the harbour. The area took its name from the kippering sheds and the rickety black towers where the fishing fleet had dried its nets when there were still fish to fish. Centuries of haphazard building had created a labyrinth of lanes and dark alleys that snaked between oddly shaped courtyards, home these days to the trinketeers and fast-foodsters who preyed on grazing tourists.

"That's *The Cat*," said Victor, pointing his finger at a nondescript building that could have been a factory or warehouse.

There was no pub sign, no cheery glow at the windows, and no door that Ginny could see—only a brick arch above a cobbled passageway that, in days gone by, would have echoed to the clatter of horses' hooves and iron-clad cartwheels.

"Don't they want customers at *The Cat*?" asked Ginny.

"Only locals," replied Albert. "Jerry doesn't warm to grockels."

Victor led the way to a patch of sunshine at the end of the passageway and, like a courtier of old, made an elegant sweep of his left hand as though presenting royalty.

"There you have it..." he announced, "*The Cat with Cream*."

The pub was a Jacobean jewel, a criss-cross of black timbers against white plaster, walls dripping wisteria, window boxes and hanging baskets ablaze with flowers. Trading insults with groups of nicotine addicts puffing away at tables below the colourful umbrellas, *The V&A* crossed the courtyard with Ginny in their wake. At the door, she stopped to look more closely at the fine mural painted on the plasterwork—a tabby cat, human-sized and wearing top hat and tails, leaning nonchalantly against the door-jamb, a smile of welcome on his furry face as he toasted new arrivals with a wineglass full to the brim with cream.

The saloon bar was divided into cosy nooks by blackened timbers supporting a low and bulgy ceiling that had been stained an ochre-brown by centuries of tobacco smoke. Drinkers were

148

standing three or four-deep around the semi-circular bar, their voices raised against the efforts of a small jazz combo which was playing in a corner of the room. From an umpire's chair at one end of the bar, an owlish figure peered at the assembled company over the top of his half-moon specs, a large whiskey in his hand and a benign smile on his lips.

"That's Jerry," said Albert, "struck-off solicitor, patron of the arts, and a living saint."

"A remarkable man," added Victor solemnly.

Ginny produced her purse and opened it.

Albert was mortified. "No, no," he insisted. "This is Victor's treat..."

Albert produced a mechanical smile for Victor. And Victor replied in kind.

Ginny ordered a St Clements and, while her escorts took their bickering to the bar, cast an eye over the room in search of DS Carmichael. A waitress passed by, carrying bowls of blue-black mussels and plates of golden chips. Breathing in the aroma of hot wine and garlic, she closed her eyes, and her mouth filled with saliva. For the first time in weeks she was ravenously hungry. She took another deep breath, then swallowed and re-opened her eyes...

The crowd at the bar was parting to allow a young woman to come through with a tray of drinks. Her head was down, and she was concentrating fiercely to avoid spillage.

Ginny's mouth went dry and her feet refused to move.

The spiky hair-do was unmistakeable.

When they were separated by little more than the width of the tray, the girl stopped and looked up, staring directly into Ginny's face. Her mouth fell open.

"Hello, Mel," said Ginny.

"Good God! I thought you were at the health farm?"

"I was," said Ginny, feeling the flush in her cheeks, "but I escaped."

The girl was uneasy, not quite her elfin-self.

"Are you feeling better, Ginny? Simon said you were in a really bad way..."

Ginny forced a smile. "Simon was glad to see the back of me, if you ask me..."

Mel made a disbelieving face. "He was really worried about you," she said, "everybody was."

Ginny searched the girl's eyes for the truth.

"I spy Sherlock," exclaimed Albert, pointing towards the pub door with a bottle of Prosecco.

DS Carmichael raised a hand in acknowledgement and headed their way, pulling himself to a dramatic halt when he saw Mel's tray of drinks. Then he advanced again and, with a shaking hand, picked up one of the pints of bitter. He put the glass to his lips and drank.

"You cheeky sod," said Mel.

Carmichael drained three-quarters of the glass in a single swallow, and wiped foam from his lip with the back of his hand.

"You just saved my life," he said.

Insults were exchanged. No one was spared, and no one took offence. Ginny was beginning to feel like the new girl at Brownies when Albert took pity and performed her initiation.

"So I discover this wonderful potter, a lady of great taste and discrimination who makes the most marvellous wonky-pots...and what do I find?" Albert paused to pout a little. "She's only having her collar felt by our resident policeman, isn't she...?" A lascivious smirk made his meaning clear.

Mel tut-tutted, and arched her eyebrows. "My, my! What will Simon say?"

Ginny managed a tentative smile, and watched as Mel took her tray to a thirsty table by the dart board.

"Can I get anything while I'm at the bar?" asked Carmichael.

"Yes, please," begged Ginny, "can you order me some mussels and chips? I feel as if I haven't eaten for weeks."

While Carmichael shouldered his way to the counter, Ginny allowed the V&A to herd her to a table in one of the bay windows where a large blonde woman was bent over the pages of a racing paper that was spread out beside her pint glass.

"Morning, Shirl," said Albert, starting to unpick the gold paper on the neck of the Prosecco bottle.

"Morning, Al," replied the blonde.

Ever the gentleman, Victor motioned for Ginny to take the comfortably padded window-seat.

"You don't mind dogs, do you, duck?" said Shirley.

Ginny looked down at the bundle of fur that was luxuriating on a cushion in a patch of sunshine.

"I certainly don't mind Captain Baxter," she said, uncertain which end to scratch.

"Well, bugger me!" said Shirley. "How come you know his name?"

The cork popped from the Prosecco.

"She's one of Sherlock's girlfriends, that's why," said Albert, catching spilt fizz in a glass.

"Hey!" said Shirley, pointing a finger. "You're not the lass who's looking out for young Billy Whizz, are you?"

"That's me," replied Ginny.

A large hand appeared in front of her.

"Put it there, duck," said Shirley. "My Captain Baxter would be down the rotten glue-factory if it weren't for that Billy Whizz."

"Huh!" grunted Victor, with evident disapproval.

By Shirley's account, Whizz was something of a hero, having risked a kicking to rescue Captain Baxter from a gang of yobbos who had been using him as a rugby ball under the Royal Pier.

Victor and Albert had a very different perspective. When it came to 'queer-bashing', Whizz was as bad as they come.

"He was tormentor-in-chief," explained Victor.

"Apart from Rivers," added Albert.

"That's true," conceded Victor, "but Whizz would do anything that Rivers told him, and that makes him just as bad."

Shirley wagged a big finger. "The kid were surviving," she argued. "When you're running wi' scum, you gotta look like scum. Take that kid out o' the gutter, gi' him a bit of time to grow up, and he'll be alright...I saw it in the regiment time and again..."

Ginny was intrigued by the dispute, but she was also keeping an eye on Carmichael. He had left the bar with two full pints held aloft for safe passage, easing himself through the crowd to deliver a replacement for the pint he had hi-jacked. The man next to Mel stood up and grabbed the glass with alacrity, saying something that made everyone laugh. He was wearing a scarlet bandana that barely kept his shock of wild black hair in check.

"What do you reckon, Sherlock?" said Shirley, when Carmichael eventually came to join their table. "Did Rivers do for that bloke in Dreamworld?"

The DS sighed. "If I knew, I certainly wouldn't tell you, Shirley."

From below her luxuriant false-eyelashes, the big transvestite glared at the policeman. "Rivers is pushing dirty gear...That's the word on the street."

Carmichael sighed. "I know—he cuts it with rat poison." He pointed an accusing finger at his neighbour. "That is an urban myth, Shirley, and you should know better."

"You say what you like, sunshine," retorted Shirley, "but young Rivers has got ambitious. He's letting the world know he's not to be messed with. That's what's going on..."

Getting to her feet, Shirley scooped up Captain Baxter in one hand, and grabbed *The Sporting Life* in the other.

"I'm off to the bookies..." she said, "and I suggest you get off your fat arse, sergeant, and get that bugger locked up before he does for somebody else."

With a neat backhand, she flicked Carmichael's head with the newspaper, and clattered away across the stone floor on her high heels.

Carmichael laughed, and shook his tired head.

Ginny smiled, and took a sip from her St Clements.

"I didn't know you knew Mel," she said, nodding her head to the table across the room. "Who's the pirate she's with?"

"That's Lazlo Fischer. He's the brains behind *The Shacks Theatre Company*. They've been trying to persuade me to come to your old man's lecture..."

Ginny laughed. "It wouldn't be your cuppa tea..."

"How would you know?" he said, summoning up some weary indignation. "*Dirty Realism* is the story of my life." He put the glass to his mouth, and then took it away. "And I can read, you know."

"Touché," said Ginny, and raised her glass an inch.

The policeman tipped back his glass and drained it, then let his head slump forwards as though he were about to fall asleep.

"You'd better fill me in on the Nolan story before you pass out," she said.

"You're right!" exclaimed Carmichael, blinking himself back into focus.

"Do you want another pint?"

He shook his head. "Better not..."

A waitress arrived and began to unload steaming bowls of food from her tray. Wasting no time, Ginny selected a pair of empty mussel shells to act as tweezers, and began to plunder the flesh of its brothers and sisters.

"So tell me about poor Kenny Nolan," she said.

The policeman shook his head, and looked doubtful. "I think I'd better wait till you've finished," he said.

"You carry on," said Ginny, dunking a piece of French stick in the broth. "Nothing's going to stop me eating."

The Nolan story was not for the squeamish. When they found Kenny's body, it had been in the rubbish skip for three days and nights, and the fairground rats had made a meal of his face. Then some greedy underling at the cop-shop had sold the story to the press, and every grisly detail had been splashed all over the media before a formal identification could be made.

Ginny had temporarily abandoned the food, and was leaning back from the table.

"So that means Jason got the full horror story before anyone knew it was his father?"

Carmichael gave a little shrug. "Mary has the TV on from morning to night..."

"And when the identification came through?"

"Social Services did their best to shield the kids. But Mary was in such a state, she blabbed the lot."

"Jesus," breathed Ginny. "Well, I'll certainly be there for Jason in the morning. Whether I can stay till home-time, I'm not so sure. I've got a visit booked to see Whizz in Fulford. It'll be up to the prison, I'm afraid."

Carmichael looked askance at her. "How come you're still giving Whizz Buckley the time of day?"

"Because I promised," said Ginny.

With a disbelieving shake of his head, Carmichael hauled himself to his feet.

"Well, while you're in the slammer," he said, "see if the young villain can make himself useful. Ask him if he's heard anything on the grapevine about this Kenny Nolan business. You never know."

"I might..." said Ginny, "if the situation presents itself."

The policeman's eyes studied her for a moment. "I think these kids are very lucky to have you," he said, and then quickly flapped a hand in farewell, as though he had inadvertently said too much. "Time for some kip—sorry I've been like the walking dead."

"Sweet dreams," said Ginny.

Carmichael chortled, and said, "Fat chance!"

When he'd gone, Ginny returned to the food, glad to see that there was plenty of everything left. Selecting a particularly plump mussel, she plucked out its flesh with her finger and thumb, and dropped it on her tongue—soft, succulent and totally scrumptious. In the pale-blue spoon of the shell, she scooped up some winey broth and leaned forwards over the bowl to slurp the still-warm liquid into her mouth.

"Can you spare a chip?"

Ginny almost choked. "Help yourself," she mumbled, wiping wine-gravy from her chin with the back of her hand.

Mel dunked a chip in the garlic mayo and took a bite. "That's about a hundred and fifty calories I've spared you," she said, and popped the rest of the chip into her mouth before licking her fingers.

She began to chat like an old friend, launching a bitchy assault on health farms and all the vain, narcissistic folk who frequented them. Coming from someone who made sculpture from her hair and painted elaborate designs on her face and body, this aversion to the cult of health and beauty seemed a bit rich. When Ginny said as much, Mel was unfazed.

"I don't know whether it's total Art, or total Bullshit," she said. "I just wannabe me, and I'm afraid 'me' is a bit weird."

"And, what about Lazlo?" asked Ginny. "Is he weird as well?"

"Very," said Mel, "mainly because he puts up with me...But then Lazlo is weirdly special..."

Lazlo, it seemed, was gifted; Lazlo was brilliant; Lazlo was Brecht and Brooke, Gielgud and Malkovich all rolled up into one gigantic ball of theatrical talent.

"There's a preview of his new play on Thursday. You should come."

"I will, if I can," said Ginny, "but Simon may be back and...

"Bring him along," said Mel, inspired by the thought. "Lazlo would value his opinion. We're all so involved with piddling performance problems that we've lost sight of the play as an entity."

Ginny dropped her pincer-shells on top of the growing pile of empty mussels, and wiped her hands on a napkin. "I don't suppose you know where Simon is, do you?" she asked. "I haven't seen him since they dragged me off to *Glebelands*..."

Mel reached for another chip. "We were rehearsing at your place yesterday, and he did say he was going to spend a few days in Town...do some work in the British Library, or something." The chip emerged from the ramekin dripping aioli. "Hasn't he phoned?"

Ginny shook her head. "His mobile's turned off."

Mel leaned forwards, taking her mouth to the chip. "He's probably switched off in the library and forgot to switch on again..." She took a bite of chip, and finished the thought with her mouth full. "It's easily done. I'm always doing it myself..."

Ginny pressed her back against the padding of the window seat and looked up at the nicotine-stained ceiling.

"What's up?" said Mel.

"Nothing's up," said Ginny. "I'm a fool for worrying, that's all."

Chapter Twenty Two

Ginny left home early to beat the morning rush hour, but arrived at school with barely enough time to programme the whiteboard before going out to meet Jason at the gate. Trust Simon to choose a moment like this to get in touch.

"I've had lots of texts to say you called...Are you alright, Ginny?"

"I'm fine, but I'm back at school, and you've caught me at a bad time."

"What are you doing at school?" he exclaimed. "I thought you were still at the health farm?"

Ginny gabbled her way through an explanation.

"Look, never mind me," she went on, "Where on earth have you been? I've been trying your phone for days."

"In Town, polishing up this damned lecture at the British Library...I forgot to switch the phone back on. Sorry."

"When are you coming back?" Ginny asked.

"I was planning to come back on Friday morning, but I'll come back today, if you like...?"

"No, no," she said, "don't change your plans for me. I've got lots on...and I'm fine, really..."

"Are you sure?"

"Positive..."

She should have ended the call there, but she found herself turning towards the corner of the room, cupping her hands around the phone, as though to shield her words from eavesdroppers.

"But we do need to talk, Simon...We haven't talked properly since we lost the baby."

There was a pause. "I know. I feel terrible about it..." he said.

"You mustn't feel terrible!" she protested. "You've been waiting for me to shake off the blues...I know you have..."

She thought she heard him swallow, as if he were blinking back tears.

"Don't worry. We'll open a bottle on Saturday, when you've got this lecture out of the way. We'll clear the air then, ok...? Now I really must dash...the poor kid will be here any minute...Bye, Simon...good luck with the lecture...We'll sort everything out afterwards...Bye..."

A young man who had been loitering to one side of the school gate hoisted a video camera onto his shoulder and pointed it towards the pedestrian crossing. Ginny opened one of the glass doors by Reception and set off down the path, pleased to see two uniformed policemen advance on the cameraman and hustle him away.

Mary Nolan was earlier than usual. She was walking slowly, like an automaton, looking neither left nor right, Jason on one side holding onto the handle of the pram, and a young policewoman or social-worker on the other, jiggling the toddler up and down on her hip to keep him amused. The mothers at the gate fell silent and turned to watch the show.

On catching sight of Ginny, Jason raised both hands in the air and jumped for joy, abandoning his mother to skip down the pavement towards her. Mary appeared not to notice. Her face was as grey and lifeless as candle-wax. The care worker leaned towards her and whispered words of reassurance, and then took hold of the toddler's hand and wagged a wave to Jason.

Ginny persuaded Jason to return his brother's wave, giving Mary a smile and a small nod of recognition. There was no response.

Refusing the offer of Ginny's hand, Jason bounced along the school path without a backward glance at his grieving mother, happy as a dog let off the leash. When Ginny prevented him from running off to the playground and steered him into the secretary's office, he looked anxious, as if he were going to be accused of some horrendous offence.

Ginny squatted down on her haunches so that they were face to face.

"If anything upsets you in school..." she began, "anything at all...you're to come straight to me. Ok?"

Behind the thick lenses, the boy's pale eyes were huge and devoid of comprehension.

Ginny glanced at the clock on the wall. "There's still some time before the bell," she said. "Do you want to come to the classroom with me...or do you want to go and play?"

"Play," said Jason, without hesitation.

Ginny opened the office door, and her charge ran out, narrowly avoiding a collision with Mrs Appleby as she emerged from the Staff Room.

"Is he ok?" mimed the secretary, hooking her thumb over her shoulder.

Ginny nodded, and spread her hands in a gesture of bewilderment.

"Oh, by the way..." called Mrs Appleby, stopping Ginny as she reached the swing-doors to the playground. "I had a call earlier from a Mr Buckley. I said you were busy. He's going to try later."

Ginny paused, the palm of her hand against the wood of the door—silly of her not to expect some ripples on *Halcyon*'s stagnant pool—she leaned her weight on the door, and what had been a low-level buzz of noise became a blast of Michael Jackson at full volume.

The Head's war on couch potatoes was underway, and this week's disco-queens were cavorting on the rudimentary stage in front of large crowd of younger children, all of them burning calories as they tried to copy the intricate choreography of their elders and betters.

It took her a moment to locate Jason. He was on the far side of the playground, sitting on the low wall that enclosed the infants' activity area. He was not alone. Several of his classmates were already clustered round, and others were deserting the ranks of dancers to join them. Class One had been given a pep-talk by the Head at the end of yesterday's lessons. Now they would be putting his words into practice, being extremely grown-up and responsible, with Chantelle and Jessica at their most excruciatingly maternal. Not that it would last. Henry Carter's appetite for gruesome detail would soon have to be assuaged. But then, kids are brave with the truth. Somehow, in their brutal, unflinching fashion, they would cope...

She was right. Jason spent the day in a state of contented bewilderment, blinking a little in the unfamiliar spotlight of celebrity. Only when Ginny picked up *The Magic Carpet* and flicked through the pages to find their going-home story, did he show signs of anxiety. With his thumb wedged tight in his mouth and his shoulders hunched, he laid his head on his folded arms and made himself as tiny as he could, as though he wished he could vanish entirely.

When the children of Baghdad had finally made their escape at the end of *The Flight to Samarkand*, Ginny went straight to his table.

"Time to go and see mummy now," she whispered.

Inside the pink frames of his glasses, the eyes moistened.

"Mummy needs you to be a good boy..."

To her surprise, Jason nodded his head. For a moment, he chewed on his lower lip, but he pushed back his chair and stood up. Ginny grabbed her bag and her coat, and took him by the hand, feeling the tug of his reluctance all the way along the corridors.

"There they are..." she said, pushing open the glass door by Reception. "Why don't you give mummy a wave?"

Jason's brother had plonked his nappy on the pavement by the gate and was having a temper-tantrum, resisting all the care-worker's efforts to placate him. Mary Nolan was behind the pram, deaf to the world around her. Other mothers were keeping a wary distance, as though the Nolans' misery were infectious.

Ginny and Jason continued down the path, the tug on her arm growing heavier with every step.

"Mrs May... Can you spare a moment?"

She knew it was Buckley before she turned her head.

"Mrs May..." he called again. He was coming from the staff car park, an imperious hand raised to attract her attention.

"Not now, Mr Buckley," she shouted, not bothering to disguise her irritation. "I'm busy."

Twitching Jason's hand, she got him on the move again, twin spots of anger scorching her cheeks. The sympathetic words she'd been rehearsing for Mary Nolan flew straight out of her head. Fortunately the care worker made a huge fuss of Jason, and held up his butterfly-painting in front of the pram so that the baby could admire it.

"He's been a very good boy," said Ginny lamely.

There was no life in Mary's eyes. If it had not been for the efforts of the young minder, who took hold of the pram's handle and pointed it to the pedestrian crossing, she would have remained rooted to the spot.

Angered by her own inadequacy, Ginny turned away. Buckley was waiting on the school path. He was wearing a fancy white shirt, a red bow-tie and matching bracers that held up the trousers of a black dress suit. He looked out of place, and not pleased to be so.

As she approached, Ginny showed him the palm of her hand. "I can't talk today, Mr Buckley..."

"My wife hasn't slept since you called..."

Ginny stopped, and looked him in the eye. "I'm very sorry about that, Mr Buckley, but I can't talk now. I've got a visit booked to see your son in prison, and I'm late...If I don't get there in time, I won't be allowed another visit for a fortnight."

She gave him a look that warned him not to argue, and hurried past, heading for the car park.

Buckley was not easily shaken off, and followed close behind. "We could talk in the car," he suggested.

"You'll have a long wait at the prison," she said.

"Not if I get my driver to follow..."

Ginny snatched a sideways glance. Irritated though she was by the ambush, there was more to Buckley's persistence than alpha male aggression.

"Ok, then," she said, "but we have to hurry."

While Buckley explained the situation to the driver of his Mercedes, Ginny cleared some debris from the Saab's passenger seat and threw it all on the back seat.

"Do you get chauffeured everywhere?" she asked, as Buckley buckled himself in.

"Good God, no!" he replied, amused by the notion. "Only when I'm going boozing for the business."

As they waited for a gap in the traffic, her passenger looked back over his shoulder at the school buildings. "I've got good memories of this place..." he mused. "It's a pity we couldn't stop the clock."

From his perch high in a juggernaut's cab, a lorry driver took pity on Ginny and waved her into the stream of traffic. The Mercedes followed, as though glued to her tail. Buckley swivelled in his seat and stared down the road ahead.

"Within a year of leaving here," he said, speaking briskly, "my son had a Police Caution for thieving; he'd been caught with drugs; and the new school was talking about Exclusion. The question is: 'Why?'"

Giving Ginny no time to speculate, he went on to give a businesslike account of his son's downward spiral. Essentially it was the same story that she had heard from his wife in *Halcyon*, but now, as told from Buckley's perspective, it was the story of a father's bitter battle to save his son. At every calamitous twist and turn, Buckley had come up with ingenious responses: When the stealing began, he persuaded the police to lock the boy in a cell to shock sense into him; when a stash of skunk was found in the boy's bedroom, he hauled him off to a drug-rehabilitation unit to confront him with addicts and their horror-stories. When the boy ran out of rope at the comprehensive school, he bought him a place at the local public school; when the public school's patience was exhausted, he hired private tutors. Nothing had worked. And Buckley blamed himself.

"Perhaps you tried too hard," said Ginny.

"Perhaps I did," Buckley conceded, "but it's not in my nature to step back and do nothing..."

"You weren't in court for him though, were you?" said Ginny, taking her eyes off the road to glance at him. "And it's not you that's going to see him in prison, is it? So why have you abandoned him?"

Buckley went quiet, and Ginny wondered if she had gone too far.

"It was getting dangerous," he said eventually. "Every time I tried to help, he did something crazy. He'd gone to war on me. All-out war, no-holds-barred." He paused, and watched the ugly suburbs spin by his window. "In the end, I decided to let him go...I didn't want to...but I had more than young Will to worry about..."

Apart from the drone of the engine, there was silence in the car. Ginny checked the mirror to make sure the Mercedes was still behind her, then indicated her intention to join the motorway and moved to the inside lane.

"How has your daughter coped with all this?" she asked.

"Badly," replied Buckley without hesitation. "We did our best to shelter her, but we failed in that as well..."

"Does she live at home?"

"Oh, no!" said Buckley, with a humourless chuckle. "She's as far away as I could get her...in Australia, at college."

Ginny risked a sideways look. "Your wife must be very lonely?" she said.

Buckley seemed engrossed in the dashboard and did not respond immediately.

"Please don't go and see her again, Mrs May. She's had too many false dawns..."

"I'm sorry," said Ginny. "It was a mistake to blunder in like that."

Indicating her intention to take the next exit, Ginny checked the mirror and saw the Mercedes do likewise.

Buckley meanwhile had returned to *Halcyon,* and was recalling his wife in happier days; her vitality; her flair for design; her love for her children. And he relived the breakdown which had left her a prisoner in her own house.

"Don't get me wrong though, Mrs May," he said. "I'm really glad you 'blundered in', as you put it... I just wish you'd come to see me rather than dredging it all up for poor Karen. You're the best hope we've got. The only hope, come to that."

A white prison transporter was approaching down the narrow road. Ginny slowed down and hugged the grass verge, aware that Buckley's eyes were fixed on the row of black window-slits as the van drove past.

"There's something you should know," he said. "No way have I abandoned my boy. Anything you can do to get him back on track...anything at all...if it costs, I'll pay...psychiatrists, counsellors, whatever it takes. The same goes for you, Mrs May. I'm more than prepared to pay you for your trouble..."

Ginny's grip tightened on the steering wheel.

"Don't be ridiculous, Mr Buckley," she said. "I'm not doing this for money. To be absolutely honest, I don't think your money can buy a solution to your family's problems. It's more complex than that."

"Don't be naive, Mrs May," said Buckley coolly. "You may not like it, but the old saying is true: 'Money talks'. I'd remember that, if I were you."

They were driving along the perimeter of the Fulford complex, and Buckley lowered his head to look up at the rolls of razor-wire that were spinning by at the top of the steel mesh that caged his only son.

Ginny was tempted to argue, but she decided to leave him to his thoughts.

Chapter Twenty Three

Ginny assumed the scarecrow posture and submitted to the searching hands. They were quick and peremptory. She was the last visitor of the day, and they were happy to see her go through.

At the Inspection Desk, she handed over her white card to the officer in charge.

"Closed Visit," he announced, and beckoned to a female colleague.

"What's that mean?" Ginny asked.

"It means he's been a bad lad," said the supervising officer, and closed the large ledger on the desk in front of him.

"This way, love," said Ginny's escort.

When they were out of earshot of the desk, the woman offered reassurance. "Don't fret, love," she said. "It's probably just handbags, but, if the lads kick off, we keep 'em apart. It's best for everyone."

They were walking down the length of the visiting area, past the queues at the WVS snack bar and the play-area where screeching children fought over plastic toys.

Today, every table was in use—inmates on the blue chairs; women and girls on the green settees, hardly a man in sight. It was a deceptively festive scene, and Ginny had to remind herself that the junky who'd raped the pensioners in High Town was here somewhere; and the boy who had smothered his foster-mum along the coast at Somerton. Or maybe they didn't get visitors. According to Bradley, lots of the boys didn't. No birthday cards, either. Not even the thought that counts.

"You can have a quiet chat in one of our executive suites," said the escort, pointing down the room.

In the far wall were six doors and six rectangular windows, like a row of small shops that were closed for business. Opening the first of the doors, the officer turned on a switch and fluorescent strip-lights flickered into life. Ginny went inside, and the door closed behind her.

It was a sparse room, divided in two by a wall and a sheet of reinforced glass that bisected a sturdy table. On her side of the glass were three green chairs, bolted to the floor, like the table. On the other side there was a single blue chair, and a heavy-duty metal door with an observation window. There would be no touching in this place—no handshakes, and no consoling hugs or kisses, not even for mothers and sons.

Ginny sat down in the middle chair, and waited. A patrolling prison officer in the Visiting Area slid his eyes across her as though she were an unremarkable fish in an aquarium. She felt exposed.

A key turned in a lock, a harsh sound, turned tinny by the microphone in the circular grille that was cut into the glass screen. The metal door on the far side of the partition opened.

"In you go, son," said a man's voice.

Whizz stepped into the room, and the door clanged shut behind him.

Ginny gaped at him. "What on earth have they done to you?" she exclaimed.

The blonde hair had been hacked off, leaving his scalp like a hayfield at the end of a botched harvest. His face had suffered too. The lower lip was bruised and swollen, and there was a graze on his cheekbone.

"Who did that to you?" Ginny demanded.

The boy slipped into the chair. He was close to tears. "I didn't think you were coming," he said.

"Do you want me to make a complaint?" she asked, ready for confrontation.

Whizz ignored the question. "I was such a knob the last time you came. I'm really sorry, Mrs May." Leaning forward, he put his face as close to the glass as the table would allow, and peered at her. "Are you feeling better now, Mrs May? You still don't look very well..."

"I'm fine," she said, "but what about you? You look awful..."

His brow furrowed. "Why do I get like that?"

The question troubled him. It was the same question that tormented his mother and father. And there was no glib response.

"Somebody was singing your praises yesterday," said Ginny, lightening the mood.

"That's a first," said Whizz, managing a painful grin. "Who was that then?"

"Shirley," replied Ginny, "the big transvestite who..."

The grin had vanished. "I know who Shirley is, and he can stick his praises!"

"He says you saved his dog."

"So what?" said Whizz, glaring at her. "I like dogs. I don't like fucking benders."

Swallowing the rebuke that sprang to her lips, Ginny said, "Shirley's not a homosexual. He's a transvestite. That's different..."

"Somebody ought to cut their cocks off."

Abruptly, Whizz pushed himself to his feet, and crossed to the cell door. For a moment she thought he was going put an end to the visit, but he simply stood at the observation window, staring out, breathing deeply, as if trying to control his temper.

Ginny waited until he seemed calmer. "I wish you'd come and sit down, Whizz. We don't have much time...It seems a shame to waste it..."

The boy raised his eyes to the breeze-block wall above the door and studied it for a moment. Then, avoiding eye-contact, he came back to the table and slumped forwards resting his head on his folded arms.

Whoever had sheared his hair, they had been quick and brutal. A sheep would have fared better. But it looked as if the wounds to his scalp had received some medical attention, and they were already beginning to heal.

"Do you remember when you were little," Ginny said, "when I used to read stories before you all went home at the end of the day?"

There was no response.

"I read one of those stories to the children today, before I came here to see you. It was from *The Magic Carpet* adventures...do you remember those?"

Still no response.

"It would be the perfect way to escape from this dump, don't you think? Up through the roof, on a magic carpet...?"

Under the thin turquoise material of his tee-shirt, the muscles of the boy's shoulders seemed to relax, and he snuggled his head more comfortably in the crook of his arm.

"Once upon a time," Ginny began, closing her eyes to the grim reality of their situation, "the poorest weaver in old Baghdad wove for his cruel master a wondrous carpet made from green silk and fine-spun gold; and with each silken thread that the weaver wove he entwined a prayer; and with each thread of gold he entwined a dream...."

"I doubt he's been raped," said Carmichael, later that evening. "The papers and the TV get excited about prison-rape, but it's not happening every day, not in the Young Offending places anyway. What do you think, Laz?"

Lazlo Fischer took the glass from his lips. "There'd have been a hell of a hoo-ha if he had been," he said.

"How would anyone know?" said Ginny. "The kid's not going to tell, is he...?"

"If they treated his cuts and bruises, they'd have done a full medical," said Carmichael, "and they'd have quizzed him hard as well."

Lazlo put down his glass, and looked at Ginny. "What colour tee-shirt was he wearing?" he asked.

Ginny sat back in her chair, puzzled. "Turquoise..." she said. "Why do you ask?"

"Because turquoise is the colour they wear in the new unit. If they've put him in there, it's a good sign. It means they're looking after him. The hard men call it the 'Sissy Wing' because it's where they put the vulnerable kids, but it's a really impressive outfit. We got a lot of our best actors from the Truman Wing. He'll be ok in there."

Lazlo was the perfect antidote to Fulford's poisonous reputation. He'd spent six years with *The Shacks Theatre* group doing drama workshops with prisoners, and recalled the productions they'd done together with genuine fondness and an enthusiasm that bordered on evangelical fervour.

"It sounds terrific," said Ginny, "exactly the kind of creative team-work those dysfunctional kids need. It's a pity you're not still there."

"Well, it wasn't the gaolers who pulled the plug," said Lazlo. "Blame the politicians! They made the cuts."

"Is there anything like that left?" asked Ginny.

"Not a lot," said Lazlo, "but there'll be something. One of the screws runs a music scene in his spare time...rock bands, rap, R&B...take your pick. Or you could point him to the chaplain...God knows whether he's still getting away with it, but when I was in there he used to let the some of the graffiti-merchants loose with spray-cans on the chapel walls. If your lad's prepared to get off his backside and go looking, he'll probably find something to light him up."

Lazlo emptied his glass of orange juice, and picked up the tricorne hat from the table.

"How do I look?" he said, preening the ostrich feather in the hat's brim.

"Very fetching," said Ginny.

"Aren't you a bit old for playing pirates?" asked Carmichael.

Reaching below his chair, Lazlo produced an angry looking stuffed parrot. "I know it's not the zenith of my theatrical career," he said, clipping the parrot to the epaulette on his right shoulder, "but it is a crust! Thank the Lord for visiting cruise ships, say I."

To a smattering of ironic applause from the early-evening drinkers, the dashing buccaneer made his exit from *The Cat*, doffing his hat and bowing to left and right, his parrot bobbing precariously on the shoulder of his frock coat.

"Feeling better?" asked Carmichael, when he'd gone.

"Much," replied Ginny.

"I had a feeling that Laz would cheer you up," he said, and clinked his pint glass against Ginny's wineglass. "Do you want another one?"

Ginny was tempted, but shook her head. "I'd love to, but I can't. I've got to go home and iron Simon's fancy dress. Tomorrow's his big day. Are you really going to come?"

"Wouldn't miss it…" said Carmichael, hiding a smile as he put the glass to his lips and drank the last inch of his beer. "Scumbags permitting, of course," he added.

Chapter Twenty Four

At precisely seven o'clock, Doc's four-by-four scrunched up the drive. Ginny quickly punched in the code for the burglar alarm, and locked up the house. As she walked down the path, Jude threw open one of the Shogun's rear doors.

"Wow!" she cried. "Don't you look expensive?"

Ginny was pleased. The new frock and the visit to the hairdresser were already paying dividends. Everyone was impressed, except for Bee, who seemed distracted and barely managed a smile of welcome...but then, to be fair, Jude's huge bulk was pressing her hard against the side window to give Ginny room on the back seat. As Doc executed a three-point turn in the Shogun, Charlie Mullen swivelled in the front passenger seat and draped his arm draped over the backrest, then launched into tonight's monologue, a pithy critique of the university's fondness for the American dollar.

"If I were the Widow Quale," he said, piling blarney on blarney, "I'd be checking the brakes on my wheelchair, so I would."

"If that old girl's got sense," chipped in Jude, "when she falls off the perch, there won't be a bean left."

And so it went, all the way to the university: Doc concentrating on his driving; Charlie holding forth; Jude supplying the occasional one-liner; and Bee oddly walled-up. Not a mention of the new professor and his moment in the sun.

When they arrived at *The Hexagon*, Doc Holroyd dropped off his passengers and went in search of a parking space. The atrium was already packed, and Charlie Mullen plunged straight into the scrum as though everyone had assembled to give him a welcome. The Senior Common Room was there in force, partners in tow, with a surprisingly large showing of undergraduates, all mingling with the usual contingent of culture-vultures from the city.

Bee and Jude embarked on an orgy of hugging and kissing, and were quickly swallowed by the crowd. Acknowledging acquaintances with a flutter of the hand, Ginny offered her cheek to anyone close enough, and smiled as they purred compliments about her hair and her dress. Everyone said how wonderful she looked. Professor Gurgieff's wife even clutched her arm and wished her the very best of luck, as though she were about to give the Quale Lecture herself.

The crowd began to edge forwards. Those with reserved seats were making for the big double doors on the ground floor, passing into the auditorium below the dedication to *The Quale Foundation* that was carved into the light oak lintel, the inscription cheapened somehow by the gold leaf. Shuffling forwards in the throng, Ginny looked up at the people climbing the stairs to the upper levels. They had no role in this strange pageant, and she envied them.

An arm waved like a hyperactive semaphore. It was attached to Mel, who was wearing a frizzy pink wig and looked like a stick of candy-floss. Lazlo had his arm around her shoulder, and was persuading her to keep moving on the stairs. Ginny grinned, and waved back. In response, Mel raised her hand in the air and began stabbing her finger back down the staircase. Ginny followed the finger and found Carmichael. He was gazing up at the pyramid of glass that crowned the atrium. In his smart charcoal jacket, with his prematurely grey hair and clean-cut features, no one would guess that he spent his days mingling with the city's low-life.

Inside the auditorium, the Quale Professor of Music, Hartley Wilcock, was at the console playing a medley of Scott Joplin rags. Below the sunburst of bronze organ pipes, occupying one of the six facets of the steeply-raked *Hexagon*, the University Choral Society sat ready, a multi-coloured trapezoid of pastel polo-necks. In the adjoining wedge of seats was the academic cohort. Near the top, among the assembled professors and spouses, was Charlie, hooded and gowned like the rest, still blathering. Bee sat beside him, mute and unsmiling. Below the Profs, the Deans of Faculties; below them, the four Pro Vice Chancellors and other academic big-wigs; below them, on a raised dais, the row of high-backed leather chairs that awaited the guests of honour.

Ginny took the reserved seat next to Jude just as a ripple of applause greeted the arrival of the great benefactor's widow. A student was pushing her wheelchair up the ramp to its place of honour beside the Vice Chancellor's throne. No stranger to applause, Mrs Quale waved a frail arm and beamed with delight. She had been a great beauty in her day, a Broadway diva who married into the wood-pulp dynasty that had funded the university library and several of the faculties that ate up the books their wood-pulp had produced.

The organ performed a quirky flourish to end the medley, and Professor Wilcock took his bow. An expectant hush fell over the hall. The great double doors were thrown open, and the Macebearer stood ready, with the Vice Chancellor's procession lined up behind him. Professor Wilcock raised both his palms towards the hexagonal lantern, and a quartet of brass instrumentalists rose to their feet.

Then, a snag: one of those delicious moments when pomp is punctured.

Old Professor Gurgieff had spotted someone he knew and scuttled across the processional aisle to say hello. He was now deep in conversation with a woman seven or eight rows up in the bank of audience, unaware that he was obstructing the Macebearer's path.

Hartley Wilcock waited to release his fanfare, arms outstretched, fingers and thumbs pinched together as though holding up a pair of grubby underpants. The audience cleared its collective throat, and someone sniggered.

Ginny gave Jude a nudge. "Don't you just love it when they cock it up?" she whispered.

But Jude was conducting a fevered search of her handbag, and Doc was leaning forwards, his elbows on his knees, hiding his face in his hands.

When a student usher arrived to explain the situation, old Prof Gurgieff went into a crouch as if seeking invisibility, and scurried across the well of *The Hexagon*. Hartley Wilcock's hands jerked skywards and the fanfare sounded. The Macebearer commenced his ponderous march and poor Professor Gurgieff, breathless and red in the face, climbed the steps beside Ginny to take his seat with the rest of the English Department somewhere behind her.

Togged out in a gown of black silk with borders of embroidered gold and sporting a mortar board gorgeously be-tasselled in yet more gold, the Vice Chancellor looked like a pantomime villain. At his side, in an unpretentious lounge suit, the American Ambassador smiled shyly, as though embarrassed that no one had given him a costume to wear. With his tricorne hat, and his furs and lace trimmings, with the mighty chain of office slung round his neck, the Lord Mayor had no such misgivings, nor did the procession that brought up the rear, a crocodile of studiously serious professors in full academic motley.

Watching the close-up coverage on one of the closed-circuit monitors that were suspended above the banks of audience, Ginny marvelled at Simon's confidence and calm, his head held high and his brow furrowed, as though his mind were already engaged in some lofty speculation.

With the fanfare dying in the echoes, the platform party performed a ritual doffing of caps and mortar boards. When everyone had bowed to everyone else, Joyce McPhee, one of the Pro Vice Chancellors, strode to the lectern and, in her clipped Edinburgh accent, got the evening off to a brisk start:

Fifty years of trans-Atlantic ties...blah, blah...honoured by the attendance of His Excellency the Ambassador...blah, blah...all thanks to the generosity of Herbert Quale... memorialised by this very building, by the scholarships that bear his name and, above all, by the great Quale Library, the very soul of this university...

The Vice Chancellor led a burst of sustained applause, and bent his head towards the Widow Quale, who now became the focus of everyone's attention. Professor McPhee thanked Mrs Quale for her continued support and generosity, and explained that, as an expression of everyone's affection, the choir had prepared a musical surprise.

With another upward sweep of his open palms, Hartley Wilcock brought the Choral Society to its feet and launched them on a spritely medley of the many show-stoppers that had featured in the old lady's Broadway career. Swaying in her wheelchair and singing-along with the youthful voices, the Widow Quale enjoyed herself mightily.

Then Joyce McPhee was back at the microphone, and the tone changed. She paid a fulsome tribute to the late, great Reuben Grossman of Colombia University, who, but for his untimely death, would have been at the podium to deliver this special, blue riband edition of the annual Herbert Quale Lecture...

Suddenly the television monitors were full of Simon in huge close-up, the new incumbent of the Herbert Quale Chair in English and American Literature, looking suitably modest as the Pro Vice Chancellor lavished praise, smiling politely as she made play with his earnest researches in the field of *Dirty Realism*, the subject of his lecture...

It was then, as the laughter resounded, that Ginny saw the woman's hand give its coded signal. She had her arms folded and the fingers of her hand moved no more than two inches from the sleeve of her coat, and yet, thanks to a conveniently placed TV screen, Ginny saw both the signal and its intended recipient. Simon's eyes widened. For an instant, his jaw sagged. Ginny turned to the platform and saw him squirm in his chair. Almost at once he recovered his poise, and looked back at the woman. His nod was barely perceptible, his smile a mere flicker. The woman seemed amused, and gave a tiny nod of her own. Then she looked away to the Pro Vice Chancellor. Message received and understood.

Ginny leaned close to Jude. "Who is that woman?" she whispered.

"Which woman?" whispered Jude.

"The woman old Prof Gurgieff was talking to?"

Jude shrugged and shook her head.

And Jude was lying.

Everyone began to clap. Ginny clapped too. So did the woman across the hall. She clapped more slowly than her neighbours and, before the applause had died away, clasped her hands together, shaking them in a gesture that spoke of triumph and affection.

Simon began to speak, his voice assured and well-modulated. He had grasped the top of the lectern with both hands in an assertion of authority, and he completely ignored his lecture notes. Ginny heard not a word he said. She could feel her cheeks burning like beacons, and felt marked out in the crowd.

The woman opposite was listening intently, drinking up Simon's words, an expression on her face that mixed admiration with pride of possession. She was not unattractive, but neither was she a beauty. Her hair was shoulder-length and well-cut, a startling silver-grey that was almost white. The coat was discreet and expensive. The silk scarf at her neck showed equally good taste...no doubt hiding some wear-and-tear. She was elegant, but past her prime...

Suddenly, everyone was clapping again. And so was Ginny.

"Wasn't he wonderful?" said a voice from the row behind.

A smile imposed itself on Ginny's face, and she turned her head to acknowledge the compliment. When she looked back, the seat across the hall was empty, and the expensive coat was disappearing through the doors at the top of the aisle.

Ginny got to her feet. There was no sign of Professor Gurgieff in the ranks of the English Department, and then she spotted him, near the top of the stairs, heading for an Exit. Turning her back on her husband's ovation, she hurried up the steps and pushed open one of the swing-doors. She was in a dimly lit corridor, and just in time to see a rectangle of bright light shrink to nothing as a door closed on its spring. It was the door to the Gents.

Not wishing to ambush the old gentleman when he emerged from the lavatory, Ginny went into the Ladies next door, and checked the cubicles to make sure she was alone. Holding the door open by a fraction of an inch, she put her eye to the crack and waited. Eventually, the old man appeared, but instead of shuffling past, he came to a halt, a mere two feet from her, polishing his spectacles on the end of his tie, humming to himself as he did so. Ginny held her breath until he moved away, then counted to five and opened the door.

"Is that Professor Gurgieff?" she called.

The old man stopped in his tracks.

"I'm sorry if I startled you," she said,

He was patting his heart with his right hand. "Good Lord!" he exclaimed, peering at her over the top of his glasses. "It's Simon's wife, isn't it? Why aren't you down there enjoying your husband's triumph?"

Ginny gave him an impish look. "I think we've been on the same mission, Professor."

Gurgieff chuckled, and grasped her by the wrist. "Well, I hope you managed to hold on until your husband had finished his most excellent lecture." The gnarled hand tightened its grip. "No better than I expected, of course...but very, very good. You must have been proud of him."

After Ginny had gushed on the subject of Simon's brilliance, she feigned an after-thought.

"By the way, Professor Gurgieff..." she began, "who was the woman you were talking to in the audience, when...?"

"When I obstructed the High Panjandrum, you mean?"

There was a mischievous gleam in the old man's eye.

"You stole the show, professor," she said, flirting a little, "...but who is that woman? The face is terribly familiar, but I can't quite place her..."

"Jane Kennedy!" said Gurgieff, announcing the name with relish, as though it evoked treasured memories. "She was one of

173

my very brightest stars when I was a young don at Cambridge...right up there with your husband, she was..." He leaned towards Ginny, and raised a forefinger. "Do you know, Mrs May, I think your Simon was more than a little sweet on young Jane back then..."

"Really?" said Ginny, agog. "You must tell me more..."

And old Professor Gurgieff proved more than happy to oblige.

In honour of the American Ambassador, Hartley Wilcock brought Quale Night to an end with an interminable, full-verse rendition of *The Stars and Stripes*, complete with an elaborate descant by the brass quartet.

Ginny waited for the music to die, pacing the corridor outside the Banqueting Suite, watching through the open door as the catering staff titivated the buffet and poured wine into glass goblets on rows of silver salvers. Two flunkeys marched to the far end of the room, and hauled open the double doors to the auditorium. On the far side of the hexagon, she saw the Macebearer bow his head to the Vice Chancellor and turn to face her. She heard the strident blast of the closing fanfare, and she saw her husband come down the steps with the rest of the platform party. Framed by two banks of audience, the procession approached with funereal solemnity, the silver mace glittering on the Macebearer's shoulder, shifting with every laboured footfall. They seemed to be on Time's treadmill, marching to nowhere, but then, by some quirk of space-time, the Macebearer was no more than two yards in front of her and his piggy-eyes were staring at her through round spectacles. A large hand, cuffed with frills of lace, took hold of the mace below its silver head, and the Macebearer presented his ceremonial burden to a waiting assistant.

Immediately, as if released from a spell, the procession disintegrated and all solemnity was cast aside. There was much laughter and shaking of hands and patting of backs. Trays of drinks arrived, and glasses were grabbed.

It would be a lie to say that Simon paled when he saw her. He was too high on glory to be shot down by a mere look. But something changed in that moment. A negative charge had passed, and in the brightness of his eyes she saw a flicker of apprehension.

The gowns and hoods parted as his colleagues ushered her through, presenting her to the hero of the hour like a garland of laurel. Ginny smiled, as was expected of her. She kissed him on the cheek, then drew him close and put her lips close to his ear.

"I want to hear all about Jane Kennedy," she whispered.

She felt him stiffen. Then his arm was around her, and he was steering her to a quiet corner of the room.

"I told her not to come..." he began, "You shouldn't have found out like this..."

Ginny ignored him. "Jane Kennedy's husband had the Chair at Leeds, didn't he? And then he died?"

Simon had screwed his eyes shut tight.

"And you were in Leeds the day I lost the baby, weren't you?"

Simon was massaging his brow with the fingertips of his left hand.

"We can't talk about this now," he pleaded.

Ginny eyed him coldly. "How thrilled you must have been when I lost the baby," she said.

Simon shook his head. "Not here," he murmured. "We can't talk about these things here."

Ginny let her eyes wander over the crowded room, watching the university feed its face. She looked back at her husband, in his red and black silks, and his stupid floppy cap. He had his eyes closed, as though praying to be spared. An eruption of loathing convulsed her, and she began to shake. Abruptly, she turned her back and ran, scything a path through the quack-quack-quack of the small-talk. In the atrium, she barged her way to the swing doors, and pushed out into the cold of the night, gulping the air, letting the rain lash her face and soak her new dress.

Chapter Twenty Five

She was wet through and shivering, hiding behind the trunk of an oak tree, listening to the cars hiss by as they left the car parks, wishing she had brought her mobile. A bedraggled return to *The Hexagon* was unthinkable, and, as far as she could remember, the nearest phone was at least four hundred, very dark yards away in the Students' Union.

"Are you there, Ginny?"

The voice startled her. It was distant, and unfamiliar.

"It's Tom..." called the voice, closer now, "Tom Carmichael."

Feeling foolish, Ginny put her hands on the rough bark and peeped around the side of the tree. He was carrying an umbrella, silhouetted against *The Hexagon*, which glowed like an outsized lantern behind him.

"I'm over here," she called, and stepped out into the open.

Carmichael swapped the umbrella from hand to hand as he approached, shrugging his way out of his raincoat. When he reached her, he draped the coat over her shoulders.

"I'm sorry to stalk you," he said, "but you looked distressed back there."

"I'm glad you did," said Ginny, letting him shepherd her towards the road. "This is not the best night of my life."

Carmichael said nothing, and they walked in silence to the car park where he had left his Mini Cooper. As he pulled out on to Erasmus, he turned the heater to maximum and switched on the fan. The tarmac was slick with rain and blotched orange with reflections from the neon street lights.

"Thank you for not asking," Ginny said.

Carmichael pointed towards the radio. "Would you like some music?"

"No thanks."

Ghostly trees passed by the window, then the immense bulk of the Science and Engineering blocks, blacker than the night and more ominous. In the darkness above, a cloud unburdened itself and the downpour hammered a deafening tattoo on the tinny roof. Glad that conversation was impossible, Ginny hugged Carmichael's raincoat around her and watched the raindrops dance a thousand furious hornpipes in the feeble beams of the headlights. It was not until they were driving below the canopy of the big copper beech, that the rainstorm began to lose its ferocity.

Carmichael stopped the Mini close to the path that led to the porch.

"I'm sorry I've been so hysterical," Ginny said.

Carmichael looked at her closely. "Are you going to be OK?"

Ginny nodded.

"You got my number?"

She nodded again.

"Don't be frightened to use it," he said.

Ginny opened the car door and looked out at the rain.

"Do you want my brolly?" offered Carmichael.

Ginny shook her head.

"You'd better run for it then," he said.

Simon did not keep her waiting long. No sooner had she dried her hair and slipped into her old blue-jeans than she heard his car on the gravel outside. She pulled the heavy-duty sweater over her head, and rolled up the frayed sleeves. As she went downstairs, she heard the key in the lock, and waited for him on the landing outside the sitting-room. She heard his footsteps on the tiled floor of the kitchen, and saw him start to climb the stairs. When he looked up and caught sight of her, he froze. He opened his mouth to speak, then closed it again, and began to bang the knuckles of his clenched fists together.

"Tonight was unforgiveable," he said eventually, still clapping his knuckles together. "It should never have happened."

Ginny looked away. She pushed open the sitting-room door and went inside. On impulse, she knelt down on the hearth rug in front of the fireplace and removed the fire-guard. She was scrunching up newspaper when he spoke, and she couldn't hear what he said. She spread the crumpled paper across the bed of wood-ash and opened the door of the little fireside cabinet in search of firelighters.

"I wanted to tell you," he said, "but you've been so beside yourself..."

The fragile cellophane was obstinately strong and when she finally ripped it apart, the stink of firelighter was intense. She broke off two white blocks from the slab, and was nestling them in the newspaper when he spoke again.

"I was frightened I'd push you over the edge. You'd been through so much already..."

Ginny reached into the log-basket and selected some small, split logs and piled them up on the slate hearth.

"I thought you might do something to harm yourself..." he said.

Ginny was building a cairn of wood around the white blocks, patiently shifting the logs until the edifice was stable, layer upon layer of wood that would tempt the flames to lick ever higher.

"I wish you'd say something..." he said.

There had been no calculation in her silence. But there was now. There was power in silence.

Leaning forwards to put the firelighters back in the cabinet, she found the matchbox and fumbled for a match. On the second attempt, with a whiff of brimstone, the match struck. She let the flame kiss the paper and watched it flare.

"I met her in Cambridge," he said, "on the first day of the first term. We weren't much more than kids..."

She heard him flop down in the armchair behind her. His story was a love-story, told with weary sadness, a story of young love...total, all-consuming passion...at least on his part...

The fire was failing. The flames had choked on their own smoke before they could enlist the help of the firelighters, leaving only a thin line of angry redness that was trying to nibble its way through the arts pages. Ginny picked up the bellows and fed the smouldering paper with a gentle breath of air.

"Guy was my best friend, and I hadn't the faintest idea what was going on..."

Ginny watched the yellow flame wrap itself around the firelighter and saw it prosper.

"I went home with glandular fever, and when I came back to college, they were already shacked up..." She heard a snort. "One boozy weekend—three lives wrecked!"

"Four!" said Ginny. "Don't forget me!"

She pumped savagely on the bellows until the logs began to spit and crackle, sending showers of sparks up the chimney. Then she put the bellows in the hearth, and watched as the fire recovered its composure.

"What happened in Leeds..." said Simon quietly, "it wasn't planned. It was one of those malicious twists of Fate..."

It was Ginny's turn to snort.

"When Guy died," Simon went on, "it was in the paper that Jane had gone to Vancouver...to be with their son. I thought she'd emigrated. Then suddenly, she turns up at the Leeds conference..."

"And suddenly she's in your bed," added Ginny, with a curious little laugh. "Quite the merry widow!"

Simon said nothing.

For a while Ginny prodded the logs with the poker, encouraging the fire to spread.

"Was she with you that morning...?" she asked, "the morning I phoned you about the baby?"

His silence was enough, but she wanted to hear the words.

"I think you owe me the truth, Simon, don't you?"

"Yes," he murmured.

"Yes, you owe me the truth? Or yes, she was in bed with me?"

"She was with me..." he said, the words escaping his mouth like unwanted tin-tacks.

Ginny nodded her head for a moment or two. "Just out of interest," she said, "what would you have done if I hadn't lost the baby?"

"I don't know," he whispered. "I really don't know."

She heard him get to his feet. She could feel his presence behind her, and she sensed that he was reaching forward to touch her shoulder.

"Do not touch me," she instructed. "Just leave, Simon."

She heard his breathing, ragged and uneven; heard the creak of a floorboard muffled by carpet; heard his hand rattle the loose doorknob.

"I know this sounds empty," he said, "but you don't deserve this, Ginny...you've done nothing but be..."

Ginny slapped her hands against her ears.

"Just go, Simon!" she shouted. "Please go..."

For a long while, she listened to the blood sing in her head. When she was convinced that he would be gone, she pulled her hands down over her cheeks, deforming her face, pinching her nose until the hands met in front of her mouth, palm to palm, finger to finger, like the children saying their prayers at school. And the reek of firelighter summoned up another odour that had lingered too long, the day their baby stained the toilet floor.

179

Chapter Twenty Six

When she pummelled the pillow or shook out the duvet, when she picked up the used tissues and dropped them in the bin, there was no tinnitus. It was strange. Whenever she stopped to listen, it whined softly in her ear, but whenever she moved it hid in the hum of the humdrum. She drew back the curtains, and it was gone again.

Nothing had changed. The world was just the same; everything in its appointed place. Even the face in the mirror was the same face, the eyes a little red, the skin a little sallow. But that was only to be expected. She had done her crying in the night.

The makeup she had used to play the loyal wife was where she had left it, arrayed beside the hand-basin in the bathroom. Once again she applied the potions and disguised her face for the watching world.

"Get a life!" she said, speaking out loud. She pulled a face at herself.

The cliché stank, but the advice was good. She angled her face, first one way, and then the other. With the tips of her fingers she tapped the soft, puffy crescents below the eyes.

"No more tears!" she instructed.

It had been years since she talked to the mirror. When she was growing up at Gran's she was always confiding in the mirror, whispering her dreams, rehearsing new personas and new voices, playing out the conflicts to come.

"Be strong, Virginia!" she advised. Then she leaned forwards until she was almost touching her reflection. "Make a new life," she whispered, and breathed hard on the mirror until her face began to vanish in the mist.

The new clay was unresponsive and cold to the touch. As Takashi had taught her, Ginny worked it hard, forming an ovoid rather like a rugby ball, then turning it on the tabletop in a rolling motion, pressing down with one hand as she twisted, producing shell-like ribs from the centre, the sixteen-petal chrysanthemum, the *kikuneri*, imperial device of the Japanese Emperor.

The tap, tap, tapping on the conservatory glass could well have been going on for some time. When awareness finally dawned, Ginny stopped kneading, and listened. The tapping stopped and a muffled voice called out her name. She swivelled her head and looked over her shoulder. It was Jude, fat as a whale, her flabby arms raised against the French doors, her moon face framed in a pane of glass.

Ginny wiped her hands on her smock, got up from the stool and went to the door. She turned the key and reached above her head to free the upper bolt, then struggled with the bolt at her feet. She greeted her visitor with a frosty stare.

"Are you alright?" asked Jude.

"Fine," said Ginny.

"Simon asked me to pop round and make sure you were ok."

"How kind!"

"Can I come in?"

"I told you, I'm fine."

"Please, Ginny..."

This was no errand of mercy. Jude wanted forgiveness.

"I suppose you'd better get it off your chest then, hadn't you?" Ginny said, and turned her back. "I've got pots to make, but say what you've got to say. I'm all ears!"

Ginny flipped the chrysanthemum and squashed its petals against the work surface, taking pleasure in its destruction.

Jude drew up a bentwood chair and sat on the opposite side of the table. "We didn't find out until we got back from *Glebelands*. Charlie let something slip at dinner, and it all tumbled out."

Working methodically and calmly, Ginny rolled the clay on the table and shaped it until the rugby ball had returned.

"Simon was terrified you might do something silly if you found out...We all were..." Jude gave a heavy sigh, and added, "I really thought he was over that wretched woman..."

Ginny's hands hesitated.

"When you came back from the States, you seemed a different couple..."

Ginny began to wedge the clay, twisting and pressing down with the heel of her right hand until the shell-spiral began to reappear.

"You were like a couple of kids on honeymoon. At that welcome-home-party, you couldn't take your eyes off each other...It was a miracle, considering the state of things before you left."

Ginny stopped wedging, and looked up. "And what exactly had been going on before we went to America?" she asked.

The flesh on Jude's face sagged.

"He hasn't told you, has he?" she said quietly.

"Told me what?"

Jude closed her eyes. "He said you knew everything..."

"Well, it's obvious there's a whole lot I don't know," said Ginny, "so I think you'd better tell me, Jude. You're supposed to be my friend."

Jude put her elbows on the modelling table and was holding her head in her hands.

"They'd had a thing at college..." she said.

With the flat of her hand, Ginny slapped the burgeoning chrysanthemum. "I know that," she hissed. "They were lovebirds at Cambridge, but it didn't end there, did it?"

Jude licked her lips. "I don't think it's for me to tell you all this..."

"By the sound of things," said Ginny, "you should have told me years ago."

While she digested this thought, Jude looked up at the sky through the tresses of vine and spread her hands on the table. When she finally lowered her eyes, they had a steely look.

"Ok, I'll tell you," she said. "I don't have all the sordid details, but I'll tell you what I know. They met up again...at a conference, I think...and it all kicked off again..."

"When?" asked Ginny.

Jude shook her head. "Don't know. But they were seeing one another for several years, I think...Off and on...Until the husband found out."

"And when was that?"

"Four years ago..."

"Just before we went to the States?"

Jude nodded.

"When Simon had his breakdown?"

Jude winced, and nodded again.

Ginny faked a chuckle. "And I thought he'd gone to pieces because he'd missed out on his Chair..."

"Kennedy was a bad man to cross," said Jude. "He knew exactly how to poison Simon's well."

Ginny found a bitter smile. "Poor Simon..." she purred, "kisses goodbye to his career and his lady-love all at the same time. No wonder he went to bits..."

Jude drew breath to speak, but Ginny had not finished.

"...And then I get dragged off to America to nurse him better. That was your doing, wasn't it, Jude? You and Charlie fixed that exchange?"

"It was a chance for you both to start again...And it worked!" There was a note of defiance in Jude's tone. "I'm not ashamed of that."

"But you let me to live a lie, didn't you?" murmured Ginny.

Jude was unrepentant. "What would you have done in my shoes? Spilled the beans and torpedoed the marriage?" She gave a vigorous shake of her head. "I don't think so. Do you?"

Ginny stared at her. Jude Holroyd had off-loaded her guilty secret. All the chutzpah was back. She had absolved herself.

"Thank you for coming, Jude," she said. "But I'd like you to go now."

Lying flat on the bed, she stared up at the blank expanse of ceiling. Anger was creeping up on her, like the incoming tide over sand-flats, steadily, ripple by ripple.

She was back in Santa Barbara. She had spent the morning with Takashi learning the rudiments of glazing, and now she was in *The Earthlings* bookshop, on a sofa, reading one of the books, putting off the dread moment when she would have to return to the house, with its oppressive silence and its air of hopelessness. A student was playing *Albeniz* on the guitar. She listened to a few bars, finished her coffee, and leaned forward to put the mug on the table. When she looked up, there he was, climbing the stairs, a hollow-eyed wreck with a tangle of unkempt beard—Simon, emerging from a dungeon of his own making.

She had taken him home, and he had wept, and he had said how sorry he was for the wasted months. And they had made love. They had made a lot of love in those remaining Californian days. That's when the Baby came into their lives. Simon had been desperate for the Baby then. The Baby had been his obsession then...not hers...

B-ring, b-ring; b-ring, b-ring; b-ring, b-ring...

Downstairs in the hall, the telephone rang out its old-fashioned ring, on and on, echoing through the house. Ginny ignored it. Eventually the ringing stopped. After a brief silence, her mobile squawked in her smock-pocket, which was no surprise. She flipped the phone open, checked the display and closed it again, feeling it tremble in her hands as the tinny ring-tone persisted.

When Simon had finally despaired of an answer, she put the mobile back in her pocket and swung her legs over the side of the bed. She went to the wardrobe, slid open the door and began to remove his clothes, the shirts first, still on their hangers, draping them over the crook of her arm until she could carry no more. Stooping down, she pinched a pair of expensive brogues between the fingers and thumb of her free hand, and headed for the Nursery, where she threw her burden on the single bed, and returned to the bedroom for a second load. When his wardrobe was empty, she began work on his chest of drawers, and when that was empty, she tipped the contents of his bedside cabinet into a wastepaper basket. It was an exercise in de-contamination.

She had often joked that Simon owned more clothes than she did. And it was true. Sitting down on the bentwood chair, she marvelled at the mountain of clobber that was piled up on the spare bed. It occurred to her that she could enjoy several happy hours with a pair of sharp scissors cutting it all to ribbons. But an altogether more imaginative scheme was already recommending itself...

How splendid a Monday morning it would be if the University awoke to find that the grounds of the English Department had been festooned with all their newly-anointed professor's clothes—his knickers and socks, his shirts and pants, his suits and shoes, his football kit, every last handkerchief and necktie, all bestrewn around the grassy knoll, like the aftermath of an air crash. And it would be easy. The campus was as quiet as the grave on a Sunday night.

The mobile rang again. This time, Ginny did not consult the display.

"Yes?" she barked.

"It's me," said an unknown voice.

"Who is that?" asked Ginny, still sharp as a knife.

"It's Whizz."

Ginny sat forward in the chair. "I'm sorry, Whizz," she said. "It's not your usual time. What's wrong?"

"I'm in hospital…"

"Why? What's the matter?"

"I'm having an X-ray, that's all."

"What's happened now?"

"I fell off a ladder."

Ginny massaged her forehead with her spare hand. "You're finding too much trouble, Whizz."

"I can handle it…"

A walking-boot chose the moment to slither from the top of the clothes-mountain, and landed with a heavy thud on the carpet.

"I think you need more help than you realise," she said.

"Bollocks."

Ginny leaned back in the chair, and swapped the phone to her other hand. "Have you thought about what you're going to do when you get out?"

"That's months away…"

"Six weeks, if you keep out of trouble…"

"Six weeks, then…" he said. "I'm no trouble."

Ginny moistened her lips. "Would you consider coming here to live?"

There was a derisive snort. "Professor Wanker Bollocks would really like that, wouldn't he?"

"The Professor doesn't live here anymore," she said.

The line went quiet.

"There will be conditions," she added.

"Like what?"

"I haven't thought them through. I'll tell you next Wednesday…

More silence.

"So? What do you think?" Ginny asked.

"I'll tell you on Wednesday," said Whizz, and hung up.

Everything she had once loved about the house was loathsome now—the wallpaper, the carpets, the curtains; every book, every picture, every stick of furniture. And yet, when she ran her fingers across the wood grain of the kitchen table, tracing the ring-stains of dead wine bottles…or when the sun glinted on the cracked glazes of the little tea-bowl they had brought back from Japan…the place was precious again, infinitely so. Several times she came close to tears, but she refused to cry. Anger steadied her.

When she was cramming the Saab with his clothes, it was pure joy. When she was throwing his books into the wheelbarrow and tipping them onto the pile in the dying orchard, picturing his shock and horror, she did the sweaty work with grim satisfaction, load after wheelbarrow-load. When she found that the petrol-can in the lean-to was empty, she was furious. If Bee hadn't made an appearance, she would have driven straight to the garage and filled it up. But Bee had appeared; Bee in a lather of sympathetic hysteria mixed with guilt and self-recrimination; Bee in the wrong place, at the wrong time, a lightning rod for yet another thrilling bolt of rage.

"Stop snivelling, Bee! I am sick of your snivelling! Be honest, Bee! Your Charlie is an egotistical shit out of the same mould as my egotistical shit. Why don't you leave him, or at least find something to do with your life that isn't running around after the self-centred bastard? Go back to your career. Get a job in a charity shop. Do something. Do any bloody thing, but please don't come round here weeping. I've had enough."

Chapter Twenty Seven

Ginny would have paid good money to see the stir that her midnight escapade had caused on campus. At lunchtime on Monday, while doing playground duty, the temptation to ring Mel for an eye-witness account proved stronger than the Head's strict rule about the use of mobiles, and she made the call, hiding herself from any prying eyes in the staffroom. She was not disappointed.

"Everyone stood around gawping..." Mel said, "upwards of twenty people, students and staff, all at a loss until Bryant showed up and waxed all pompous. Then the poor secretaries were dragged out to play washerwomen. It took them ages..."

A shrill dispute over a skipping-rope flared up in the playground.

"Hang on," cried Ginny, and went to separate the warring parties. "Sorry about that," she said, looping the confiscated rope over the wall beside her.

"Sounds like a war-zone?" said Mel.

"It is," said Ginny. "But what about Simon..? I don't suppose you...? "

"Bull's Eye!" said Mel. "To be honest, I felt quite sorry for him...What on earth's been going on between you two?"

Keeping a watchful eye on the playground, Ginny supplied an abbreviated account of her troubles in terse, unemotional language.

"My God, that's awful!" Mel exclaimed. "Do you want to come and stay for a few days?"

"That's kind," replied Ginny, "but I've got things to do...Can you get me a couple of tickets for *The Follies*?"

"You're kidding!"

"No, I'm not," said Ginny firmly. "I'll ask Carmichael if he'll take me...No way am I hiding myself away to spare that bastard."

It was a moment before Mel spoke again. "After what's happened, I'm not sure I want to be up on stage acting the fool, not with..."

"Don't you dare pull out, Mel!"

A wayward football whacked Jason Nolan between the shoulder-blades.

"Hang on..." said Ginny, "more trouble..."

Instead of running to clutch her skirt, Jason scampered after the ball and made a clumsy attempt to boot it back. It looked as though Daddy's death had enlivened him no end.

Ginny put the phone back to her ear. "False alarm," she said.

"Are you two going to try and patch things up?" asked Mel doubtfully.

The bell for the end of lunch went off like an old-time fire-engine.

"No way!" shouted Ginny, pitching her voice against the din. "They call it 'Irretrievable Breakdown', and that's what it is. Kaput! Finished! I'm seeing my solicitor at four o'clock...."

Joe Bradley leaned back in his swivel chair and stroked his droopy moustache, giving an occasional shake to his shaggy head. To keep her voice steady, Ginny was larding her tale with heavy irony and she was in danger of sounding flippant.

"She's not some young thing with tits and teeth, Joe. She's an old bag he knew at Cambridge a hundred years ago... I've been swapped for an older model, Joe. How's that for a new twist?"

Joe reached for a notepad and began to scribble.

"I wish I could help you," he said, "but I wouldn't know how to find the divorce courts if I needed one myself." He consulted a small box-file on the desk, and wrote down a telephone number. "It's a shame, because I'd enjoy a few rounds with your old man." He unpeeled the note from the pad and passed it across the leather skiver. "This guy will fight your corner, and he won't rob you blind. Mention my name, if you like."

"You've helped already, just by listening...and to be honest, Joe, I didn't come here looking for a divorce lawyer."

While the lawyer listened impassively, grooming his moustache, Ginny explained her plans for Whizz when he was released from Fulford. Bradley's response was rather less than enthusiastic.

"I admire your guts," he said, "but you're crackers. That kid's more trouble than a bag of snakes." He stabbed a finger in her direction. "You are in no fit state to play Mother Theresa. Don't be a dumb-ass!"

Ginny marshalled her arguments while the lawyer leaned back in his chair, thumbs hooked under his red braces, eyeing her with frank scepticism. When she had finished, he put his hands on the desk and leaned forwards.

"It ain't going to happen," he pronounced. "The kid will need his Probation Officer's say-so, and he won't get it. No way!"

"Why not?"

"Well, apart from the fact that you are an attractive woman, living alone, and he is a convicted felon well past puberty, they'll be looking to get the little sod back into education or get him a job..."

"I'm a teacher," Ginny protested, "and, as it happens, I'm the only person that he'll take teaching from. As far as a job goes— our garden's in a mess, and there's a whole orchard that needs grubbing out. There'll be no shortage of work for the lad, that's for sure...and I'll be paying him."

"But you're not going to have a man about the house, are you?" said Joe, giving her a challenging stare.

Ginny glared back defiantly, but she had no reply.

Abruptly, the lawyer got out of his chair and strode to the door behind Ginny's chair.

"We're dying of thirst in here, Vanessa," he shouted. "Have you been to China for that tea, or what?"

An exasperated voice shouted something about 'having to go out for biscuits'.

Bradley closed the door behind him.

"That's me in the dog-house," he said, and crouched down beside Ginny's chair. Putting an arm around her shoulder, he smothered her hands with his own bear-like paw. "Now come on, Ginny," he coaxed, "there are plenty of ways you can help that undeserving little shit, without putting yourself at risk. You've got to be sensible. You've just had an earthquake in your life...deal with that...it's enough..."

Tears were welling-up, and the more of the fatherly wisdom that Joe Bradley dispensed, the closer Ginny came to letting them go.

The knock on the door rescued her.

"Thank you, nurse," said Bradley, taking the tea-tray from the toothy secretary.

"Sorry to keep you waiting, O Lord and Master," said Vanessa icily.

Bradley poured the tea and offered the plate of biscuits. Then he surprised Ginny by reaching for the squeeze-box that was hanging by its strap on a wooden coat stand. Leaning back in his chair, he swung his cowboy boots up on the desk and began to pick out some wheezy Cajun melodies while he dispensed more cracker-barrel wisdom in the style an English *Atticus Finch*. It was an eccentric performance, calculated to calm and amuse her. And it succeeded.

By the time she was back behind the steering wheel, Ginny had accepted an invitation to partake of Molly Bradley's 'legendary gumbo' and had 'volunteered' to be an unpaid roadie for *The Swamp Rats*' next gig in the city. She was also less frantic, and more focused. Thanks to Joe's clear analysis of the problem, she knew precisely what to do about Whizz Buckley. But she must tell no one else. It would be their secret... and they would conspire together to bring their plans to fruition. In this, she would not be thwarted.

She drove home as fast as the traffic would allow. The day was beginning to look uncertain, and she was anxious to beat the rainclouds that were massing out to sea. It was a race that she almost lost. The first drops of rain were already spattering down as she began to load the wheelbarrow with the last of the books. There had been casualties – the odd spine broken, some pages creased or torn, and one or two hard covers had detached themselves from their texts. Fortunately, the damage was not apparent when the shelves were full again. She had been unable to remember exactly where each volume had its rightful place in Simon's meticulous shelving policy, but then, as long as the Probation Officer could smell an academic in the house, she could not care less.

She poured herself a glass of Merlot and sat in her armchair by the unlit fire. After taking a sip, she put the glass on the coffee table, and picked up her mobile.

Simon was quick to answer. "Ginny...are you alright?"

"I've been better."

Simon gushed out his remorse. Ginny cut him off.

"The stunt at the university was uncivilised," she said. "I'm sorry."

"It's the least I deserve..."

"I want to ask a favour," she cut in.

"Anything..." he said.

"When I've got my head round what has happened," she began, "I will sell up and move away from this place. But right this moment, I can't bear the idea of change. I'd like everything left just as it is...pictures, books, furniture... I need some sense of permanence in my life..."

"Of course you do..." he said.

"Except for the piano," she said. "The piano upsets me..."

"I'll get it shifted..." he said.

The climb up the rickety loft-ladder was a mistake. She had never visited the attic at the back of the house, and there were ghosts waiting.

The discarded junk was harmless enough—posters that had cheered up the walls before they could afford paintings; the hideous table-lamp they'd once thought chic; the figurine that only saw daylight when Simon's aunt came visiting; that vase...

But the cardboard boxes stacked below the eaves were too pristine to have been consigned as junk. They were a mystery. She tipped one of the flat boxes onto its side, surprised by its weight. She looked at the label, and immediately let the box fall back. It was the baby's cot, flat packed, awaiting assembly. They had bought it with the high-chair and the carry-cot the first time the clinic had good news.

Ginny wiped her hands on her thighs, and turned away. Moving quickly, she threw open the lid of the trunk that Gran had helped her pack when she left for university. It was crammed with more detritus from their marriage. Simon's fedora was on top of the pile, crushed flat, but serviceable. The trench coat and the Norfolk jacket that Simon had forbidden her to dump were hiding below old curtains and tablecloths. She punched up the crown of the hat and put it on her head to free her hands, then snatched up the two coats and dropped them through the open trapdoor.

In the hallway, she hung the coats on the pegs next to her raincoat and the hat she wore for winter walks. After pressing out the dents in the felt, she placed the fedora on the peg above the trench coat, and stood back to admire her composition. It was a 'his and hers' arrangement that made a perfect marriage.

Chapter Twenty Eight

From the moment he set foot in the Visiting Room, Whizz was at his most truculent. He blanked her when she asked about the hospital; curled his lip when she told him her plans for the summer; sneered about the job she was offering him. Now he was examining the nails on his left hand looking for something to chew.

Ginny exhaled noisily. "I am trying to help you, Will..." she said, wearily.

"My name is Whizz," he said, and went to work on his thumbnail.

"Sorry..." said Ginny, "I am trying to help you...Whizz."

He eyed her scornfully. "Am I supposed to get excited about doing a bit of gardening?"

Ginny rubbed her forehead. "Well, it might not be a major career-move, but I bet your Probation Officer will be amazed that you've got any kind of a job at all."

The kicking may have cracked a rib or two, but it hadn't kicked out the cussedness. Physically though, he was looking better than she had expected. There was a healthy sheen on his skin as though he'd been out in the sun, and the new-grown fuzz of hair was a great improvement.

"Where's your old man gone?" he asked.

The question took Ginny aback. After a pause, she said, "He's found somebody else."

"Are you glad he's gone?"

She frowned, and screwed her eyes shut. It was a strange question, but worth thinking about.

"Yes, I am..." she said, hearing a note of surprise in her voice. "I'm really glad he's gone. I haven't admitted that before, but it's true."

"Why are you crying then?"

Ginny pressed her fingertips to the corners of her eyes. They were wet, and they should not have been. Inside she was not tearful, if anything she was in a giddy state close to euphoria. It was like one of those paradoxical days when the rain tips down and the sun keeps on shining.

"I don't know why I'm crying," she said, and smiled.

Whizz was not smiling. He did not believe her.

Ginny bowed her head, and asked herself the question again.

"I'm crying because I feel useless," she said. "I'm trying to be brave and not show it, but inside I feel useless. I've been wasting my life in a marriage that was a sham...and I can't even have a baby. How useless can you get?"

She put her fingertips over her eyelids, and pulled them roughly towards her temples, wiping away the tears and feeling the soft skin stretch. When she opened her eyes, the boy was scanning the family groups on their green and blue islands.

"You're going to mess with my head, aren't you?" he said.

Ginny sniffed, and wiped her nose on the back of her hand. "No, I'm not," she said, "but you will have to come clean about the things that bug you. That won't be easy."

He looked into her eyes. "No shrinks," he said, "I don't want shrinks poking around in my head."

"No shrinks," agreed Ginny. "It'll be just the two of us...playing the Truth Game...secret for secret." She attempted a smile. "I've already made a good start, don't you think?"

"How much are you going to pay me then?" he asked.

"Minimum wage," replied Ginny. "I can't afford any more."

"What about rent?" he asked.

"Don't be silly," said Ginny. "There is no rent."

For a while they squabbled. Whizz wanted to pay rent; Ginny said no. It was a silly haggle, but Whizz insisted. In the end, they did a deal, and shook hands across the table that divided them.

Ginny had enjoyed the sparring. She liked his playfulness, and she liked his sense of fairness. It augured well. Even the cussed streak was hard to hate.

"You'd better tell your Probation Officer about the gardening job and the wages you're going to get...and the rent you're going to pay. And you'd better tell him what a great teacher I am, and how you're going to make a start on your GSCEs..."

"Am I bollocks," said Whizz.

Ginny laughed and leaned back against the backrest of the sofa, crossing her legs at the ankles and folding her arms across her chest.

"I wouldn't say anything about my split with Simon though..."

There was a beat of silence. "Why's that then?" he asked.

"Well..." Ginny began, "they might think it's a bit odd...you and me sharing a house when there's no bloke about the place."

Whizz leaned back against the blue upholstery and hooked his thumbs into the pockets of his prison trousers. After a moment's thought he gave a little snort, then cocked his head to one side and eyed her with gleeful admiration.

"We'd better pretend he's still about then...hadn't we?" he said.

Chapter Twenty Nine

Mel's instincts had been sound. The grand gesture at *The Follies* was pure bravado, and she should never have gone through with it.

She had enjoyed the frisson when she made her appearance in the foyer with Carmichael on her arm. But the moment the curtains parted to reveal Simon at the honky-tonk, dressed up in his silly, striped blazer and his straw boater, somebody at the back of the hall gave a loud hiss. It was a hiss that Simon probably didn't hear, but it triggered in Ginny an upsurge of emotion that engulfed her.

To run out of the theatre was embarrassing enough, but to sit sobbing in Carmichael's mini outside the house, for the second time in as many weeks, was too much. The thought of that expensive bottle of Sancerre in the fridge, and the clean sheets that she had carefully spread on the big double bed, made her face burn.

"Don't be so bloody daft," said Mel, when she phoned the next day. "Sherlock's been through a divorce himself. He's a big boy, Ginny. Get yourself down to *The Cat* this evening and we'll have a good laugh about it. Lazlo and I have got things to celebrate. And bring a bag. You're going to spend the weekend with us."

Lazlo watched fondly as his partner's bottom bobbed its way to the bar in an outrageous ra-ra skirt.

"Every day is a celebration for Mel," he said admiringly. "Today she's celebrating the Arts Council's miserly contribution to the new play. Tomorrow she'll find something else to celebrate...the rain...the sunshine...could be anything."

"How lovely to wake up to happy surprises," said Ginny, but then pulled back from the brink of self-pity, asking brightly, "So what's the new play, Lazlo?"

"It's our play," he replied, "the one what we wrote, Mel and me. It's the play we're taking to Edinburgh in two months time—the play that's going to make my fortune. Goodbye *Shacks Theatre Company*! Hello Big Time! Ha! Ha! Ha!"

Surprised, Ginny said, "Are you really giving up *The Shacks*?"

Lazlo gave a nod, and grimaced. "I'm going to miss it like hell," he said, "but they've cut the soul out of community theatre. One more *Summer Spectacular* with the local Am-drams, and I'm off!"

"Is Mel going with you?" asked Ginny, suddenly anxious.

"Not for the full bumpy ride," said Lazlo. "When I turn up skint with my tail between my legs, which probably won't be that long, we'll both have to live on Mel's ill-gottens at the Uni. That's the plan, anyway."

After two glasses of spritzer and a graphic account of Mel's on-stage love affair with an out-sized stick of rock, Ginny was managing to laugh at yesterday's indignities, exactly as Mel had promised. Even so, when Carmichael showed up at the table, she felt the colour rise to her face. The policeman appeared not to notice.

"Right then, you lot?" he cried, rubbing his hands together. "I've just passed the exams for DI...so I'm in the chair. What are you all having?"

No one needed a second invitation, and, while Carmichael took himself off to the bar with a long order, Lazlo commandeered more tables and chairs to accommodate the growing party of regulars who had sniffed free drink. Ginny swigged back her spritzer and was swept along on the festive tide.

From behind her back, a hand lowered a piece of paper directly in front of her eyes.

"Everything's gone, darling," explained Albert's falsetto, "...except for that ghastly ewer-thing."

Ginny took the cheque from his hand, and gaped at it. It was for a hundred and fifty pounds.

Albert wagged a finger. "You're a naughty girl though. You still haven't been in touch with old Ma Carfax..."

"Oh, yes I have," said Ginny, triumphantly. "I phoned her this afternoon and I'm seeing her tomorrow. I need the money, Albert, I really do." And then she was on her feet, planting a fruity kiss on the gallery owner's lips, causing Victor to run for cover at the bar in case he was next.

Ginny sat down and looked again at the cheque, then folded it carefully and zipped it away in her bag. Everything was coming good. Whizz might even get his wages without making a hole in her savings.

Mel began clapping her hands to bring the rowdy gathering to order. "Ladies and gentlemen..." she cried, pausing as though about to make a speech, then turning rapidly to her partner and extending her hand. "Lazlo would like to say a few words..."

Lazlo took the pint glass from his mouth and his head slumped forwards until his chin touched his chest. Cries of 'Speech...speech!' and some table-thumping brought him reluctantly to his feet.

"Thank you, my treasure, for that kind introduction," he began, and assumed an ostentatiously oratorical pose. "Friends and fellow Cat-lovers, I would like you all to raise your glasses to our own master-sleuth...to that scourge of the criminal classes...our bulwark against the tides of anarchy...that direct descendant of the incomparable Mr Sherlock Holmes...the one and only, Detective Inspector Carmichael."

"No, no, no," protested Carmichael, holding up a hand. "It's only the exams. Don't jinx me, for God's sake. I've got to go back to Police College to 'widen my skills-base'. They could still blow me out."

Nobody was listening. By the end of the evening DS Carmichael had been promoted to Chief Constable, and a huge *meze* had been consumed in a remarkably tolerant Lebanese restaurant, together with countless bottles of red wine. Mel had performed another filthy monologue, and Ginny had danced like a dervish to the intoxicating rhythms of a wild *bouzouki*. Then she passed out.

A hand touched her bare shoulder, and shook her gently.

"There's coffee on the table," said a man's voice.

Ginny flinched. She had no idea where she was.

"It's black, no sugar. But there's a sugar bowl if you want some."

Slowly, she opened her eyes, just a fraction, squinting against the pain of the headache.

"My God, what's that?" she cried, and sat up, covering her nakedness with the duvet.

A huge crocodile was rearing up from behind an armchair in the bay window.

"That's *Tick-Tock*," said the man's voice, "he's the star of our *Peter Pan*...."

Ginny hugged the duvet tighter to her chest, grimacing as the curtains twitched and a dagger of sunshine attacked her eyes. She seemed to be on a sofa in the middle of what could have been a junk shop.

Lazlo was standing beside the crocodile, tickling its tummy with a finger. "Don't tell Sherlock," he said, "but Mel steals any of the props that take her fancy. The house is stuffed with them."

"Is that really the time?" asked Ginny, pointing to the old-fashioned alarm clock that was wedged in *Tick-Tock*'s open jaws.

"That's right," said Lazlo, "you've slept half the day away."

"Oh, Christ," Ginny groaned, "I'm going to be late..."

Chapter Thirty

Ginny switched off the engine and opened her window. The entire queue of traffic had despaired of movement, and the street was unnaturally quiet. Picking up the swatch of material from the passenger seat, she draped it over the steering-wheel and, for the umpteenth time, contemplated the drab colours. Late for the old lady and devoid of a single creative idea, she began to panic. If she was to blow this commission, the summer she had schemed so hard for would make a big hole in her bank balance. With divorce looming, the road ahead looked rocky enough without money-worries on top. Taking advantage of her pessimistic mood the hangover tightened its clamp on her brain, causing the blood to throb her temples and her eyes to ache.

Ten minutes later, still with no flash of inspiration, she had made stuttering progress but was held up by yet more road works on the Esplanade. Leaning over the passenger seat to look past the van in front, she could see her destination a few tantalising yards beyond the temporary traffic light which seemed to spend most of its life at red.

Cranbrook Square was not strictly a square at all because the terraces of handsome Regency houses occupied only three sides. On the south, it was open to the Esplanade and, beyond that, to the ocean. In its heyday, it had been a fashionable address, but that was long ago.

Tail-gating dangerously, Ginny followed the van through the red light, swung the Saab into the Square and began a desperate search for what turned out to be the one and only parking space. After feeding the meter, she checked the number of the nearest house and realised with sickening clarity that her patroness lived on the opposite side of the Square. In search of a short-cut, she explored the gate to the jungle that had once been a communal garden, but was denied by a rusty padlock and chain, and set off at a half-run, causing her hangover to protest...and causing some mirth in the multi-ethnic crowd of youngsters who were taking a cigarette break outside the *Express English* language school.

In a terrace of houses that had been colonised by solicitors and accountants, the Carfax house stood out from its neighbours as brightly as the highly polished brass-work on the lacquered blackness of its front door. It was pristine. The antique bell-pull moved with silky smoothness, and a well-tuned bell chimed musically inside the house. Ginny steadied her breathing, half-expecting a butler to open the door, but was surprised by a cheerful young woman in jeans and kaftan.

"Hi," she said, "I am Martina. Mrs Carfax think she gonna miss you…"

Ginny launched into her apology, but was interrupted by a distant voice inside the house.

"Come in, my dear, come in…"

Ginny stepped into the porch and peered up the impressive staircase. An elderly woman was riding side-saddle on a stair-lift, gliding slowly down towards the chequered tiling of the hall, her walking-stick held aloft like a sabre.

"Tally-ho!" she cried. "I'm afraid I'm going to have to scoot, Mrs May. I'm going to the Dogs with the lads from The King's Head."

"I'm terribly sorry to be so late, Mrs Carfax…" began Ginny.

"Oh, don't you worry your pretty head," said the old lady, leaning on her stick for leverage as she got to her feet. "You will be in Martina's very capable hands."

Mrs Carfax hobbled across the tiles and clasped Ginny's wrist in a firm grip. "I'd almost given up on you, my dear," she said, lowering her head in order to peer over her spectacles into Ginny's eyes. "But I'm glad you've come because I really love your pots. They've got mischief in 'em, and I like a bit of mischief very much."

Outside in the road, someone beeped a car-horn.

"That'll be Terry," said Mrs Carfax. "Wish me luck."

Martina offered the old lady her arm and, with the help of the burly man who was waiting on the doorstep, eased her down the stone steps to the minibus that was double-parked in the road outside. From inside the coach, a loud cheer greeted Mrs Carfax as she was pulled and pushed aboard.

"I hope she win," said Martina, skipping up the steps to rejoin Ginny under the portico. "She give me twenty quids one time."

The bus tooted and began its journey, and the two women waved until it turned the corner on to the Esplanade. Ginny followed the girl back into the house and they began to climb the grand staircase.

It was then, as her eyes travelled across the myriad watercolours hanging on the wall of the stairwell that something stirred in her memory. She looked closely at one of the landscapes. The quality of the painting was familiar, a touch old fashioned perhaps, maybe a little sentimental, but there was something magical in its other-worldliness...

And then she knew.

"Does Mrs Carfax write books for children?" she asked.

Martina turned round on the landing. "Oh, yes," she said, her face alight with pride and pleasure. "Mrs Carfax is a very famous writer..."

"Called 'Dulcie Davenport'?" added Ginny.

"Yes," confirmed Martina, "that was her girl-name."

In the dining room, above an impressive Regency fireplace, hung a large oil painting of *The Winsome Witch*, posed like a duchess with a manic gleam in her eye, a large spider suspended by a thread from the crooked tip of her witch's hat. Around the walls were other wizards and witches from *The Witchy Wood* in faux-aristocratic poses, all of them painted by the same brush that had enlivened the staircase. On the sideboards, in silver frames were some of the same characters, but rendered in the garish colours of *The Witchy Wood* cartoon series that was watched on television by millions of children across the world.

"What sort of dinner-parties does Mrs Carfax have up here?" asked Ginny, suspecting that she already knew the answer.

"She have the little witches and wizards from the *Coven Clubs*," said Martina. "Mrs Carfax read stories from the books, and then they all have bean-feasts."

Ginny let her eyes travel over the weird aristocrats on the walls, and experienced a strong sense of kinship with Mrs Carfax. Her Dulcie Davenport stories, dreamed up so many years ago, were still enlivening young minds. And the words on the page would always work their magic more vividly than their flashy offspring on the TV screens and the play-stations. The old lady believed that. And so did Ginny. It was her mission every afternoon at Murray's Road, where *Tales from the Witchy Wood* had been a favourite with the children since she began teaching

Instantly, Ginny knew what she would do with the clay. She would use strong primary colours that would please the children and sing brightly on the dark mahogany of the table and sideboards...but she would splash them with lustres to make them glisten and gleam, especially in candlelight....from a forest of twisted candlesticks ...perhaps another nest of snakes with candles in their greedy mouths...with toads for salt and pepper pots...and a cauldron for the soup. And every plate and every bowl would feature a spider...or a spider's web... like the portrait of *The Winsome Witch* above the fireplace...

Chapter Thirty One

The long silence from the *Youth Offending Team* began to prey on Ginny's composure. Every night when he called from prison, Whizz nagged her to phone Mr Beresford and push the arrangement through. Ginny resisted the temptation, terrified that she might appear too eager and sabotage their plan. With every passing day, the anxiety intensified, whining at the periphery of her consciousness like a mosquito in a darkened room.

At school, she broke the rule again and left her mobile switched on during lessons, becoming distracted by its obstinate refusal to ring, losing her grip on the children and growing fractious. At home, she tried to engross herself in experiments with lustres, mixing potions with the fevered zeal of an alchemist in search of gold...but even as she laboured, she was fretting for a call from Whizz, or she was chewing over the call he'd just made. At night, if she managed sleep at all, the dream would send an avalanche of rubber tyres to wake her up, and her mind would be ensnared by the futile, endlessly repetitive speculations about the YOT's interminable silence. There was no escape. As her rational-self told the haggard face that looked back from the mirror, she was behaving irrationally, but her fixated-self refused to listen.

The call finally came when she was least expecting it—on a Saturday afternoon, when all good bureaucrats should be at home with their spouses. She was with Mel in the deserted auditorium of *The Old Fish Market Theatre*, sitting in the front row of the stalls for a run-through of *Like Rabbits,* the black and bawdy farce that Lazlo was taking to the Edinburgh Festival.

For Ginny, the play was a much needed tonic. From the moment the curtains opened, she'd been convulsed with laughter, or rendered breathless by shock and horror. After a brief interlude of sanity, the pace of the comedy picked up again, growing ever more frenetic in a crescendo of expertly timed gags and culminating in a tense silence, a moment of epiphany when the bombastic character played by Lazlo was to be revealed in all his vulnerability...

In the empty theatre, the mobile's bleat was as loud as an air raid siren. The entire cast turned to stare at her. Ginny gaped back, uncomprehending. When she finally managed to pin the blame on her own coat pocket, instead of apologising and turning the phone off, she ran away, making an ungainly exit up the centre aisle with the mobile repeating its stupid jingle ever louder.

Bursting through the doors to the foyer, she flicked the phone open. "Yes," she gasped, sounding fiercer than intended.

"Is this a bad time?" said a woman's voice. "It's the Youth Offending Team."

Ginny leaned her back against the wall, and breathed deeply. "No, it's fine... I had to run to the phone..."

"Sorry to call at the weekend, Mrs May, but we're trying to catch up on a backlog of work. Do you think Mr Beresford could come and see you later on this afternoon? He's got another call to make in your neck of the woods, and his diary is..."

"No, no, no..." Ginny broke in, "that should be fine. I can be home in an hour. Any time after four will be great..."

The secretary was grateful, and spent a few minutes explaining how overworked her colleagues were, especially the unfortunate Beresford. When the goodbyes were done with, Ginny feigned an afterthought:

"By the way..." she said, "just a thought. My husband won't be around this afternoon. I hope that's not a problem..?"

The nursery was already spotless, but she sprayed polish anyway for the smell of cleanliness. The guest bathroom was stocked with clean towels, a towelling dressing gown, and a generous supply of male toiletries. She sprayed room-freshener. On the kitchen table, she arranged a few academic books as though Simon had been having profound thoughts. In one of the drawers in the dresser she found the framed photograph taken at their wedding reception and propped it up beside the portrait of Simon in his doctoral clobber that she'd found at the top of the wardrobe. From the cupboard in the playroom, she retrieved the shoebox containing the pictures of Will at Murray's Road, and placed it on the dresser.

Beresford was more or less what she expected a probation officer to be: a scrawny man in his mid-forties, with the puffy eyes of an insomniac and the crumpled look of someone too busy to care.

"Mike Beresford," he said, offering his hand, and showing his ID in the other. "Nice house you've got."

"We were lucky to get it," Ginny said. "The way prices have gone, we couldn't afford it now…Do come in…"

Beresford declined her offer of tea, and checked his wristwatch. Ginny removed a handful of photographs from the shoebox.

"Look at these," she said. "This is Will, aged five. He was in my very first class at Murray's Road. He was a real charmer then…"

Beresford quickly riffled through pictures. "That police car that rammed you did the kid a big favour," he said.

Ginny was surprised. "He told you about that, did he?"

"Calls it his lucky day," said Beresford, handing the photographs back to Ginny. "Look, I don't mean to be rude, Mrs May, but could I take a quick peep at the room?"

It was a lightning visit, a classic exercise in ticking boxes. Beresford barely glanced at the bedroom, or the bathroom.

"We have our own bathroom *en suite*," Ginny said, "so this one is all for him…."

Beresford seemed impressed. "I wish all my clients had you for a fairy godmother."

"Is there anything else you'd like to see?"

"No, no…everything's fine," he said. "According to the terms of his licence, this will be his address. He shouldn't be anywhere else without letting us know. If he starts going AWOL, we'll need to know. And he'll have to come and see me, or one of my colleagues, every week. If he's seriously in breach of his licence, he'll be back inside pronto, so he'd better be good." Beresford reached into the breast pocket of his jacket and retrieved a business card. "This is where you'll find me. To be honest, the way he talks about you and your husband, I doubt he's going to give you any grief. But if you have any problems, give me a bell."

It was as easy as that. Ginny escorted Beresford to the front door and waved him goodbye. Either her scheming had paid dividends, or she had squandered weeks of nervous energy. On its hook above the trench coat, the fedora looked theatrical and vaguely silly. She did not remove it. If Simon's vanity had helped her cause, she was more than pleased. The hat could stay.

On her next visit to Fulford, Ginny was determined to be businesslike. She came straight to the point

"No drugs, no cigarettes and no alcohol."

Whizz leaned back against the blue upholstery, hands in pockets, his face impassive.

"These are absolutes, Whizz. Set in stone. Ok?"

The boy shrugged, and muttered, "No problem."

Ginny wanted no misunderstandings, and pressed him. "Any drugs, soft or hard, and I go straight to see Beresford. Understood?"

Whizz nodded.

She told him that he would not be a prisoner in her house; that he would have a key to the door; that he would be free to come and go, as long as he was home to sleep. That was a 'must'. It would be specified in the terms of his licence. He must be home every night, without fail.

"I've got to be honest though," she added, "there's not much point in us trying to get your life back on track if you spend any time with the likes of Moon Rivers...What say we put the city out of bounds?"

To her surprise, he nodded his head.

"And you really are serious about trying to get to the bottom of your problems?"

"Yep," he muttered, and nodded again, "I'm serious."

He looked her directly in the eye, and Ginny left the prison convinced that he had spoken the truth.

Mike Beresford's letter confirmed everything he had told her on his visit, this time spelled out in long paragraphs of turgid office-speak. The only news was in the penultimate paragraph, and it came as a shock. The Date of Release was several days earlier than she had expected. Either by miscalculation or by some self-deluding wish, she had assumed that the school term would be finished before the boy was released. In reality, there was a disturbing three-day gap when Whizz would be alone in the house.

Her first thought was to call her 'job-share' and negotiate a solution—but when she needed her, Jenny would be honeymooning somewhere in the wilds of Thailand. For a rash moment, she considered asking Beresford if the Date of Release could be changed, but dismissed the idea as preposterous. She would have to go 'sick'. But she couldn't. Not after taking so much time off already this term. And anyway, who was the loudest voice in the staffroom when it came to bad-mouthing the skivers?

That evening, when Whizz made his regular call, Ginny steeled herself and confessed her anxieties frankly. The response was indignant.

"You said you weren't going to watch me like a screw."

"I'm not going to watch you like a screw," she protested. "All I want is a promise that you won't leave the house while I'm at school..."

"In case I go out and mug old ladies..."

Ginny massaged her forehead. "It's only three days, Whizz..."

"You don't trust me, do you?"

"You, I trust..." she said. "It's your friends I don't trust."

"That's crap. You don't trust me."

"I trust you enough to put a roof over your head, isn't that enough for you?"

"No, it's not."

"Look..." she said, preparing a shift of emphasis, "trust doesn't arrive by magic. It's something we've got to work at, both of us. This time I need a bit of help, that's all..."

She paused, hoping for a response, but nothing came.

"I need your promise, Whizz...for my peace of mind..."

Again, he kept her waiting.

"OK," he said, at last, "I'll stick to the house when you're at school."

"Is that a promise?"

"Yeah, it's a promise."

Chapter Thirty Two

Her sleep was fitful, and she was awake before dawn. To fill the empty hours she went down to the playroom and tried to lose herself in a slab of clay, searching out its textures as she wedged, communing with the earth just as Taka had taught her. It was a fruitless exercise. Wrapping the clay in a wet cloth, she went back upstairs and ran a bath, then lay under the carpet of scented bubbles and rehearsed the lie that she would tell to Mrs Appleby.

"I can't believe I'm going sick yet again...but I really daren't risk it...not with the trots. Can you tell Colin I'm sorry to lumber him again? If I starve this bug into submission over the weekend, I should be fit as a flea by Monday..."

She gave a good performance, and even managed to feel genuinely queasy as the untruths slipped off her duplicitous tongue. Three months ago such a fib would have been unthinkable...but it was, after all, a single day's truancy, and her very first 'sicky' in ten years of teaching.

Taking her time, she got dressed and made herself eat a bowl of muesli for breakfast, idly turning the pages of yesterday's *Guardian,* digesting nothing. Despite her dallying, she was in the car too early and had to dawdle in the slow lane to spin the journey out. Even then, she was in the prison car park with half an hour to spare.

At nine twenty five, she got out of the car and went to wait outside the gates. Nothing moved on the other side of the steel mesh, and the officer who usually manned the gatehouse was nowhere to be seen. There was an ominous stillness, as though some great catastrophe had caused the whole encampment to be shut down and abandoned.

At exactly nine thirty, two figures appeared in the distance, blurred by the close weave of the steel-mesh fence, walking towards her down a long path between two cellblocks. Eventually she recognised Whizz by his blonde hair, and raised a hand in greeting. There was no response.

When they reached the inner fence, the escorting officer selected a key from the bunch at his waist, and unlocked the first gate. He motioned Whizz through, and searched out another key. With a squeal from its hinges, the final steel gate swung open, and Whizz stepped out.

"Good luck to you, lad," said the officer. "Try not to come back!"

In an odd way, the grubby puffer jacket and baggy jeans gave Whizz a bulk that only drew attention to the slender boyish frame they were meant to disguise. Ginny's instinct was to give him in a hug. Instead, she offered him a shy smile.

"Welcome to freedom," she said. "How does it feel?"

Whizz unfolded the piece of paper he was clutching in his hand and examined it carefully. "I ain't free," he said. "I've got to go and see Beresford at twelve-thirty."

"Can I have a look?" asked Ginny, holding out her hand.

The paper was headed *Notice of Supervision*, and laid out the terms and conditions for his release from prison.

"Never mind..." she said, brightly. "We've got plenty of time to celebrate. And we're going to buy you a whole new outfit as well

Ginny began to thread her way through the crowded car park. Whizz followed.

"How come you've got the day off?" he asked. "Taken a sicky, have you?"

"No, I have not," said Ginny, telling the fib with a convincing note of indignation. "Mr Croft owes me a favour."

When they reached the old Saab, Ginny put the key in the lock.

"Bit of a wreck, innit?" said Whizz.

The central locking clicked open.

"Don't you be rude about my old Saab," Ginny warned, "I am very attached to this old car."

As soon as he was in his seat, Whizz put his hand on the dashboard radio.

"Saab was one of the first to do the integrated radio," he said, "...they're a real sod to get out, they are." He watched her disengage the parking gear. "And that gear-lock is a bugger an' all if you're in a hurry…"

Ginny gave him a sideways look. "I'm glad to hear it," she said.

Whizz grinned. "No need to worry about this old heap, Mrs May. Nobody in their right mind would want to nick this."

Ginny pursed her lips. "I was going to drive you to the nearest MacDonald's and buy you a feast, but now you've insulted the old Saab, I'm not so sure."

Whizz leaned forward to look at the car's mileage. "I suppose it might have antique value..." he said.

The tricky morning that Ginny had half-expected was proving easy, all thanks to the boy, who had taken charge of the ice-breaking. And he was clearly enjoying himself, teasing her about his life of crime, shocking her with unsavoury truths. All she had to do was tut-tut a little and look scandalised, which, in the circumstances, was not too difficult.

In MacDonald's, he made her stomach churn. While he wolfed down the cheeseburgers and gulped his milkshake, she made the mistake of asking what the food had been like in prison. He did not address the question directly.

"We was having our grub one day when this dickhead rolls up his sleeve and bites a bloody great chunk out of his arm." He mimed the action gleefully. "Chewed it up an' all, and swallowed it!"

"You're kidding?"

He beamed at her, relishing her disgust.

"No, I'm not. There are loads of fruit-cakes inside."

In *T K Maxx,* while he was working his way through the rails in search of clothes, he boasted how his posse used to bribe younger kids to do their shoplifting for them.

"They'd do anything for some puff or a few pills. And if they got nicked, the pigs would only give 'em a Caution...not even that if they was first timers..." He held up a coat-hanger to inspect the graphic on a tee-shirt. "Good way to do your shopping, innit?" he added, giving her another grin.

While he was trying on a pair of trainers, he continued his crash course in the economics of street-life.

"When I was a kid, I had my trainers nicked by some bigger kids. That's called 'taxing'." He paused to make sure she had understood. "Then when I grew up, I did some taxing of my own. Everybody gets taxed. It's the way it works."

Even though the bill at the cash-desk was almost twice what she had planned to spend, Ginny walked out of the store convinced she'd had good value. She hadn't expected such openness from the boy, at least not so soon. No profound revelations yet, but he seemed to have made a down-payment, with an unspoken promise of more to come.

"Time to go and see Beresford," said Ginny, as they hauled the bags across the car park.

As soon as Whizz closed the car door, he was a different person. No more tales of derring-do. No more gallows humour. Slouched in the passenger seat, his body-language spoke of boredom and aggression. His mouth confined itself to directions, issued in grunts that took her unerringly through a lattice of back streets until they joined a shabby main thoroughfare with more than its fair share of boarded-up shop fronts.

"That's it," he said, pointing across the road to a two-storey office block with stained concrete render and chipped paintwork.

A group of teenaged lads were congregated in the street outside, shoulders hunched, roll-ups cupped in their hands.

"Shall I come in with you, or shall I...?"

"No fucking way," snapped Whizz. "Drive round the corner."

Ginny's knuckles whitened on the steering-wheel, but she obeyed the instruction. Every parking space in the road was occupied, except for one directly outside a greasy spoon called *Tano's Cafe*.

"If you're a long time, I'll be in the caff, having a cuppa," she said.

Whizz got out of the car and slammed the door. In the driving mirror, she watched him saunter back down the road in the direction of the YOT, shoulders rolling, trying to look dangerous.

The tea was treacle brown, but tasty. Ginny turned the pages of a borrowed *Sun* and immersed herself in the latest celebrity scandal. This would be a weekly treat. She had better get used to it. No thrill for her, and bad news for the boy. Every week he would be plugged back into the world that he badly needed to escape. It was a Kafkaesque way to run Youth Justice.

Half way through a second cup of treacle, *Tano*'s steamed-up door swung open, and Whizz showed himself on the threshold. Ginny waved, but the door was already swinging shut. She found him leaning against a lamp post next to the Saab, a study in teenage angst.

"How did it go?" she said, searching for the car-key.

Whizz grunted something unintelligible, and back-heeled the base of the lamppost with one of his trainers.

They drove in a silence that quickly became oppressive. Ginny switched on the car radio.

"Help yourself to some music..." she said, wagging her finger across the row of buttons, "...the choice is yours."

For a while she thought he was going to tolerate the news on Radio 4, but after a few seconds a hand shot out and he began to stab the pre-sets, sampling each station, rejecting them instantly. When he had exhausted the stored options, he began to spin the manual control with his finger, listening to snatches of every random station, and then spinning the control again and again. When he finally found something he liked, he flicked the volume control, and an all-girl gospel choir filled the car, backed by a rhythmic underlay from a drum machine. A gravelly voice, close to the microphone, began to rap.

> *You say I'm a misfit, and you ain't wrong*
> *Coz who'd wanna fit in a crock o' shit*
> *I want out*

Ginny suppressed a smile. It could have been the boy's anthem.

> *You say I'm a loser, which bring me no shame*
> *Coz your dumb-ass rules*
> *are for lame-brain fools*
> *And I proclaim...Yeah, I proclaim...*
> *That I don't wanna play your lousy game*
> *No, I don't wanna play in your lousy game*
> *I want out*

Whizz sat hunched against the window, but the world-weary performance was not entirely convincing. Unable to resist the catchy beat, his fingers were tapping out the syncopations on the denim of his jeans, and the pirate station pumped out ear-splitting hip-hop all the way home.

Ginny reversed the Saab into the lean-to and switched off the engine. Silence returned. When she had loaded her surly house-guest with shopping bags, she prattled on about the wonderful summer she had planned for him and led the way to the house. Whizz trudged behind, dragging the black cloud of his sulk with him.

"Don't worry about the soppy wallpaper," Ginny explained, when they reached the nursery. "You can have it however you like...black with blue spots, if you want..."

Whizz dumped the bags on the floor, and threw himself down on the single bed.

"Why can't I have your old man's room?" he asked, pointing a finger at the ceiling.

"Simon's study, do you mean?" exclaimed Ginny, surprised. "How do you know about that?"

Whizz produced a sly smirk. "I nicked a tenner from his wallet last time I was here."

Ginny put her hand over her face to hide the dimples.

The boy's eyes widened. "I've got a great idea," he said, and rolled off the bed. "Come on, I'll show you."

Running out into the passage, he took the steps to Simon's eyrie two at a time.

"I'm going to cover the whole place in graffiti," he shouted, spinning round and round, miming squirts of spray-paint all over the gabled ceiling and the walls. "It'll be cool. The whole room Banksied! A proper work of art!"

Ginny folded her arms across her chest. "Are you any good?" she asked.

"I'm fucking brilliant!" he replied.

"Brilliant will do," she said. "Let's have a little less of the F-word, if you don't mind."

"Sorry," he said. "Can we go and buy the paint then?"

Ginny grimaced. "What, now?"

Whizz started to wheedle, as if he were a little boy at school again. "Please, Mrs May...please...it won't take long...Please, Mrs May...I'll be good, Mrs May...."

Ginny shook her head and pretended to be stern.

When they returned from the Industrial Estate with a large, and surprisingly expensive, box of spray-cans, Ginny cooked the meal that Whizz had requested on her last visit to Fulford: a small piece of rump steak, two lamb chops, three sausages and a fried egg, with a hill of chips and a small lake of baked beans on the side.

"That was great," he said, wiping the plate clean with a piece of bread.

"Sure you can manage some pudding?" she asked doubtfully.

"Watch me," he said, and patted his stomach with both hands.

Ginny took out the bowl of tiramisu and was searching the fridge for the cream jug when an electronic beep announced the arrival of a text. Straightening up, she scanned the kitchen, trying to remember where she had left her mobile. And then she noticed Whizz, tapping out a reply on a more up-to-date cell phone than her own.

"Who was that?" she asked, as she put the tiramisu on the table.

With a flick of his thumb, Whizz dispatched his message and returned the phone to his pocket. "Just a mate," he said, and picked up his spoon.

Ginny busied herself in the galley, feeling foolish and not a little alarmed. An umbilical to the street had not been factored into her calculations.

After a lesson in loading the dish-washer, she took her new lodger into the playroom to show him the sample pots that she had made for Mrs Carfax. There were three designs for the old lady to consider, all different, and all eccentric in their different ways.

"What do you think?" she asked.

Without hesitation, Whizz pointed to Ginny's own favourite.

"Why that one?" she asked.

"Dunno," he said, with a shrug. "It's weird, but not too weird."

"And you don't like this one?" she asked.

She passed him a plate that seemed to be in the process of melting away.

"No, I don't like that," he said. "You've nicked the idea from Dali, and I don't like Dali. He's a freak."

Ginny was impressed—but then his parents had probably dragged him around some of the world's best galleries.

"Did your mum and dad take you to Figueres, to that strange Dali museum?" she asked.

Whizz gave her a chilly, sidelong stare, and ignored the question. He picked up another bowl and turned it in his hands, examining the glazed spider's web that clung to the copper lustres on the outer surface.

"How come you don't make 'em round and smooth like everyone else?" he wondered.

"Sometimes I prefer them wonky," Ginny said. "Machines make pots that are polished and perfect, and I'm not a machine."

"Can I have a go?" he asked.

"Of course you can." she said, pleased by his curiosity.

The damp muslin cloth had done its job and the ball of clay she had worked at dawn was still moist. Digging her fingers into the centre of the mound, she began to gouge out the crude shape of a bowl, working fast and without much care.

"It's as simple as that..." she said, and collapsed the bowl, folding the sides down and pressing it back into a rough ball. "You can make your bowl as rough or as smooth as you want...big and thin, or small and fat... do it fast, or do it slow...whatever you fancy..." She dumped the clay in front of him, and began to wipe her hands on a scruffy piece of towel. "There's a catch, though..." she added, and untied the scarf that was holding her hair back. "I want you to do it blindfold..."

"What for?" asked Whizz.

"Because..." she said, folding and refolding the scarf, "I want you to 'see' the bowl with your fingers, and I want you to smell the clay."

"Why?"

"Just try it!" she instructed, and tied the blindfold round his head. "Play with it. There's nothing childish about play. Play is a way of finding out. I do it all the time."

Whizz extended his arms and his hands began a tentative exploration of the clay, gently at first, then more confidently, clawing out a basin in the centre of the mound, digging deeper, smoothing the surfaces. He was soon engrossed, head bent to the clay, tongue stuck in the corner of his mouth, nose sniffing obediently.

Ginny was amused. He was still the child he'd been ten years before.

Chapter Thirty Three

"Why don't you make a start on your room?"

Whizz wrinkled his nose. "Don't fancy it," he grunted, hammering the keys on his mobile with his thumbs.

On Friday, graffiti had been top priority. Today, it was anathema. Today, nothing engaged him. He was bored, sprawled out in the old leather armchair, hooked on that stupid game, while she slapped glazes on pots, unable to focus and becoming increasingly anxious. What sixteen year-old would not be bored, locked up with a thirty-six year-old schoolteacher on a wet weekend, with no company of his own age? If she couldn't find ways of energising him, Fulford could soon become a fond memory.

"I'm sure you'll find better games on the computer upstairs. Why don't you give it a go?"

It was a lame suggestion, and it didn't help.

"Stop nagging," he muttered. "I'm alright."

Ginny looked out through the rain-spattered glass at the garden beyond.

As gardens go, it was a decent size, but it was hardly a full-time job. Once the shaggy lawns had been tamed and the borders thinned, a few hours a week would be plenty. She'd been fooling herself...worse; she'd been fooling the boy.

"The rain's easing," she said, "...shall we take a look at the garden...work out what you can do tomorrow when I'm at school?"

There was no reply. She repeated the question, loudly, making sure she had his attention. He did not look up.

"I just want to finish Level 7," he said, thumbs twitching.

Ginny waited until Level 7 had been successfully accomplished, then prised him out of the armchair and shooed him into the garden. On cue, the rain came down in earnest and they took shelter in the garden shed.

"If it clears up tomorrow, you can mow the lawns," she said, "if not, you'd better get on with your room."

Her lesson on how to operate the lawnmower was not a success.

"I know how a bleeding lawnmower works," Whizz said.

Ginny gave him her withering look. "Well, you might not know how this particular lawnmower works."

After a guided tour of the machine, she showed him how to start the motor, and tugged hard on the starter cable. Nothing happened. She tried again. Not a cough. Ginny cursed under her breath.

"Someone's left the choke out," said Whizz, squatting down on his haunches. "The plug's probably knackered, as well. Have you got any tools?"

Ten minutes later, when he tugged on the starter-cable, the engine sputtered into life, uncertainly at first and with a nasty puff of acrid black smoke. Whizz adjusted the choke, and the engine chugged contentedly.

"Sounds a bit like your Saab," he said.

Ginny planted a friendly kick in the seat of his jeans.

"Come on, smart-arse, the rain has stopped...Let's see how good you are at real gardening."

In the months of neglect, the big flower bed by the patio had run riot. Ginny planted a wellington boot near a patch of unwanted ground ivy and tugged out a handful. "All this stuff has got to go," she said, "and that sticky stuff over there... it's called bindweed...and that..."

The distinction between flowers and weeds seemed to hold little fascination for her less-than-attentive student.

"I hope you're listening," she said. "I don't want you ripping out my flowers..."

With extreme nonchalance, Whizz began to bounce his finger over the big flower bed. "Weed... weed...weed..." he announced, "weed..."

"No!" cried Ginny. "That's a late flowerer, and so is that. You'd better stick to the ivy, and the bindweed, and the thistles, and the dandelions. If in doubt, leave it, or I won't have a garden left. OK?"

"What about the orchard?" Whizz demanded.

Ginny suppressed a groan. The orchard was another blunder; eight trees to be felled, and all the roots to be grubbed up. It was a job for a professional tree surgeon, not a boy.

"I'm an ace with a chainsaw," Whizz said, and proceeded to scythe down an imaginary tree with his hands held palm-to-palm, making screeching noises with his mouth.

Tossing a handful of bindweed onto the patio, Ginny wiped her hands together. "You've got to get rid of all this stuff before we even think about the trees," she said.

But her new gardener was already crossing the lawn, heading for the gate in the slate wall and the little orchard beyond.

With his imaginary chainsaw at the ready, Whizz looked up into the branches of a dying Bramley apple, and prepared to demonstrate. "You do the lower branches first..." he said, supplying another burst of screeching, "...then you move up the tree, stripping all the branches till you've just got the trunk left and a knobbly bit on top..."

"What about the roots?" Ginny asked. "If we leave anything in the ground, the honey-fungus will just keep eating..."

For a second, Whizz seemed nonplussed. "We'll hire a machine," he said. "They'll tell us what we need when we get the chainsaw. You'll have to give me a hand, but we'll get it done ok."

Ginny smiled. His eagerness to please was engaging, and she had no wish to put him down.

"So where did you learn to be a lumberjack?" she asked.

Whizz frowned. For a moment he was back at *Halcyon*, alongside his father in the woods. Then he gave her a sly grin.

"The vicar at St Stephen's taught me," he said. "I learned a hell of a lot from him..."

"Oh, pull the other one," said Ginny, eyeing him sideways. "DS Carmichael told me all about your vicar..."

Whizz looked shocked. "I dunno," he said. "You try to be a good Christian and you get persecuted for it..."

Hiding her smile, Ginny turned away, and headed back to the house.

"Hey...Mrs May..." cried Whizz, running to catch her up, "...how about we have a bonfire when I've got those trees down? We could stuff your old man's coat with newspaper and stick his hat on top of a turnip or something, and then we could send the fucker up in smoke."

Ginny stopped in her tracks. "I've had just about enough of your bad language," she said. "I'm serious, Whizz. Will you please cut it out?"

"Sorry," he said, looking contrite.

Ginny glared at him, and then turned away, cross with herself. Playing the schoolmarm was not the answer.

"I'll tell you what though, Whizz..." she called out, marching off and throwing her voice over her shoulder, "...that bonfire's not a bad idea."

Monday dawned cloudless, and Whizz was in a suitably sunny mood. Not Ginny. She had slept badly. As she cooked his sausage, bacon and eggs, she even toyed with the idea of phoning the school and calling in sick.

Whizz read her mind. "Don't worry about me," he said, "I won't be going anywhere. And I will look after the place...promise!"

With the morning sun in his hair, he looked positively cherubic.

"I know you will," she said, and gave him a smile that she hoped was convincing.

Despite the best efforts of thirty infant jack-in-the-boxes, the faint whine of anxiety was like persistent tinnitus. While she supervised the playground at lunchtime, she hid herself from watching eyes in the staffroom and phoned the landline at home, regretting that she hadn't asked the boy for his mobile number. With mounting alarm, she listened to the bell ring and ring. She was about to give up in despair when the phone was answered.

"I'm fine," Whizz said. "Did a bit of mowing. Now I'm gonna look at my room..."

At the end of the afternoon, when Jason Nolan came tugging at her skirt Ginny rejected him, palming him off on Jan Lockwood while she made a guilty escape. She drove home as fast as the gauntlet of speed cameras would allow. It was irrational, bordering on hysterical, but when she finally rounded the bend in the drive, she was relieved to find the house still standing. And there was more good news. The lawn in front of the rose garden had been immaculately shorn in orderly stripes, its edges neatly trimmed. In the garden shed, she found the lawnmower, wiped cleaner than she could ever remember it.

Music was leaking from the open windows—not the squabbling string quartets that had so often greeted her homecomings in the past, but a heavy bass line thumping a pulse into the air. It was a welcome change.

There was more good news waiting on the stairs to the attic. Her lodger had had the good sense to clear the room before starting to paint. On each tread there was a neat stack of Simon's books, and the futon's wooden base had been up-ended on the landing, with its mattress slumped drunkenly beside it.

The music from within was so loud, it was hardly surprising that her knock went unnoticed. She tried again, knocking harder. Receiving no response, she tugged on the cord to lift the latch, and pushed the door open. The rap lyric slapped her in the face.

> *Hey, deedle-deedle*
> *The cat's got a needle...*
> *And the cow's on a trip to the moon.*

Like a flower opening in time-lapse, a patch of scarlet burgeoned on the sloping ceiling. The spray-can was moving to the rhythm of the rap. Ginny watched, mesmerised, failing for a moment to observe that the hand that held the spray-can did not belong to Whizz.

> *And Li'l Boy Blue has lost his horn*
> *Cos his pussy's done fell down the well*

Whizz was at the far end of the room. He was dancing—a robotic routine, eyes closed, oblivious to everything but the music.

> *So hump me, dump me,*
> *See if I care*

Ginny looked back at the graffiti artist. He was standing on one of her kitchen chairs, spraying scarlet from his right hand, and yellow from his left, alternating the cans with casual abandon, on her ceiling.

> *I take no shit*
> *From no hypo...crit*

The rap-chorus ended, and the horns stole the tune from the glockenspiel. Whizz doubled the tempo of his dance, performing a series of spin turns while his arms executed an elaborate semaphore. Then, mid-frenzy and for no apparent reason, he froze, staring straight at Ginny.

She stabbed a finger in the direction of the graffiti artist.

"Who...is...he?" she mouthed.

As if a puppeteer had relaxed his strings, Whizz crumpled and he was on his hands and knees, reaching for the ghetto-blaster. The music stopped.

"What the fuck...?" shouted the artist into the silence.

"That's Cee-Jay," said Whizz. "Cee-Jay, this is Mrs May."

The graffiti artist turned to Ginny and gave a pathetic wave with one of the paint-cans. He had a pale baby-face, framed by a Napoleonic fringe and a wisp of black beard that drew a thin line around his chin. He clearly wanted to be somewhere else.

Ginny gave him an ironic salute. "Hi, Cee-Jay," she said.

Turning back to Whizz, she crooked her finger and beckoned. Then she pointed to the door. When they had reached the privacy of the landing, she put her face close to his.

"Why didn't you ask?" she said, in an angry whisper.

"Cos you'd have said 'no'," he replied, holding her gaze.

"And you call that 'trust', do you?" she said.

Whizz did not blink. "I kept my promise... I told you I wouldn't leave the house, and I didn't."

Chapter Thirty Four

For all that Ginny understood of their street-patois, the two boys could have been speaking Swahili. "Please, Mrs May..." and "Thank you, Mrs May..." seemed to be the only words of English in Cee-Jay's vocabulary, and he used them frequently. Whizz was not speaking at all...at least not to her.

Leaving them to their fish and chips, Ginny slipped out of the kitchen and took her cheese sandwich upstairs for a more considered appraisal of Cee-Jay's murals. She was impressed. He had a good eye, and a flair for draughtsmanship. Either side of the windows, in bold, black outline, he had sketched two cartoon faces: a boy and a girl, both with the almond eyes and spiky hair that she had seen on manga comics in the kiosks of Tokyo. They were not original, but they were striking. On another wall, he had sprayed a sci-fi figure reminiscent of a Jedi knight. It was a less successful design, but she could tell from the faint pencil markings on the plaster that it was work in progress.

"I really like your murals, Cee-Jay," said Ginny, as she came back into the kitchen. "They do wonders for that room... When can you come and finish them?"

Whizz stopped a spoonful of cheesecake on its journey to his mouth.

"If he's allowed to come back," he said, "why can't he sleep-over tonight, and do it tomorrow?"

"How many more times?" said Ginny, with a weary sigh. "Because I take these licences seriously, even if you don't...and I don't want to be responsible for getting Cee-Jay sent back to prison. As soon as you've finished your grub, we're taking him home. Ok?"

"Nobody would know," Whizz grumbled.

"I would know," said Ginny, "and that's an end of it."

To her surprise, Cee-Jay piped up. "Could I come back tomorrow, please, Mrs May?"

It was the first full sentence that Cee-Jay had uttered in English, and he seemed as surprised as Ginny by his boldness.

"Of course you can," Ginny said, "I'll give you some money for the bus fare."

The amusement arcades, the ice-cream parlours and the bingo dives lit up the seafront with their garish lights and poured a cacophony of trashy music into the good sea air. It was a cooked-up gaiety that seemed to fool none of the glum punters on the pavement.

Whizz directed Ginny to take a right turn at a sign that alternately flashed the words '*Skin*' and '*Art*' down the side of the tattooist's emporium on the corner. She pulled up the Saab onto the crown of the road, and waited for the on-coming traffic—a bus, two taxis and then the *Thomas-the-Tank-Engine* train that toured the Old Town. It was on its way home to the *Fat Controller*, and Ginny watched the jolly smile trundle past, wondering how many children it had managed to disappoint that day.

"Look, Whizz..." shouted Cee-Jay from the back seat. "There's the Moon-man!"

Whizz snatched a look across the road, and quickly ducked his head below the level of the windscreen.

"Which one is Moon?" said Ginny, scanning the pavement.

A pointing hand appeared over her shoulder. "The guy in the shades," said Cee-Jay, "the one with the ponytail by the *Caribbean*."

She saw him for only a moment. He was holding open the door to the *Caribbean Club* and ushering two older men inside. Then he was gone. She would never have recognised him. In a dark blazer, with his hair pulled back, he looked nothing like the little creep she'd met in the arcade with Carmichael.

An impatient car horn jolted Ginny to her senses and, in her confusion, she almost stalled the Saab. Pulses of green and yellow light briefly stained the windscreen as they passed the tattoo-parlour, and they were quickly swallowed in the gloom of a narrow one-way street.

Whizz sat up in the passenger seat. "It's the third road on the right," he said.

Ginny held back the questions. That he wanted to stay clear of Rivers was reassuring enough for now.

With the exception of a man walking his dog and a couple necking in a doorway, there was nobody about. The roads to right and left were similarly deserted, but when she followed

Whizz's pointing finger and turned into Zealand Road, the dark and desolate world went suddenly haywire.

A conga-line of skimpily clad females was snaking its way towards them in the middle of the road. It was led by a fat girl in a bridal veil, and she was being cheered on by a drunken crowd that had spilled out of Zealand Arms.

Ginny slowed the Saab to a crawl.

The bride-to-be stood like a colossus in front of the Saab, barring the way.

Ginny braked to a halt.

To ever louder cheers from the crowd, the fat girl ripped open her blouse and, with surprising agility, draped herself across the bonnet, flattening her immense breasts on the windscreen. Another girl kissed the passenger window next to Whizz. Soon, girl after girl was puckering-up to leave their lipstick smeared on the glass. Then the yobs arrived, pushing the girls aside, squashing their faces against the windows, glassy-eyed and tongues lolling, ugly as gargoyles.

Whizz raised his middle finger and dispensed the insult to every window.

Ginny reached across and smacked him on the arm.

"Stop that!" she cried. "Try and look happy, for God's sake!"

But the crowd was already turning nasty. Palms slapped the windows and fists hammered on the roof. Then the car began to rock.

With a flick of a switch, Ginny engaged the central-locking system.

A youth with steel staples in his ears peered into the car and seemed to recognise her passengers. He smiled unpleasantly, then pursed his lips and blew Whizz a kiss.

"Do nothing," Ginny instructed.

Whizz put the flat of his hand against the glass to block the youth from view.

Fortunately, the siege ended as quickly as it began. Someone hauled the fat girl off the bonnet and, like a wind-up toy, she was off again, gyrating unsteadily, shaking her bare breasts and wagging her formidable backside. The yobs around the car fell back and plugged their mouths with bottles of lager, lurching towards the pub and the whooping crowd.

Ginny edged the Saab forwards, cautiously increasing her speed as the road cleared.

"Who was the guy with the studs in his ears?" she asked.

Whizz ignored her.

"That was nasty back there," Ginny said, glancing at Whizz, "and you could have made it worse..."

Whizz curled his lip and muttered something unintelligible.

Ginny concentrated on the road. Fifty years ago, this place would have been home to a fierce breed of seaside landlady. Not now. Most of the three-storey terraced houses were boarded-up and waiting for the demolition squad. Only a few showed signs of life, with prams and bicycles parked behind rusty railings, and occasional glimmers of light behind tatty curtains.

"That's it, over there," said Cee-Jay, from the back seat. He was pointing to the only boarding house in the road that appeared to be still open for business.

Ginny drew up at the kerb opposite. An eco-friendly light bulb dimly illuminated a sign which read: *Braemore Guest House*. In its heyday, the white pebble-dash would have been smart. Now it was grey, and blackened by the overflow from blocked guttering. Somehow you could smell the damp inside, picture the cracked linoleum, the faded wallpaper, the stained sinks and the filthy lavatories. The sign that hung at a drunken angle in one of the downstairs windows proudly proclaimed *No Vacancies*.

Goodbye buckets-and-spades. Welcome Social Services. *The Braemore Guest House* was doing ok. And it was a disgrace.

Ginny reached for the glove compartment where she had put her purse. "I expect you could do with some more paint, Cee-Jay?" she said.

"No, it's alright, Mrs May," said the voice in the back.

She pulled out a twenty-pound note and held it over her shoulder. "Take this anyway," she said, "you've earned it. I'll give you some more when you're finished."

The money disappeared from Ginny's hand.

It was a small act of kindness that she would soon regret. Next day, when she returned home from school, the house had been trashed.

Chapter Thirty Five

Someone had performed hand-brake turns on the newly-mown lawn. There were black ruts gouged deep in the turf. The gravel drive had been churned as well...churned and churned again. And the front door was wide open.

Ginny sat in the car for several minutes. She felt strangely calm, as though her capacity for feeling had blacked out.

The discarded spray-cans that littered the path were no surprise. The up-turned Noh mask in the flowerbed was. Ginny picked it up, and turned it round. It was the *Hannya* mask, the once-beautiful princess soured and turned ugly by unrequited love, its twisted features the quintessence of bitterness and evil.

Scattered along the hallway were the *Hannya*'s playmates...a multi-coloured hell of Japanese devilry: demons with bulging eyes; demons fanged and horned; others blank-faced or smiling, no less malevolent.

The kitchen had been blitzed. Walls, ceiling and most of the furniture were defaced by zigzags of spray-paint. The staircase and the first-floor landing had suffered the same mindless desecration. The only evidence of skill was on the sitting-room door, where the letters 'C' and 'J' had been entwined in a graphic love-knot.

Expecting the worst, she opened the door. But the sitting room was unscathed. It was exactly as she had left it that morning. Her hands began to shake, as though this happy discovery had kick-started her nervous system. She pressed her back hard against the door, hugging her arms to her chest, trapping her hands in her armpits and fighting to keep her breathing steady.

Where was the boy? Had they beaten him again? Was he...?

The thoughts hit her like hammer blows, driving her out onto the landing, with adrenalin flooding her veins, calling his name, opening door after door, searching every corner where he could be lying, barely registering the wreckage in the rooms. At the foot of the stairs to Simon's eyrie, breathless, with the blood pounding in her temples, she called his name again and began to climb.

The room was empty...except for the kitchen chair, the box of spent spray-cans and Cee-Jay's ghetto-blaster. But something had changed. Above her head, on the flat section of the ceiling, a jagged bolt of lightning had been sprayed from one corner to the other. That was new. The Jedi figure had been given its highlights, and looked quite different. On the far wall, another tag, also new: the 'C' and the 'J' again, but in block letters, using four colours to create a 3-D effect. Compared to this, the tag on the sitting-room door was scribble.

Cee-Jay must have been up here for two or three hours, maybe more, doing his best work with a steady hand. It was hardly the behaviour of a mad vandal...

So who did trash the house? And where have they taken the boy?

Taking her mobile from the pocket of her cardigan, Ginny sat on the kitchen chair and scrolled through her contact list until she found Carmichael's number. After a couple of rings, his voice-mail replied. Feeling sick with disappointment, she waited until the beeps cued her to speak.

"I've got a problem..." she began, "and I need to talk it through, Tom...as a friend, please...nothing official. Could you call me back, please...as soon as you can? It's about Whizz Buckley."

For a while she sat perfectly still, feeling the weight of the phone in her hand. Weighing the embarrassment against the seriousness of her predicament, she went back to her contacts list and found Joe Bradley's name.

The toothy secretary told her that Mr Bradley was with a client. Fortunately, the girl detected the panic in Ginny's voice and interrupted the meeting, bringing the lawyer to the phone.

"Please don't say, 'I told you so!'" Ginny began, "but I've had Whizz Buckley living in the house..."

She heard a sound that was part sigh, part groan. Aside from that, and the occasional 'Jee-sus!' muttered under his breath, the lawyer listened quietly while she told her story.

"I don't suppose I can persuade you to call the police?" he said.

"No way," replied Ginny. "This business is not the boy's fault. I'm sure of it."

"Your faith is touching..." said Bradley, drily, "but whether the kid had a hand in it or not, you should let the police sort it out."

"No!" said Ginny. "They'll have him straight back inside, and I'm not having that."

The lawyer made clicking noises with his tongue while he considered the problem. "The person you really need is Sticks Munro," he said.

Ginny slapped her forehead with her spare hand. "For God's sake, Joe, what are you on about?"

"He's a painter and decorator, and that's what..."

Ginny got to her feet. "Joe," she shouted, "I am beside myself with worry about the kid..."

"Hold your horses, lady," said Bradley. "The kid will turn up...He always does...Now, what you need is someone to come round and hold your hand."

"I don't need my hand holding..." said Ginny.

"Yes, you do," Bradley insisted. "I've got thieves to see, or I'd be there myself...Hang on..."

She could picture him consulting the pocket-watch in his fancy waistcoat.

"...I'll be with you about seven o'clock...and I'll round up Sticks if I can. Meantime, Mrs May, will you please, just for once, take some advice? Phone a friend!"

The line went dead.

Once again, Ginny was left staring at her mobile. A few months ago she would have called Jude, and Jude would have waddled round straight away. And if Jude had been out, she would have tried Bee. Not now.

Expecting that Mel would be on one of her many zany creative missions, she keyed in her number without much hope of success, but was rewarded by an immediate response.

"Hello," said a whisper on the other end.

"It's Ginny...I'm in a mess, Mel..." she gabbled. "Is there any chance you could get in a taxi and come round to the house? I'll pay, of course..."

"No need," whispered Mel, "I'm at the university library. What's the problem?"

Ginny sighed, and made her confession.

"Ten minutes," said Mel. "Get the kettle on."

Ginny felt better. As she made her way downstairs, the scrawls and daubs on the walls were no longer shocking. But they remained a rebuke. Which fool had left two troubled kids in the house alone, with cans of spray paint? And which fool had bought the paint?

Making a collection of the scattered *Noh* masks, Ginny dumped them on top of the badly drawn swastika that adorned the surface of the big pine table. Picking up the *Hannya* mask, she ran her fingertips across the sharp, pinched features. It was a convincing replica made of hardened plastic, not cheap, but lacking magic. In the *Noh* plays that she had seen with Simon in Japan, the ancient masks seemed to be inhabited by spirits, and the authentic *Hannya* had chilled her bones. Up close and in the light of day, her plastic sister was just a harmless fraud.

"Bloody hell!" exclaimed Mel, when she saw the devastation. "The bastards!"

To Ginny's surprise, the girl went straight into the galley, and opened the fridge door.

"What on earth are you doing?" asked Ginny.

"Just checking," said Mel, peering at the shelves. "Sherlock told me that burglars sometimes leave nasties in the fridge. It's a revenge thing, apparently." She shut the fridge door. "At least they spared you that."

"This lot weren't burglars," said Ginny, "they were making mischief for the boy."

"Nice friends, he's got," said Mel. "Have they trashed the whole house?"

"Most of it," replied Ginny.

Mel gave her a searching look. "What about your bedroom?"

Ginny pulled a face. "Not good, I think...Not sure I want to look..."

Mel extended her hand. "Come on," she said, "let's get it over with..."

On one of the wardrobe's mirror-doors they had daubed the icon of a thousand school toilets: a penis, with testicles, spitting semen; on the other door, a crude vagina, doughnut-like, with a scribble of pubic hair.

"That's nice," said Mel.

Ginny turned her back on the mirror. The floor was littered with bras and panties, camisoles and slips, nighties, tights...and tampons, scattered like confetti, some of them stripped of their paper wrappings, some lying in pools of wine next to abandoned bottles.

"Hey, look at this..." said Mel, holding up the mask of a geisha girl, "I found it with this..."

With her free hand, Mel shook out a piece of blue material, and let it hang below the mask. It was the frock that Ginny had bought for Simon's inaugural, ripped at the bodice and minus buttons.

"Looks like someone's been playing lady-boys," said Mel.

"Bin it!" said Ginny. "Anything they've had fun with, we bin. Everything else, we wash, or send to the cleaners."

"I think they've been on the funny fags," said Mel, fishing out the stub of a roll-up from an up-turned Noh mask on one of the bedside tables. Gingerly, she put it to her nose and sniffed. "It's not weed, though."

"Christ, it's not heroin, is it?" exclaimed Ginny.

Mel shrugged her shoulders. "Could be...or it could be crack. How would I know?"

With a shudder of distaste, she dropped the dog-end back in the mask.

"Come on," said Ginny, newly energised, "let's wash every damn thing we can see...starting with the bed linen! By the look of it, they've been in the bed as well..."

The washing machine was at work on its second load when the doorbell rang. Ginny opened the door as far as the security chain would allow and was pleased to see Joe Bradley. He was accompanied by a shambling figure in white that she would never have recognised if she hadn't been given advance warning. Without his Stetson, Sticks Munro had a head like an egg, and in his paint-stained overalls he looked twice the size of the man behind the drum kit in *The Swamp Rats* line-up.

A cursory glance at the kitchen was more than enough for Joe Bradley. "You can't stay here," he said. "You'd better pack a few things, and come to our place."

"That's kind, Joe," said Ginny, "but I've got to be here in case the boy shows up."

Bradley sucked in a noisy breath and tugged on his moustache.

"She won't budge," said Mel, "but I'm going to stay the night. If you guys could give me a hand to get a couple of mattresses down, we'll set up a girls' dorm in the sitting room."

Sticks Munro had been prowling around the kitchen inspecting the damage, giving special attention to the scrawl on the dresser, touching the paint respectfully, like a connoisseur of antiques preparing an expert valuation.

"What do you make of it, Sticks?" asked Ginny.

"Not as bad as it looks," he replied. "Where you got plaster, we can cover up wi' BIN Primer and whack on some emulsion....Where you got paper, it might get more expensive...The pine's a bit tricky, 'specially the dresser...But I got an idea..."

Pulling his specs down to the tip of his nose, Sticks Munro surveyed his audience over the top of the frames, and launched into a technical explanation that he knew was beyond them.

"If there's silver lining to all this mayhem," said Ginny, "it's the chance to get some colour into this dreary house...It's never been how I wanted it."

"The bad news is..." added Joe Bradley, angling his head to emphasise his scepticism, "...you're not going to be able to claim on your insurance unless you report all this to the police."

"I am not letting that boy go back to prison," said Ginny, fixing the lawyer with a glare.

Sticks Munro refused to be deflected from his mission. "It don't have to be an arm-and-a-leg," he said, "not if we all mucks in..."

Joe Bradley slapped a hairy hand over his heart. "Am I hearing straight?" he said.

Sticks rearranged his specs. "I didn't say I'd do it for nowt, Joe, but if the rest of *The Rats* are up for it, I'll adjust my rates."

Bradley gave Ginny another sideways look. "Sounds like you've got yourself a house-painting-party."

"That's very sweet of you, Sticks," Ginny said, "but before you make any promises, you'd better take a look upstairs."

Like student doctors following a consultant on his rounds, they all followed Sticks as he made his diagnosis of the stairwell's ailments and wrote prescriptions in his notebook. They were all on the first floor landing, when Ginny's mobile rang.

She flicked open the phone. To her intense relief, it was Carmichael.

"Can you show Sticks the bedroom, Mel?" said Ginny, and hurried into the sitting room.

"I've got a problem," she began, "I do hope you can help, Tom..."

As she limped through her explanation, Ginny could sense that she was getting a chilly reception.

When she'd finished, Carmichael said, "What do you expect me to do, Ginny?"

"I want you to find him please, and bring him home."

"And what if he's up to no good? I'm a policeman, Ginny. I can't turn a blind eye."

"Why not, for God's sake?" Ginny snapped. "This is not the boy's fault. Somebody is trying to get him sent back to Fulford."

There was a long silence.

"Are you still there?" Ginny asked.

"I'm thinking," said Carmichael, testily. "Can you tell me anymore about this Cee-Jay character?

"I can tell you where the little sod lives...He's in a dump called *The Braemore Guest House* on Zealand Road."

There was another pause, presumably, while he made a note of the address.

"OK. I'll see what I can do," he said.

"Thank you, Tom," she said, sighing with relief.

"You've put me in a spot, Ginny...and I'm making no promises..."

"But if you get any news...you will ring, won't you? However late...just to let me know he's alright."

Chapter Thirty Six

They arranged the two mattresses side by side in front of the fire and covered themselves with spare duvets from the airing cupboard, lying on their stomachs, arms folded on top of pillows so they could watch the flickering flames. Ginny reached across and topped up Mel's glass from the bottle of *Moulin à Vent* she had found in the pantry.

It must have appeared as cosy and companionable as one of those midnight feasts in a story by Angela Brazil, but it wasn't. Anxiety was coiled inside her like an over-wound spring, jangling the senses, making the blood sing harmonics in her ears, energizing every nerve ending in her fingertips.

"You're making a lot of sacrifices for this boy," Mel said. "Are you sure he's worth it?"

Ginny took a sip of wine. "It feels Fated," she said, holding up the glass so that the fire burned in a burgundy lens. "It's my role in the gods' great game."

"You don't really believe that crap?" Mel said.

"No, of course I don't. But it does feel like that...Take the way it all started, the day my life collided with his crazy life...If I hadn't done a stupid right turn at the Clock Tower roundabout, none of this would have happened..."

Mel shook her head, and buried her smile in the wineglass.

"You can laugh all you like," said Ginny, "but it's spooky...Take the dream I had in hospital. It drew me to his mother like a magnet..."

She told the story of the few past months, finding destiny at work in strings of accidents, weaving a myth out of her own existence in much the same way that Homer must have spun yarns around a fire on some Greek island. And whether it was the wine, or the flickering flames, or whether she was bewitched by her own story-telling, by the time her tale had reached the present moment, she was a believer.

Her audience was unconvinced.

"I don't buy it," said Mel. "You could have walked away. You still could. It's called free will."

"But that's the problem," said Ginny, "I don't think I can. This is what my life is for..."

The phone rang, and Ginny's hand had snatched it up before it could ring a second time.

"Ginny May," she announced.

"Sorry to ring you so late, duck," said a man's voice, "but Sherlock said it wouldn't matter."

Ginny screwed up her face into a mask of puzzlement. "Is that Shirley?" she asked.

"That's right...and I've found your lad."

Ginny threw the duvet to one side. "Is he alright?"

"He'll be fine. He's away with the fairies at the moment, but when he comes down he'll be fine."

Ginny was on her knees beside the mattress. "What do you mean, Shirley? When he comes down?"

"I mean he's as high as a bloody kite. God knows what he's been on, but he's still tripping."

"Where are you, Shirley? I'll come and fetch him."

"I were going to let him sleep it off at my place..."

"No!" said Ginny, getting to her feet. "He's supposed to be here. That's what his licence says."

"Come on, duck," said the transvestite, trying to calm her. "It wouldn't matter for one night."

"No," Ginny repeated. "It does matter."

"Ok, then," conceded Shirley, "no sweat! I'll bring the kid to you. How do I find you?"

Through the kitchen window, Ginny watched the headlights blinking on and off as the car passed behind the screen of rhododendrons. She raced to the front door in time to see Carmichael's Mini Cooper draw up at the end of the path. When she stepped out into the night, the scene was bathed in the harsh whiteness of the security lights. A tall man, dressed in black, got out of the driver's side, went around the car and ducked out of sight. After a few moments he emerged into the light, half-carrying, half-dragging his young passenger. Ginny ran forwards to offer help, and between them they managed to lift Whizz into a standing position.

"I'd best carry the little bugger," said Shirley, letting the boy flop over his shoulder in a fireman's lift.

"Where did you find him?" asked Mel.

"In a right den of thieves," replied Shirley, shifting his load to a more comfortable position. "The whole crew were out of their skulls, so I just picked the kid up and buggered off. No problem!"

With every stride that Shirley took, the boy grumbled incoherently, groaning as air was expelled from his lungs.

"Was Moon Rivers there?" asked Ginny, scurrying to keep up.

"No, he weren't," grunted Shirley, "more's the pity..."

As he negotiated the narrow hallway, Shirley slowed down to avoid bumping his cargo against the walls. When he reached the kitchen, he came to a standstill and stood gawping at the vandals' handiwork.

"I hope none o' this were your doing, sunshine," he exclaimed, addressing the remark to Whizz's backside.

"I'm pretty sure it wasn't his fault," said Ginny. "I think they got him stoned, and trashed the place to get him sent back to prison."

Shirley gave her a bleak look. "Aye, well let's hope so...Now, where do you want him?"

Ginny and Mel had dragged one of the mattresses across the sitting room floor, hiding the three craters that Simon's baby-grand had bequeathed to the carpet. Shirley knelt down by the mattress and twisted at the waist, bending forwards so that the boy's head and shoulders tipped over, ready to be caught by Ginny's waiting hands. Whizz gave another disgruntled mumble, but fell silent as soon as they had his head on the pillow.

"Do you think he's alright?" whispered Ginny.

"It's a trip, that's all..." said Shirley, "...LSD, or the like...Not the best thing for his health, but not the end of the world."

Unconvinced by Shirley's diagnosis, Ginny peered anxiously at the pale young face and smoothed the hair from his brow. The boy's mouth was slack and his eyelids were half-open, revealing two disconcerting crescents of whiteness.

She felt a hand on her shoulder.

"If it's ok with you, Ginny," said Mel, "I'm going to take Shirley upstairs to see the rest of the mess. Then I'll make us all a cuppa tea, ok?"

"Fine," said Ginny, distractedly.

Picking up the duvet from the floor, Ginny reached across the unconscious boy and spread it over him, taking care not to disturb him. Then she leaned forwards and put her lips close to his ear.

"You mustn't worry, Whizz," she whispered. "Whatever has happened, we're going to put things right."

When Mel and Shirley re-appeared carrying mugs of tea and a box of biscuits, Ginny was sitting on the sofa, wrapped in her duvet.

"We've been making decisions," announced Mel, offering a mug to Ginny.

Ginny put a finger to her lips and shushed her, nodding her head towards the sleeping boy. Shirley put his mug down on the coffee table, and sat beside her on the Chesterfield.

"If it's ok wi' you, duck," he said quietly, peeling off one of his gloves, "I'm going to kip upstairs in your room tonight. Mel reckons you could do wi' a man about the house. And I'm your man." He grinned, and waggled his scarlet fingernails in front of Ginny's face. "Apart from Shirley's claws, I'm all bloke today. You can call me Frank, if you like."

Ginny cupped a hand over her mouth and smothered a laugh. "Do you mind if I call you Shirley, Frank? It's too confusing."

"Course not," he said. "I get confused myself when Frank turns up and pokes his nose in."

Without the wig and the make-up, Shirley made a good-looking man, with sturdy features that were in no way effeminate.

"Come on, then," Ginny whispered, "What else have you two cooked up?"

"Well," began Mel, teasing her, "...when you're at school tomorrow..."

"Don't be silly," said Ginny, dismissively, "I can't possibly go to school tomorrow."

"Oh yes, you can," Mel insisted. "You said yourself you'd already taken too much time off this term...and you can't miss the last day."

"And you need to be out of this place," chipped in Shirley. "You don't want to be stuck here fretting, wi' all this crap on the walls..."

"So while you're at school," said Mel, "we're going to make a start clearing up."

"And we'll rope the kid in and all," added Shirley. "It'll do the bugger good."

"And what about Captain Baxter?" said Ginny. "What's he going to do?"

"As long as Sherlock gives him his grub and lets him out to do his business, the Captain will do ok."

"So, that's it," said Mel, rubbing her hands together. "No more arguments, ok?"

But Ginny was not convinced. There were more arguments, not least about who should forgo the comfortable mattress and sleep on the Chesterfield. Eventually, as the hands on the mantelpiece clock were pointing to two o'clock, a bargain was struck. Mel would allow Ginny to sleep on the sofa in exchange for a solemn promise that she would definitely go to school in the morning. Surprisingly, in spite of the tribulations of the day and the sofa's lumpy upholstery, Ginny did not spend long awake.

Chapter Thirty Seven

As was traditional on the last day of the school year, Ginny consigned the National Curriculum to the wastepaper basket. Before break, she raided the store cupboard for a supply of board-games and let the children play while she and Mrs Lockwood began to take down the rich collage of colourful paintings and teaching-aids that had accumulated on the walls over the year. Afterwards they all played *Simon Says* and *I-Spy*, and then went outside to the school field to burn off excess energy with hoops and skipping ropes and footballs.

It was lunchtime before she had a chance to use the phone. The news from home was good. The hangover that had rendered Whizz speechless at breakfast time was being sweated away, thanks mainly to Shirley, who had stuck a paint-roller in his hand and was working him like a slave. Better still, according to Mel, her hunch about yesterday's invasion by the vandals had been more or less accurate. The boy's memories were vague and patchy, but he remembered the hands that had wrenched his jaws apart, and he remembered the gang's laughter as they waited for him to swallow whatever it was they forced down his throat. As to who was responsible—Whizz was saying nothing, except that Cee-Jay was whiter than white.

Ginny returned to the classroom feeling vindicated and better able to enjoy her last afternoon with the children whose tears she had mopped up, whose noses she had wiped, whose cuts and bruises she had tended for an entire year. For them, this last encounter with Mrs May was a Rite of Passage.

She told them how well they had done, and what a lovely class they had been. And she told them that when they came back to school after the holidays, they would no longer be the little ones in the school. They were growing up. Bottoms wriggled on seats, and chests were puffed out. But as well as joy, there was sadness in those saucer-eyes, perhaps even a flicker of fear, and a vague understanding that something precious was slipping away, to be gone forever.

For their final story, Ginny had chosen one of the *Tales from Witchy Wood*. If Dulcie Davenport, aka Mrs Carfax, had been at the back of the class, she would have been pleased, because thirty-three infants – all of them computer-literate, TV-addicted, play-station devotees – had eagerly clambered aboard her ancient broomsticks and let their imaginations fly.

Loaded with two carrier bags full of home-made thank-you cards, various boxes of sweets and chocolates, plus enough cloyingly scented soap to wash an army, Ginny walked through the school with Jason Nolan for the last time. Having been told he was growing up, the little boy had refused her hand, but he shuffled along behind her, subdued and white-faced, making no response as she jollied him along.

Standing apart from the other mothers, Mary Nolan was waiting by the gate, her toddler perched on the end of the pram, screaming as if a wasp had stung him. From behind the pram, a man appeared, brandishing a dummy which he had apparently retrieved from the pavement. He was thickset and bald, with a drinker's gut that strained the red fabric of a Man U shirt.

Jason's small hand took hold of Ginny's wrist, and once again she felt the tug of his reluctance.

After giving the dummy a cursory wipe on his jeans, the man stuffed it into the child's mouth, then grasped the child by the scruff of his neck with his other hand, and forced him to submit to the pacifier. Mary Nolan bent at the waist and screeched like a banshee at the struggling infant, who suddenly went quiet and raised a podgy arm to point down the path towards Jason. Mary turned her head, and swayed. Her glassy gaze took time to find focus, but her lurching advance down the path was swift. Without a word to Ginny, she grabbed Jason by the elbow and plucked him away, leaving behind her the whiff of alcohol.

With Jason dragging his heels in the rear, Mary and her new beau propelled the pram towards the pedestrian crossing, his right hand caressing her right buttock, her raucous laughter loud above the noise of passing traffic.

Before the lights had changed, Ginny was on the mobile, and by the time the Nolan family had reached the far side of Murray's Road, DS Carmichael had picked up.

"I am so angry," Ginny hissed, going on to explain what she had witnessed. "Do we report this to Social Services, or what? There may be no bruises, but why wait? These kids are at risk."

"I wouldn't worry," said Carmichael. "Social Services are on the case already. The guy's a known villain."

"What next then?" Ginny spluttered. "Put them in 'Care', I suppose. Most of Joe Bradley's clients have been in bloody 'Care'."

"This is the real world, Ginny. They can't all have fairy godmothers... How is young Mr Buckley, by the way?"

Ginny drew a breath to steady herself. "Whizz is going to be fine," she said, "thanks to you..."

"Thanks to Shirley, you mean... If we'd been involved, the kid would have been back in Fulford."

"But it was your idea, Tom..."

Carmichael laughed. "Don't you dare tell that to the Chief Constable or I'll never make DI..."

When Ginny arrived home the Mini Cooper was still parked in the drive, and hip-hop was blaring from the open windows in the eyrie. It was a happier return than yesterday.

The kitchen was still in chaos, but the crumpled dust-sheets along the passage to the stairs were signs that restoration was underway. Somewhere, someone was whistling. Ginny dropped her schoolbag on the table, and went to explore.

She found the whistler half way up the stairs. It was Shirley, stripped to his boxer-shorts, reaching high above his head with a long-handled paint-roller gripped in gloved hands.

"Hi, Shirley," she called, "I'm back!"

"Hello, duck," he shouted, looking over his shoulder. "Watch yourself wi' this primer stuff. Don't want you spattered."

Shirley's muscular body was flecked white from head to toe, and he seemed totally unembarrassed by his state of manly nakedness.

"Good stuff this Bin Primer," he said, giving a demonstration with the roller. "I'll leave the tricky jobs for your drummer-bloke, but we'll have most of the place ready for emulsion by the end of tomorrow."

The first-floor landing was already a pristine white and shiny wet. With the exception of Cee-Jay's tag on the sitting-room door, there was not a trace of graffiti to be seen.

"Have you done all this on your own?" asked Ginny, incredulous.

"Not quite. The kid's done his bit."

"Where is he?" she asked.

Shirley hooked a thumb towards the pulse of music. "Up there wi' Mel," he growled, "cavorting around while muggins is working."

The door to the eyrie was wide open. Whizz was dancing in front of the open windows, flanked on either side by Cee-Jay's manga portraits, his back to the door. Behind him and slightly to his left, Mel was doing her best to shadow his routine, her feet and arms a fraction behind the beat. Swivelling at the hip, Whizz turned to the left and performed an elaborate series of arm movements. Mel followed suit. Whizz swivelled again, this time to the right, repeating the semaphore with crisp precision. Mel followed suit...and caught sight of Ginny as she turned.

"You should try this..." she shouted. "It's impossible!"

Crouching down, Mel reached out for Cee-Jay's boom-box and turned it off.

Whizz stopped dancing, and spun round. Twin blotches of red appeared on his cheeks. He looked clumsy and uncertain what to do with his hands.

Ginny took a step towards him and scrutinised his face. "You're looking better," she said.

"He's fine..." said Mel, "bounced back in no time." She draped an arm across the boy's shoulders, and gave him a friendly hug. "And he's been working like a demon, haven't you, Whizz?"

"I feel a total prat," the boy said. "I should never have let them in..."

Ginny was about to make reassuring noises, when a voice behind her said, "Are we on strike, or what?" Shirley pointed a finger at Whizz, and beckoned. "Come on, sunshine, shift your arse!"

Glad of an excuse to leave, the boy squeezed past his taskmaster and led the way downstairs. Ginny closed the door after them, and turned to Mel.

"What do you make of my delinquent, then?" she asked.

Mel was examining a stripy jumper to establish its back from its front. "I've changed my mind about him," she said, and put the woolly over her head. "At first I thought he was making a monkey out of you..."

Her head made a re-appearance through the polo neck.

"So what changed your mind?" asked Ginny.

Mel pushed an arm through a sleeve. "His reaction to the damage....That crude stuff in the bedroom really got to him. He did his best to hide it, but he was close to tears...I don't think he could fake that."

Pulling the hem of the jumper down to her tiny waist, Mel began smoothing out creases with her hands.

"How come the dancing?" asked Ginny.

"I came up to see these," Mel said, looking up at the lightning flash on the ceiling, and spreading her hands to encompass the whole room. "Aren't they fantastic?" She looked back at Ginny, cocking her head to one side. "I bet you didn't know that Whizz had dancing lessons when he was in prison?"

Ginny was piqued. "No, I didn't," she said. "He didn't say a word."

"Teenagers don't tell Mum anything..."

"I am not his mother!" said Ginny, defensively.

Mel lifted an eyebrow. "Oh, but I think you are, in a surrogate-sort-of-a-way...That kid listens to everything you say. He knew all about Lazlo...all about the drama workshops in Fulford...all about the new play...He even knew about me."

Ginny pulled a face. "I'm amazed," she said. "I didn't think he took a blind bit of notice of anything I said..."

"It's not cool to be keen at that age, is it?" said Mel. "But look at the dancing...He's no Billy Elliot, but he's not bad...and you don't get to be as good as that if you're not keen, do you? All these kids need is a bit of encouragement..."

For a moment it seemed as though Mel had more to say, but for some reason she changed the subject.

"Have you looked at your bedroom yet?" she asked.

Ginny shook her head.

"Well, you'd better come and see..." said Mel. "We've worked a miracle in there..."

Holding up a hand, Ginny stopped Mel as she made for the door. "You were going to say something else about Whizz, weren't you?."

"No, I wasn't..."

"Oh yes, you were..."

Mel screwed up her eyes, and ran her fingers through her hedgehog hair. "No," she said, "I really should talk to Lazlo first..."

Ginny grimaced. "You're being a pain, Mel..."

The girl clenched her fists and gritted her teeth. "Ok," she conceded, "but no promises...I was wondering if Lazlo could find something for Whizz in this *Summer Spectacular* malarkey that they're putting on at the Drill Hall..."

Ginny stared at her.

"He'd only be a gofer, doing a bit of fetching and carrying...and he'd have to be up for it. It would be no good if we had to twist his arm..." Mel frowned, and gave Ginny a quizzical look. "What's up? Have you got other plans?"

Ginny shook her head. "If you must know, I've been praying that Lazlo would give the boy a chance, but I didn't have the nerve to ask...Is that spooky, or what?"

"Oh, please..." groaned Mel. "Don't go writing me and Laz into your stupid Greek myth. I'm a free spirit, and I like it that way."

Chapter Thirty Eight

The Drill Hall would have looked at home in the sprawl of buildings at Fulford prison—dull red brick, dull metal-framed windows with grimy glass, and dull paintwork in institutional green. Not a penny had been spent to please the eye. Inside, the space was cavernous, apparently designed to produce maximum clash and clamour for the Territorial Army at play. Every tiny sound bounced off the polished concrete floor and boomed up through steel girders to the corrugated roof, bouncing back to ricochet around a squadron of coolie-hat lampshades with dull, low-wattage light bulbs fighting a losing battle in the vast gloom. It was hard to imagine a less congenial place to celebrate the Community's creativity.

"You can get back to the house now, if you like," said Whizz, "I'll be alright."

"No," replied Ginny, "I'll wait till Lazlo shows..."

She had felt guilty leaving Joe and his *Swamp Rats* to divide up the brushes and rollers. Not that they seemed to mind. When she left, Molly had already commandeered the kitchen to produce the first batch of bacon and sausage butties, and Sticks Munro was revelling in his unaccustomed leadership of the band.

"I'm not a kid, you know," said Whizz.

Ginny gave him a rueful look. "You won't get rid of me, so please don't try," she said.

With deafening squeals and scraping noises, one of the giant concertina doors was pulled open by unseen hands, and a builder's lorry made a noisy entrance, driving the entire length of the Hall to stop beside Whizz and Ginny. The passenger door opened and Lazlo jumped out.

"What do you think of the theatre, then?" he said, spreading his arms out as though he was about to catch a huge football. "Believe it or not, we've got two weeks to turn this dump into a Dream Factory....And it's gonna be..." Lazlo tipped his head back and bellowed at the metal rafters, "...FUN, FUN, FUN..."

Fun, fun, fun doubled and re-doubled itself in the empty spaces.

Lazlo pointed a finger upwards. "That acoustic is our biggest problem. Last year we tried to damp it down with clouds of balloons, but so many of the damned things went off pop, it was like trying to act in the middle of a gunfight. This year we've sold our soul to a local company that makes inflatable giants for advertisers. They're letting us have fifty blow-up monsters, and they'll be up there grinning down at us. We're going to write them into the story and give every one of them a voice, and then we'll bring 'em to life with some tricksy lighting..."

Lazlo's exuberance rolled over Whizz like a wave. An uncertain smile came and went on the boy's face as cavemen and smugglers, sea-monsters and dragons, marching bands and choral societies were conjured up in the vast empty spaces.

"We're calling the show *The Ozone Overdose* because we intend to get off our heads making entertainment. Some of it will be crap, and some of it will be brilliant, but it's all gonna be FUN, FUN, FUN..."

Once again, 'fun' reverberated around the vast hall, until it was drowned out by the roar of a second lorry which arrived at breakneck speed and screeched to a halt on the far side of the hall, brakes squealing.

"That's the scaffolding crew," said Lazlo, "they're gonna build the audience seating, which is one lousy job that's not down to you." He put his arm around Whizz's shoulder. "You, my lucky man, are going on a magical mystery tour with old Curly there..." He nodded his head toward the bald man behind the lorry's steering wheel. "Curly is gonna take you out into the highways and byways collecting scenery from all the local Am-drams and Op-Socs. It'll be a doddle."

Easing Whizz towards the cab's open door, Lazlo did the introductions.

"Curly, this is your assistant, Whizz...Whizz, this is Curly. He's the scene-master..."

The bald-headed man behind the steering-wheel leaned across the passenger seat and offered Whizz his hand, then turned the welcome into a heave and helped the boy to climb aboard. The cab door slammed shut, and the engine roared into life.

"Bye..." called Ginny, raising her hand as the truck pulled away.

"Don't worry about the kid," said Lazlo, "he's in good hands."

"I know he is," said Ginny, giving up on the futile wave, "and I am so grateful that you're giving him a chance..."

"Don't be," said Lazlo, flatly. "To be honest, I need all the help I can get."

Arriving back home, Ginny found Carmichael's Mini parked behind Joe Bradley's rusty old heap of a van, two *Swamp Rat* motorbikes and Sticks Munro's gleaming new transit. There was barely room to park the Saab.

In the kitchen, Molly Bradley was standing by with a bucket of soapy water, waiting to wash the grime from the wall, while Carmichael and Shirley struggled to shift the heavy oak dresser. Ginny called out a cheery hello and thanked them both for coming.

"It's a real pleasure," groaned Carmichael, straightening his back to lift his burden.

Shirley had left Frank at home today, and was dressed for the painting-party in a pretty housecoat over blouse and slacks, with a floral headscarf to protect her blonde wig from splash. Captain Baxter was watching proceedings from the comfort of a basket near the door to the playroom.

In little more than two hours, *The Swamp Rats* had transformed the stairwell and most of the first floor landing with a first coat of emulsion. Instead of the lack-lustre 'Parchment' shade that she had lived with for so long, the walls now had a warm and honeyed glow. Sticks shrugged off her compliments, but she could tell he was pleased.

"Would it be a good time to give me that lesson with the sander?" Ginny asked.

Sticks rubbed his cloth vigorously on the sitting-room door, and the last vestige of Cee-Jay's tag disappeared.

"What's so special about that table then?" he asked.

"I'm wiping the slate clean, I suppose," replied Ginny. "It's a symbol."

As far as Sticks was concerned, all power-tools were well beyond female understanding. Ginny bit her lip and listened patiently while he delivered an idiot's guide to the *Black & Decker* sander. To prove that she had been paying attention, she performed a short and deeply satisfying pass with the whirling sand-paper, erasing the ghost of an ancient wine-spill. Satisfied with his pupil's progress, Sticks finally left her alone, but before the assault on the swastika could get properly underway, a ring on the doorbell brought a halt to proceedings.

Ginny opened the door. "Good God!" she exclaimed.

Bee Mullen had a spark in her eye and a wry smile on her lips. It was the look of someone who knows they're not expected.

"Hello," she said.

Ginny felt the blood flush her cheeks. "You're supposed to be in France!"

"I was in France," replied Bee, "but I flew back for an interview..."

Ginny winced, remembering their last meeting.

"Don't worry," Bee continued, "you were absolutely right. I needed a kick in the bum, and you gave me one..."

"But I shouldn't have said what I said..."

"I should have gone back to work years ago..."

"But it wasn't for me to say…"

The competition in contrition continued a while, ending in a lengthy hug, with both women close to tears.

"Excuse me, ladies," said *The Swamp Rats'* banjo-player, squeezing past with two empty cans of emulsion in each hand.

Bee looked surprised. "You having the place done up?" she asked.

Ginny chuckled. "You could say that...Come and see..."

Although the graffiti was vanishing fast, there was enough damage on view to make Bee cover her mouth and gasp in horror. But as the two women made their tour of the house, meeting painters up step-ladders and painters on their hands and knees, it was the workforce that seemed to make the most enduring impression on Bee.

"What a wonderful bunch of oddballs!" she whispered, as they were coming downstairs.

"Well, if you've nothing else on, why don't you come and join us?" said Ginny.

"Could I?" said Bee, as if she had been awarded a prize.

"Of course, you can."

As they walked through the kitchen, Bee stopped by the table and ran her hand across the patina of interlocking ring-stains bequeathed by dead wine bottles.

"We've had so many good times in here," she said.

"And we'll have more," said Ginny, feeling unexpectedly guilty.

"I hope so," said Bee, giving her a sad smile.

When the wine-stains and the swastika were dust on the floor, and the pine tabletop was virgin-white, it was too clean to touch. It had become alien. Ginny could scarcely wait to find the can of wood-stain.

Bee made her reappearance in a grubby boiler suit, tucked into red wellingtons, with a cloche hat to cover her curls. Despite the strange garb, she could have been on her way to take tea with the vicar. After she had donned her yellow *Marigold* gloves, she took a bowl of wood-stain and began to apply it in slow, circular sweeps of her cloth. Ginny worked on the opposite side of the table, adopting the same, mesmeric rhythm so that the two cloths performed a stately pavane, dispensing a light shade of tan to the pasty wood as they danced together.

Molly had brought a salad picnic, with cold meats and *fruits de mer*, and after a sumptuous lunch, *The Swamp Rats* staged an impromptu concert on the patio—Joe Bradley on squeezebox, Molly on mouthorgan, Fat Boy on fiddle, Bean-pole on banjo, and Sticks Munro beating time on an array of upturned flower-pots. After a couple of foot-tappers, Joe crooned a lilting ballad and, when the old French words finally petered out, the sentimental melody was passed from *Swamp Rat* to *Swamp Rat*.

Bee was stretched out on a garden bench swigging beer from the bottle. Shirley was feeding morsels of sausage to Captain Baxter. And Carmichael had his hands clasped behind his head, leaning back in a canvas chair, soaking up the sad old tune. Propped up against the garden wall, with her bare legs stretched out on the warm York stone, Ginny watched them all through half-closed eyes, feeling safe and cocooned in friendship.

Then Joe's gruff baritone stole back the melody from the band and, after a final refrain and a few minor chords on the squeezebox, he brought the ballad to a sweet and wheezy conclusion.

The applause may have been thin, but it was generous. Shirley whistled her appreciation through a gap in her teeth.

"Not bad for a lawyer," called out Carmichael, clapping his hands above his head.

"God knows what they're gonna make of it in Cajun country," said Joe Bradley. "It'll be like taking guacamole to Mexico."

Ginny opened her eyes. She had forgotten *The Swamp Rats'* pilgrimage to Louisiana. They would soon be gone. So too would Carmichael, off to 'widen' his wretched 'skills-base' at some police college up north. Bee would be back in France, listening to non-stop Charlie. And Mel would be with Lazlo at the Festival in Edinburgh. Come August, only Shirley and Captain Baxter would be left in town. And Whizz, of course.

Chapter Thirty Nine

From that first moment in the Drill Hall, Whizz was stage-struck. He became obsessed with 'The Show', and Ginny became his slave, ferrying him to and fro in the Saab, cooking his meals, washing his clothes, and listening to daily bulletins on 'The Show': Lazlo's battle with the drum-majorettes who couldn't smile and dropped batons; Lazlo's brilliant idea for the caveman sketch; Lazlo directing the army of giants in the rafters; Lazlo persuading the Choral Society to hand-jive as they sang their sea-shanties. While it was wonderful to see him so motivated and to dream giddy dreams of his brilliant future on the stage, at the same time Ginny felt excluded from his new-found happiness, and his dog-like devotion to Saint Lazlo was beginning to grate. After a stern word with herself, she resolved to stop behaving like a jealous schoolgirl, and to concentrate on making some money.

It was while she was packing the box with a few samples of spider-ware for Mrs Carfax to consider...to be precise, at the moment she shrouded a large dinner-plate in bubble-wrap...that Simon made his unannounced and unwelcome reappearance. The flashes of red as the Mazda passed the screen of rhododendrons gave her warning and anyway she was not entirely taken by surprise. The moment Bee put her foot over the threshold of the French cottage and told Charlie about her adventures back home, the jungle drums were bound to beat.

Hurrying down the hall, Ginny put her ear to the front door and listened until the crunch of footsteps came to a stop. Before her visitor could ring the bell, she threw the door open.

"Come to check on your investment?" she asked, looking him straight in the eye.

It was gratifying to see Simon wrong-footed.

"I've come to make sure you're ok," he said.

Ginny did not believe him.

"Well, come on in," she said, waving him inside, "I've finally got the place as I wanted it..."

She was proud of the new decor. The colours were warmer, more imaginative, more daring in every way. Simon looked and made polite noises. They sat at the history-free pine table with their cups of coffee, and they talked of divorce, a civilised conversation in the best tradition of civilised break-ups. Joe Bradley would have been proud of her.

"I don't want to put the house on the market until the boy has served out his licence," she said.

"When will that be?" Simon asked.

"October the second," she replied.

"And then what?"

"I'm going to try to get him away from here...give him a fresh start if I can."

"I wish you luck," he said.

It was an ambiguous remark, and not as kindly meant as his smile pretended.

"Thank you," she said.

Simon opened his old leather satchel and took out two A4 sheets of paper. "We've taken a house down the coast...would you mind forwarding any mail that comes?"

His new address was printed on the sticky labels, twenty-one per sheet, she noticed. It was a posh address, and not far from *Halcyon*. His lady-love had come well-provided for...

"Thank you," she said. "Some letters arrived yesterday. They're on the dresser. I threw everything else away. I'm sorry."

"Please don't apologise," he said. "God knows, I don't deserve any apologies from you."

Ginny looked at him intently, and nodded her head in agreement.

She smiled, and said, "I'm afraid I took out my fury on your books..."

She told him about the bonfire of books she had prepared, and finished off the tale with another apology.

"They're only books," he said, "but I do miss them. Would you mind if I took some away with me?"

"Help yourself," she said, "you know where we keep the cardboard boxes."

Driving into town, she pictured Simon, back in his eyrie, searching through piles of books on his hands and knees, fussing over the broken bindings, filling boxes. He would have noticed the lightning flash on the ceiling and the manga portraits; and he would have shaken that distinguished head of hair, and he would have congratulated himself on the escape he had made. He was getting off lightly...far too lightly...

But then Joe was right. Revenge costs money, and isn't worth the spleen. Besides, their life together was already fading in the memory, becoming unreal—an undeniable fact, and yet insubstantial, like an old movie half-remembered.

Mrs Carfax held up one of the sample serving bowls, turning it slowly in her veiny hands.

"The colours are perfect," she said, "and I love the roughness of the lustres. The web motif is perfect, quite brilliant!" Turning to Ginny, she lowered her chin, and peered at her over the gold-rimmed spectacles, her watery eyes alive with mischief. "Only one thing to add, my dear...Your beautiful spiders are all on the outside of the bowls and the goblets..." She gave Ginny a sly smile that could have belonged to a character in the *Witchy Wood*. "But, you see, my little witches would quite like some of their spiders on the inside, where the food is. In my experience, children squeak and squeal and pretend they are squeamish, but in reality they like nothing better than a good shudder. It's the secret of my success."

After two cups of Earl Grey tea and a compulsory slice of date and walnut cake, followed by another generous helping of flattery, Ginny departed the fine house in Cranbrook Square with her commission secured, almost convinced that she was the finest ceramic artist in the country, if not in Europe.

She was still buoyed up when the Saab drew up outside the Drill Hall, but her euphoria was to be short-lived. From the moment Whizz opened the car door, she knew something was wrong. When she asked him how his day had been, he did not reply. Not that he was truculent or even sullen. He seemed paralysed by sadness, and stared blankly out of the windscreen, his hands resting on a fat script that he nursed in his lap.

"What's the matter?" she asked, gently.

"Nothing," he mumbled.

Ginny reached out and touched the script with her index finger. "I haven't seen this before—has Lazlo offered you a part?"

It was as though she had detonated a bomb.

"I don't want a part. I didn't ask for a fucking part. I don't even want to be in the fucking chorus...I didn't ask for a fucking part..." He was screaming, repeating his mantra over and over again.

Ginny found it hard to breathe. This was no ordinary tantrum. It was as though some inner volcano had blown him apart in a psychic eruption. When the screaming finally stopped, the confines of the car still seethed with rage and distress. The boy's hands were trembling and his face was paper-white.

Ginny laid her hand on his forearm. "Can you tell me why you're so upset?" she whispered.

"Because I'm stupid..." he said, in a voice that was low and hoarse, "because I can't learn anything...because I never could learn anything...because he wants me to learn some stupid fucking songs, and I can't...because I'm stupid... cos I'm stupid and thick...and I'm sick of looking a prat... I'm sick of looking a prat..."

He was in tears now, crying quietly, with his head bowed and his whole body quivering.

Gently, Ginny gave his arm a squeeze. "Nobody is going to make you do anything you don't want to do," she said, and switched on the engine.

Nothing more was said on the drive home. The shock of what she had witnessed remained with Ginny, making her flesh tingle and her heart race. She had heard tales of troubled children whose psychic storms caused poltergeists to crash about the house, made temperatures plummet and conjured foul smells. They were tales she had always dismissed as crackpot, but now they seemed all too plausible...And yet her reason shrank from the easy nonsense of the supernatural. The only demon that possessed this boy was the demon of inadequacy. Deep down, below the bluster, there was no self-belief.

"It's not true you can't learn anything."

She spoke as the Saab turned into the shadow of the copper beech, and the thought had arrived without conscious process.

"I've seen your lips move when you dance," she said. "I bet you know every word of those raps."

She took a sideways glance. Her passenger was poker-faced, but he was listening.

"Maybe you're different," she continued, "maybe you do your learning through your ears?"

Ginny reversed the Saab into the lean-to, and switched off. They sat side by side in the gloom in an expectant silence. It felt as though there was a charge of static in the air, like the hum and buzz around a pylon.

"Have you got an i-Pod, Mrs May?" he asked.

"I got it for jogging," said Ginny, "but, as I never go jogging, I haven't the foggiest idea where it is."

"Could you have a look for it, please?"

"Sure."

"And does the computer have a built-in mike?"

"Yes," she said, "I think it does."

Next morning Whizz came down to breakfast with his usual appetite for grease. He said nothing about the previous day's events, nor did Ginny. In the car he asked if he could have music on the radio, and all the way to the city he played drummer on the script for *Ozone* which rested on his lap. When they arrived at the Drill Hall, he disappeared inside with a cheery wave—crisis over. It was not until the evening that Ginny learned how close his embryonic stage-career had come to termination.

When she collected him at the end of rehearsals, he was so intoxicated by the success of his day that he did not want it to end. Lazlo and his faithful disciples were adjourning to *The Cat* and Whizz was desperate not to be left out.

Secretly delighted to be spared another session with the chip-pan, Ginny complied with her lodger's wishes and, while he played darts with the electricians, she and Mel found a quiet alcove just off the main bar.

"Did Whizz tell you about the fight?" asked Mel.

Ginny frowned. "What fight?"

Mel took a swallow from her pint of bitter. "Happened yesterday...He went for one of the black kids from the Belsize Estate and it got quite nasty. Blood was spilled, I'm afraid, and Lazlo had to pull him off."

"Oh God, I am sorry," said Ginny. "What was it about?"

"Lazlo's not sure..." Mel turned her head and squinted at Ginny. "Does he have problems with reading?"

Ginny shook her head. "No. I taught him myself, and he's very good. Why do you ask?"

"Well, according to Laz, he was fine until they gave him a script...and then he lost the plot. According to Laz, there were lots of kids in the nick who were just the same, and it was usually because they couldn't read...scared rotten that their mates would find out."

"No, it's not reading that's the problem," said Ginny. "I'm pretty sure it's his memory." She took a sip of her wine, and went on to explain what had happened the previous evening. "When he was up in his room with the i-Pod, I googled a bit for 'learning difficulties' and, from what I've been reading, I think he's dyspraxic."

Mel took the glass away from her mouth. "And what's that when it's at home?" she asked.

"They used to call it *Clumsy Child Syndrome* when I was doing my teacher-training, and if Whizz had tripped over his feet and dropped balls like the clumsy kids, we'd probably have spotted the problem at school and all this mayhem could have been avoided. The problem is: not all dyspraxic kids are clumsy. They can have a whole ragbag of difficulties, some of them very hard to live with...In Whizz's case, it's a dodgy memory. Can't remember from the blackboard to the book; and probably can't remember from the book to the brain." Ginny tapped her finger on her forehead. "A bit of faulty wiring up here...and way beyond me, I'm afraid."

"Sounds like you need an Ed Psych on the case," said Mel.

"Fat chance!" exclaimed Ginny. "The kid's allergic to shrinks."

Mel picked up her pint. "Well, however you deal with it... he can't go on punching the lights out of the actors. Much as we love him, Ginny, it can't happen again."

Chapter Forty

For the most part, Lazlo's *Ozone Overdose* lived up to expectations. Despite the uncomfortable seating and an acoustic only partially tamed by airborne giants, the audience seemed to enjoy the proceedings almost as much as the cast. Once Ginny had located Whizz in the vast chorus, she could not take her eyes off him. Not that he was especially dazzling. He was just one kid in a mass of other kids. But the joy on his face as he belted out *The Ozone* anthem, and the confident way he moved in the swirl of the choreography, brought her close to tears.

It was pantomime history, brash and gaudy, like the city it celebrated. And if the performance lacked expertise, it didn't matter. The audience was determined to be entertained. Collapsing scenery and faulty microphones were cheered as lustily as the brilliant Civil War battle and the sweet singing of the Operatic Society's troupe of Pierrots. Even so, as the 21st Century loomed, the palms of Ginny's hands moistened and her mouth went dry. She need not have worried. The entire Belsize Estate had turned out to support their kids, which ensured Whizz and his street-dancers one of the noisiest receptions of the night. Ginny felt sick with pride, and clapped till her hands were sore.

At the end of the Grand Finale, when the applause was finally dying down, the Lord Mayor left his front row seat and was handed a stick-microphone. A collective groan rumbled through the tiers of audience, but His Worship the Mayor was no mean showman himself and, with a rather good joke at his own expense, soon had everyone's attention. He had come to pay tribute to the man 'who had pumped more ozone into the city's lungs than all the good sea breezes.' A spotlight picked out Lazlo, who was forced to run a gauntlet of back-slapping until he was centre-stage. The Lord Mayor thanked him for the contribution he had made to the cultural life of the city, wished him well as he embarked on a new phase of what, everyone knew, would be 'a glittering theatrical career', and presented him with the twin masks of Comedy and Tragedy carved from bleached driftwood washed up on the city's foreshore.

While Lazlo posed for local press photographers holding his trophy aloft, the audience and cast bellowed out *For He's a Jolly Good Fellow,* with Whizz in the front rank, singing as lustily as anyone, as high as he had ever been on speed, but this time on a healthy *Ozone Overdose.*

Ginny allowed herself to fantasize about his brilliant future on the stage, and decided to start a scrap-book, making a mental note to visit the local paper in search of photographs.

Whizz had been dreaming the same dreams. When she found him in the middle of a scrum of fellow actors, all too excited to strip off their costumes and come back to earth, he was ecstatic.

"I asked Lazlo if I could help out on the new play, and he said yes!"

"But they're going to Edinburgh," she said, taken aback.

"Not for weeks," he said, "and there's still loads to do." The joyous expression on his face crumpled. "You're not going to stop me, are you?"

"Of course I'm not," said Ginny, "but..."

Before she could go on, the boy had enveloped her in a hug and was whispering in her ear. "Thank you, Mrs May. You've rescued me..."

Ginny pulled away from him. "Not yet," she said, grasping him by the shoulders. "It's not as easy as that."

But Whizz was not listening.

Instead of trips back and forth to the Drill Hall, Ginny's taxi now yo-yoed between home and the *Old Fish Market Theatre.* Although a mere gofer and probably supernumerary to Lazlo's needs, in his own mind Whizz quickly became an indispensible member of the production crew. Ginny was pleased and amused by his full-blooded commitment. At the same time, she dreaded the withdrawal symptoms when *Like Rabbits* finally took the highroad to Scotland leaving the boy behind.

One morning while he toyed with his bacon and eggs, Whizz raised the subject, casually, with as much nonchalance as he could manufacture.

"Lazlo says I'm doing ok. He doesn't know how they're going manage without me when they get to Edinburgh..."

"I'm sure they're going to miss you," said Ginny.

There was a pause before he asked the question she was expecting.

"Why can't I go with them?"

"Because you're still serving your sentence," she replied. "Your licence says you have to live here, with me. It's what the court specified, I'm afraid."

Whizz gave this some thought. "I bet it would be ok if I asked Mr Beresford."

"Well, you can try, if you like," she said, "but I think I know what he'll say."

No more was said, and Ginny assumed that the boy had swallowed the bad news and moved on. She was wrong. The next time she took him to the YOT, she was waiting for him in the caff, contemplating a second mug of mahogany tea, when he breezed through the door full of fizz.

"You're right," he said, "I'm stuck here till the end of my licence. But afterwards..." His index fingers tapped a tattoo on the Formica table, like the drum-roll before a magician reveals his big surprise. "...afterwards, I can do the tour. Beresford's well up for it. It'll get me right away from all the shit I've been in...Make a new start..."

Ginny had already dreamed this dream. It was the fairytale solution.

"He's right," she said. "It would be wonderful. But the tour may not happen. Lazlo's not got the finance in place yet. And lots of theatres won't book a show until they know they've got a winner..."

"It'll be a winner," said Whizz, "I know it will."

Ginny put her hand on his forearm. "Look, even if the show's a hit and the tour gets off the ground, the budget's going to be very tight. How is Lazlo going to find the cash to pay you, on top of everything else?

Whizz removed his arms from the table, and hooked his thumbs in his jeans' pockets.

"I'll work for nothing," he said.

"I'm sure you would," said Ginny, picking up her mug of tea, "but you'll have to eat, and you'll have to have somewhere to sleep."

"I'll sleep in the bus," he said, eyeing her defiantly.

Ginny sipped her tea. How many times had she rehearsed in her mind the visit to the Chief Executive of William Buckley Motors? It was a scene that always began with an eloquent submission quoting Lazlo on the redemptive power of drama. And the scene always ended with a drawer being opened in the huge executive desk, and the emergence of an impressively large corporate cheque book.

Putting the mug down on the Formica, Ginny leaned forward and looked Whizz in the eye.

"I will do everything I can to make this happen for you," she said. "That is a promise. But I want a promise from you in return. You are not to say a word about this to Lazlo, or to Mel. This is not the time to ask for a favour, because the answer would almost certainly be 'No'. We have to pick our moment. Do you understand?"

Whizz nodded his head.

"And you promise?"

"Yes, I promise."

"Besides," added Ginny, "we have unfinished business. Do you remember the other promises you made...about facing up to your problems?"

Again, Whizz nodded.

"Well, it's more important than ever now," she said. "What is the point of dreaming of fresh starts and bright new futures, if you take all that poison with you when you go?"

Chapter Forty One

When Lazlo's double-decker bus rounded the horseshoe of the harbour taking his cast and crew on the road to Edinburgh, Ginny had been relieved to see them go. Carmichael was up north, 'widening his skills-base'; Joe Bradley was teaching Cajuns how to play their music; and even the Ghetto had emptied for the long vacation. She had been looking forward to having Whizz to herself, to begin unpicking the tangle of his problems and set him truly free. Instead she experienced an irrational sense of abandonment, as though she had been marooned with the boy on some God forsaken island.

Since Lazlo's departure, Whizz had been subdued. She had done her best to woo him with the beach and the bowling alley, even the wretched go-kart track, but he remained beyond her reach...polite enough, but distant. Perhaps, now that the time had come, he was wary of coming too close... Or perhaps it was the oppressive, unrelenting heat of August, which had come in as hot as her kiln.

The blade of the hoe bit scratchily into the baked earth, and Ginny bent down to pull the thistle from its deep anchorage, drips of sweat falling like meagre rain on her gardening glove. She straightened her back and tossed the thistle into the wheelbarrow, then took off the straw hat and used it to fan herself. Across the parched lawn, the wizened branches of the dead fruit trees were a paradoxical glimpse of winter in the heat of summer. They would all have to come down sometime. So why not now?

As she entered the kitchen the fridge shuddered and took a rest. There was not a sound in the house. She called out the boy's name, then climbed the stairs, checked that he was not asleep in the sitting-room, then continued her climb to the eyrie. The door was ajar. She called his name again, and rapped her knuckles on the door. There was no response.

She knocked again, waited a moment, and pushed open the door.

"Whizz…if I got hold of a chainsaw…"

He was naked, stretched out on the futon with a book held in the air above his head.

Ginny turned her back. "If I got a chainsaw, would you cut down the fruit trees for me?"

She waited a moment for a reply, and then tiptoed out to the landing.

It was possible he had the iPod plugged in his ears, so she raised her fist and was preparing to administer a more demanding knock when his voice broke the silence.

"I thought you weren't going to trust me with a chainsaw…?"

Ginny felt ridiculous, like the victim of a schoolboy prank. It was not easy to keep some lightness in her tone:

"You said you'd cut down lots of trees."

"I have cut down lots of trees," he shouted.

There was a pause. "So, what about it then?" she called. "Shall I get hold of a chainsaw, or shall I call a tree-surgeon?"

"Please yourself…"

"Ok then," said Ginny, irritated. "If you're such a wonderful lumberjack, I'll get a chainsaw."

When she returned from the industrial estate an hour later, Whizz took the chainsaw from its box and inspected it with a reverence.

"How come you got a new one?" he asked.

"They wouldn't let me hire one without a Forester's Licence, but they were happy to sell me one in the shop next door…silly, isn't it?"

"Did it cost a lot?"

He seemed genuinely concerned.

"Not that much…" she replied, "surprisingly cheap really."

"I'll tell you what…" he said, "When we've done the job, I'll flog it for you on eBay."

He was like a six year-old with a new toy, desperate to go out into the garden and play. Ginny had a knot of anxiety in her stomach and wished she could take back the last hour of her life. But the display of machismo she'd been dreading did not materialise. Whizz read the safety instructions with care, and put on the plastic goggles and the heavy-duty gauntlets without protest. The chainsaw came to life with an angry whine, and he approached the dying Bramley with respectful caution. He raised the saw and, as the teeth bit into the wood, the old tree screamed.

His father had taught him well. He was perfectly balanced, with his feet well apart to grip the earth. His slim torso twisted as he applied the blade to the bough, the sinews standing proud in his back and arms and his lean flesh quivering as the tree fought back.

As gravity began to drag the branch downwards, a wound opened in the wood. Whizz raised his blade, and the tree stopped screaming. Then with two carefully angled cuts, he dispatched the branch, which fell to earth with a crackling of dead twigs. Ginny moved in to drag away the debris, and Whizz moved on to another branch. The tree shrieked again.

By the end of the morning they had two trees down, and they were working as a team, stacking boughs and trunks to make logs for winter, making a bonfire-pile of the twigs and smaller branches.

"That's enough for today," said Ginny, wiping sweat from her brow with her forearm. "Do you fancy a swim?"

At the Long Naze they made camp in the dunes and walked across the tide-crinkled sand-flats to the faraway sea, then floated side by side in the shallows, gazing up at the hazy sky. The water was warm and the air was still, and the silence between them seemed to grow heavy with unspoken thoughts. Ginny waited for the boy to begin...but, in a frantic windmill-ing of arms, he broke into a splashy backstroke and swam out to sea.

When they had towelled down, she applied sun-oil to the pale-gold skin of his back, and knelt in the sand while he returned the favour. She lay face down on her beach-towel. Whizz shook out his towel and lay down beside her. They were profile to profile, not more than a metre apart. Again she sensed his need to speak, but resisted the temptation to pry. The moment to begin was his to choose.

To her disappointment, Whizz propped himself up on an elbow and reached for his jeans, rummaging in his pockets until he found the iPod. Lying back on the towel, he plugged himself in, and soon his lips were ghosting the lyrics. Ginny opened her novel, and found her place. She would have to wait.

That evening, as she sat at the wheel with her hands on the wet clay, Whizz came into the playroom carrying a large cardboard box.

"Do you fancy being somebody different for a change?" he asked.

Ginny took her hands off the clay and let the unfinished bowl spin on the wheel. "What do you mean?" she exclaimed.

Whizz put the box on the modelling table, and took out a Noh mask.

"I could be this old geezer," he said, holding up a grandfatherly character with a droopy white moustache and long chin whiskers. "And you could be Madame Butterfly..." He showed her the demure features of a young Japanese woman.

"Sounds like a good game," said Ginny, cleaning her hands on a piece of towel. "How do we play?"

Whizz began to take out the Noh masks, laying them face-up on the modelling table until the entire surface was a patchwork of grotesques.

"You stand that side," said Whizz, pointing, "and I'll stand here. We take it in turns, and we change character any time we like."

"Who starts?" she said.

"You do," he said, and held the old man's face over his own.

Ginny disguised herself with the geisha mask. "I have bad news, Honourable grandfather," she began. "When I was picking wild flowers with Honourable Grandmother, the demon of the wild woods turned her into a chicken and tried to catch her for his cooking pot..."

Grandfather had a laughing-fit, and then began to make lots of "Oh dear! Oh dear!" noises while Whizz floundered for a proper reply.

"Then I will turn you into a Monkey Goblin," he said at last, "and you must go in search of Honourable Grandmother. Do not come back without her, Honourable Granddaughter."

It was a hesitant start, but as they snatched up mask after mask self-consciousness vanished. Devils roared, birds squawked and maidens swooned. From the chaos, a ramshackle narrative began to take shape. It featured the *Hannya* princess, played by Whizz in the style of a pantomime witch, and the penis-nosed demon, played by Ginny in a gruff bass voice. After an exchange of venomous curses, the penis-nosed demon decided that he would never meet an uglier and more compatible soul-mate, and

263

the two monsters fell passionately in love. Turning away in surprise, the *Hannya* princess forgot that she was doomed to a life of rancour and bitterness, and became a white-faced geisha-girl.

"Can we do another one?" pleaded Whizz, as Ginny took away the green mask, emerging red-faced and laughing.

"Another day," she said, breathing deeply.

"Oh, please..." he persisted.

"Tomorrow..." she said. "That was great, but I've got a bowl to finish..."

Whizz examined the geisha mask, tilting it back and forth to observe the subtle changes in expression as the light played on the facets of the face.

Ginny returned to the wheel and the unfinished bowl. The play-acting had been fun, but there had been no coded messages... not one that she could decipher anyway. She was disappointed.

Wetting her hands with slip, she kicked the treadle to set her wheel in motion, and let the clay slither between her open palms.

"I haven't been happy like this since I was six."

Ginny's foot came off the treadle, and she looked up. Whizz had slipped the black *Hannya* mask over his face.

"Could you say that again, please?" she said.

"I haven't been happy since I was six."

If circumstances had been different, she would have taken him in her arms and hugged him, as sad little boys ought to be hugged.

"Why is that, do you think?" she asked.

"I dunno..." he said. "I sometimes think I'm not right in the head..."

"What makes you say that?"

"I do mad things..."

"Like what?"

"Smashing things up, burning things...Lots of things..."

The *Hannya*'s hideously twisted features were framed by a halo of blonde hair. Focusing on the narrow eye-slits, Ginny searched in the shadows for the gleam of human eyes.

"I don't think you're mad," she said, "I think you've been doing crazy things because you're confused, and because you're angry. Since you were a little boy, people have been telling you that you're stupid, or lazy, or disobedient. But you're not, are you, Whizz? You're actually an extremely bright person. Your brain has a different way of doing things, that's all. It's no wonder you get angry. Anyone would!"

The *Hannya*'s baleful stare was unmoving. Ginny held its gaze, waiting for a response.

"Could I have a go on your wheel?" said the *Hannya*.

Ginny snorted with laughter.

"What's the matter?" Whizz asked.

Ginny shook her head. "Nothing's the matter. Of course you can have a go. But I want a deal. If I teach you how to raise a pot, you've got to teach me some street-dance...ok?"

The small electric wheel she had used as a beginner was gathering dust behind stacks of unused clay. When they had pulled it out, she switched on and gave him a short demonstration.

"Don't expect miracles," she said. "Just play around. Wet your hands, and see what it feels like to have the clay spinning through your fingers"

Ginny stood behind the boy and watched as the clay slithered and slipped between his clumsy fingers.

"It's not as easy as it looks, is it?" she said.

"No, it's not," said Whizz, and flattened the clay with the palm of his hand.

"I think it's time you felt the magic," she said, and rolled the clay into a ball before centring it again on the wheel. "We're going to pretend that your hands are my hands." She stood behind her pupil and leaned over him, reaching out so that she could grasp his hands. "Now, open your fingers..." she instructed, and placed her hands on top of his hands until they were finger to finger. "That's it," she said quietly, "now when I move, you move, as though your hands are the shadows of my hands."

She lifted her hands, and his hands followed. Slowly she took his hands to the spinning ball of clay and cupped it protectively in the palm of his left hand. With the fingers of his right hand, she pressed down deep into the clay. Slowly and patiently, she brought his right hand towards his left hand and raised them as though in prayer. And the clay responded, silky wet, and compliant...

"That's great," breathed Whizz, as a new pot began to rise from the wheel.

Ginny closed her eyes. His body was warm against her breast, and his hair was soft on her cheek.

She felt his body go tense and immediately removed her hands from his hands. She stepped back.

"You see," she said, "it's easy when you know how. All you need is practice."

Chapter Forty Two

The next day was sultry and oppressive. Ginny abandoned her gardening jeans for some loose tie-at-the-waist jogging pants and put on a flimsy blouse. When she appeared in the kitchen, Whizz was already ensconced, poring over the pages of *The Guardian* which was spread out on the pine table.

"It's a bit soon..." she said, looking over his shoulder, "I don't think they open for another week."

Whizz dabbed his forefinger around the page, counting under his breath. "Jesus!" he exclaimed. "How many shows have they got up there?"

"Hundreds," said Ginny, "and most of them don't make the papers. There's no guarantee that Lazlo will get a review."

"He will," said Whizz, in flat contradiction, "and it'll be a good one."

Ginny put the kettle under the tap and turned on the cold water.

"Do you think we could manage with cereal today?" she asked. "It's too hot for bacon and egg."

"It's never too hot for bacon and egg," said Whizz, "and anyway...you can't expect me to chop down trees if you don't feed me properly."

By mid-morning Ginny was drenched in sweat, and ready to call a halt. Whizz accused her of being a wimp and wielded the chainsaw with renewed vigour, stopping occasionally to wipe the fog from his protective goggles, then returning to the cull as though levelling the orchard were his goal in life.

The solitary drop of rain that splashed Ginny's forearm was a gift from the gods.

"Best get inside..." she said, frowning up at the surly sky, "it looks like a downpour."

On cue, the rain intensified, spattering her face with heavy globules, mingling with her sweat, soaking her blouse, soaking her skin.

Somewhere out to sea a low grumble of thunder rolled towards the coast.

"That's God moving his piano," she said.

"I suppose that's your Granny talking?" said Whizz, as he slipped the plastic sheath over the blade of the chainsaw.

"She loved a good storm," said Ginny. "It's better than going to the pictures, according to her!"

Another growl from the sea was quickly followed by a loud snarl, much closer and more ferocious, as though the cloud masses were muttering to each other, ganging-up to make mischief.

"Shall we watch from the playroom?" said Ginny. "With all that glass, we'll get a fantastic view..."

A pulse of blue lightning lit up the entire sky, as quick as a blink—a trailer for the big feature to come.

"I've got a better idea..." said Whizz, a wayward glint in his eye. "We're gonna dance through it..." Picking up the chainsaw, he started to sprint for the lean-to, but pulled up and turned around. "Go and make some room, Mrs May," he shouted. "It'll be off the hook!"

Ginny squinted against the downpour and marvelled at the shifting mountains of cloud. Why not? There was anarchy in heaven. Why not join Nature in her wild excess?

She had just dragged the heavy modelling table across the stone flags, when Whizz appeared in the doorway carrying Cee-Jay's ghetto-blaster. He was holding out the plug as though to ask where the sockets were, but, before he could speak, lightning lit up the conservatory as if it were the bulb in a flash-gun. They both froze, held spellbound in the unearthly light, too scared to move as twin thunderclaps cracked like rifle shots in the sky above.

Ginny looked up. The glass had held. Rain was hammering down as if furious to be left outside, turning every pane into a fluid lens, smudging the ochre from the hidden sun with the greys and purples of the cloud mass.

Whizz was on his hands and knees scrabbling for a socket, frantic to begin his rain-dance before the storm had spent its fury.

The boom-box boomed; trumpets blared against the thunder, and an insinuating voice began to chant.

Come on now Satan, make your stew
You got a long line for the brimstone brew.

Whizz took a baseball cap from the waistband of his jeans and crowned Ginny, adjusting the angle of the peak until he had made her sufficiently 'street'.

Hey there, sinner, bring that bowl.
Gonna feed your greed for the price o' your soul.

He put his mouth close to her ear. "Just a few basic steps...then we go for it...just let go...hang loose..."

Whizz stepped back and began to jump up and down, feet together, bouncing on the balls of his feet. Ginny copied, self-conscious to begin with, but then, as the pulse took her and she felt the joy of it, she bounced higher and higher. Whizz pointed up at the tumult in the sky, first with one hand, then with the other, shaking his hands as though ringing hand-bells.

Take a bucket o' rye and a can o' coke
An' as much gutter-glitter as a man can smoke.

Thunder pealed, and the bouncing stopped. Whizz was a broken puppet, bent double at the waist, arms hanging loose. Slowly, as though climbing an imaginary rope, he began to pull himself upright, hand over hand, swaying at the hip with each throb of the bass. Ginny followed, raising her face to the storm, squinting as a pulse of sheet lightening shattered to silver smithereens in the watery-prisms.

Demons holler, devils dance
We all at the ball with Beelzebub...

Whizz was climbing an invisible ladder, onwards and upwards, as though trying to climb out of their glass bowl into the chaos beyond.

Read my lips, dumb mother fucker,
We gonna kiss the apocalypse.

Ginny stopped dancing. Whizz had gone where she couldn't follow. He was in the throes of some ecstatic rite, and the rapt expression on his face was strangely familiar.

> *Come hear'nly choirs, come join the jig,*
> *An' shake your ass with Mr Big,*
> *Let's clip them angel wings.*

On impulse, she went to the big storage cupboard and retrieved the shoebox from the disarray on the bottom shelf, then sat on the stone floor, splaying out her legs and leaning back against the old armchair. She put the shoebox on the floor beside her, took out a handful of photographs and began to sift through them.

The storm was beginning to rumble away down the coast, and shafts of hot sun were finding gaps in the scudding clouds. Whizz seemed unaware of the world, and danced on tirelessly.

Ginny looked at the six-year-old, frozen mid-skip as he whirled round the Maypole. Then she looked across at the sixteen-year-old, moon-walking to nowhere.

> *Take the Keys to the Kingdom, sinner man,*
> *An' we'll all sit down to the Devil's Dinner.*

Shuffling the photographs, Ginny found the Buckleys at the sack-race—his mother, quite unlike the shell-of-a-woman that she'd met at *Halcyon*; and his father, fist clenched, urging him on...always urging him on...

> *Yeah, we'll all sit down to the Devil's Dinner,*
> *We'll all sit down to the Devil's Dinner.*

The hypnotic voice had rapped its last, and after a final salvo from the drum-machine Whizz stopped dancing. He put his hands on his knees and began to gulp air. Then he kicked off his trainers, and fell to his hands and knees, still panting.

"Was that as good as it looked?" Ginny asked.

Whizz rolled over onto his back and spread-eagled himself on the cold flag floor.

"That was..." he said, exhaling as he spoke, and panting some more, "...off da fucking hook, man."

"Good as that, eh?" said Ginny, with a chuckle.

"Better," he said, and took several deep breaths.

While she waited for him to recover, Ginny organised the sports day photographs into a neat stack, putting all the pictures of his parents towards the middle of the pile and the Maypole Dance on the top.

"Jesus, I'm hot," said Whizz, and scrambled to his feet. "Let's get some air in this place."

Undoing French windows, he pushed them open and breathed in the fecund smell of garden wetness. To Ginny's surprise, his upper body began to twist and writhe. For a moment, she thought that he was going to dance again, but then she saw that he was trying to wriggle free of his sodden tee-shirt, flexing his back with the effort. When his hands were high above his head, he tossed the shirt away like a used rag, and his hands fumbled with his belt. With a shake of his hips he encouraged the baggy jeans to concertina at his feet and kicked them to one side. Naked now, except for his boxer-shorts, he raised his arms to the sun and let the cool breeze play on him.

"Come and see what I've found." Ginny called.

Whizz turned round. "Can we go swimming later on?" he asked.

"Yes, if you like," she replied. "But have a look at these…" She held up the photographs. "They were taken at your first sports day at Murray's Road, when you were six. You were into dancing even then."

Whizz sat down on the floor beside her and took the pile of photographs in his hand.

"That's my favourite," Ginny said, pointing. "You were the only boy who would dance the Maypole…everyone else thought it was sissy."

Whizz stared at the photograph, a little smile on his lips.

"You were a lovely little boy," she said. "Do you remember that day?"

He didn't need to speak. He was back in the playground, weaving the ribbons with the girls.

Ginny took the Maypole photograph from the top of the pile. "Have a look at the others," she said, "You'll find me in there somewhere, looking podgy, and very young…"

Taking his time, Whizz leafed through the photographs. "That's you," he said, turning a grin on her. "You look just the same."

"No, I don't," she protested.

"Yes, you do," he insisted. "I think you're just the same." He brought the photograph close to his face and studied it, adding, "It's only me that's different."

Whizz continued to browse, barely glancing when he came to the picture of his parents at the sack race.

"They were very proud of you, you know," she murmured.

Whizz held out the pile of photos and, before Ginny could take them, let them spill on the floor.

Ginny began to gather up the pictures. "Don't you think it's time we talked about your family?"

Whizz began to move his hands up and down his bare thighs, from the shorts to the knees, and back again.

Ginny held out one of the photographs at arms' length. It showed the entire Buckley family in the refreshment tent: Will and Chloe, Mum and Dad, all posing for the camera with slices of cake, their mouths wide open, ready to gorge themselves.

"You were all so happy then. And now you can't bring yourself to look at them..."

The hands continued their pointless massage.

Ginny brought the photo closer, and peered at the boy's mother. She had such a zest. It shone in her eyes, and she was beautiful.

"You hurt your mother badly when you cut yourself out of those photographs..."

The hands stopped moving.

"Why did you do it, Whizz?"

In an instant the hands were round her throat and she was keeling over, propelled by the rush of his bodyweight, her head thudding on the stone floor.

"You shouldn't have gone there..." he screamed. "You shouldn't have fucking gone there..."

He was kneeling astride her, his hands tightening their grip on her throat. Ginny took hold of his wrists and struggled, croaking as she begged him to relent. His hands came off her throat, but he shook off her grasp and clenched his fists. Ginny flinched. The fists began to flail about, punching the air as if fighting phantoms.

Ginny massaged her throat with one hand, and laid the other gently on his chest.

"Listen..." she said, in an urgent whisper, "please listen..."

He was crying now, his breath stuttering so that his whole frame trembled under her touch.

"Listen...please listen..." she whispered again.

She ran her hands up and down the flanks of his body, repeating the mantra over and over until he grew quiet.

"I did go to see your mother, but it was a long time before we made our bargain...."

He was wiping away tears with the heels of his hands.

"I'd just lost my baby and I was in hospital, and I had a strange dream about your mother...I don't know why...I suppose I was worrying about you going to prison...But it was the dream that took me there..."

He had placed one of his forearms across his eyes, as though he fending off the thoughts that troubled him.

"I haven't broken any promises. And that's the truth... Do you believe me, Whizz?"

Behind the raised forearm, the boy nodded.

Ginny reached up and slipped her hands around his back, pulling him towards her. "Come here..." she murmured.

Whizz leaned forwards and, in the same movement, slithered along her body until his head was buried in the crook of her neck. Ginny cradled him in her arms, rocking him gently from side to side, kissing his hair, letting her fingertips give comfort on the satin skin of his back. Slowly the tension in him ebbed away, and the sobs subsided.

For a long time they lay still and his body grew comfortably heavy, his heart beating against her heart. And then they became aware of the closeness, each alert to the other, scarcely daring to breathe. Whizz turned his head and his breath was on her neck. She felt his lips graze the soft skin behind her ear. An ambiguous caress: maybe an accident of proximity; maybe a question?

Letting her hands slide down the flanks of his slim body, she hooked her thumbs inside the waistband of his shorts and raised the cotton from his flesh, asking a question of her own. In response, the boy raised his hips, and she eased his shorts over his buttocks.

There was a moment of awkwardness while she wriggled free of her sweatpants and her briefs, but then he was between her thighs, urgent and clumsy. Reaching down, she took hold of his penis and helped him to find her.

Her body was ready, and she felt full of him. But there was to be no fulfilment. After a second thrust, his back arched like a longbow and he let out a groan that was more anguished than ecstatic.

Ginny held him close, holding him inside her, placing kisses on the side of his face and neck. For a moment he lay still, breathing deeply. Then, without warning, he pulled out of her, and scrambled to his feet. Too shocked to speak, she watched him snatch up his jeans and make his escape into the house.

Lying back on the flagstones, Ginny looked up through the vine-tresses at the broken white cloud and the blue sky, marvelling at how quickly the storm had blown itself out. She let her head fall to one side and looked at the garden through the open French windows. Water was dripping from the guttering and the hot sun was teasing wisps of vapour from the lush grass. A bright-eyed starling was keeping watch for a thirsty worm.

Chapter Forty Three

Ginny tapped her knuckle gently on the door. Receiving no response, she eased the door open a fraction.

"Can I come in?"

She peeped round the edge of the door. He was lying on the futon, half-covered by a sheet, his back towards her and his face to the wall.

"I think we should talk, don't you?" she said.

The reply was muffled.

"What did you say?" she asked.

"I said, leave me alone!"

Ignoring the aggressive tone, Ginny crossed the room and stood beside the huddled shape on the futon.

"I'm going to get into bed," she said.

She waited a while, giving him the chance to reject her, then slipped out of her dressing gown and let it fall to the floor. As she peeled back the sheet, the boy did not move. He was naked, curled up like a foetus and just as vulnerable. Lying down beside him, she wrapped an arm around him and shaped her body to his body as best she could.

"You've done nothing wrong," she said, whispering into the soft down at the nape of his neck. "If anybody has done wrong, it's me...What happened after the storm should never have happened. But it did. For whatever crazy reason, we reached out to each other, and now things cannot be the same. Either we try to make something good come out of this madness, or we find somewhere else for you to live. It's your choice. If you want, I'll call Beresford and tell him that things haven't worked out between us... Whatever you decide, I shall understand. All I want is to do what's right by you."

What she had said she meant. But what she could not voice, except in her nakedness, was her need for him, a hunger more powerful and mysterious than mere lust. It was a primordial imperative that she did not understand, a challenge to her reason and her power to choose, as though the Fates were at work again.

They lay together, scarcely daring to breathe, as though a breath could blow the fragile moment away; skin to skin, warmth to warmth, waiting until the distance between them had melted to nothing. The boy was the first to move, reaching for her hand and clasping it to his chest, unwinding the curl of his body so that she was able to tuck her knees behind his thighs. Ginny let out a long sigh of relief, an exhalation of hot breath that rustled the hair behind his ears.

Whizz raised his head from the pillow. "You needn't worry," he said. "You're not going to get AIDS."

Ginny stiffened. "I wasn't thinking any such thing."

"You did think I'd been raped though, didn't you?"

She paused. "I suppose it had occurred to me...but..."

"Well, I wasn't..."

His head was back on the pillow, but there was a new tension in him.

"So what did happen then?" she asked.

"They rammed a bar of soap up my arse..."

The crudeness of his reply robbed Ginny of words.

"Aren't you going to laugh?" he said. "Everybody else did."

"No, I am not laughing," said Ginny, pulling him to her. "What happened to you was awful...as bad as rape."

"They put me in the Sissy Wing, so I couldn't get my hands on the bastards that did it. But I'll get them one day."

Ginny pressed her mouth to his ear. "You mustn't talk like that. It's over, and done..."

"No, it's not," he said. "If they give you shit, you've got to give them double shit back."

"Forget all that Moon Rivers nonsense," she whispered, "that's all in the past. You're moving on..."

For a long time she held him close, murmuring words of reassurance, nuzzling the back of his head, kissing his shoulders until she felt the tension and the anger ebb away. Then she turned onto her back.

"Turn round, Whizz," she said, "let me see your face."

With a show of reluctance, Whizz turned and propped himself up on his elbow. His eyes were drawn irresistibly to her naked breasts but immediately skittered away to inspect the mural of the Jedi knight.

Ginny smiled. "Don't be shy," she said, and pulled him down so that his head was on her breast. "We must be as honest and open as we can."

Taking hold of his hand, she placed it palm down on her thigh, covering it with her own hand, finger to finger, so that once again his hand became the shadow of her hand.

He was a responsive and eager pupil. Once he had discovered her pleasure, he was anxious to please, and they made love frequently, day and night at first, always at her instigation, on the futon below Cee-Jay's lightning flash.

When they were not in bed, Ginny slaved on the Carfax commission, hand and eye working with speed and confidence to produce pots that were full of verve and spontaneity. Sometimes Whizz worked as her assistant, loading and unloading the kiln, wrapping and boxing the finished pots; more often than not, he worked in the garden, soaking up sun and growing stronger. To her great relief and gratitude, when they were away from the bedroom he did not pester her with furtive caresses or flirtations, nor even look at her with lust in his eye. Their uninhibited couplings seemed to take place in a world apart from the everyday-ness of life. But there was more kindness in his manner, as if, in the humdrum of existence, he were able to cast aside the mask of Whizz and live for a while as Will.

It was not long before he realised that there was insufficient work to keep him occupied in the garden and he volunteered to become the maid-of-all-work in the house, wielding a duster with more enthusiasm than diligence and knocking chunks out of the new paintwork with the vacuum cleaner. Ginny hid her winces, and let him loose, observing him from a discreet distance. At first she attributed his slap-dash housework to the incorrigible sloppiness of the teenage male, but patterns began to emerge in the chaos he created: cupboards, once opened, would have their contents thrown into disarray, and their doors would be left open; likewise the drawers... every single drawer, once opened, would be ransacked for whatever it was he wanted, then left unclosed. The house always looked as though a burglar had been disturbed at his business. Whizz seemed utterly unaware of the mayhem he created, and continued with work cheerfully. In the interests of harmony, Ginny tried hard not to nag, but her patience was often tested.

The dishwasher was a particular source of irritation. Exasperated by finding unwashed pans and mugs full of dirty water when she unloaded the machine, Ginny watched him carefully the next time he offered to clear up after supper. Everything was piled into the machine haphazardly... dinner plates laid flat, instead of in their racks...mugs the wrong way up or covered with upturned saucepans...pots piled on pans, pans piled on plates. He was either blind to the logic of the layout, or he couldn't care less – it was hard to tell. But when she gently pointed out the correct way to proceed, he gave her a mouthful of abuse and refused to load the machine again.

The lawn was an exception. So proud was he of his razor-edged stripes that the lawn was cut more frequently than strictly necessary. Was it the unambiguous simplicity of that straight line which guaranteed him success...or was it the praise that came with it? Probably both.

Ginny renewed her vow to stem the flow of criticisms and promised to praise every achievement, however trivial. This was a difficult oath to keep. Tired of crunching her way through a scatter of spilled sugar on the floor of the galley, she watched him transport a teaspoon piled high on a perilously long journey from the sugar bowl to his coffee mug, and could not resist a word of advice.

"You would save yourself a lot of mess if you moved the sugar bowl to the mug, or the mug to the sugar bowl."

Fortunately, the boy was concentrating so hard on his problem that the implied criticism went unnoticed. From his vantage point, the physical world made perfect sense. A spoonful of sugar was required elsewhere, so why not move it? To the observer, he looked incompetent and stupid...which he was not.

To Ginny's surprise, he began to pore over the news pages in *The Guardian* and quizzed her about the happenings in the world. Unafraid to reveal his ignorance, he seemed anxious to learn, as if he knew that he had wasted precious time and had catching-up to do. Once, on the way home from the cinema, they argued about the film they'd seen...the plot, the acting, the music, the sound design...little escaped his shrewd eye, and he voiced his opinions clearly and cogently. Another evening, he raided the bookshelves for a volume of short stories by one of Simon's *Dirty Realists*, and read her a bleak story about a recovering alcoholic in an American accent that would have impressed even Simon.

Observing him as he made a hash of some menial task, or listening to his childish curses as he played games on his mobile, Ginny's conscience would sometimes spring an ambush, leaving her dry-mouthed and sick with guilt. That she was sleeping with this damaged boy was tantamount to child abuse. She knew that, and hated herself. But as the sun began to dip in the sky and the night threatened, she wanted him again. She wanted to hold him close, and bring him comfort. At the same time, she wanted his body with an appetite that alarmed her, and brought her shame.

They had abandoned Simon's eyrie by now, and were sleeping in the big double bed. And every night, when their passions were spent, they would lie back and talk to the ceiling, playing the Truth Game that they had invented in the prison Visiting Room, swapping truth for truth in accordance with rules that Whizz had devised. Rule One: he would begin, quizzing Ginny about some secret corner of her life. Rule Two: she would reply with the stark truth, however painful. Sometimes his cross-examination bordered on cruelty, and she would be left on the verge of tears. When he had exacted enough truth, he would volunteer a confidence of his own. But he was not especially generous with his offerings, sometimes making her wait for days before he found his voice. If Whizz was going to quarry in dark places, it would only be when he was ready and on his terms.

And then, one night he said, "Have you ever thought you were going nuts?"

"Yes," replied Ginny, without pause for thought.

"When?"

"If you must know, I don't think I'm quite sane right now...at this very moment, lying here in bed with you. If this isn't madness, what is?"

The question seemed to hang in the air defying a response.

"Why is it madness?" he asked.

"Because I'm old enough to be your mother," she said, "Because I'm supposed to be helping you find a way out of your problems. Because it's wrong for an older woman to take advantage of a boy like you."

"It was an accident," he said.

"Sex is never an accident," she contradicted. "Whatever part of me it was that let this happen...it was a part of me. I'm a grown woman. I'm responsible for my actions, and I'm ashamed..." Reaching out, she grasped his forearm. "Not of you..." she went on hastily, "you have no blame in this. A judge would say that you were my innocent victim...and he'd be right."

Whizz turned his head on the pillow. "I'm sixteen," he said, "and the Law says I'm old enough."

"That doesn't stop me feeling guilty," countered Ginny. "But the terrible thing is...the guilt doesn't stop me wanting you. That's why I feel so torn in two...as if I'm in the grip of a great madness...and I don't understand what's happening to me..."

There was a pause, and then he murmured, "That's how I feel..."

Ginny gave his arm an encouraging squeeze. "What a pair!" she said. "Two corks adrift on a stormy sea...Perhaps, if we cling together, we can both be saved?"

Whizz said nothing. He had gone to that inner place beyond her reach, and it was a while before he found his voice.

"I knew they'd gone away for the weekend, so I came home to nick a few things..."

Instantly, Ginny knew that she had paid his price.

"...I was off my head on speed, and when I came across the albums, I lost it...I went looking for matches...to burn them...maybe set fire to the house..."

Ginny waited for him to go on, but it seemed as though his memory had stalled.

"Why didn't you burn them?" she asked. "Why go to the trouble of cutting yourself out of all those pictures? It must have taken ages..."

"That were Moon's idea. He thought it would be a good laugh."

The tiny hairs on Ginny's arms bristled and her skin crawled.

"And Moon did the cutting?" she asked.

"Yeah, Moon used his blade on one book, and the other guys done the rest with a pair of scissors."

"And why was it such a 'good laugh'?"

"Moon reckoned if the cutting was neat and tidy they wouldn't notice at first...and then, when they saw all those little white holes where my face should be, they'd feel like shit...and all those 'happy memories' they were always going on about wouldn't be 'happy memories' anymore, would they? They'd just be memories."

"That's cruel," said Ginny.

"Yeah," agreed Whizz, "it was meant to be cruel. Why should they remember 'happy' days when I was fucking miserable?"

"And let me guess..." began Ginny, "you didn't let them damage the ones when you were very little, because you were happy then?"

"You got the message," said Whizz. "I hope they did."

"Oh, they got the message alright. Of all the terrible things you did, I think those photographs hurt them the most—especially your mother."

Whizz gave a mirthless chuckle. "After we'd fucked up the albums, we went up to my bedroom and we demolished it, broke every window, smashed every piece of furniture, ripped down the wallpaper, cut the carpet to ribbons...And then we tidied up the mess into nice neat piles, like they were always nagging me to do...How's that for 'nuts'?"

His grin was invisible in the half-light, but she knew it was there.

"I don't think you're crazy, Whizz—I think you're angry. You have a dangerous amount of anger locked up inside you. And the silly thing is, there are people who could help you flush it away...if you'd only let them."

"I've told you before. No Shrinks! I don't want no creepy gits poking around in my head."

"These people are psychologists, not psychiatrists. And you don't have to see any of them. You can read what they have to say on the computer. What's the harm in that?"

He was listening, but he made no response.

"Would you read the website I've found?" she asked. "I really think it could help you..?"

Before he could answer, a cat screamed in the garden. It was the long, agonised yowl of feline passion which silenced the early dawn chorus and shattered the mood of the confessional.

"I'm tired," said Whizz, and turned away from her.

Ginny put an arm around his huddled form and kissed the soft skin of his shoulder. For the first time he had acknowledged the existence of his family. It was a good beginning.

"There's something you should know," she whispered. "Your mum and dad still care for you. In spite of all the terrible things that have happened and although she is sick with worry, your mother still loves you very much. You must remember that..."

Again she brushed her lips against the boy's shoulder, and wished him good night. Then she lay back on the pillow, and pictured Moon Rivers in the *art deco* luxury of *Halcyon*, knife in hand, bent over the photograph album, intent on stealing so much more than Buckley's precious trinkets.

Chapter Forty Four

The tyres were rolling down the hill, an inexorable tide of black rubber, rank upon rank, growing huge, blotting out the fierce sun...And her sandals were stuck in the ticky-tacky tarmac...And the tyre-treads were like teeth...And the breath of the beast was hot in her face...

Gasping for air, Ginny opened her eyes and stared wildly about her.

"It's alright...it's alright..." said a voice beside her. "Don't be frightened..."

In the no-man's-land between nightmare and the half-light of dawn, Ginny groped for reality. And then she remembered the boy. She turned her head on the pillow.

He was propped up on his elbow gazing down at her, his expression troubled.

She attempted a smile. "I'm sorry," she said, still breathing in spasms. "It's only my silly dream..."

His fingers began to move aside the strands of her hair that were plastered sweatily across her face.

"You're soaked," he murmured, caressing her brow and drawing his hand slowly down the line of her chin.

The tenderness of his touch was disconcerting. "I'd better have a shower," Ginny said, making to get up.

"Not yet," said Whizz, laying his hand on her shoulder. "Tell me about the dream..."

She looked away.

"You've been thrashing around for ages..." he said. "It must be lousy?"

Lying back on his pillow, he slipped an arm behind her head and drew her to him, so that she lay with her head above his heart.

"It must be scary...?" he said. "Tell me about it."

"It's been plaguing me since I was very little," Ginny began, and went on to recount the nightmare in every minute detail.

When she had finished, Whizz said, "Do you know what it means?"

"I'm not sure you can interpret dreams like that," Ginny replied. "But my father was killed in a car accident, and I've always wondered if it was something to do with that."

"Do you remember him?"

"Not really...I was only about five when it happened, and my memories are foggy. I can remember my mother though. They took her away in a big black car...and I remember her face in the window, looking sad. I've always had the nagging feeling that everything was my fault...the accident, the taking-away of mummy...everything."

His fingertips had stopped stroking the nape of her neck, and his hand was warm against the skin of her back.

"You were too little..." he said. "It couldn't have been your fault."

"That's what Gran always said, but something put the idea in my head and I can't shake it out."

After a moment's silence, he said, "Was that the last time you saw your mum?"

Ginny gave a barely perceptible nod of her head. "They didn't tell me that she'd died until I was a lot older...and I've always wondered if she might have killed herself."

"What made you think that?"

"Because in the stories that Gran used to tell me, mummy was always having such a lovely time it was all too good to be true—the stories couldn't possibly be true. They were just fairy tales, like the *Merry Maid* stories. Something really bad must have happened."

"And she never told you the truth?"

Ginny shook her head against his chest. "She was protecting me, I suppose...doing her best..."

Whizz nuzzled her hair and his hand moved softly back and forth on the skin of her arm.

Ginny savoured the compassion in his touch. In this reckless intimacy he was discovering something good and kind in himself. Will was emerging from the shadows.

For a merciful instant, this consoling thought drowned out the guilty whispers in her divided self. And then the moment was spoiled. Whizz was back.

"Do you think you married old Prof Wanker Bollocks because you lost your dad when you were little?"

Ginny lifted her head, and then propped herself up so that she could look at him. "My grandma didn't use foul language like you, but funnily enough that's exactly what she always said."

"Well, the old fart is a lot older than you, isn't he?"

Ginny flopped back on her pillow and addressed the ceiling.

"I've been thinking about that a lot recently, and you're probably right... Maybe I married him for all the wrong reasons...poor bloke."

"He's a bastard. You said so yourself."

"Maybe he is...but we all screw up sometimes. Look at me."

"He's a shit."

"Maybe he is...but maybe he's just a bloke who fell in love when he was very young and never got over it..."

"He's a shitty bastard."

"Well, I've got to move on..." said Ginny, forcefully, "because if I don't, I'm going to turn into an embittered old hag with a face like that *Hannya* mask, and I'm not going to let that happen."

Yet again the morning trawl through *The Guardian*'s arts pages produced nothing. It was hard to say who was more disappointed.

Ginny turned back a page to double-check that she hadn't missed a mention in the Edinburgh Diary. "Dammit!" she said. "I thought today would be the day."

Whizz said, "Why don't you ring Mel...see how it's going?"

Ginny shook her head. "I don't want to push our luck."

Whizz cocked his head, and gave her one of his lopsided grins. "You're frightened you're going to get stuck with me, aren't you?"

"Don't be silly," she said, and busied herself with the dirty breakfast dishes. "Why don't you get yourself into the garden and give that tree-surgeon a hand?" She tugged at the back of Whizz's chair. "Come on..." she said, "shift your bones! Go and build your wretched bonfire!"

While the PC was booting-up, Ginny went to the window and looked out across the lawn to the orchard where the tree surgeon was manhandling his infernal digging-machine in a battle with an obdurate tree-stump. He was on his own, but then, from the back of the bonfire pile, Whizz appeared, and began to harvest more debris.

Ginny selected the tiniest key on her key-ring and unlocked the escritoire, lowering its angled lid to make the writing-desk. From an inside drawer, she removed the file she was preparing for Whizz's father. It was already a substantial dossier. Putting to one side the photographs of *The Ozone Overdose* from the *Evening Echo*, and the American article on *Learned Helplessness*, she retrieved the copy of *Borka* which Whizz had stolen from her classroom, and examined the address that he had scrawled on the back cover. Even making allowances for his haste, the writing was babyish and ill-formed.

Googling the *Dyspraxia Society*'s website, Ginny scrolled to the page that dealt with handwriting, and held up the copy of *Borka* to one side of the screen. She began to cross-reference. The comparison was startling. In every minute particular, the boy's writing conformed to type—letters back to front; the tails of letters like 'b', 'p' and 'd' confused or non-existent. And her address was written in tiny, malformed letters, as though he'd been too ashamed to make them larger.

Ginny printed out the relevant pages and put them in the folder with the copy of *Borka*. This was exactly the kind of concrete evidence that would impress a businessman—graphic, clear, and conclusive. All she needed now were rave reviews from Edinburgh, and her case would be complete.

The stink from the garden assaulted Ginny's nose as soon as she opened the kitchen door. It was a toxic marriage of disinfectant and coal-tar, and she could taste it on her tongue.

"You'll have the pong for quite a while," said the tree surgeon, flicking his horny thumb through the wad of ten pound notes. "It'll be worth it though. That Honey Fungus is a bugger."

When the truck had trundled away up the drive, Ginny gazed down at the poisoned earth beneath her feet, and sniffed with distaste.

"What say we go and get a blast of sea air?" she said.

"I don't fancy a swim," Whizz replied, "not in this wind."

"What about *The Dragon's Back* then?" she suggested. "There should be some hang-gliders up on a day like this..."

"That'd be cushty!" said Whizz, "I haven't been up there since we pushed a four-by-four over the top..."

"You did what?"

"We pushed a Toyota right off the top...It was fantastic."

Ginny looked at the glee on the boy's face. "Why on earth would you do a stupid thing like that?" she asked.

Whizz shrugged. "For a laugh, I suppose."

"Was it one of your father's?"

Ginny was braced for trouble, but an amused smile flickered on the boy's lips.

"It might have been," he said, "or it might not have been... I can't remember."

Ginny folded her arms, and looked at him askance. "Why did you go to war with your dad?"

"Why not?" he said. "He was at war with me..."

"Tell me more," she said.

Whizz shook his head. "Maybe I'll tell it to the ceiling sometime..."

From the topmost point of the jagged limestone ridge, a hang-glider launched itself into space and began to search for thermals above the pastel patchwork of the fields below. Whizz shaded his eyes from the low sun, and followed the glider with rapt attention.

"It's not my idea of fun," said Ginny, "being strung up in a kite with a thousand feet of nothing underneath."

"Must be a hell of a buzz..."

"You like being on the edge, don't you, Whizz? That's the real reason you do all these crazy things, isn't it?"

"It's better than drugs," he said, and gave her a sideways glance. "Doing a ton with a pig on your tail beats a line of coke any day."

In the past, whenever she'd tried to talk to him about drugs, he had pulled the shutters down. This was a first.

"Have you done lots of coke?" she asked.

"Not enough to put a hole in my snout."

"So what were you on the day they wrecked the house?"

"Acid..." he replied. "They held me down and stuffed some tabs down my neck."

"Was it Rivers?"

That was a mistake. His look was sharp as a knife.

"I've told you before..." he said, "I don't grass."

"Joe Bradley thought they were on crack..."

"Some of them were, but most were on ketamine..."

"Have you ever done crack yourself?"

Whizz gave a vigorous shake of his head. "No crack, no smack. Moon taught me that."

The wind gusted, catching hold of Ginny's hair and wrapping it around her face. She pulled the strands from her mouth and swept her hair back, turning to face the wind, careful to keep sight of the boy in the corner of her eye.

"Did Moon look after you when you went on the streets?" she asked.

"Without Moon, I'd have been dead by now. He was a good mate...found me somewhere to doss down; taught me to survive on the streets."

Ginny anchored her hair with one hand, and turned to face him. "So why did you fall out with him then?"

"Dunno," said Whizz.

He had spoken without thinking, and he looked sad. It was the simple truth.

"It's time you were honest about Moon," she said. "I know for a fact that he got you 'banged-up' in Fulford, and I wouldn't mind betting he made trouble for you when you were in there...He's probably still after you, isn't he?"

"Look," cried Whizz, pointing down into the chasm, "he's found a thermal..."

The hang-glider was soaring skywards. When he reached their altitude, he levelled out and hovered, close enough for them to see his goggle-eyes and hear the wind shiver the membranes of his wings.

"I'm like him..." Whizz said. "If I'm going to kill myself, I want to see it coming... Crack and smack are for the brain-dead...Give me speed any day..."

The glider banked and began another spiral descent, plummeting towards the dinky cars on the ribbon-roads and the ant-cows on the painted pasture. Ginny felt giddy, and stepped back from the precipice.

"Do you think the theatre's going to give you the buzz you need?" she asked.

"It's got to, hasn't it?" he said.

He was silhouetted against the glory of the setting sun, gazing down into an abyss of his own thoughts. Ginny hugged her coat against the wind, and waited.

"Can we go home and talk to the ceiling?" he said.

They followed their long shadows down the hillside to the Saab. Ginny switched on the radio and they drove home through the quiet country roads, grateful to the music that made talk unnecessary.

When they reached the house, they dispensed with supper and went straight to bed. Whizz was impatient, as though love-making were a tiresome preamble to what really mattered. When it was over and they were lying back on their pillows, she reached out under the sheet and took hold of his hand, sending a signal through the flesh that he was not alone.

They lay side by side, for a long time; Ginny waiting; Whizz summoning the courage to begin.

"Have you been with lots of blokes?" he asked.

"No, I have not," she retorted angrily.

Swallowing her irritation, she made the confessions that the truth-game demanded, telling him about the shy lad from school and their clumsy couplings in the shed on the allotment. When she described her many 'tutorials' in Simon's study his interest quickened. Whether it was his deep loathing for Simon or whether it was sheer dirty-minded curiosity was hard to tell, but she did not like his prurience and brought the cross-examination to an end as quickly as she could.

"So the answer to your question is 'Two'," she said. "It's not a very impressive total is it? What about you?"

"Only one..."

Ginny turned her head on the pillow. "Do you mean I'm your first?"

"No," he replied, "there was somebody else."

Ginny waited.

"It was Chloe..."

The room was so quiet that she could hear the blood sing in her ears.

"Do you mean your sister?" she said quietly.

"She's not my real sister," Whizz said. "They adopted Chloe because they couldn't have kids...and then, straight away, I came along. Mum always said I was her 'little miracle'."

Chapter Forty Five

The newspaper boy was late, and they almost ran him down as his BMX turned into the drive at racing speed. Ginny braked to a halt, and the boy performed an impressive skid-turn to come alongside. The newspaper appeared through Ginny's open window, and Whizz reached across to snatch it away. He was already leafing through the pages before the Saab escaped the shadow of the copper beech.

"This is it," he said, and lowered his head to the print.

"Well?" snapped Ginny. "What's it say?"

"It's brilliant," said Whizz, and went back to his feverish reading.

The review for *Like Rabbits* was indeed brilliant. The critic loved the bawdy bits, and loved the language more. It was a triumph. Even before Whizz had finished reading it out, Ginny was making plans to phone his father. If she had sat at the computer to write a testimonial for Lazlo, she could not have produced anything so lavish.

"I'm gonna need new clothes," said Whizz, talking to himself.

"Hey! Hold on there, mister...This tour isn't on yet..."

"It will be..."

His optimism was premature...and yet she couldn't help sharing his excitement. Every piece of the jigsaw was sliding neatly into place, as if the gods were smiling on them.

"Can I take this to show Beresford?" Whizz asked, holding up the folded newspaper.

"Of course, you can. But don't count your chickens—it could still all go wrong."

Having dropped him off on the opposite side of the road to the YOT, she watched him negotiate the heavy traffic before heading for her usual parking place outside Tano's Cafe. There would be no mahogany tea today. The mobile was in her hand before she had switched off the engine.

Mel answered her phone after three rings. The company had just finished reading the papers, and everyone was ecstatic. Ginny gushed out her congratulations, and asked about the tour.

"It's still not a cert," said Mel, "but if the money-bags don't cough after this, it would be a real bummer..."

"And what about my delinquent?" said Ginny. "Is Lazlo still up for taking him along?"

"You'd better ask him yourself," said Mel.

There was a pause and a mumbling of voices as the phone was handed over.

"I'm feeling bad about this, Ginny," Lazlo began, "but even if we get a green light, I won't have the cash to spare...It was stupid of me to raise the kid's hopes."

"Don't worry about the cash," Ginny said. "If I come up with enough to pay his bed and board, and give him some pocket money, would you take him then?"

"Of course, I would," Lazlo said, "but how can you possibly afford to...?"

"It won't be my money. Look...I can't say anymore. But keep your fingers crossed."

Ginny closed her phone and drew a deep breath. From the zipped pocket in her purse, she retrieved Buckley's business card. On the back, he had written his mobile number. The numerals were boldly written, so different to his son's puny efforts on the cover of *Borka*.

The phone rang, hiccupped a couple of times as though the signal was being passed along a line of relays, and was finally answered.

"Buckley," he announced, ploughing on before she could introduce herself, "I'm in Germany and I'm rather busy. Could you be brief, please?"

"It's Mrs May..."

There was a moment's pause, and then he said, "With good news, I hope?"

"Could be..." Ginny said. "I need to see you urgently."

There was another pause while Buckley flicked through his mental diary.

"The earliest I can do is tomorrow," he said, "six o'clock, at the Hillbrook showroom, will that do?

"That will do fine...see you tomorrow."

Ginny snapped her phone shut, and checked her wrist watch. There was a newsagent almost directly opposite the YOT, so if the session with Beresford finished early, she was almost certain to run into Whizz on his way back. Deciding to risk it, she checked that the boxes of pots on the back seat were looking innocuous under the old coat she'd thrown over them, and locked the car.

Surprisingly for a down-at-heel neighbourhood, the newsagent's racks were stacked with foreign newspapers, as well as all the national dailies. Ignoring the red-tops, Ginny selected two copies of each, and added The Scotsman and The Daily Record for good measure. She was taking her burden of newsprint to the door when, through the metal lattice that protected the shop window, she caught sight of Cee-Jay. Her own personal graffiti artist was squatted down on his haunches with his back against the wall of the YOT building. As she watched, he took a roll-up from behind his ear and slipped it between his lips, then hid his little chin beard behind his cupped hands until a puff of smoke appeared.

Moving aside to let a customer come into the shop, Ginny pretended to engross herself in the personal ads that covered half of the shop window. She was tempted to cross the street and see what Cee-Jay had to say for himself, but she had a hunch that he was waiting for Whizz, and she was curious. As expected, Whizz soon appeared from the side of the building, and squatted down beside Cee-Jay. They began to talk...at least Cee-Jay talked, with great urgency, as though confiding a state secret. Whizz listened, speaking rarely, and only to ask questions as far as she could tell. Not once did his eyes leave the pavement at his feet, and there was something stony in his look.

The shop-bell rang again as another customer came into the shop. Ginny caught the door before it swung back on its spring and went outside, watching the two boys through the traffic that thundered by. A taxi, followed by a white van and a motorbike; then two saloon cars going the other way; then a gap... and, in that instant, Cee-Jay looked up to take a drag on his roll-up. His eyes widened in recognition, and Ginny raised a hand in acknowledgement. A slow-moving single-decker bus wiped both boys from view and, by the time it had trundled past, Cee-Jay had left the scene. Whizz was waiting at the kerb, anxious for the traffic to abate and let her cross.

She had barely reached the central white line, when he shouted his question.

"What did Mel say?"

Ginny waited until she reached the pavement. "They're still haggling about money, but things are promising."

"Yessss!" hissed Whizz, and punched the air with two clenched fists, raising his eyes to the sky.

"And what did Leonardo de Vinci want?" she asked.

"Not a lot...he'd got a bit of goss from the nick, that's all."

Whizz turned away and began walking back to the car.

Ginny raised an eyebrow, and followed. "So why did he do a runner then?"

Whizz looked over his shoulder and flashed his lopsided smile. "Scared you'd cut his bollocks off for wrecking the house..." He nodded his head towards the bundle of newspapers. "Why all the papers?"

"Half for you, and half for me," Ginny replied, "According to Mel, the reviews are even better in *The Times* and *Independent*..."

Whizz broke into a dance, shaking his hips and clicking his fingers for the sheer joy of it. "Five more visits to this poxy dump, and I'll be free..."

Ginny laughed. "So what did Mr Beresford have to say?"

Whizz fell into step beside her. "Same as you—said I shouldn't get too excited; said people let you down sometimes." He looked across, and frowned. "Lazlo's not like that though, is he?"

Ginny shook her head and smiled. "No, he's not. I don't think Lazlo will ever let you down...but he might not get the money together. And that's why you shouldn't start celebrating. Not just yet."

When they reached the Saab, Ginny handed the pile of newspapers to Whizz, and pretended to search for her car-keys, complaining about the junk she had accumulated in her bag.

"Did you arrange to meet Cee-Jay?" she asked, watching his reaction closely.

There was no hesitation.

"No, I didn't..." Whizz replied, "he'd got a meeting with his social worker." He gave her another crooked grin. "All the best villains get down the YOT."

Leaving Ginny to navigate her way through the criss-cross tangle of back streets, Whizz buried his head in the newspapers, reading out choice morsels when he came to them. Apart from a vague sense that she was heading towards the sea, Ginny was lost and it was a pleasant surprise when they eventually emerged on the Esplanade, not five hundred metres from her destination. In

Cranbrook Square, her luck held. There was a parking space directly outside the old lady's house.

"We're here," she announced, and pulled on the handbrake.

Whizz looked up from the newspaper, and took in his surroundings. "Is this Cranbrook Square?" he asked.

"That's right," she said. "Why so surprised?"

Whizz gave a snort.

"What's so funny?" she asked.

Whizz treated her to a sly grin. "We knocked off one of these houses. That's all."

Ginny pointed a finger at the Carfax mansion. "Not this one, I hope."

Lowering his head so that he could see up to the roofline, Whizz gave her a professional critique of the expensive burglar alarm.

"It's too good for us," he said, and turned back to Ginny. "A pity really...looks like she's loaded."

"She is," said Ginny, "and she made it all from *The Witchy Wood.*"

Martina answered the door, and took them back down the portico steps to show them a concealed entrance to the subterranean servants' quarters. She also produced an old-fashioned porter's trolley so that, after two creaky journeys in an arthritic service lift, almost all the boxes of pots had been stacked in the *Winsome Witch*'s dining room.

"I'll get the last two," said Ginny. "Must lock the car, there may be thieves about." To underscore her feeble jest she flashed Whizz a phony smile, and pushed the trolley back to the lift.

Minutes later, when she returned, she regretted that smile. Martina was standing in a sea of discarded bubble-wrap, and Whizz was deep in conversation with Mrs Carfax.

The old lady waved her stick in greeting, and cried, "Your son is a real charmer, Mrs May."

Ginny's mouth dropped open.

"Do you know, the lad remembers more about *The Witchy Wood* than I do?"

Ginny formed an inane smile.

"Where do you want these, mum?" asked Whizz, holding up a nest of vipers. "On the table or on the sideboard?"

Ginny flapped her hands distractedly. "Oh...the table will do," she muttered, and then busied herself with the pots, biting down hard on her lower lip.

When everything had been unwrapped, Martina produced a set of table mats and a canteen of antique cutlery, and began to set the table for dinner. Mrs Carfax helped Whizz to feed rolled-up napkins into the coiled serpent-rings which Ginny had made as a surprise. Not once did Whizz miss an opportunity to call her 'Mum'. He was without mercy.

With all the spider-pots and all the snakes and toads in their appointed places, the table was ready for the witches and wizards on the walls to leap out of their ormolu frames and take their places for a weird feast.

"It's perfect, Mrs May!" cried Mrs Carfax, clapping her hands.

Martina was instructed to close the curtains, and Whizz was sent to find matches in one of the sideboards. When the lustrous pots were bathed in the gentle light of two dozen candles they glowed and gleamed, as rich and sumptuous as any treasure trove.

"Oh, yes...!" said Mrs Carfax, in a voice that was part growl and part whisper. "That's beautiful...and rather sinister. My little witches are going to love it. Thank you so much, Mrs May."

Turning to Whizz, the old lady clutched his arm in a gnarled claw. "And now, young man...what say we have some tea, eh?"

Although it was barely noon, the fireside table in the sitting-room was already laid with plates of delicate sandwiches and a cake-stand loaded with éclairs and cup-cakes. Mrs Carfax dispatched Martina to make the tea, and then pulled Whizz towards the huge Regency window where two wing-backed armchairs sat side by side, facing a panoramic view over the Square to the strip of sea beyond the Esplanade.

Mrs Carfax pointed down into the garden wilderness. "That is *The Witchy Wood*," she said, and turned the pointing finger to a chair. "I used to sit there, making up all the stories, and my dear old Jolyon used to sit in this one with his sketch-pad..."

She laid her hand on the antimacassar. For a moment it seemed that memories would steal her away, but she quickly collected her thoughts, and gave the top of the chair a brisk slap.

"Best thing we ever did moving to Cranbrook Square. 'If it works for Lewis Carroll, why not for the Carfaxes?' that's what Jolyon used to say...and, by golly, he was right."

Ginny moved closer to the window. "Tell me more, Mrs Carfax..." she said. "What has Lewis Carroll got to do with your *Witchy Wood?*"

"Oh, it's silly really," said the old lady, with a chuckle, "but Mr Dodgson found his *Wonderland* in a garden just like this one a little further down the coast, and we thought we'd be copy-cats." Seeing the puzzled look on Ginny's face, the watery old eyes twinkled mischief over the top of the spectacles, and she added, "You don't know the story, do you?"

Ginny shook her head.

"Well, apparently, the Reverend Mr Dodgson was taking a stroll in the garden when a little girl scampered across the grass and vanished into thin air...He was rather partial to little girls, was Mr Dodgson..." She paused, and gave a wheezy chuckle. "...but anyway, when the reverend gentleman went to investigate, he found that the child had disappeared down a tunnel that ran from the garden, under the Esplanade, right down to the beach...And what did the clever old thing do? He turned the tunnel into a rabbit warren and the little girl into the White Rabbit..."

"And that's how he found *Wonderland*?" said Ginny. "That's a great story!"

Mrs Carfax wagged her finger. "We have our own tunnel down in Cranbrook Square...but do you know..." She edged closer and lowered her voice. "One dark night, when the witches moved into the garden, that tunnel was mysteriously bricked up, and all the padlocks on all the gates were suddenly thick with rust..."

"Tea's ready, Mrs Carfax," sang out Martina.

The glitter of menace left the blue eyes, and an elderly hand took hold of Ginny's elbow.

"Come along, Mrs May... Let's get some cake into that lad of yours..."

Braced for more torment, Ginny glanced at her persecutor. But this time Whizz had missed his cue. He was standing by the big Regency window, gazing down into *The Witchy Wood* as if he too had been bewitched.

Chapter Forty Six

The number rang for so long Ginny began to wonder if the Holroyds were still in Italy. She was on the point of hanging up when Doc replied.

"Sorry," he said, breathlessly, "just got in…"

"Hi, Doc," said Ginny, "is Jude with you?"

"She's on her way from the car…and she'll be so pleased to hear from you. How are you, Ginny?"

"I'm fine. Busy making a new life…"

"Well, don't forget your old friends, eh? We still care about you, you know…"

"Don't worry, Doc, you're still my very favourite quack…"

"I'm glad to hear it…Hang on, Jude's here…"

Ginny pictured Doc's hand over the mouthpiece, and the eyebrows rising on Jude's plump face as she took in the news.

"Well, hello stranger," Jude purred. "Am I forgiven?"

"No, you're not," said Ginny, "but I'm working on it. I need you to settle an argument…"

"My role in life, darling…fire away…"

"What were the fees at St Ninian's when you worked there? Can you remember?"

Jude thought for a moment. "Can't be exact, but it was in the region of twenty grand for boarders, probably more now. Why do you ask?"

"You've just helped me win 50p," Ginny lied.

After the jokey opening, the conversation began to stutter, but each time it threatened to expire Jude breathed new life into it.

"And how's that lodger of yours?" she asked. "According to Bee, you've had your hands full…"

Ginny winced…if only Jude knew…

"We've got along just fine," she said, then babbled on to cover her confusion. "When his licence expires, we're going to have a big shindig to celebrate. Would you and Doc like to come?"

The lawn was having yet another stripy trim. When Whizz saw her approach, he let go of the handle and the engine sputtered into silence, sending a puff of exhaust fumes into the summer air.

"You're looking very nice," he said.

"Thank you, kind sir," said Ginny, bobbing a curtsy. "I want my horrible husband and his evil lawyer to see what a delectable creature he's dumped."

It was important that she looked businesslike for her meeting with Buckley, so she'd settled for the silk blouse with a Chinese collar and the pale linen suit that she'd worn for a reception at the Senate House.

"I hope your lawyer gives him a hard time," said Whizz.

"There's a Salade Niçoise in the fridge, with a big dollop of that trifle we had the other day...I shouldn't be too late, but I may go for a drink with the lawyer afterwards. Ok?"

"Don't worry about me," said Whizz, "just make sure you take that creep to the cleaners."

With a vigorous jerk on the starting cord, he brought the lawnmower back to raucous life and carefully aligned the blades with the nearest green stripe.

Ginny followed the receptionist across the shiny floor, past an echelon of sleek motors fragrant with the scents of new rubber and vanilla car-wax. The girl knocked on an office door marked *Chief Executive*, and a voice within called, "Come!"

William Buckley Senior was on his feet, walking round his enormous desk, his hand outstretched. The greeting was friendly, but the hand was moist.

"I'm sorry I'm so early," she began, "but…"

"No problem," Buckley said, and indicated one of the armchairs that were grouped around a low coffee-table in a corner of the office. "It's good of you to come."

"Can I get you any tea or coffee?" asked the receptionist.

"Nothing for me, thanks," replied Ginny.

"Nor me, Carrie…" said Buckley, "and can you get the desk to hold the calls, please? No exceptions."

Buckley closed the door behind the girl. He was perfectly groomed, in a crisp white shirt and silk tie, with cufflinks to match the gold wedding ring. He slapped the back pockets of his well-cut trousers in a brisk, down-to-business gesture, and then dried his palms on his backside.

"Does Will know you're here?" he asked.

Ginny gave a vigorous shake of her head. "Oh no, no, no..." she said, "if he knew I was meeting you, all bets would be off."

"No change there then," said Buckley, sitting in the chair beside her. "So, what have you got?"

Ginny opened the flap on the shoulder bag and took out the file.

"I'd like to get something straight," she began. "I'm not an expert, Mr Buckley. If I had my way, Will would be seeing a specialist. But he's adamant. No psychologists, no psychiatrists!"

Buckley was impatiently eyeing the folder. "Come on, you've got something there for me. What is it?"

Ginny opened the file and took out the copy of *Borka*.

"Take a look at this..." She pointed out the handwritten scrawl inside the back cover. "That's Will's handwriting, done a few months ago..."

"It's like a five-year-old's," said Buckley.

"Now look at this."

She handed him the handwriting analysis that she'd found on the internet and let him read for a moment.

"I think Will suffers from Dyspraxia."

For ten minutes Buckley listened quietly while Ginny explained her amateur diagnosis, feeding him sheets of paper to support her findings. He seemed impressed and handled the documentary evidence with some reverence, stacking the pages in a neat pile on the coffee table.

Ginny drew a deep breath, and handed him the thick American report on *'Learned Helplessness'*.

"This makes a link between learning difficulties and delinquency," she said. "The trigger is usually some form of abuse."

As she had calculated, Buckley's reaction was swift, rapping his forefinger so loudly on the table that it must have been painful.

"Stop there, Mrs May!" he said. "Every snooping jobs-worth has tried to imply that Will had been abused. And it's just not true."

"I'm sure you're right. Nobody intended to abuse him..."

"And what does that mean?" asked Buckley, still tetchy. "Nobody intended to abuse him?

"It means that it's perfectly possible to damage a child without meaning to..."

Buckley shook his head, not bothering to hide his scepticism and irritation.

"Take a kid like Will..." Ginny went on, "his brain has got a few minor kinks in the wiring. He can't remember things. He can't write things down properly. The teachers know he's not stupid, so they're on his back...so are his parents...nag, nag, nag...Why don't you do this? Why did you do that? You're lazy; you're thick; you're disobedient; you're uncooperative... From the kid's point of view, that's abuse."

Ginny pointed to the American report. "It's all in there. These kids end up feeling useless and helpless. Then, they get angry. Sometimes, they get very angry.

Buckley riffled the pages. "This is going to take time to read," he said.

Ginny nodded. "I've highlighted the crucial sections, so it won't take that long. But before you tackle that, it's time for some good news. Take a look at these."

She passed across three of the photographs that the local newspaper had taken at the Drill Hall, shifting in her chair so that she could point out the details. "Do you recognise anyone?"

Buckley's finger went straight to his son. "When was this taken?" he asked.

Ginny told him everything: about the street-dancing classes in prison; about *The Ozone Overdose*; and about Lazlo...

Buckley had stopped listening. He was holding the photographs close to his face, moving from still to still and back again, feasting his eyes.

"You know, his mother always wanted to be an actress," he murmured, then looked up from the photographs and fixed Ginny with a keen look.

"Is he any good?" he asked.

"Does it really matter?" said Ginny. "He loves it. That's the main thing."

From her file, she pulled out the photograph of Lazlo with the Lord Mayor, and tapped it with her index finger.

"This is the man who could be your son's saviour," she said.

Buckley was listening now.

Ginny told him about the workshops that Lazlo had run in Fulford, about his passionate belief in the power of drama to transform.

"But he's not a social worker, Mr Buckley. Lazlo is an actor, and a writer, and a director, and he's got a crust to make like the rest of us. He's taken a big gamble and started his own theatrical company. He's invested every penny he has..."

Reaching into the file, Ginny took out the wad of press cuttings from Edinburgh, and, while Buckley browsed, she explained Lazlo's plans for the tour.

"If they can raise the money, and get this show on the road," she said, "it could be the making of Will..."

Buckley thought for a moment, and produced the same wry smile that she had seen many times on his son's face.

"This is where you're going to ask me to get out the cheque book, isn't it?" he said.

"Not quite yet," Ginny said.

"Come on, Mrs May! Don't be coy! How much?"

"It's not for me to say," Ginny replied, meeting his gaze directly, "but I'll tell you how you could make the calculation, if you like?"

Buckley smiled, but his eyes narrowed. "Ok, fire away," he said.

"Suppose Will hadn't gone off the rails..." she began, "he'd have been at St Ninian's, and you would have been shelling out twenty...maybe twenty-five thousand a year for what...three or four years? That's a lot of money. And he'd still have a couple of years to go..."

The businessman said nothing, but he was doing the sums.

"Does he have any talent?" he asked.

Ginny shrugged. "Maybe he does, maybe he doesn't...who knows? He's not going to be the star of the show, Mr Buckley. He's going to be the gofer...the lowest form of animal life; humping lights about; packing costumes; making tea...But he'll be in a professional team, so there'll be no slacking and no time for mischief...and if he does have any talent, then Lazlo will find it, and Lazlo will nurture it...He's worked with hundreds of kids like Will. You couldn't find a better mentor for the boy if you advertised for one."

They locked eyes. After a pause, Buckley said, "What about Will? Is he up for this?"

Ginny gave a little nod. "Desperate," she said.

The businessman put his hand over his mouth and began to massage his cheekbones with a finger and thumb.

"Please don't make your mind up until you've read this," said Ginny, tapping the American report on *Learned Helplessness*.

"I don't need to," said Buckley, "I'm convinced."

"Please," Ginny begged, "...it's important."

Buckley spread his hands in puzzlement. "But I'm ready to go for the chequebook..."

"Not yet," Ginny insisted, "you haven't got the full picture."

Buckley sighed. "You're a good saleswoman, Mrs May, but you've got to know when to close a deal."

"I'm not selling a car, Mr Buckley. This is a damaged boy we're talking about, and I want you to understand exactly what he's been through..." She went on to explain that he would find the American case-studies more than a little distressing, and that she wanted him to read them in private.

Eventually, Buckley shrugged and raised his hands in surrender. "Ok, ok...I'll do as I'm told."

They had been talking for more than two hours, and the sun had set behind the buildings opposite, leaving just a stain of redness in the sky. If it were not for the spill from the security lights outside, the showroom would have been in darkness. The unsold motors had lost their gleam and seemed to be hunkered down for the night like a herd of sleeping beasts. In the eerie silence, Buckley's shoes squealed softly on the polished floor and Ginny's heels clicked officiously.

At the glass door by Reception, Buckley said, "Give me half an hour. Just ring the bell when you want to come in."

Ginny unlocked the Saab and sat behind the wheel. She switched on the radio and found a Promenade Concert on Radio 3. A viola and a violin were love-making in Mozart's Sinfonia Concertante. She tipped her seat back and listened. The music was exquisite, but it was impossible to concentrate. Through half-closed eyes she watched the ghostly green digits on the dashboard clock measuring out the minutes, and began to count off the seconds in her head, trying to hit sixty as the next minute was marked. Three times she failed, and gave up.

She decided to ring home and check on the boy. The mobile accepted the code, and the screen welcomed her back. There were two messages; the first from Joe Bradley, who had brought his *Swamp Rats* home from Louisiana; the second from Carmichael, back from Police College with a widened skills-base...Without instruction, her thumb pressed hard on the red button, and the screen went black again.

302

She got out of the car and click-clacked her way along the empty neon-lit street, past the *Automatic Car Wash*, and *The Carpet Warehouse*, and the *Sleep Easy Centre*... counting her steps until she reached four hundred. Then, she returned, counting backwards from four hundred until she reached the showroom. She looked at her wristwatch. There were ten more minutes to burn. She set off in the other direction, past *Tool Hire*, and *The DIY Mall*, and the *Bathroom Boutique*...walking just as quickly, counting again...then re-counting.

When she finally came back into the harsh lighting of the forecourt, she was breathing heavily and would have liked a moment to catch her breath. To her surprise though, the showroom door opened to greet her.

"Come in, Mrs May," Buckley called. He held up a wad of white paper. "Thank you for making me read this. It's Will's story...every nightmare we lived through...every lunatic thing that happened..."

In the office he motioned Ginny to sit down and took the chair opposite. His tie was askew and his shirt was open at the neck. His eyes had an unnatural brightness, and he looked drained, as though the muscles that gripped the mask of his face had despaired of the struggle.

He sniffed. "Ain't life a shitty business?" he said. "You love your kids. You do the very best by them. And you push 'em a little bit, just to make sure they make the most of themselves...And all the time it's as if you were pulling out their fingernails..."

Ginny began to make consoling noises, but Buckley cut across her.

"Fifty Thousand," he said. "Will that do for starters?"

Ginny frowned, not quite able to comprehend.

Buckley leaned forward and snatched up a piece of paper from the coffee table.

"If Will is still with them after three months, I'll chuck in another twenty-five. If they get a theatre in London at the end of the tour, another twenty-five...I've put it in writing..."

Ginny accepted the paper and shook her head as she read the figures. "That's incredibly generous of you," she said.

"No, it's not," Buckley countered. "If I get my son back, it's cheap at the price. And I'll get the satisfaction of watching young Lazlo What's-His-Name make his way in the world...Mind you..." He raised a cautionary forefinger, and squinted at her. "My accountants will want to squeeze some tax advantage out of this..."

Ginny smiled. "You'd better make sure the boy doesn't find out that you're the one that's pulling his strings..."

"We'll be discreet, don't worry." Buckley got to his feet, and spread his hands. "I really don't know how to thank you, Mrs May. You've worked a miracle..."

Ginny raised her palms. "Not yet Mr Buckley. The boy's got a long, long road to travel..."

There was something else that Ginny was determined not to shirk, but she allowed Buckley to lead her into the welcome darkness of the showroom before she began.

At the door by Reception, she said, "By the way, there's something I've forgotten."

"What's that?" asked Buckley.

"Will's going to need a good laptop with a built-in microphone, and a printer...and a state-of-the-art Dictaphone."

"No problem," Buckley said. "Buy the best you can get, and send me the bill."

Ginny made as though to leave as Buckley opened the door, but at the last moment she turned her back on the bright forecourt, leaving her face in shadow.

"One other thing..." she said. "Will told me how he got the scar below his eye..."

The security lights gave Buckley's face a bleached-out, sickly look.

"It was the only time I ever hit the boy," he said.

"I know," said Ginny.

Buckley raised his gaze and looked directly at her. "But did he tell you why I hit him?"

"Yes," she said, "and I think you got it wrong. When Will was at his lowest ebb, Chloe was the only person who was really listening to him. That's why they became so close...too close, perhaps. But it's one of the perils of intimacy, I suppose. It's dangerous to get close."

"I had a duty to protect her..."

"I know you did," Ginny said, interrupting, "but you blamed Will...and as far as he's concerned, that is yet another injustice."

There was a long pause. Buckley hung his head, and gave a weary sigh.

"I'd better talk to Chloe, hadn't I?" he said.

"No!" said Ginny, quickly. "I think your wife should talk to Chloe. I think you should let the women do some of the work." She extended her hand. "Goodnight, Mr Buckley...and thank you. You've been very generous. If it's any consolation, I really wish I'd had a dad like you."

Chapter Forty Seven

Ginny was euphoric. The mobile was in her hand before she had unlocked the Saab, and while the number rang her fingers drummed impatiently on the steering wheel.

At first the news reduced Mel to silence, but then she began to whoop. When she finally came down to earth, it was clear that Buckley's largesse was much more than a welcome bonus.

"The tour was looking dead in the water," Mel confessed. "We'd almost given up. Now this! It's a reprieve, Ginny! You've saved our bacon."

As she drove out of the deserted industrial estate, Ginny watched the patch of bright light that was Buckley Motors dwindle in the rear-view mirror. How right he had been when he accused her of being naive. His filthy lucre had bought his son another chance. Pity she couldn't tell the boy who his saviour was...And pity the poor kids banged up in prison with no one rich to rescue them. What chance have the Jason Nolans of this wicked world?

The moment the Saab rounded the bend in the drive, she knew that she had been celebrating her triumph too soon. The house was black as pitch. All her instincts told her that a search was futile, but she searched anyway and proved her instincts sound - Whizz had gone walkabout. Given his track record, it would be a waste of imaginative resource to invent an innocent explanation for his absence. Whizz would not be visiting the sick.

With anger building like methane in a mine, Ginny prepared for a vigil. First, she set the burglar alarm and made sure that Simon's virtual guard dog was on its leash. Then she grabbed a bottle of Rioja from the larder and a glass from the dresser. In the sitting room, she moved an armchair close to a window that overlooked the garden and the drive. Turning the television set around, she switched it on and sat in the glow from the screen, trying to engage with a glossy no-talent show, alert for the flash of the security lights on the patio.

The wine was a mistake. When the alarm jangled and the rabid dog went berserk, her fuddled brain wrote them into the dream that was troubling her, and when reality finally disentangled itself, she discovered a glass in her hand and a wet patch on her thigh. Immediately she was on her feet, wiping the skirt, spreading the wine stain on the linen.

The bell stopped ringing, and the dog stopped barking.

She was on the landing just as Whizz reached the foot of the stairs. She switched on the lights

"Where the hell have you been?" she demanded.

Whizz pulled off a woollen hat and shook his hair free. He was dressed in the baggy black jeans and black puffer-jacket that he'd worn on his release from Fulford.

"Cee-Jay wanted his boom-box back," he said.

"And that took you till two in the morning?"

"We got chatting..."

Ginny's grip tightened on the banister rail. "I hope you haven't done anything stupid."

He spread his hands. "I've just been to see a mate..."

"It would be a shame if you'd fouled up," Ginny said, "because I've been in touch with Lazlo, and..."

"Is it on?" asked Whizz, his face lighting up.

Ginny nodded. "Unless you've done something to make it impossible?"

Whizz clenched his fists. "Great!" he exclaimed.

Bounding forwards, he took the stairs three at a time and approached her, arms outstretched. Ginny planted a hand on his chest to prevent an embrace.

"What have you been up to?" she said.

There was a flush to his face, and the pupils of his eyes were hugely dilated.

"Nothing much..." he said, offering one of his sly grins. "But if anybody asks, you'd better say we were in the playroom making pots..."

Ginny screwed up her face, and stared at him. "You have done something stupid, haven't you?"

Whizz opened his mouth to speak, then closed it again, tilting his head coyly to one side. "Best you don't know..." he said, "it's nothing serious, but..." Reaching out his hand, he touched her lightly on the shoulder and began to caress her upper arm. "Can we go and talk to the ceiling?"

"No, we can't," Ginny snapped, and shrugged off his hand. "You can sleep in your own room."

Without the benefit of those violet-flecked irises, his eyes were pools of tar, inscrutable, devoid of reason.

"We'll talk in the morning," said Ginny, and turned away. "I'm going to bed."

Whizz said nothing, but she could feel his eyes on her back as she climbed the stairs.

Wishing there was a key in the lock, she closed her bedroom door and sat down on the stool by the dressing table, keeping her eyes fixed on the gap at the bottom of the door. As she had feared, a shadow arrived, bisecting the bar of light. For several anxious minutes, scarcely daring to breathe, she watched until the shadow backed away. Still she waited, straining her ears for any clue to his movements.

Eventually, from along the corridor came a drumming sound, faint, yet intense...then softer, and sporadic. It was the shower in the spare bathroom, peppering the plastic of the bath, at two-fifteen in the morning.

Since the trashing of the house, he had given her no cause to be frightened...anxious, yes...infuriated, yes...but not frightened. Tonight was different.

Silence. And then, above her head, a floorboard creaked. Panic over. He was going to bed. On impulse, Ginny went to the chest of drawers and, for the first time in weeks, pulled out a nightdress. From the medicine cabinet in the *en suite,* she took out the box of sedatives that Doc had prescribed when she lost the baby. With one of Simon's razor blades, she chopped a tablet in two, and swallowed the smaller of the two pieces with a swig of water.

Lying in bed, with the duvet pulled up to her chin, she waited for sleep, letting thoughts and half-thoughts come and go, competing for attention, drowning each other out, merging and meshing until a stream of white noise carried her to oblivion.

Then a hand was shaking her shoulder, and a voice was whispering urgently in her ear.

"That'll be the police. You'd better let them in."

Ginny sat bolt upright, clawing sleep from her eyes.

Downstairs, someone had jammed his finger in the doorbell.

"I've done something crazy," said Whizz, kneeling beside her on the bed, close to tears. "If they get me for it, I'll be straight back inside..."

Ginny ran her fingers through her hair, struggling to find her wits.

"Just tell them you were teaching me the pottery..."

Rolling off the bed, Ginny hurried to the bedroom door, and snatched her dressing-gown from the hook.

"Please, Mrs May..."

As she reached the bottom of the stairs, the doorbell stopped ringing and a fist began to hammer on the front door.

"Alright..." she screamed, as she ran through the kitchen, "Alright, I'm coming!"

Half way along the hallway, the hammering stopped. She turned the knob on the Yale lock, and opened the door an inch. A fleshy face announced itself as 'Police' and hid behind a Warrant Card.

Thankful it wasn't Carmichael, Ginny shouted, "What the hell do you mean hammering at my door at this hour of the morning?"

Then another voice spoke. "Sorry to get you out of bed, Ginny, but we need a word with Whizz..."

Instinctively, she took cover behind the door.

"Can we come in, please?"

Paralysed by shame and embarrassment, it required an effort of will to pull open the door.

"What is this all about?" she asked.

Carmichael looked as though he wished he wasn't there.

"There's been an incident," he said. "Is the boy in?"

"As far as I know, he's in his room," she said, and stepped back give the two men access.

But she was wrong about the boy. As the police crossed the kitchen, he made an entrance from the stairs, naked except for his boxer-shorts.

Ginny pulled the dressing gown tight around her body, and swallowed dryly as a flush of blood suffused her neck.

"What's up?" asked Whizz, giving a convincing performance as the bewildered innocent.

"Where were you last night?" asked Carmichael.

"I was here, with Mrs May," said Whizz.

Carmichael turned to Ginny. "Is that right?"

Ginny nodded.

"What time did he go to bed?"

"Quite late," she said, "after midnight, I think...I was working late in my studio."

"What am I supposed to have done?" asked Whizz.

Carmichael eyed him closely. "Another car got torched last night...the first for quite a while..."

"Not me," said Whizz, "I was here...all night."

Carmichael put his head to one side. "Wouldn't be the first time you got a mate to strike the match, would it? Can we take a look at your mobile?"

"I haven't got one..."

"You'd got one the last time I was here..."

"I've lost it."

Carmichael held the boy's gaze, and then glanced at Ginny. "Do you mind if my DC takes a look in the boy's room?"

Ginny shrugged. "Help yourself. He's in the study at the top of the house..."

"I'd better go as well," chipped in Whizz. "We don't want Mr Plod finding things that aren't there, do we?"

He flashed a sarcastic grin at DC Parker, who hooked his thumb skywards. "Up the stairs, sonny-boy!"

When they were alone, Carmichael turned to Ginny and gave an apologetic shrug of his shoulders. "I'm sorry about all this..." he said. "It's not the return I'd got in mind..."

Ginny looked down at the floor, still hugging the dressing-gown about her, biting down on her lower lip.

"For what it's worth, there's not a snowflake's chance we'll get him for it..."

Ginny looked up. "Then, for goodness sake, why are you hassling the boy?"

Carmichael raised his eyebrows, and issued a long-suffering sigh.

"Because the car that took a nosedive from *The Dragon's Back* was your old man's Mazda..."

Chapter Forty Eight

The month of August had passed like a fevered dream, and September dawned clear and fresh. The world had shifted on its axis. At night they slept alone; Whizz in his attic; Ginny in her double bed. Occasionally, as they moved about the house, their eyes would meet and they would remember, vaguely puzzled that, by some quirk of Nature, they had shared the same delirium.

Ginny's eyes were firmly on the future. She made preparations for the new school year, and surprised her divorce lawyer with her impatience for a quick settlement, consulting estate agents and combing the Old Town for a cottage. Whizz seemed newly liberated, as if he had packed all his demons into Simon's car and pushed them screaming from the top of *The Dragon's Back*. During the days, he mowed and pruned and grubbed out borders, building his bonfire ever higher, waiting for Lazlo's return and the start of a new life.

They enjoyed a companionable day touring the charity shops so that Whizz could select a bohemian wardrobe that befitted his new self-image. After they had filled the old Saab's boot with his bizarre collection of cast-offs, they drove to *Computer World*, where Whizz flatly refused to accept the gifts that Ginny proposed.

Placing her forefinger over his lips, she said, "When you are rich and famous, you can pay me back. No arguments. You need this technology. It's your equalizer."

They spent a great deal of his father's money on a laptop and a digital speech-recorder, both of them top-of-the-range, plus the most compact printer she could find. Whizz played non-stop with his new toys for several days, and showed off by reeling off several speeches from *Julius Caesar* that Ginny had challenged him to learn.

A few days before the school term began, Lazlo returned from Edinburgh buzzing with ideas for a second play that would run back-to-back with *Like Rabbits* when they took to the road at the beginning of November. Improvisations began immediately in the upstairs function-room at *The Cat*, and the trainee dogsbody started work on the new project as unfamiliar with the material as everyone else in the company. Whizz could not have asked for a better baptism, and Ginny was able to devote herself to the new cohort of babies in Class One without a moment's worry for what might be happening back home.

The only nagging concern was the fast-approaching bonfire party, which had grown and grown like the mountainous heap of debris that the boy had piled up in the orchard. Taking her bravado at face value, Bee and Jude had invited half the university, and Mel and Whizz had issued invitations to *The Cat's* entire clientele. If the heavens were unkind on the big night, the house would be in danger of bursting at the seams.

Fortunately, the Fates were benign. Although October 13th dawned dreary, with the garden shrouded in a damp mist, the pale autumn sun did its work, and by the afternoon the sky was clear. Feeling bemused and under-employed, Ginny watched as an invasion of helpers descended on her house. Lazlo's double-decker bus arrived and disgorged trestle tables and chairs, and lighting equipment, and a tangle of ancient bunting that had once done coronation-duty at *The Cat*. The set-designer supervised the erection of an open-sided pavilion to house Joe Bradley and his *Swamp Rats*, and the lean-to was requisitioned for use as a bar, with a sign hung from its tin roof that read: *The Cat's Away*. The sainted landlord togged himself out in a chef's hat and stripy apron and set a pig to roast in the rose-garden, while Shirley humped crates of ale and boxes of wine from the pub van, leaving *The V&A* to bicker as they polished glasses.

Retreating to the kitchen in the hope of being useful, Ginny was instantly rebuffed by Jude, who was trying so hard to restore good relations that she had taken sole charge of the puddings and salads, determined to be a martyr.

Ginny busied herself in the playroom, tidying away the mess she had made, and creating space for guests who might need refuge from the chill night air.

Mel stuck her head through the French window. "I don't suppose you'd let us burn that horrible *Hannya* mask, would you?" she asked.

Ginny pulled a puzzled face. "Why on earth would you want to do that?"

"Come and see," said Mel, offering her hand.

As they came round the great bonfire heap in the orchard, they found Tom Carmichael and Whizz crouched over what appeared to be a scarecrow tied to a wooden cross on the bare earth.

"I'm going to torch the 'old me'," explained Whizz.

Ginny looked down at the effigy. It was wearing the black jeans and the black bomber jacket she had last seen the night that Simon's car took its fiery dive from *The Dragon's Back*.

"Mel's got a blonde wig I can burn," said Whizz, "but if it's gonna be me, we need the wickedest face we can get..."

Ginny studied the roguish grin, and questioned the innocent blue eyes with their strange flecks of violet.

"You can burn the *Hannya*, provided you burn Whizz Buckley with it," she said. "I think it's time we had Will Buckley back."

Whizz screwed up his face while he considered the offer.

"Ok, Mrs May," he said. "You can call me Will, if you like. It's a deal."

There was a crescent moon in a velvet sky and the trees that ringed the garden were ablaze with the colours of autumn, flaunting themselves in the soft light of Lazlo's artful lamps. On the lawns and on the patio, Town and Gown danced together, new friends and old, drunk on the sweet music of old Louisiana—the healing of wounds and the flowering of a new life. Ginny wished she'd had the courage to invite Simon and his lady-love.

She danced a jaunty polka with the Doc, who told her she looked radiant. Then she danced an eccentric waltz with Will, remembering the child he'd been in the whirl of the Maypole. And later still, as Joe and Molly crooned a Cajun love song, she danced with Tom.

But for all the magic of the night, the image that Ginny took to her pillow, and the image that was with her when she woke, was the *Hannya* mask, unrepentantly malignant; defying the flames long after the scarecrow had turned into a cross of fire.

Chapter Forty Nine

Lowering her head over the steaming saucepan, Ginny shut her eyes and breathed in the scent of childhood.

"What's the pong?" called out Will, as he rattled the wheels of his suitcase across the kitchen tiles.

"Porridge..." replied Ginny. "We had it the first morning you were here. Remember?"

The rattling noise stopped. "What about the fry-up?"

"Don't panic," she said, "you'll get your grease as well."

Breakfast was a silent affair. Neither of them knew what to say because everything had already been said.

"Are you sure I can't come with you to the road?" asked Ginny, when the table had been cleared.

"I've told you," he said, with a faint note of exasperation, "I'm not a kid."

A quarter of an hour before Lazlo's bus was due to arrive they were in the hallway by the open front door with his suitcase and his enormous backpack and the satchel for his laptop.

Will cleared his throat nervously, as though about to deliver a speech.

Ginny placed her forefinger over his lips. "Don't say a word," she said. "Just make me proud of you."

Feeling tears prick at her eyes, she drew him to her, and for a long time they held one another close. She felt him stretch out his arm and reach behind her.

"Would you mind if I took this?" he said.

He stepped back and showed her the fedora, which he had taken from the hat-peg.

"Of course you can," she said, and laughed. "It'll suit you."

Will put Simon's hat on the back of his head, and the wide brim became a dark halo around the tangled straw of his hair.

"What do you think?" he said, posing for her appraisal.

The deep tan of summer had faded leaving his skin a pale gold, and there was a faint trace of beard, so downy that she hadn't noticed it before. Her delinquent protégé would soon be a full-grown man, and a handsome one at that.

"I think you're going to break some hearts," she said.

"I hope so," he said, with a grin. "I've had a brilliant teacher."

Loading himself with the heavy rucksack, he extended the handle on the suitcase, and hitched the strap of his computer satchel over his shoulder.

"I'm off then," he said.

"Be good," said Ginny, "and if you ever need me, you have my number."

With a nod, Will turned away and walked down the path to the driveway. In his chequered chef's trousers and his coat of many colours he looked ridiculous, but he was hauling his baggage into the future with such magnificent swagger that it was hard not to admire him.

At the little gate, he stopped, just as she had imagined he would. Now he would turn round, and with that crooked grin on his face, he would say, "Thank you for having me, Mrs May." And she would give him a rueful shake of her head, and tell him to behave himself.

But she had underestimated him again. When he looked back over his shoulder, he said: "You can call me 'Will', Mrs May. But I think I'll keep 'Whizz Buckley' as my stage-name. 'Whizz' has got more balls than 'Will', and I'm gonna need all the balls I've got if I'm gonna be a star."

Coda

Escaping its elderly master, a white Jack Russell terrier squeezed itself through the iron railings that surrounded the jungle at the heart of Cranbrook Square and went in search of wild life. Two days later its plaintive yelps were heard by a rough-sleeper, bedding down for the night in an arched recess in the wall that ran the length of the promenade. Despite the sea grumbling on the shingle beach and late-night traffic hissing through the drizzle on the Esplanade high above, it was a peaceful spot and one of his regular haunts. The dog's faint cries appeared to come from deep within the solid breeze-block wall and defied explanation, so the drunk concluded that he was hallucinating again, and went to sleep. Only at three o'clock in the morning, when a passing police constable nudged him awake with the toe of his boot, was the derelict able to put his sanity to the test. The dog's bleats were faint now and intermittent, but, to the vagrant's considerable surprise, the policeman could hear them too.

And so it was that, by the end of the night, Tom Carmichael, newly promoted to the rank of Detective Inspector, had been given his first major enquiry—an investigation into the murder of Charles Henry Rivers, better known as 'Moon'.

The body was sitting in a film-director's folding chair, legs stretched out, arms dangling, the head tilted back so that the ponytail drooped towards the paved floor. Bulging eyes gazed in apparent terror at the curved roof of the brick-lined tunnel, and the livid welt around his neck explained why. The pathologist's face-mask was a poor defence against the sickly, all-pervasive stench of decomposition.

"Been dead for three months...maybe longer," he speculated, swatting away the swarm of angry bluebottles to peer closely at the wound.

By the harsh light of the photographer's lamps, the hideaway looked makeshift and tawdry. Swags of looted fabric hung from nails in the walls, and a matching drape turned a wrought-iron garden seat into an unlikely sofa. Four silver candelabras dripped frozen wax on to upturned flower-urns. Beer-crates had become occasional tables and were littered with enough stolen knick-knacks to stock a flea-market. Paintings and photographs adorned the breeze-block arch that denied access to the promenade; two gloomy Scottish landscapes of doubtful value and a vibrant still-life; and dominating the wall, a collection of faded Daguerreotypes, stern portraits and unsmiling family groups in oval cut-outs—the kind of affluent Victorians who might have lived in Cranbrook Square, strolling the garden with their parasols, taking their children through the private underpass to the bathing-machines and the sea.

The SOCO peered intently at the neck-wound. "Done us a favour, if you ask me," she said.

It was a view that was shared by the entire nick. There would be few mourners at Moon's funeral—although, as a matter of curmudgeonly principle, Joe Bradley would be there, and in the front pew.

"He wasn't evil when they slapped his little arse in the maternity unit," the lawyer said, confronting Carmichael over the rim of his wine-glass.

"He always had choices," replied the policeman, "and Moon chose to be wicked, that's the truth of it. He was a menace."

"Just look where you found him..." countered Bradley, "the poor kid had dreamed himself the decent home he never had, and a decent family to fill it."

Ginny May had already left the table. She was lying down on the bed, her hands resting on her swollen stomach, fingers spread. She was staring up into the criss-cross of wooden timbers that supported the roof of her new home, trying to clear her head of unwanted thoughts by counting the dozens of crude iron nails that had been hammered into the blackened oak. Something had hung from them long ago, something fishy no doubt...God knows what.

"Can I come in?"

It was Tom Carmichael, looking contrite.

"Joe and I have buggered up your dinner-party, haven't we?" he said.

Ginny shook her head. "The sad truth is: you're both right." She raised a hand and massaged forehead, adding, "Ain't it a shitty world?"

"You feeling rough?"

"The baby kicked me," she said, and patted the duvet. "Come and feel…"

Carmichael sat on the bed and allowed Ginny to place his hand on the tight drum of her belly. Eyes closed, he waited, frowning a little. Then a smile flickered on his lips.

"That's it…" he said, "I felt it."

Ginny's hand squeezed his hand. "I wish it was yours," she said.

"So do I…" he said, "but like you say, it's a shitty old world…"

Notes On
'The Jocasta Complex'

The Jocasta Complex is a variation of the Oedipal theme which mainly operates between mother and son. The emotional relationship of an adoptive mother to her adopted son is normally the same as that of a natural mother to her natural son, and therefore an emotional Oedipus situation exists between them even in the absence of blood relationship. But it is just the factor of absence of blood relationship which increases the danger of a break-through of unconscious incestuous tendencies. This danger is further increased if the marital relationship between adoptive parents is disturbed, which is more often the case in adoptive than natural parents. Parental discord is a very important factor in the development of a pathological Oedipus situation.

J. C. Fluegel   *The Psycho-analytic Study of the Family* (1921)

Acknowledgements

To Bridget Hawkins for her expertise in the treatment of infertility; to Wingham Primary School and its then headmaster, Gary Davis, who allowed me to join the reception class; to William Styles, the enlightened governor of HM YOI Wetherby; to Ian Bond, a solicitor who has defended hundreds of wayward teenagers in court; to Detective Sergeant Scott Lynch, who has locked more of them up than he would have wished; to Rick Carter of the Ramsgate Youth Offending Team, who strives to keep his many clients out of further trouble with the Youth Justice System; and to Cherry Tewfik who taught me about clay...to all of them, sincere thanks. Without their input, the book would have been impossible. If there are errors of fact, the responsibility is entirely mine.

My thanks are also due to Patricia Debney, Lawrence Tuck and Patience Agbabi who helped me take my first tentative steps as a writer at the University of Kent. The book began to take shape on a Creative Writing MA at Canterbury Christ Church University with guidance from Andrew Palmer, Sarah Grazebrook and Michael Baldwin. Publishing the early chapters to fellow students enabled me to gauge a variety of reader-responses. Their critiques, positive and negative, were all helpful. And I am especially grateful to Michael Irwin, Emeritus Professor of English at the University of Kent, who put aside his own writing to be my mentor. His eye for my shortcomings was unerring, but his encouragement spurred me to do better.

The following brave souls read the drafts: Lynne Hapgood, Karen Russell-Graham, John Crook, Jay McCue, and my daughter, Holly. They did not flatter or put me down, and the amendments made in response to their observations greatly improved the book.

David Pick
Canterbury 2012

18058836R00170

Made in the USA
Charleston, SC
14 March 2013